THE BEAUTIFUL MYSTERY

Louise Penny

WINDSOR
PARAGON

First published 2012
by Sphere
This Large Print edition published 2013
by AudioGO Ltd
by arrangement with
Little, Brown Book Group

Hardcover   ISBN: 978 1 4713 2036 1
Softcover   ISBN: 978 1 4713 2037 8

British Library Cataloguing in Publication Data available

Printed and bound in Great Britain by
TJ International Ltd.

This book is dedicated to
those who kneel down,
and those who stand up.

ACKNOWLEDGMENTS

The Beautiful Mystery started as a fascination with music, and a very personal and baffling relationship with it. I love music. Various pieces have inspired each of the books, and I'm convinced music has had a near magical effect on my creative process. When I sit on planes, or go for walks, or drive and listen to music I can see scenes from the book I'm about to write, or am writing. I can feel the characters. Hear them. Sense them. It's thrilling. Gamache and Clara and Beauvoir come even more alive when I'm listening to certain music. It's transformative. Spiritual, even. I can feel the divine in the music.

I'm far from alone in this, I know.

In preparing for this book I read widely, including a book by McGill University professor Daniel J. Levitin called *This Is Your Brain on Music,* about the neuroscience of music — its effects on our brains.

I wanted to explore this beautiful mystery. How just a few notes can take us to a different time and place. Can conjure a person, an event, a feeling. Can inspire great courage, and reduce us to tears. And in the case of this book, I wanted to explore the power of ancient chants. Gregorian chants. On those who sing them, and those who hear them.

I had a great deal of help in writing *The Beautiful Mystery*. From family and friends. From books and videos and real-life experiences, including a remarkable and very peaceful stay at a monastery.

I'd like to thank Lise Desrosiers, my amazing assistant, who makes it possible for me to concentrate on writing, while she does all the rest. Thank you to my editors, Hope Dellon, of Minotaur Books in New York City, and Dan Mallory, of Little, Brown in London, for all their help with *The Beautiful Mystery*. Thank you, Teresa Chris and Patty Moosbrugger, my agents. To Doug and Susan, my first readers. To Marjorie, for always being so willing and happy to help.

And thank you to my husband, Michael. If there's one mystery even more baffling and powerful than music in my life, it's love. It's one mystery I'll never solve, and never want to. I just enjoy where loving Michael takes me.

And thank you, for reading my books and giving me a life beyond imagining.

PROLOGUE

In the early nineteenth century the Catholic Church realized it had a problem. Perhaps, it must be admitted, more than one. But the problem that preoccupied it at that moment had to do with the Divine Office. This consisted of eight times in the daily life of a Catholic community when chants were sung. Plainchant. Gregorian chant. Simple songs sung by humble monks.

Not to put too fine a point on it, the Catholic Church had lost the Divine Office.

The different services throughout a religious day were still performed. What were called Gregorian chants were sung here and there, in the odd monastery, but even Rome admitted the chants had strayed so far from the originals that they were considered corrupt, even barbaric. At least, in comparison to the elegant and graceful chants of centuries earlier.

But one man had a solution.

In 1833 a young monk, Dom Prosper, revived the Abbey of St. Pierre in Solesmes, France, and made it his mission to also bring back to life the original Gregorian chants.

But this produced another problem. It turned out, after much investigation by the abbot, that no one knew what the original chants sounded like. There was no written record of the earliest chants. They were so old, more than a millenium, that they predated written music. They were learned by heart, passed down orally, after years of study, from one monk to another. The chants were simple, but there was power in that very simplicity. The first chants were soothing, contemplative, magnetic.

They had such a profound effect on those who sang and heard them that the ancient chants became known as "the beautiful mystery." The monks believed they were singing the word of God, in the calm, reassuring, hypnotic voice of God.

What Dom Prosper did know was that sometime in the ninth century, a thousand years before the abbot lived, a brother monk had also contemplated the mystery of the chants. According to Church lore, this anonymous monk was visited by an inspired idea. He would make a written record of the chants. So that they'd be preserved. Too many of his numbskull novices made too many mistakes when trying to learn the plainchants. If the words and music really were Divine, as he believed with all his heart, then they needed to be safer than stored in such faulty human heads.

Dom Prosper, in his own stone cell in his own abbey, could see that monk sitting in a room exactly like his. As the abbot imagined it, the monk pulled a piece of lambskin, vellum, toward him then dipped his sharpened quill in ink. He wrote the words, the text, in Latin, of course. The psalms. And once that was done he went back to the beginning. To the first word.

His quill hovered over it.

Now what?

How to write music? How could he possibly communicate something that sublime? He tried writing out instructions, but that was far too cumbersome. Words alone could never describe how this music transcended the normal human state, and lifted man to the Divine.

The monk was stumped. For days and weeks he went about his monastic life. Joining the others in prayer and work. And prayer. Chanting the Office. Teaching the young and easily distracted novices.

And then one day he noticed that they focused on his right hand, as he guided their voices. Up, down. Faster, slower. Quietly, quietly. They'd memorized the words, but depended upon his hand signals for the music itself.

That night, after Vespers, this nameless monk sat by precious candle-light, staring at the psalms written so carefully on the vellum. Then he dipped his quill in ink and drew the very first musical note.

It was a wave above a word. A single, short, squiggly line. Then another. And another. He drew his hand. Stylized. Guiding some unseen monk to raise his voice. Higher. Then holding. Then higher again. Hanging there for just a moment, then swooping and sweeping downward in a giddy musical descent.

He hummed as he wrote. His simple hand signals on the page fluttered, so that the words came alive and lifted off. Became airborne. Joyous. He heard the voices of monks not yet born joining him. Singing exactly the same chants that freed him and lifted his heart to Heaven.

In trying to capture the beautiful mystery, this monk had invented written music. Not yet notes, what he'd written became known as neumes.

Over the centuries this plain chant evolved into complex chant. Instruments were added, harmonies were added, which led to chords and staffs and finally musical notes. Do-re-mi. Modern music was born. The Beatles, Mozart, rap. Disco, *Annie Get Your Gun,* Lady Gaga. All sprang from the same ancient seed. A monk, drawing his hand. Humming and conducting and straining for the Divine.

Gregorian chant was the father of western music. But it was eventually killed by its ungrateful children. Buried. Lost and forgotten.

Until the early 1800s when Dom Prosper, sickened by what he saw as the vulgarity of the Church and the loss of simplicity and purity, decided it was time to resurrect the original Gregorian chants. To find the voice of God.

His monks fanned out across Europe. They searched monasteries and libraries and collections. With one goal. To find that original ancient manuscript.

The monks came back with many treasures lost in remote libraries and collections. And finally Dom Prosper decided one book of plainsong, written in faded neumes, was the original. The first, and perhaps only, written record of what Gregorian chant

15

would have sounded like. It was on a piece of lambskin almost a thousand years old.

Rome disagreed. The pope had conducted his own search and found another written record. He insisted his piece of tattered vellum recorded how the Divine Office should be sung.

And so, as often happens when men of God disagree, a war erupted. Volleys of plainsong were hurled between the Benedictine monastery of Solesmes and the Vatican. Each insisting theirs was closer to the original and therefore, closer to the Divine. Academics, musicologists, famous composers and humble monks weighed in on the subject. Choosing sides in the escalating battle that soon became more about power and influence and less about simple voices raised to the glory of God.

Who had found the original Gregorian chant? How should the Divine Office be sung? Who possessed the voice of God?

Who was right?

Finally, after years, a quiet consensus arose among the academics. And then was even more quietly suppressed.

Neither was correct. While the monks of Solesmes were almost certainly far closer to the truth than Rome, it appeared even they were not there yet. What they found was historic, priceless — but it was incomplete.

For something was missing.

The chants had words and neumes, indications of when monastic voices should be raised, and when they should be hushed. When a note was higher, and when it was lower.

What they didn't have was a starting point. Higher, but from where? Louder, but from where? It was like finding a complete treasure map, with an X for exactly where to end up. But not where to begin.

In the beginning . . .

The Benedictine monks of Solesmes quickly established themselves as the new home of the old chants. The Vatican eventually relented and within a few decades the Divine Office had regained favor. The resurrected Gregorian chants spread to monasteries worldwide. The simple music offered genuine comfort. Plainsong in an increasingly noisy world.

And so the abbot of Solesmes passed away quietly, knowing two things. That he had achieved something significant and powerful and meaningful. He'd revived a beautiful and simple tradition. He'd restored the corrupted chants to their pure state, and won the war against a gaudy Rome.

But he also knew, in his heart, that while

he'd won, he hadn't succeeded. What everyone now took to be genuine Gregorian
chants were close, yes. Almost Divine. But
not quite.

For they had no starting point.

Dom Prosper, a gifted musician himself,
couldn't believe the monk who had codified
the first plainchants wouldn't tell future
generations where to start. They could
guess. And they did. But it wasn't the same
as knowing.

The abbot had argued passionately that
the Book of Chants his monks had found
was the original. But now, on his deathbed,
he dared to wonder. He imagined that other
monk, dressed exactly as he was now, bending over candle-light.

The monk would have finished the first
chant, created the first neumes. And then
what? Dom Prosper, as he drifted in and
out of consciousness, in and out of this
world and the next, knew what that monk
would have done. That anonymous monk
would have done what he'd have done.

Dom Prosper saw, more clearly than his
brothers chanting soft prayers over his bed,
that long dead monk bending over his desk.
Going back to the beginning. The first
word. And making one more mark.

At the very end of his life, Dom Prosper

knew there was a beginning. But it would be up to someone else to find it. To solve the beautiful mystery.

ONE

As the last note of the chant escaped the Blessed Chapel a great silence fell, and with it came an even greater disquiet.

The silence stretched on. And on.

These were men used to silence, but this seemed extreme, even to them.

And still they stood in their long black robes and white tops, motionless.

Waiting.

These were men also used to waiting. But this too seemed extreme.

The less disciplined among them stole glances at the tall, slim, elderly man who had been the last to file in and would be the first to leave.

Dom Philippe kept his eyes closed. Where once this was a moment of profound peace, a private moment with his private God, when Vigils had ended and before he signaled for the Angelus, now it was simply escape.

He closed his eyes because he didn't want to see.

Besides, he knew what was there. What was always there. What had been there for hundreds of years before he arrived and would, God willing, be there for centuries after he was buried in the cemetery. Two rows of men across from him, in black robes with white hoods, a simple rope tied at their waists.

And beside him to his right, two more rows of men.

They were facing each other across the stone floor of the chapel, like ancient battle lines.

No, he told his weary mind. *No. I mustn't think of this as a battle, or a war. Just opposing points of view. Expressed in a healthy community.*

Then why was he so reluctant to open his eyes? To get the day going?

To signal the great bells that would ring the Angelus to the forests and birds and lakes and fish. And the monks. To the angels and all the saints. And God.

A throat cleared.

In the great silence it sounded like a bomb. And to the abbot's ears it sounded like what it was.

A challenge.

With an effort he continued to keep his eyes closed. He remained still, and quiet. But there was no peace anymore. Now there was only turmoil, inside and out. He could feel it, vibrating from and between the two rows of waiting men.

He could feel it vibrating within him.

Dom Philippe counted to one hundred. Slowly. Then opening his blue eyes, he stared directly across the chapel, to the short, round man who stood with his eyes open, his hands folded on his stomach, a small smile on his endlessly patient face.

The abbot's eyes narrowed slightly, in a glare, then he recovered and raising his slim right hand, he signaled. And the bells began.

The perfect, round, rich toll left the bell tower and took off into the early morning darkness. It skimmed over the clear lake, the forests, the rolling hills. To be heard by all sorts of creatures.

And twenty-four men, in a remote monastery in Québec.

A clarion call. Their day had begun.

"You're not serious," laughed Jean-Guy Beauvoir.

"I am," nodded Annie. "I swear to God it's the truth."

"Are you telling me," he picked up another

piece of maple-cured bacon from the platter, "that your father gave your mother a bathmat as a gift when they first started dating?"

"No, no. That would be ridiculous."

"Sure would," he agreed and ate the bacon in two big bites. In the background an old Beau Dommage album was playing. *"La complainte du phoque en Alaska."* About a lonely seal whose love had disappeared. Beauvoir hummed quietly to the familiar tune.

"He gave it to my grandmother the first time they met, as a hostess gift, thanking her for inviting him to dinner."

Beauvoir laughed. "He never told me that," he finally managed.

"Well, Dad doesn't exactly mention it in polite conversation. Poor Mom. Felt she had to marry him. After all, who else would have him?"

Beauvoir laughed again. "So I guess the bar is set pretty low. I could hardly give you a worse gift."

He reached down beside the table in the sunny kitchen. They'd made breakfast together that Saturday morning. A platter of bacon and scrambled eggs with melted Brie sat on the small pine table. He'd thrown on a sweater this early autumn day

24

and gone around the corner from Annie's apartment to the bakery on rue St-Denis for croissants and *pain au chocolat.* Then Jean-Guy had wandered in and out of the local shops, picking up a couple of *cafés,* the Montréal weekend papers, and something else.

"What've you got there?" Annie Gamache asked, leaning across the table. The cat leapt to the ground and found a spot on the floor where the sun hit.

"Nothing," he grinned. "Just a little *je ne sais quoi* I saw, and thought of you."

Beauvoir lifted it into plain sight.

"You asshole," Annie said, and laughed. "It's a toilet plunger."

"With a bow on it," said Beauvoir. "Just for you, *ma chère.* We've been together for three months. Happy anniversary."

"Of course, the toilet plunger anniversary. And I got you nothing."

"I forgive you," he said.

Annie took the plunger. "I'll think of you every time I use it. Though I think you'll be the one using it most of the time. You are full of it, after all."

"Too kind," said Beauvoir, ducking his head in a small bow.

She thrust the plunger forward, gently prodding him with the red rubber suction cup as though it was a rapier and she the swordsman.

Beauvoir smiled and took a sip of his rich, aromatic *café.* So like Annie. Where other women might have pretended the ridiculous plunger was a wand, she pretended it was a sword.

Of course, Jean-Guy realized, he would never have given a toilet plunger to any other woman. Only Annie.

"You lied to me," she said, sitting back down. "Dad obviously told you about the bathmat."

"He did," admitted Beauvoir. "We were in Gaspé, in a poacher's cabin, searching for evidence when your father opened a closet and found not one but two brand-new bath-mats, still in their wrapping."

As he spoke he looked at Annie. Her eyes never left him, barely blinked. She took in every word, every gesture, every inflection. Enid, his ex-wife, had also listened. But there was always an edge of desperation about it, a demand. As though he owed her. As though she was dying and he was the medicine.

Enid left him drained, and yet still feeling inadequate.

But Annie was gentler. More generous.

Like her father, she listened carefully and quietly.

With Enid he never talked about his work, and she never asked. With Annie he told her everything.

Now, while putting strawberry *confiture* on the warm croissant, he told her about the poacher's cabin, about the case, the savage murder of a family. He told her what they found, how they felt, and who they arrested.

"The bathmats turned out to be the key pieces of evidence," said Beauvoir, lifting the croissant to his mouth. "Though it took us a long time to figure it out."

"Is that when Dad told you about his own sad history with bathmats?"

Beauvoir nodded and chewed and saw the Chief Inspector in the dim cabin. Whispering the story. They weren't sure when the poacher would return, and they didn't want to be caught there. They had a search warrant, but they didn't want him to know that. So as the two homicide investigators deftly searched, Chief Inspector Gamache had told Beauvoir about the bathmat. Of showing up for one of the most important meals of his life, desperate to impress the parents of the woman he'd fallen hopelessly in love with. And somehow deciding a bathmat was the perfect hostess gift.

"How could you have thought that, sir?" Beauvoir had whispered, glancing out the cracked and cobwebbed window, hoping not to see the shabby poacher returning with his kill.

"Well, now," Gamache had paused, obviously trying to recall his own thinking. "Madame Gamache often asks the same question. Her mother never tired of asking either. Her father, on the other hand, decided I was an imbecile and never mentioned it again. That was worse. When they died we found the bathmat in their linen closet, still in its plastic wrapping, with the card attached."

Beauvoir stopped talking and looked across at Annie. Her hair was still damp from the shower they'd shared. She smelled fresh and clean. Like a citron grove in the warm sunshine. No makeup. She wore warm slippers and loose, comfortable clothing. Annie was aware of fashion, and happy to be fashionable. But happier to be comfortable.

She was not slim. She was not a stunning beauty. Annie Gamache was none of the things he'd always found attractive in a woman. But Annie knew something most people never learn. She knew how great it was to be alive.

It had taken him almost forty years, but Jean-Guy Beauvoir finally understood it too. And knew now there was no greater beauty.

Annie was approaching thirty now. She'd been a gawky teenager when they'd first met. When the Chief Inspector had brought Beauvoir into his homicide division at the Sûreté du Québec. Of the hundreds of agents and inspectors under the Chief's command, he'd chosen this young, brash agent no one else had wanted as his second in command.

Had made him part of the team, and eventually, over the years, part of the family.

Though even the Chief Inspector had no idea how much a part of the family Beauvoir had become.

"Well," said Annie with a wry smile, "now we have our own bathroom story to baffle our children with. When we die they'll find this, and wonder."

She held up the plunger, with its cheery red bow.

Beauvoir didn't dare say anything. Did Annie have any idea what she'd just said? The ease with which she assumed they'd have children. Grandchildren. Would die together. In a home that smelled of fresh citron and coffee. And had a cat curled around the sunshine.

They'd been together for three months and had never talked about the future. But hearing it now, it just seemed natural. As though this was always the plan. To have children. To grow old together.

Beauvoir did the math. He was ten years older than her, and would almost certainly die first. He was relieved.

But there was something troubling him.

"We need to tell your parents," he said.

Annie grew quiet, and picked at her croissant. "I know. And it's not like I don't want to. But," she hesitated and looked around the kitchen, and out into her book-lined living room, "this is nice too. Just us."

"Are you worried?"

"About how they'll take it?"

Annie paused and Jean-Guy's heart suddenly pounded. He'd expected her to deny it. To assure him she wasn't the least bit worried whether her parents would approve.

But instead, she'd hesitated.

"Maybe a little," Annie admitted. "I'm sure they'll be thrilled, but it changes things. You know?"

He did know, but hadn't dared admit it to himself. Suppose the Chief didn't approve? He could never stop them, but it would be a disaster.

No, Jean-Guy told himself for the hundredth time, *it'll be all right. The Chief and Madame Gamache will be happy. Very happy.*

But he wanted to be sure. To know. It was in his nature. He collected facts for a living, and this uncertainty was taking its toll. It was the only shadow in a life suddenly, unexpectedly luminous.

He couldn't keep lying to the Chief. He'd persuaded himself this wasn't a lie, just keeping his private life private. But in his heart it felt like a betrayal.

"Do you really think they'll be happy?" he asked Annie, and hated the neediness that had crept into his voice. But Annie either didn't notice or didn't care.

She leaned toward him, her elbows and forearms resting on the croissant flakes on the pine table, and took his hand. She held it warm in hers.

"To know we're together? My father would be so happy. It's my mother who hates you. . . ."

Seeing the look on his face she laughed and squeezed his hand. "I'm kidding. She adores you. Always has. They think of you as family, you know. As another son."

He felt his cheeks burn, to hear those words, and felt ashamed, but noticed that once again Annie didn't care, or comment.

She just held his hand and looked into his eyes.

"Sort of incestuous, then," he finally managed.

"Yes," she agreed, letting go of his hand to take a sip of *café au lait.* "My parents' dream come true." She laughed, sipped, then set the cup down again. "You do know he'll be thrilled."

"Surprised too?"

Annie paused, thinking. "I think he'll be stunned. Funny, isn't it? Dad spends his life looking for clues, piecing things together. Gathering evidence. But when something's right under his nose, he misses it. Too close, I guess."

"Matthew 10:36," murmured Beauvoir.

"Pardon?"

"It's something your father tells us, in homicide. One of the first lessons he teaches new recruits."

"A biblical quote?" asked Annie. "But Mom and Dad never go to church."

"He apparently learned it from his mentor when he first joined the Sûreté."

The phone rang. Not the robust peal of the landline, but the cheerful, invasive trill of a cell. It was Beauvoir's. He ran to the bedroom and grabbed it off the nightstand.

No number was displayed, just a word.

32

"Chief."

He almost hit the small green phone icon, then hesitated. Instead he strode out of the bedroom and into Annie's light-filled, book-filled living room. He couldn't speak to the Chief standing in front of the bed where he'd just that morning made love to the Chief's daughter.

"Oui, allô," he said, trying to sound casual.

"Sorry to bother you," came the familiar voice. It managed to be both relaxed and authoritative.

"Not at all, sir. What's up?" Beauvoir glanced at the clock on the mantle. It was 10:23 on a Saturday morning.

"There's been a murder."

It wasn't, then, a casual call. An invitation to dinner. A query about staffing or a case going to trial. This was a call to arms. A call to action. A call that marked something dreadful had happened. And yet, for more than a decade now every time he heard those words, Beauvoir's heart leapt. And raced. And even danced a little. Not with joy at the knowledge of a terrible and premature death. But knowing he and the Chief and others would be on the trail again.

Jean-Guy Beauvoir loved his job. But now, for the first time, he looked into the kitchen, and saw Annie standing in the doorway.

33

Watching him.

And he realized, with surprise, that he now loved something more.

Grabbing his notebook he sat on Annie's sofa and took down the details. When he finished he looked at what he'd written.

"Holy shit," he whispered.

"At the very least," agreed Chief Inspector Gamache. "Can you make arrangements, please? And just the two of us for now. We'll pick up a local Sûreté agent when we arrive."

"Inspector Lacoste? Should she come? Just to organize the Scene of Crime team and leave?"

Chief Inspector Gamache didn't hesitate. "No." He gave a small laugh. "We're the Scene of Crime team, I'm afraid. Hope you remember how to do it."

"I'll bring the Hoover."

"*Bon.* I've already packed my magnifying glass." There was a pause and a more somber voice came down the line. "We need to get there quickly, Jean-Guy."

"*D'accord.* I'll make a few calls and pick you up in fifteen minutes."

"Fifteen? All the way from downtown?"

Beauvoir felt the world stop for a moment. His small apartment was in downtown Montréal, but Annie's was in the Plateau

Mont Royal *quartier,* a few blocks from her parents' home in Outremont. "It's a Saturday. Not much traffic."

Gamache laughed. "Since when did you become an optimist? I'll be waiting, whenever you arrive."

"I'll hurry."

And he did, placing calls, issuing orders, organizing. Then he threw a few clothes into an overnight bag.

"That's a lot of underwear," said Annie, sitting on the bed. "Are you planning to be gone long?" Her voice was light, but her manner wasn't.

"Well, you know me," he said, turning from her to slip his gun into its holder. She knew he had it, but didn't like to actually see it. Even for a woman who cherished reality, this was far too real. "Without benefit of plunger I might need more tighty whities."

She laughed, and he was glad.

At the door he stopped and lowered his case to the ground.

"Je t'aime," he whispered into her ear, as he held her.

"Je t'aime," she whispered into his ear. "Look after yourself," she said, as they parted. And then, as he was halfway down the steps she called, "And please, look after

my father."

"I will. I promise."

Once he was gone and she could no longer see the back of his car, Annie Gamache closed the door and held her hand to her chest.

She wondered if this was how her mother had felt, for all those years.

How her mother felt at that very moment. Was she too leaning against the door, having watched her heart leave? Having let it go.

Then Annie walked over to the bookcases lining her living room. After a few minutes she found what she was looking for. The bible her parents had given her, when she'd been baptized. For people who didn't attend church, they still followed the rituals.

And she knew when she had children she'd want them baptized too. She and Jean-Guy would present them with their own white bibles, with their names and baptism dates inscribed.

She looked at the thick first page. Sure enough, there was her name. Anne Daphné Gamache. And a date. In her mother's hand. But instead of a cross underneath her name her parents had drawn two little hearts.

Then Annie sat on the sofa and sipping

the now cool *café* she flipped through the unfamiliar book until she found it.

Matthew 10:36.

"And a man's foes," she read out loud, *"shall be they of his own household."*

TWO

The open aluminum boat cut through the waves, bouncing every now and then, sending small sprays of fresh, frigid water into Beauvoir's face. He could have moved back, toward the stern. But Beauvoir liked sitting on the tiny, triangular seat at the very front. He leaned forward and suspected he looked like an anxious and excited retriever. On the hunt.

But he didn't care. He was just glad he didn't have a tail. To put the lie to his slightly taciturn façade. Yes, he thought, a tail would be a great disadvantage to a homicide investigator.

The roar of the boat, the bounce, the occasional jolts were exhilarating. He even liked the bracing spray and the scent of fresh water and forest. And the slight smell of fish and worms.

When not ferrying homicide investigators, this small boat was obviously used to fish.

Not commercially. It was far too small for that, and besides, this remote lake wasn't for commercial fishing. But for enjoyment. The boatman casting into the clear waters of the craggy bays. Sitting all day, casually casting. And reeling in.

Casting. And reeling in. Alone with his thoughts.

Beauvoir looked to the stern. The boatman had one large, weathered hand on the handle of the outboard motor. The other rested on his knee. He too leaned forward, in a position he'd probably known since he was a boy. His keen blue eyes on the water ahead. Bays and islands and inlets he'd also known since he was a boy.

What pleasure there must be, Beauvoir thought, in doing the same thing over and over. In the past the very idea had revolted him. Routine, repetition. It was death, or at least, deadly dull. To lead a predictable life.

But now Beauvoir wasn't so sure. Here he was zooming toward a new case, in an open boat. The wind and spray on his face. But all he longed to do was sit down with Annie and share the Saturday papers. To do what they did every weekend. Over and over. Over and over. Until he died.

Still, if he couldn't be there, this was his second choice. He looked around, at the forests. At the rock cuts. At the empty lake.

There were worse offices than this.

He smiled a little at the stern boatman. This was his office too. And when he dropped them off would he find a quiet bay, pull out his rod, and cast?

Cast, and reel in.

It was, now that Beauvoir thought of it, not unlike what they were about to do. Cast for clues, for evidence, for witnesses. And reel them in.

And eventually, when there was enough bait, they'd catch a killer.

Though, unless things became terribly unpredictable, they probably wouldn't eat him.

Just in front of the boatman sat Captain Charbonneau, who ran the Sûreté du Québec station in La Mauricie. He was in his mid-forties, slightly older than Beauvoir. He was athletic and energetic and had the intelligent look of someone who paid attention.

He was paying attention now.

Captain Charbonneau had met them at the plane and driven them the half kilometer to the dock and the waiting boatman.

"This is Etienne Legault." He introduced the boatman, who nodded but didn't seem inclined to a fuller greeting. Legault smelled

40

of gasoline and smoked a cigarette and Beauvoir took a step back.

"It's about a twenty-minute boat trip, I'm afraid," Captain Charbonneau explained. "No other way to get there."

"Have you ever been?" Beauvoir had asked.

The captain smiled. "Never. Not inside anyway. But I fish not far from there sometimes. Like everyone else, I'm curious. Besides, it's great fishing. Huge bass and lake trout. I've seen them at a distance, also fishing. But I've left them on their own. I don't think they want company."

They'd all climbed into the open boat and now were halfway through the trip. Captain Charbonneau was looking ahead, or appeared to be. But Beauvoir realized the senior Sûreté officer wasn't focused completely on the thick forests or into the coves and bays.

He was stealing glances at something he found much more riveting.

The man in front of him.

Beauvoir's eyes shifted and came to rest on the fourth man in the boat.

The Chief Inspector. Beauvoir's boss and Annie's father.

Armand Gamache was a substantial man, though not heavy. Like the boatman, Chief

Inspector Gamache squinted ahead, creating creases at his mouth and eyes. But unlike the boatman, his expression wasn't glum. Instead his deep brown eyes were thoughtful, taking everything in. The glacier-stunted hills, the forest turning brilliant autumn colors. The rocky shoreline, unbroken by docks or homes or moorings of any kind.

This was the wilderness. Birds flew over them who might never have seen a human being.

If Beauvoir was a hunter, then Armand Gamache was an explorer. When others stopped, Gamache stepped ahead. Looking into cracks and crevices and caves. Where dark things lived.

The Chief was in his mid-fifties. The hair at his temples curled slightly above and behind his ears and was graying. A cap almost hid the scar at his left temple. He wore a khaki-colored waxed field coat. Beneath that was a shirt and jacket and gray-green silk tie. One large hand clasping the gunwale was wet with cold spray, as the boat chopped across the lake. The other rested absently on a bright orange life preserver, on the aluminum seat beside him. When they'd stood on the dock looking at the open boat with its fishing rod and net and tub of squiggling worms, and the outboard motor that looked like a toilet, the Chief had handed a life preserver, the newest, to Beauvoir. And when Jean-Guy had scoffed, he'd insisted. Not that Beauvoir had to wear it, but that he had to have it.

In case.

And so, Inspector Beauvoir's life jacket sat on his lap. And with each bounce he was privately happy to have it there.

He'd picked up the Chief at his home before eleven. At the door, Gamache paused to hug and kiss Madame Gamache. They lingered a moment before breaking the embrace. Then the Chief had turned and walked down the steps, his satchel slung over his shoulder.

When he'd gotten into the car Jean-Guy had smelled his subtle cologne of sandalwood and rosewater and been overwhelmed at the thought that this man might soon be his father-in-law. That Beauvoir's infant children might be held by this man, and smell that comforting scent.

Soon Jean-Guy would be more than an honorary member of this family.

But even as he thought that he heard a low whisper. *Suppose they aren't happy about that? What would happen then?*

But that was inconceivable, and he shoved

43

the unworthy thought away.

He also realized, for the first time in more than a decade together, why the Chief smelled of sandalwood and rosewater. The sandalwood was his own cologne. The rosewater came from Madame Gamache, as they'd pressed together. The Chief carried her scent, like an aura. Mixed with his own.

Beauvoir then took a long, slow, deep breath. And smiled. There was the slightest hint of citron. Annie. For a moment he was fearful her father would also smell it, but realized it was a private scent. He wondered if Annie now smelled a little of Old Spice.

They'd arrived at the airport before noon and had gone straight to the Sûreté du Québec hangar. There they'd found their pilot plotting the course. She was used to taking them into remote spots. Landing on dirt roads and ice roads and no roads.

"I see we actually have a landing strip today," she said, climbing into the pilot's seat.

"Sorry about that," said Gamache. "Feel free to ditch in the lake if you'd prefer."

The pilot laughed. "Wouldn't be the first time."

Gamache and Beauvoir had talked about the case, shouting at each other over the engines of the small Cessna. But eventually the Chief looked out the window and lapsed into silence. Though Beauvoir noticed that he'd put small earplugs in and was listening to music. And Beauvoir could guess which music. There was the trace of a smile on Chief Inspector Gamache's face.

Beauvoir turned and looked out his own small window. It was a brilliantly clear day in mid-September and he could see the towns and villages below. Then the villages got smaller, and sparser. The Cessna banked to the left and Beauvoir could see that the pilot was following a winding river. North.

Further and further north they flew. Each man lost in his own thoughts. Looking at the earth below, as all sign of civilization disappeared and there was only forest. And water. In the bright sunshine the water wasn't blue, but strips and patches of gold and dazzling white. They followed one of the golden ribbons, deeper into the forest. Deep into Québec. Toward a body.

As they flew, the dark forest began to change. At first it was just a tree here and there. Then more and more. Until finally the entire forest was shades of yellow and red and orange, and the dark, dark green of the evergreens.

Autumn came earlier here. The further north, the earlier the fall. The longer the fall, the greater the fall.

And then the plane started its descent. Down, down, down. It looked as though it would plunge into the water. But instead it leveled off and skimmed the surface, to land at a dirt airstrip.

And now Chief Inspector Gamache, Inspector Beauvoir, Captain Charbonneau, and the boatman were bouncing across that lake. The boat banked to the right slightly and Beauvoir saw the Chief's face change. From thoughtful to wonderment.

Gamache leaned forward, his eyes shining.

Beauvoir shifted in his seat and looked.

They'd turned into a large bay. There, at the end, was their destination.

And even Beauvoir felt a *frisson* of excitement. Millions had searched for this place. Looking all over the world for the reclusive men who lived here. When they'd finally been found, in remotest Québec, thousands had traveled here, desperate to meet the men inside. This same boatman might have even been hired to take tourists down this same lake.

If Beauvoir was a hunter, and Gamache an explorer, the men and women who came here were pilgrims. Desperate to be given what they believed these men had.

But it would have been for nothing.

All were turned away at the gate.

Beauvoir realized he'd seen this view before. In photographs. What they now saw had become a popular poster and was, somewhat disingenuously, used by Tourisme Québec to promote the province.

A place no one was allowed to visit was used to lure visitors.

Beauvoir also leaned forward. At the very end of the bay a fortress stood, like a rock cut. Its steeple rose as though propelled from the earth, the result of some seismic event. Off to the sides were wings. Or arms. Open in benediction, or invitation. A harbor. A safe embrace in the wilderness.

A deception.

This was the near mythical monastery of Saint-Gilbert-Entre-les-Loups. The home of two dozen cloistered, contemplative monks. Who had built their abbey as far from civilization as they could get.

It had taken hundreds of years for civilization to find them, but the silent monks had had the last word.

Twenty-four men had stepped beyond the door. It had closed. And not another living soul had been admitted.

Until today.

Chief Inspector Gamache, Jean-Guy

47

Beauvoir and Captain Charbonneau were about to be let in. Their ticket was a dead man.

THREE

"Want me to wait?" the boatman asked. He rubbed his stubbly face and looked amused.

They hadn't told him why they were there. For all he knew they were journalists or tourists. More misguided pilgrims.

"Oui, merci," said Gamache, handing the man his payment, including a generous tip.

The boatman pocketed it and watched as they unloaded their things then climbed onto the dock.

"How long can you wait?" asked the Chief.

"About three minutes," laughed the boatman. "That's about two minutes more'n you'll need."

"Can you give us," Gamache checked his watch. It was just after one in the afternoon. "Until five o'clock?"

"You want me to wait here until five? Look, I know you've come a long way, but you must know it won't take four hours to walk to that door, knock, then turn round and come back."

"They'll let us in," said Beauvoir.

"Are you monks?"

"No."

"Are you the pope?"

"No," said Beauvoir.

"Then I'll give you three minutes. Use 'em well."

Off the dock and up the dirt path, Beauvoir swore under his breath. When they reached the big wooden door the Chief turned to him.

"Get it out of your system, Jean-Guy. Once through there the swearing stops."

"Oui, patron."

Gamache nodded and Jean-Guy raised his hand and hit the door. It made almost no sound, but hurt like hell.

"Maudit tabernac," he hissed.

"I think that's the doorbell," said Captain Charbonneau, pointing to a long iron rod in a pocket chiseled out of the stone.

Beauvoir took it and hit the door a mighty whack. That made a sound. He hit it again and noticed the pockmarks, where others had hit. And hit. And hit.

Jean-Guy looked behind him. The boatman raised his wrist and tapped his watch.

Beauvoir turned back to the door and got a start.

The wood had sprung eyes. The door was looking at them. Then he realized a slit had been opened, and two bloodshot eyes looked out.

If Beauvoir was surprised to see the eyes, the eyes seemed surprised to see him.

"*Oui?*" The word was muffled by the wood.

"*Bonjour, mon frère,*" said Gamache. "My name is Armand Gamache, I'm the Chief Inspector of homicide with the Sûreté. This is Inspector Beauvoir and Captain Charbonneau. I believe we're expected."

The wooden window was rammed shut and they heard the unmistakable click as it was locked. There was a pause and Beauvoir began to wonder if they really would get in. And, if not, what would they do? Ram the door down? Clearly the boatman would be no help. Beauvoir could hear a soft chuckle coming from the dock, mingling with the lapping of the waves.

He looked into the forest. It was thick and dark. An attempt had been made to keep it at bay. Beauvoir could see evidence of trees chopped down. Stumps dotted the ground around the walls, as though there'd been a battle and now an uneasy truce. The stumps looked, in the shadow of the monastery, like tombstones.

Beauvoir took a deep breath and told himself to get a grip. It wasn't like him to be so fanciful. He dealt in facts. Collected them. It was the Chief Inspector who collected feelings. In each murder case, Gamache followed those feelings, the old and decaying and rotting ones. And at the end of the trail of slime, Gamache found the killer.

While the Chief followed feelings, Beauvoir followed facts. Cold and hard. But between the two men, together, they got there.

They were a good team. A great team.

Suppose he isn't happy? The question snuck up on Beauvoir, out of the woods. *Suppose he doesn't want Annie to be with me?*

But that was, again, just fancy. Not fact. Not fact. Not fact.

He stared at the door and saw again the pockmarks, where it had been beaten. By someone, or something, desperate to get in.

Beside him, Chief Inspector Gamache was standing solid. Calm. Staring at the door as though it was the most fascinating thing he'd seen.

And Captain Charbonneau? Out of the periphery of Beauvoir's vision he could see the outpost commander also staring at the door. He looked uneasy. Anxious to either enter or leave. To come or go. To do something, anything, other than wait on the stoop like some very polite conquerors.

Then there was a noise, and Beauvoir saw Charbonneau twitch in surprise.

They heard the long, drawn-out scrape of wrought iron against wood. Then silence.

Gamache hadn't moved, hadn't been surprised, or if he was he hadn't shown it. He continued to stare at the door, his hands clasped behind his back. With all the time in the world.

A crack appeared. It widened. And widened.

Beauvoir expected to hear a squeal as old, rusty, unused hinges were finally used. But instead there was no sound at all. Which was even more disconcerting.

The door opened completely, and facing them was a figure in a long black robe. But it wasn't totally black. There were white epaulettes at the shoulders, and a small apron of white partway down the chest. As though the monk had tucked a linen napkin into his collar and forgotten to remove it.

Tied at his waist was a rope, and attached to that was a ring with a single giant key.

The monk nodded, and stepped aside.

"Merci," said Gamache.

Beauvoir turned to the boatman and barely resisted giving him the finger.

Had his passengers levitated, the boatman could not have looked more surprised.

On the threshold Chief Inspector Gamache called back.

"Five o'clock then?"

The boatman nodded and managed, *"Oui, patron."*

Gamache turned back to the open door, and hesitated. For a heartbeat. Unnoticeable by anyone other than someone who knew him well. Beauvoir looked at Gamache and knew why.

The Chief simply wanted to savor this singular moment. With one step, he would become the first nonreligious ever to set foot into the monastery of Saint-Gilbert-Entre-les-Loups.

Then Gamache took that step, and the others followed.

The door closed behind them with a soft, snug thud. The monk brought up the large key and placed it in a large lock, and turned.

They were locked in.

Armand Gamache had expected to need a few moments to adjust to the dark interior. He hadn't expected that he'd need to adjust

54

to the light.

Far from being dim, the interior was luminous.

A long wide corridor of gray stones opened up ahead of them, ending in a closed door at the far end. But what struck the Chief, what must have struck every man, every monk, who entered those doors for centuries, was the light.

The corridor was filled with rainbows. Giddy prisms. Bouncing off the hard stone walls. Pooling on the slate floors. They shifted and merged and separated, as though alive.

The Chief Inspector knew his mouth had dropped open, but he didn't care. He'd never, in a life of seeing many astonishing things, seen anything quite like this. It was like walking into joy.

He turned and caught the eye of the monk. And held it for a moment.

There was no joy there. Just pain. The darkness Gamache had expected to find inside the monastery was not in the walls, but in the men. Or, at least, in this man.

Then, without a word, the monk turned and walked down the hallway. His pace was swift, but his feet made almost no sound. There was just a slight swish as his robe brushed the stones. Brushed past the rainbows.

The Sûreté officers hiked their packs securely over their shoulders and stepped into the warm prisms.

As he followed the monk, Gamache looked up and around. The light came from windows high up the walls. There were no windows at head height. The first were ten feet off the ground. And then another bank of windows above that. Through them Gamache could see blue, blue skies, a few clouds, and the tops of trees, as though they were bending to look in. Just as he was looking out.

The glass was old. Leaded. Imperfect. And it was the imperfections that were creating the play of light.

There was no adornment on the walls. No need.

The monk opened the door and they walked through into a larger, cooler space. Here the rainbows were directed to a single point. The altar.

This was the church.

The monk rushed across it, managing to genuflect on the fly. His pace had picked up, as though the monastery was slightly tilted and they were tumbling toward their destination.

The body.

Gamache glanced around, quickly taking in his surroundings. These were sights and sounds never experienced by men who actually got to leave.

The chapel smelled of incense. But not the musky, stale scent of so many churches in Québec, that smelled as though they were trying to hide something rotten. Here the scent was more natural. Like flowers or fresh herbs.

Gamache took it all in, in a series of swift impressions.

There was no somber and cautionary stained glass here. He realized the windows high on the walls were angled slightly so that the light fell to the simple, austere altar first. It was unadorned. Except for the cheerful light, which played on top of it and radiated to the walls and illuminated the farthest corners of the room.

And in that light Gamache saw something else. They weren't alone.

Two rows of monks faced each other on either side of the altar. They sat with their heads bowed, their hands folded in their laps. All in exactly the same position. Like carvings, tipping slightly forward.

They were completely and utterly silent, praying in the prism of light.

Gamache and the others passed from the church and entered yet another long hallway. Another long rainbow. Following the monk.

The Chief wondered if their guide, the hurrying monk, even noticed the rainbows he was splashing through anymore. Had they become humdrum? Had the remarkable become commonplace, in this singular place? Certainly the man in front of them didn't seem to care. But then, the Chief knew, violent death did that.

It was an eclipse, blocking out all that was beautiful, joyous, kind or lovely. So great was the calamity.

This monk who was leading them was young. Much younger than Gamache had expected. He quietly chastised himself for having those expectations. It was one of the first lessons he taught new recruits to his homicide division.

Have no expectations. Enter every room, meet every man, woman and child, look at every body with an open mind. Not so open that their brains fell out, but open enough to see and hear the unexpected.

Have no preconceptions. Murder was unexpected. And often so was the murderer.

Gamache had broken his own rule. He'd expected the monks to be old. Most monks and priests and nuns in Québec were. Not many young people were attracted to the religious life anymore.

While many continued to search for God, they'd given up looking for Him in a church.

This young man, this young monk, was the exception.

In the brief moment Chief Inspector Gamache and the monk had stared at each other, locked eyes, Gamache had realized two things. The monk was barely more than a boy. And he was extremely upset, and trying to hide it. Like a child who'd stubbed his toe on a rock but didn't want to admit to the pain.

Strong emotions were the rule at a murder scene. They were natural. So why was this young monk trying to hide his feelings? But he wasn't doing a very good job.

"Jeez," puffed Beauvoir, coming up beside Gamache, "what do you wanna bet Montréal is through there?"

He nodded to the next closed door, at the far end of the corridor. Beauvoir was more winded than Gamache or Captain Charbonneau, but then he carried more baggage.

The monk took a wrought-iron rod, like the one at the front door, from the side of the door and hit the wood. There was a mighty thump. He waited a moment, then hit again. They waited. Finally Beauvoir took the rod and gave the door a mighty rap.

Their wait ended with a familiar rasp, as again a deadbolt was pulled back. And the door opened.

FOUR

"My name is Dom Philippe," said the elderly monk. "The abbot of Saint-Gilbert. Thank you for coming."

He stood with his hands up his sleeves and his arms across his midsection. He looked exhausted. A courteous man, trying to hold on to that courtesy in the face of a barbaric act. Unlike the young monk, the abbot wasn't trying to hide his feelings.

"I'm sorry it was necessary," said Gamache, and introduced himself and his men.

"Follow me, please," said the abbot.

Gamache turned to thank the young monk who had shown them the way, but he'd already disappeared.

"Who was the brother who brought us here?" Gamache asked.

"Frère Luc," said the abbot.

"He's young," said Gamache, as he followed the abbot across the small room.

"Yes."

Dom Philippe was not being abrupt, Gamache believed. When men take a vow of silence a single word was a great offering. Dom Philippe was, in fact, being very generous.

The rainbows and prisms and cheerful light of the corridor didn't penetrate to here. But far from being glum, this room managed to feel intimate, homely. The ceilings were lower and the windows here were little more than slits in the wall. But through the diamond mullions Gamache could see forest. It was a comforting counterpoint to the rambunctious light of the hallway.

The stone walls were lined with bookcases and one wall was taken up with a large, open fireplace. Two chairs with a footstool between them flanked the fire. A lamp added to the light.

So there is electricity here, thought Gamache. He'd been uncertain.

From that small room they passed into an even smaller one.

"That was my study," the abbot nodded toward the room they'd just left. "This is my cell."

"Your cell?" asked Beauvoir, adjusting the now almost unbearably heavy duffel bags hanging from his drooping shoulders.

"Bedroom," said Dom Philippe.

62

The three Sûreté officers looked around. It was roughly six feet wide by ten feet long. With a narrow single bed and a small chest of drawers that seemed to double as a private altar. On it was a carving of the Virgin Mary and Christ Child. A tall, slender bookcase was against one wall and beside the bed was a tiny wooden table with books. There was no window.

The men turned around. And around.

"Forgive me, *mon père*," said Gamache. "But where is the body?"

Without a word the abbot tugged on the bookcase. All three men put out their arms in alarm, to grab the bookcase as it fell, but instead of tumbling over, it swung open.

Bright sunshine poured through the unexpected hole in the stone wall. And beyond it the Chief could see green grass scattered with autumn leaves. And bushes in different stages of fall colors. And a single, great tree. A maple. In the middle of the garden.

But Gamache's eyes went directly to the far end of the garden, and the figure crumpled there. And the two robed monks standing motionless a few feet from the body.

The Sûreté officers stepped through the last door. Into this unexpected garden.

■ ■ ■ ■

"Holy Mary, mother of God," the monks intoned, their voices low and melodic. *"Pray for us sinners . . ."*

"When did you find him?" Gamache asked as he carefully approached the body.

"My secretary found him after Lauds." On seeing the look on Gamache's face, the abbot explained. "Lauds ends at eight fifteen. Brother Mathiew was found at about twenty to nine. He went to find the doctor, but it was too late."

Gamache nodded. Behind him he could hear Beauvoir and Charbonneau unpacking the Scene of Crime equipment. The Chief looked at the grass, then reached out and gently guided the abbot back a few paces.

"*Désolé,* Dom Philippe, but we need to be careful."

"I'm sorry," said the abbot, stepping away. He seemed lost, bewildered. Not just by the body, but by the sudden appearance of men he didn't know.

Gamache caught Beauvoir's eye and subtly gestured to the ground. Beauvoir nodded. He'd already noticed the slight difference between the grass here and the rest of the garden. Here the blades were bent. And pointed to the body.

Gamache turned back to the abbot. The man was tall and slender. Like the other monks, Dom Philippe was clean-shaven, and his head, while not shaved to the scalp, had just a bristle of gray hair.

The abbot's eyes were deep blue and he held Gamache's thoughtful gaze as though trying to find a way in. The Chief didn't look away, but he did feel quietly ransacked.

The abbot again slipped his hands up the sleeves of his robe. It was the same pose as the other two monks who were standing not far from the body, eyes closed and praying.

"Hail Mary, full of grace . . ."

The rosary. Gamache recognized it. Could say it himself in his sleep.

". . . the Lord is with thee. . . ."

"Who is he, *Père Abbé?*"

Gamache had placed himself so that he was facing the body, and the abbot was not. In some cases the Chief wanted the suspects to be unable to avoid seeing the dead person. The murdered person. He wanted the sight to fray and tear and rend.

But not in this case. He suspected this quiet man would never forget that sight. And that perhaps kindness would be a more rapid road to the truth.

"Mathieu. Brother Mathieu."

"The choirmaster?" asked Gamache. "Oh."

The Chief Inspector lowered his head slightly. Death always meant loss. Violent death tore the hole wider. The loss seemed greater. But to lose this man? Armand Gamache looked back at the body on the ground, curled into a ball. His knees as far up to his chin as he could get them. Before he died.

Frère Mathieu. The choir director of Saint-Gilbert-Entre-les-Loups. The man whose music Gamache had been listening to on the flight there.

Gamache felt as though he knew him. Not by sight, obviously. No one had seen him. There were no photographs, no portraits of Frère Mathieu. But millions, including Gamache, felt they knew him in ways far more intimate than physical appearance.

This was indeed a loss, and not just to this remote and cloistered community.

"The choirmaster," the abbot confirmed. He turned around and looked at the man on the ground. Dom Philippe spoke softly. Almost whispering. "And our prior." The abbot turned back to Gamache. "And my friend."

He closed his eyes and became very still. Then he opened them again. They were very blue. The abbot took a deep breath. Gathering himself, thought Gamache.

He knew the feeling. When there was something deeply unpleasant, painful, to do. This was that instant, before the plunge.

On the exhale Dom Philippe did something unexpected. He smiled. It was subtle, almost not there. He looked at Armand Gamache with such warmth and openness the Chief Inspector found himself almost paralyzed.

"All shall be well," said Dom Philippe, looking directly at Gamache. *"All shall be well; and all manner of thing shall be well."*

It wasn't at all what the Chief had expected the abbot to say and it took him a moment, looking into those startling eyes, to respond.

"Merci. I believe that, *mon père,"* said Gamache at last. "But do you?"

"Julian of Norwich wouldn't lie," said Dom Philippe, again with that slight smile.

"Probably not," said Gamache. "But then Julian of Norwich wrote of divine love and probably never had a murder in her convent. You have, I'm afraid."

The abbot continued to watch Gamache. Not, the Chief felt, in anger. Indeed, the same warmth was there. But the weariness had returned.

"That is true."

"Would you excuse me, *Père Abbé?*"

The Chief stepped around the abbot and examined the ground, picking his way carefully across the grass and through the flower bed. To Frère Mathieu.

There he knelt.

He didn't reach out. Didn't touch. Armand Gamache just looked. Taking in the evidence, but also the impressions.

His impression was that Frère Mathieu had not gone gently. Many people he knelt beside had been killed so quickly they barely knew what happened.

Not the prior. He knew what had happened, and what was going to happen.

Gamache looked back to the grass. Then to the dead man. The side of Frère Mathieu's head had been bashed in. The Chief Inspector leaned closer. It looked like at least two, perhaps three blows. Enough to mortally wound. But not enough to kill instantly.

The prior, Gamache thought, must have had a hard head.

He sensed, rather than saw, Beauvoir kneel beside him. He looked over and saw Captain Charbonneau beside Beauvoir. They'd brought their evidence kits.

Gamache glanced back to the garden.

Scene of Crime tape had been put up around the grass and outlined a trail to the flower bed.

The abbot had rejoined the other monks and together they were reciting the Hail Mary.

Beauvoir brought out his notebook. A fresh one for a fresh body.

Gamache himself did not take notes, but preferred to listen.

"What do you think?" the Chief asked, looking at Charbonneau.

The captain's eyes widened. *"Moi?"*

Gamache nodded.

For a horrible moment Captain Charbonneau thought nothing. His mind went as blank as the dead man's. He stared at Gamache. But far from being haughty or demanding the Chief Inspector was simply attentive. This was no trap, no trick.

Charbonneau felt his heart slow and his brain speed up.

Gamache smiled encouragingly. "Take your time. I'd rather have a thoughtful answer than a fast one."

". . . pray for us sinners . . ."

The three monks intoned while the three officers knelt.

Charbonneau looked around the garden. It was walled. The only entrance and exit through the bookcase. There was no ladder, no evidence anyone had climbed into or out of there. He looked up. The garden wasn't overlooked. No one could have witnessed what had happened here.

What had happened here? Chief Inspector Gamache was asking for his opinion. His educated, thoughtful analysis.

Christ, he prayed. *Christ, give me an opinion.*

When Inspector Beauvoir had called and asked that one of the local Sûreté officers meet the plane and accompany them to the monastery, Captain Charbonneau had taken the job himself. As head of the detachment he could have assigned anyone. But that was never a consideration.

He wanted it for himself.

And not just to see the inside of the famous abbey.

Captain Charbonneau also wanted to meet Chief Inspector Gamache.

"There's blood on the grass over there." Charbonneau waved to a section cordoned off with crime scene tape. "And by the marks on the grass it looks as though he dragged himself a few feet, over here."

"Or was dragged," suggested Gamache, "by his killer."

"Unlikely, *patron.* There're no deep foot-

70

prints on the grass or in the flower bed here."

"Good," said Gamache, looking around. "Now why would a dying man drag himself here?"

They all considered the body again. Frère Mathieu was curled into a fetal position, his knees up, his arms wrapped tightly around his stout stomach. His head tucked in. His back was against the stone wall of the garden.

"Was he trying to make himself small?" asked Beauvoir. "He looks like a ball."

And he did. A quite large black ball that had come to rest against the wall.

"But why?" Gamache asked again. "Why not drag himself toward the monastery? Why move away from it?"

"Maybe he was disoriented," said Charbonneau. "Was going more on instinct than thought. Maybe there was no reason."

"Maybe," said Gamache.

All three continued to stare at the body of Frère Mathieu. Captain Charbonneau glanced across at Gamache, who was deep in thought.

He was inches from the man. Could see all the lines of his face. Both natural and man-made. He could even smell the man. The slightest hint of sandalwood and something else. Rosewater.

He'd seen the Chief Inspector on television, of course. Charbonneau had even flown to Montréal to attend a police conference where Gamache was the keynote speaker. The topic was the Sûreté motto, *"Service, Intégrité, Justice."*

That was always the keynote topic and over the years it had become a pep rally, an orgy of self-congratulations to end the annual Sûreté conference.

Except when Chief Inspector Gamache had given the talk, just a few months earlier. At first Gamache had shocked the thousand officers in the audience by talking about his own failings in each of those areas. Where he could have done better. Where he'd failed to do anything at all.

And he made clear the failures of the Sûreté itself. Bringing home with precision and clarity where the police force had let down, even betrayed the trust of the people of Québec. Time and again. It was a merciless indictment of a force Gamache believed in.

And that's what became clear.

Armand Gamache believed in them. He believed in the Sûreté and in Service and Integrity and Justice.

He could do better.

They could do better.

As individuals and as a force.

By the end of the talk the thousand officers were on their feet, cheering. Revitalized. Inspired.

Except, Captain Charbonneau had noticed, a small cadre. In the front row. They too stood. They too clapped. How could they not? But from his position off to the side, Charbonneau could see their hearts were not in it. And God only knew where their heads were at.

These were the superintendents of the Sûreté. The leadership. And the Minister of Justice.

He wanted now to lean forward. Over the body. To lower his voice and say, *"I don't know why this man crawled away. But I do know something you should hear. You might not have as many friends in the force as you think. As you believe."*

He opened his mouth to speak, but closed it again on looking into the Chief's face. At the scars, and the deep, intelligent eyes.

This man knows, Charbonneau realized. Chief Inspector Gamache knows his days on the force might be numbered.

"What do you think?" Gamache asked again.

"I think he knew exactly what was going

to happen to him."

"Go on," said the Chief.

"I think he did his best, but it was too late. He couldn't get away."

"No," agreed Gamache. "There was nowhere to go."

The two men stared at each other for a moment. Understanding each other.

"But why didn't he leave a message?" asked Beauvoir.

"I'm sorry?" Charbonneau turned to the younger man.

"Well, he'd seen his killer, he knew he was dying. He had the strength to crawl all this way. Why didn't he use some of that last energy to leave us a message?" Beauvoir asked.

They looked around, but the earth had been trampled. Not by them, but by a bunch of monks, well meaning or otherwise.

"Maybe it's simpler than that," said Charbonneau. "Maybe he was like an animal. Curling up to die alone."

Gamache felt an overwhelming sympathy for the dead man. To die alone. Almost certainly struck down by someone he knew and trusted. Was that the alarm on this man's face? Not that he was dying, but that it was at the hands of a brother. Was that how Abel had looked, as he fell to the earth?

74

They bent over the monk again.

Frère Mathieu was in late middle age, and rotund. A man who didn't appear to deny himself much. If he mortified his flesh it was with food. And maybe drink. Though he didn't have the ruddy, bloated complexion of the dissolute.

The prior simply looked well satisfied with his life, though clearly more than a little disappointed by his death.

"Could there have been another blow?" asked the Chief. "To his abdomen, perhaps?"

". . . and blessed is the fruit of thy womb . . ."

Beauvoir also leaned closer and nodded. "His arms are wrapped around his stomach. Do you think he was in pain?"

Gamache stood up and absently brushed dirt from his knees.

"I'll leave him to you, Inspector. Captain."

The Chief Inspector retraced his steps, careful not to wander from the path he'd already created.

"Holy Mary, mother of God . . ."

The monks continued to repeat the Hail Mary.

How did they know when to stop, Gamache wondered. When was it enough?

He knew what his goal was. To find whoever had killed Frère Mathieu.

"... *pray for us sinners* ..."

But what was theirs, these three black-robed figures?

"... *now and at the hour of our death. Amen.*"

FIVE

The Chief watched the monks for a few moments, then he turned and watched Beauvoir.

He'd put on weight, and while still lean he was no longer gaunt. Jean-Guy's face had filled out and the shadows under his eyes had disappeared.

But more than the physical change, Beauvoir now seemed happy. Indeed, happier than Gamache had ever seen him. Not the feverish, giddy highs of the addict, but a settled calm. Gamache knew it was a long and treacherous road back, but Beauvoir was at least on it.

Gone were the mood swings, the irrational outbursts. The rage and the whining.

Gone were the pills. The OxyContin and Percocet. It was one of the terrible ironies that medications meant to relieve pain would finally cause so much.

God knew, thought Gamache as he

watched his Inspector, Beauvoir had had genuine pain. Had needed those pills. But then he'd needed to stop.

And he had. With help. Gamache hoped it wasn't too soon for his Inspector to be back on the job, but suspected what Beauvoir needed now was normalcy. To not be treated as though he was handicapped.

Still, Gamache knew Jean-Guy needed watching. For any cracks in the calm.

For now, though, Gamache turned away from the agents, knowing they had a job to do. And he turned away from the monks, knowing they also had their job.

And he had his.

Gamache looked around the garden.

It was the first chance he'd had to really take it in.

It was square. Roughly forty feet by forty. Not meant for sports or large gatherings. The monks would not be playing soccer here.

Gamache noticed a wicker basket with gardening implements dropped on the ground. There was also a black medical bag, close to the praying monks.

He began to wander, looking at the perennials, at the herbs all marked and named.

Echinacea, meadowsweet, St. John's wort, chamomile.

Gamache was no gardener, but he suspected these weren't just herbs or flowers, but medicinal. He looked around again.

Everything here seemed to have a purpose. To be thought out.

Including, he suspected, the body.

There was a purpose to this murder. His job was to find it.

A curved stone bench sat under the maple in the center of the garden. Most of the tree's autumn leaves had fallen. Most had been raked up, but some were scattered on the grass. And a few, like forlorn hope, clung to the mother tree.

In summer, in full leaf, there would be a magnificent canopy, throwing dappled light over the garden. Not much of this garden would be in full sun. Not much in complete shade.

The abbot's garden had achieved a balance between light and dark.

But now, in autumn, it seemed to be dying.

But that too was the natural cycle. It would be deviant, abnormal, if all was in perpetual flower.

The walls were, Gamache guessed, at least ten feet high. No one climbed out of the garden. And the only way in was through the abbot's bedroom. Through the secret door.

Gamache looked back at the monastery. No one inside the monastery could come into, or even see into, the abbot's garden.

Did they even know it was here? Gamache wondered. Was that possible?

Was this not only a private garden, but a secret one?

Dom Philippe repeated the rosary.

"Hail Mary, full of grace, the Lord is with thee. . . ."

His head was bowed but his eyes were open, just a slit. He watched the police officers in the garden. Bending over Mathieu. Taking his picture. Prodding him. How Mathieu, always so fastidious, so precise, would have hated this.

To die in the dirt.

"Holy Mary, mother of God . . ."

How could Mathieu be dead? Dom Philippe mouthed the rosary, trying to concentrate on the simple prayer. He said the words, and heard his brother monks beside him. Heard their familiar voices. Felt their shoulders against his.

Felt the sunshine on his head, and smelled the musky autumn garden.

But now nothing seemed familiar anymore. The words, the prayer, even the sunshine felt foreign.

Mathieu was dead.

How could I not have known?

". . . pray for us sinners . . ."

How could I not have known?

The words became his new rosary.

How could I not have known that it would all end in murder?

Gamache had come full circle and stopped in front of the praying monks.

He had the impression as he approached that the abbot had been watching.

One thing was obvious. In the few minutes Gamache had been in the garden, the abbot's energy had diminished even further.

If the Hail Marys were meant to comfort, it wasn't working. Or perhaps, without the prayers Dom Philippe would be in worse shape. He seemed like a man on the verge of collapse.

"Pardon," said Gamache.

The two monks stopped their prayers, but Dom Philippe continued, to the end.

". . . now and at the hour of our death."

And together they intoned, *"Amen."*

Dom Philippe opened his eyes.

"Yes, my son?"

It was the traditional greeting of a priest

to a parishioner. Or an abbot to his monks. Gamache, though, was neither. And he wondered why Dom Philippe would use that term with him.

Was it habit? An offer of affection? Or was it something else? A claim to authority. A father's over a child.

"I have some questions."

"Of course," said the abbot while the other two remained silent.

"I understand one of you found Frère Mathieu."

The monk to the right of the abbot shot Dom Philippe a look, and the abbot gave a very small nod.

"I did." The monk was shorter than Dom Philippe and slightly younger. His eyes were wary.

"And you are?"

"Simon."

"Perhaps, *mon frère,* you can describe what happened this morning."

Frère Simon turned to the abbot, who nodded again.

"I came in here after Lauds to tidy up the garden. Then I saw him."

"What did you see?"

"Frère Mathieu."

"*Oui,* but did you know it was him?"

"No."

82

"Who did you think it might be?"

Frère Simon lapsed into silence.

"It's all right, Simon. We need to speak the truth," said the abbot.

"Oui, Père Abbé." The monk didn't look happy or convinced. But he did obey. "I thought it was the abbot."

"Why?"

"Because no one else comes in here. Only him and me now."

Gamache considered that for a moment. "What did you do?"

"I went to see."

Gamache glanced over at the wicker basket, on its side, the contents tumbling out onto the autumn leaves. The rake thrown down.

"Did you walk, or run?"

Again that hesitation. "I ran."

Gamache could imagine the scene. The middle-aged monk with his basket. Preparing to garden, to rake up the dead leaves. Entering this peaceful garden to do what he'd done so many times before. Then seeing the unthinkable. A man collapsed at the base of the wall.

Without doubt, the abbot.

And what had Frère Simon done? He'd dropped his tools and run. As fast as his robed legs would take him.

"And when you got to him, what did you do?"

"I saw that it wasn't *Père Abbé* at all."

"Describe for me please everything that you did."

"I knelt down." Every word seemed to cause him pain. Either because of the memory, or just their existence. The very act of speaking. "And I moved his hood. It'd fallen across his face. That's when I saw it wasn't the abbot."

It wasn't the abbot. That was what seemed to matter to this man. Not who it was, but who it wasn't. Gamache listened closely. To the words. The tone. The space between the words.

And what he heard now was relief.

"Did you touch the body? Move him?"

"I touched his hood and his shoulders. Shook him. Then I went to get the doctor."

Frère Simon looked at the other monk.

He was younger than the other two, but not by much. The stubble on his close-cropped head was also graying. He was shorter and slightly rounder than the other two. And his eyes, while somber, held none of the anxiety of his companions.

"Are you the doctor?" Gamache asked and the monk nodded. He seemed almost amused.

But Gamache wasn't fooled. One of Reine-Marie's brothers laughed in funerals and wept at weddings. A friend of theirs always laughed when someone yelled at him. Not from amusement, but an overflow of strong emotion.

Sometimes the two got mixed up. Especially in people unused to showing emotion.

The medical monk, while appearing amused, might in fact be the most devastated.

"Charles," the monk offered. "I'm the *médecin*."

"Tell me how you found out about the death of the prior."

"I was with the animals when Frère Simon came to get me. He took me aside and said there'd been an accident —"

"Were you alone?"

"No, there were other brothers there, but Frère Simon was careful to keep his voice low. I don't think they heard."

Gamache turned back to Frère Simon. "Did you really think it was an accident?"

"I wasn't sure and I didn't know what else to say."

"I'm sorry." Gamache turned back to the doctor. "I interrupted you."

"I ran to the infirmary, grabbed my medical bag and we came here."

Gamache could imagine the two black-robed monks running through the sparkling halls. "Did you meet anyone on the way?"

"Not a soul," said Frère Charles. "It was our work period. Everyone was at their chores."

"What did you do when you arrived in the garden?"

"I looked for a pulse, of course, but his eyes were enough to tell me he was dead, even if I hadn't seen the wound."

"And what did you think when you did?"

"At first I wondered if he'd fallen off the wall, but I could see that was impossible."

"And then what did you think?"

Frère Charles looked at the abbot.

"Go on," said Dom Philippe.

"I thought someone had done this to him."

"Who?"

"I honestly hadn't a clue."

Gamache paused to scrutinize the doctor. In his experience when someone said "honestly" it was often a prelude to a lie. He tucked that impression away and turned to the abbot.

"I wonder, sir, if you and I might talk some more."

The abbot didn't look surprised. He looked as though nothing could shock him anymore.

"Of course."

Dom Philippe bowed to the other two monks, catching their eyes, and the Chief wondered what message had just passed between them. Did monks who lived silently together develop a form of telepathy? An ability to read each other's thoughts?

If so, that gift had sorely failed the prior.

Dom Philippe led Gamache to the bench under the tree. Away from the activity.

From there they couldn't see the body. They couldn't see the monastery. Instead the view was to the wall, and the medicinal herbs and the tops of the trees beyond.

"I'm finding it hard to believe this has happened," said the abbot. "You must hear that all the time. Does everyone say that?"

"Most do. It would be a terrible thing if murder wasn't a shock."

The abbot sighed and stared into the distance. Then he closed his eyes, and brought his slender hands to his face.

There was no sobbing. No weeping. Not even praying.

Just silence. His long elegant hands like a mask over his face. Another wall between himself and the outside world.

Finally he dropped his hands into his lap. They rested there, limp.

"He was my best friend, you know. We're not supposed to have best friends in a monastery. We're all supposed to be equal. All friends, but none too much. But of course that's the ideal. Like Julian of Norwich, we aspire to an all-consuming love of God. But we're flawed and human, and sometimes we also love our fellow man. There are no rules for the heart."

Gamache listened and waited, and tried not to overinterpret what he was being told.

"I can't tell you how often Mathieu and I sat here. He'd sit where you are now. Sometimes we'd discuss the business of the monastery, sometimes we'd just read. He'd bring his scores for the chants. I'd be gardening, or sitting quietly and hear him humming under his breath. I don't think he even knew he was doing it or that I could hear. But I could."

The abbot's gaze drifted to the wall and the tips of the forest, like dark steeples, beyond. He sat quietly for a moment, lost in what was now and forever the past. The scene he described would never be repeated. That overheard sound would never be heard again.

"Murder?" he finally whispered. "Here?" He returned to Gamache. "And you've come to find out which of us did it. The

Chief Inspector, you said. So we get the boss?"

Gamache smiled. "Not the big boss, I'm afraid. I also have bosses."

"Don't we all," said Dom Philippe. "At least yours can't see everything you do."

"And know everything I think and feel," said Gamache. "I'm grateful for that every day."

"Though neither can they bring you peace and salvation."

Gamache nodded. "That much is certain."

"Patron?" Beauvoir was standing a few feet away.

Excusing himself, Gamache walked over to his Inspector.

"We're ready to move the body. But where should we take him?"

Gamache thought about that for a moment, then looked at the two praying monks. "That man over there," Gamache pointed to Frère Charles, "is the *médecin.* Go with him to get a stretcher and take Frère Mathieu back to the infirmary." Gamache paused for a moment, and Beauvoir knew him well enough to wait. "He was the choir director here, you know." Gamache looked once again at the balled-up body of Frère Mathieu.

To Beauvoir this was just another fact. A

piece of information. But he could see it meant more to the Chief.

"Is that important?" asked Beauvoir.

"It could be."

"It's important to you, isn't it," said Beauvoir.

"It's a shame," said the Chief. "A great loss. He was a genius, you know. I was listening to his music on the way in."

"I thought maybe you were."

"Have you ever heard it?"

"Hard not to. It was everywhere a couple years ago. Couldn't turn on a damned station without hearing it."

Gamache smiled. "Not a fan?"

"Are you kidding? Of Gregorian chants? A bunch of men singing without instruments, practically in a monotone, in Latin? What's not to love?"

The Chief smiled at Beauvoir and returned to the abbot.

"Who could have done such a thing?" Dom Philippe asked under his breath when Gamache resumed his seat. "I've been asking myself that all morning." The abbot turned to his companion. "And why didn't I see it coming?"

Gamache was silent, knowing the question wasn't directed at him. But the answer would come from him, eventually. And he realized something else.

Dom Philippe had not tried to imply that an outsider had somehow done this. He'd not even tried to convince Gamache, or himself, that it was an accident. An unlikely fall.

There was none of the usual squirming away from the awful truth.

Frère Mathieu had been murdered. And one of the other monks had done it.

On the one hand Gamache admired Dom Philippe's ability to face reality, no matter how terrible. But Gamache was also puzzled that this man so easily accepted it.

The abbot claimed to be astonished that murder should happen here. And yet he didn't do what would be most human. He didn't look for another explanation, no matter how ludicrous.

And Chief Inspector Gamache began to wonder just how shocked Dom Philippe really was.

"Frère Mathieu was killed between eight fifteen, when your service ended, and twenty to nine, when he was found by your secretary," said the Chief. "Where were you at that time?"

"Right after Lauds I went to the basement to discuss the geothermal system with Frère Raymond. He looks after the physical plant.

The engineering of the monastery."

"You have geothermal here?"

"That's right. Geothermal heats the monastery and solar panels power it. With winter coming I had to make sure it was working. I was down there when Brother Simon found me and told me the news."

"What time was that?"

"Close to nine, I think."

"What did Frère Simon say?"

"Only that it appeared Frère Mathieu had had some sort of accident in my garden."

"Did he tell you that Frère Mathieu was dead?"

"Eventually. As I rushed back he came out with it. He'd gone to get the doctor first and then me. By then they knew it was fatal."

"But did he tell you any more?"

"That Mathieu had been killed?"

"That he'd been murdered."

"The doctor did. When I arrived here the doctor was standing at the door waiting. He tried to stop me from going closer, and said Mathieu wasn't just dead, but that it looked as though someone had killed him."

"And what did you say?"

"I can't remember what I said, but I suspect it was something not taught at the seminary."

Dom Philippe cast his mind back. He'd shoved by the doctor and run, stumbling, to the far end. To what looked like a mound of dark earth. But wasn't. As he saw it in his memory he described it to the large, quiet Sûreté officer beside him.

"And then I dropped to my knees beside him," said Dom Philippe.

"Did you touch him?"

"Yes. I touched his face, and his robe. I think I straightened it. I don't know why. Who would do such a thing?"

Again, Gamache ignored the question. Time enough for the answer.

"What was Frère Mathieu doing here? In your garden?"

"I have no idea. It wasn't to see me. I'm always out at that time. It's when I do my rounds."

"And he'd know that?"

"He was my prior. He knew it better than most."

"What did you do after you'd seen his body?" Gamache asked.

The abbot thought about that. "We prayed first. And then I called the police. We have only one phone. It's a satellite thing. Doesn't always work, but it did this morning."

"Did you consider not calling?"

The question surprised the abbot and he

studied this quiet stranger with new appreciation. "I'm ashamed to admit it was my first thought. To keep it to ourselves. We're used to being self-sufficient."

"Then why did you call?"

"Not for Mathieu, I'm afraid, but for the others."

"What do you mean?"

"Mathieu is gone now. He's with God."

Gamache hoped that was true. For Frère Mathieu there were no more mysteries. He knew who took his life. And he now knew if there was a God. And a Heaven. And angels. And even a celestial choir.

It didn't bear thinking about what happened to the celestial choir when yet another director showed up.

"But the rest of us are here," Dom Philippe continued. "I didn't call you in for vengeance or to punish whoever did this. The deed is done. Mathieu is safe. We, on the other hand, are not."

It was, Gamache knew, the simple truth. It was also the reaction of a father. To protect. Or a shepherd, to keep the flock safe from a predator.

Saint-Gilbert-Entre-les-Loups. Saint Gilbert among the wolves. It was a curious name for a monastery.

The abbot knew there was a wolf in the

fold. In a black robe, and shaved head, and whispering soft prayers. Dom Philippe had called in hunters to find him.

Beauvoir and the doctor had returned with the stretcher and had placed it beside Frère Mathieu. Gamache stood and gave a silent signal. The body was lifted onto the stretcher and Frère Mathieu left the garden for the last time.

The abbot led the small procession, followed by Frères Simon and Charles. Then Captain Charbonneau at the head of the stretcher and Beauvoir behind.

Gamache was the last to leave the abbot's garden, closing the bookcase behind him.

They walked into the rainbow corridor. The joyful colors played on the body, and the mourners. As they arrived at the church, the rest of the community stood and filed from the benches. Joining them. Walking behind Gamache.

The abbot, Dom Philippe, began to recite a prayer. Not the rosary. Something else. And then Gamache realized the abbot wasn't speaking. He was singing. And it wasn't simply a prayer. It was a chant.

A Gregorian chant.

Slowly the other monks joined in and the singing swelled to fill the corridor, and join with the light. It would have been beautiful, if not for the certainty that one of the men singing the words of God, in the voice of God, was a killer.

Six

Four men gathered around the gleaming examination table.

Armand Gamache and Inspector Beauvoir stood on one side, the doctor across from them and the abbot off to the side. Frère Mathieu lay on the stainless steel table, terrified face to the ceiling.

The other monks had gone off to do what monks did at a time like this. Gamache wondered what that might be.

Most people, in Gamache's experience, groped and stumbled, barking their shins against familiar scents and sights and sounds. As though struck with vertigo, falling over the edge of their known world.

Captain Charbonneau had been detailed to search for the murder weapon. It was, Gamache believed, a long shot, but one that needed to be taken. It appeared the prior had been killed by a rock. If so, it had almost certainly been tossed over the wall, to be lost in the old-growth forest.

The Chief Inspector glanced around. He'd expected the infirmary to be old, ancient even. He'd privately prepared himself to see something out of the Dark Ages. Operating tables made of stone slabs, with open gutters for the fluids. Wooden shelves with dried and powdered herbs from the garden. Hacksaws for surgery.

Instead, this room was brand-spanking-new, with shining equipment, orderly cabinets filled with gauze and bandages, pills and tongue depressors.

"The coroner will do the autopsy," said Gamache to the doctor. "We don't want you doing any medical procedures on the prior. All I need is for his clothes to be removed so we can properly search them. And I need to see his body."

"Why?"

"In case there are other wounds or marks. Anything else we should see. The faster we can collect the facts the sooner we can get at the truth."

"But there's a difference between fact and truth, Chief Inspector," said the abbot.

"And one day you and I can sit in that lovely garden of yours and discuss it," said Gamache. "But not now."

He turned his back on the abbot and nodded to the doctor, who got to work.

The dead man was no longer curled in the fetal position. Though rigor mortis was setting in, they had managed to lay him flat on his back. The prior's hands, Gamache noted, were still buried up the long black sleeves of his cassock, and wrapped around his midsection, as though gripping in pain.

After untying the cord around the prior's middle, the doctor pried the dead man's hands from his sleeves. Both Gamache and Beauvoir leaned forward, to see if they had hold of anything. Was there anything under his nails? Anything in those balled-up fists?

But they were empty. The nails clean and tidy.

The doctor carefully placed Frère Mathieu's arms at his side. But the left arm slipped off the metal table and dangled. Something dropped from the sleeve and drifted to the floor.

The doctor stooped to pick it up.

"Don't touch that," Beauvoir ordered, and the doctor stopped.

Putting on a pair of gloves from the Scene of Crime kit, Beauvoir bent and picked a piece of paper off the stone floor.

"What is it?" The abbot stepped forward. The doctor leaned across the examination table, the body forgotten in favor of what

Inspector Beauvoir held.

"I don't know," said Beauvoir.

The doctor came around the table and the four men stood in a circle, staring at the page.

It was yellowed and irregular. Not store-bought. Thicker than commercial-grade paper.

On it, in intricate script, were words. The black letters calligraphied. Not ornately, but in a simple style.

"I can't read it. Is it Latin?" asked Beauvoir.

"I think so." The abbot leaned forward, squinting.

Gamache put on his half-moon reading glasses and also bent toward the paper. "It looks like a page from an old manuscript," he finally said, stepping back.

The abbot looked perplexed. "It's not paper, it's vellum. Sheepskin. You can tell by the texture."

"Sheepskin?" asked Beauvoir. "Is that what you use for paper?"

"Not for hundreds of years." The abbot continued to stare at the page in the Inspector's hand. "The text doesn't seem to make sense. It might be Latin, but not from any psalm or Book of Hours or religious text I know. I can only make out two words."

"What are they?" asked the Chief.

"Here," the abbot pointed. "That looks like *'Dies irae.'*"

The doctor made a small noise that might have been a guffaw. They looked at him, but he fell completely silent.

"What does that mean?" asked Beauvoir.

"It's from the Requiem Mass," said the abbot.

"It means 'day of wrath,'" said Gamache. *"Dies irae,"* he quoted, *"dies illa.* Day of wrath. Day of mourning."

"That's right," said the abbot. "In the Requiem Mass the two are said together. But here, there is no *dies illa.*"

"What does that tell you, Dom Philippe?" asked the Chief.

The abbot was quiet for a moment, considering. "It tells me this isn't the Requiem Mass."

"Does it make any sense to you, Frère Charles?" Gamache asked.

The doctor's brow was creased in concentration as he stared at the vellum in Beauvoir's hand. Then he shook his head. "I'm afraid not."

"Neither of you have seen this before?" Gamache pressed.

The doctor glanced at the abbot. Dom Philippe continued to stare at the words and finally shook his head.

There was a pause then Beauvoir pointed to the page. "What're those?"

Once again the men leaned forward.

Above each word there were tiny squiggles of ink. Like little waves. Or wings.

"I think they're neumes," said the abbot, at last.

"Neumes?" asked Gamache. "What's that?"

Now the abbot was clearly bewildered. "They're a musical notation."

"I've never seen it before," said Beauvoir.

"You wouldn't." The abbot stepped away from the page. "They haven't been used for a thousand years."

"I don't understand," said Gamache. "Is this page a thousand years old?"

"It might be," said Dom Philippe. "And that might explain the text. It might be plainchant using an old form of Latin."

But he didn't seem convinced.

"By 'plainchant' do you mean Gregorian chant?" asked the Chief.

The abbot nodded.

"Could this be," the Chief pointed to the page, "a Gregorian chant?"

The abbot looked again at the page and shook his head, "I don't know. It's the words. They're Latin, but they're nonsense.

Gregorian chants follow very old and pre-scribed rules and are almost always from the psalms. This isn't."

Dom Philippe lapsed into his habitual si-lence.

There seemed no more to be learned from the paper at the moment. Gamache turned to the doctor.

"Please continue."

Over the next twenty minutes Frère Charles stripped Brother Mathieu, taking off the layers of clothing. Struggling with the rigor.

Until lying before them on the examina-tion table was the naked man.

"How old was Frère Mathieu?" Gamache asked.

"I can show you his file," said the doctor, "but I believe he was sixty-two."

"In good health?"

"Yes. A slightly enlarged prostate, a slightly elevated PSA but we were monitoring that. He was about thirty pounds overweight, as you can see. Around the middle. But he wasn't obese and I'd suggested he take more exercise."

"How?" asked Beauvoir. "He could hardly join a gym. Did he pray harder?"

"If he did," said the doctor, "he'd hardly be the first person to decide they could pray themselves thin. But, as it happens, we put together a couple of hockey teams in the winter. Not NHL caliber, but we're surprisingly good. And quite competitive."

Beauvoir stared at Brother Charles as though he'd just spoken Latin. It was almost indecipherable. Monks playing competitive hockey? He could see them on a rink on the frozen lake. Cassocks flying. Barreling into each other.

Muscular Christianity.

Maybe these men weren't quite the oddities he'd presumed.

Or perhaps that made them all the odder.

"Did he?" asked the Chief.

"Did he what?" asked the doctor.

"Did Frère Mathieu get more exercise?"

Brother Charles looked down at the body on his table and shook his head, then met Gamache's eyes. Once again the monk's eyes were tinged with amusement, though his voice was solemn.

"The prior was not a man to take suggestions easily."

Gamache continued to hold the doctor's eyes, until Brother Charles dropped his and spoke again. "Beyond that, he was in good health."

The Chief nodded and looked down at the naked man on the table. He'd been anxious to see if there was indeed a wound to Brother Mathieu's abdomen.

But there was nothing there. Just flabby, graying skin. His body, except for the crushed skull, was without a mark.

Gamache couldn't yet see the blows that led up to the final, catastrophic crushing of this man's skull. But he'd find them. This sort of thing never came out of the blue. There'd be a trail of smaller wounds, bruises, hurt feelings. Insults and exclusions.

The Chief Inspector would follow those. And they would lead, inevitably, to the man who'd made this corpse.

Chief Inspector Gamache looked over to the desk and the yellowing sheet of thick paper. With its squiggles of, what was that word?

Neumes.

And its nearly unintelligible text.

Except for two words.

"Dies irae."

Day of wrath. From the mass for the dead.

What had the prior been trying to do, at the hour of his death? When he could do only one more thing in this life, what had he done? Not written in the soft earth the name of his killer.

No, Frère Mathieu had shoved that sheet

of paper up his sleeve and curled himself around it.

What did this jumble of nonsense and neumes tell them? Not much, yet. Except that Frère Mathieu had died trying to protect it.

SEVEN

The chair beside Dom Philippe was empty.

It had been years, decades, since the abbot had looked to his right in the Chapter House and not seen Mathieu.

Now he didn't look to his right. Instead, the abbot kept his steady eyes straight ahead. Looking into the faces of the community of Saint-Gilbert-Entre-les-Loups.

And they looked back at him.

Expecting answers.

Expecting information.

Expecting comfort.

Expecting him to say something. Anything.

To stand between them and their terror.

And still he stared. At a loss for words. He'd stored up so many, over the years. A warehouse full of thoughts and impressions, of emotions. Of things unsaid.

But now that he needed words, the warehouse was empty. Dark and cold.

Nothing left to say.

Chief Inspector Gamache leaned forward, his elbows on the worn wood desk. His hands casually holding each other.

He looked across at Beauvoir and Captain Charbonneau. Both men had their notebooks out and open and were ready to report to the Chief.

After the medical examination, Beauvoir and Charbonneau had interviewed the monks, fingerprinting them, getting initial statements. Reactions. Impressions. An idea of their movements.

While they did that, Chief Inspector Gamache had searched the dead man's cell. It was almost exactly the same as the abbot's. Same narrow bed. Same chest of drawers, only his altar was to a Saint Cecilia. Gamache had not heard of her, but he determined to look her up.

There was a change of robes, of underwear, of shoes. A nightshirt. Books of prayers and the psalms. And nothing else. Not a single personal item. No photographs, no letters. No parents, no siblings. But then, perhaps God was his Father, and Mary his mother. And the monks his brothers. It was, after all, a large family.

But the office, the prior's office, was a gold

mine. Not, sadly, of clues to the case. There was no bloody stone. No threatening, signed letter. No murderer waiting to confess.

What Gamache did find in the prior's desk were used quill pens and a bottle of open ink. He'd bagged and put them in the satchel along with the other evidence they'd collected.

It had seemed a major find. After all, that sheet of old paper that had fallen from the prior's robes had been written with quill pen and ink. But the more the Chief thought about it the less certain he was that this would prove significant.

What were the chances the prior, the choirmaster, a world authority on Gregorian chant, would write something almost unintelligible? The abbot and the doctor had both been baffled by the Latin, and those neume things.

It seemed more the work of some unschooled, untrained amateur.

And it was written on very old paper. Vellum. Sheepskin. Stretched and dried, perhaps hundreds of years ago. There was plenty of paper, but no vellum in the prior's desk.

Still, Gamache had been careful to bag and label the quills and ink. In case.

He also found scores. Sheets and sheets of

sheet music.

Books filled with music, and histories of music. Learned papers on music. But while Frère Mathieu was Catholic in his belief, he was not small "c" catholic in his taste.

Only one thing interested him. Gregorian chant.

There was a simple cross on the wall, with the crucified Christ in agony. And below and surrounding that crucifix was a sea of music.

That was the passion of Brother Mathieu. Not Christ, but the chants he floated above. Christ might have called Frère Mathieu, but it was to the tune of a Gregorian chant.

Gamache had had no idea so much had been, or could be, written about plainchant. Though, to be fair, he'd given it no thought. Until now. The Chief had settled in behind the desk and while waiting for Beauvoir and Charbonneau to return, he'd begun reading.

Unlike the cell, which smelled of cleaning fluid, the office smelled of old socks and smelly shoes and dusty documents. It smelled human. The prior slept in his cell, but he lived here. And Armand Gamache began to see Frère Mathieu as simply Mathieu. A monk. A music director. Perhaps a genius. But mostly a man.

110

Charbonneau and Beauvoir eventually returned and the Chief turned his attention to them.

"What did you find?" Gamache looked at Charbonneau first.

"Nothing, *patron.* At least, I didn't find the murder weapon."

"I'm not surprised," said the Chief, "but we had to try. When we get the coroner's report we'll know if it was a stone or something else. What about the monks?"

"All fingerprinted," said Beauvoir. "And we did the initial interviews. After the seven thirty service they go to their chores. Now," Beauvoir consulted his notes, "there're four main areas of work at the monastery. The vegetable garden, the animals, the physical repairs to the monastery, which are endless, and the cooking. The monks have an area of expertise, but they also rotate. We found out who was doing what at the crucial time."

At least, thought Gamache, listening to the report, the time of death was fairly clear. Not before Lauds finished at quarter past eight, and not after twenty to nine, when Frère Simon found the body.

Twenty-five minutes.

"Anything suspicious?" he asked.

Both men shook their heads. "They were all at their work," said Charbonneau. "With

111

witnesses."

"But that's not possible," said Gamache, calmly. "Frère Mathieu didn't kill himself. One of the brothers wasn't doing what he was assigned to do. At least, I hope it wasn't an assignment."

Beauvoir raised a brow. He presumed the Chief was joking, but perhaps it was worth considering.

"Let's try to get at this another way," suggested the Chief. "Did any of the monks tell you about a conflict? Was anyone fighting with the prior?"

"No one, *patron,*" said Captain Charbonneau. "At least no one admitted there was conflict. They all seemed genuinely shocked. 'Unbelievable' was the word that kept coming up. *'Incroyable.'* "

Inspector Beauvoir shook his head. "They believe in a virgin birth, a resurrection, walking on water and some old guy with a white beard floating in the sky and running the world, but this they find unbelievable?"

Gamache was quiet for a moment, then nodded. "It is interesting," he agreed, "what people choose to believe."

And what they'd do in the name of that faith.

How did the monk who'd done this reconcile the murder with his faith? What, in his quiet moments, did the murderer say to the old man with the white beard floating in the sky?

Not for the first time that day, the Chief Inspector wondered why this monastery had been built so far from civilization. And why it had such thick walls. And such high walls. And locked doors.

Was it to keep the sins of the world out? Or to keep something worse in?

"So," he said, "according to the monks, there were no conflicts at all."

"None," said Captain Charbonneau.

"Someone is lying," said Beauvoir. "Or all of them are."

"There is another possibility," said Gamache. He brought the yellowed page toward him, from the middle of the table. Examining it for a moment he lowered it again and looked into their faces.

"Maybe the murder had nothing to do with the prior himself. Maybe there really was no conflict. Maybe he was killed because of this."

The Chief placed the page on the table again. And again he saw the body, as he'd first seen it. Curled into a shady corner in the bright garden. He hadn't known then, but he did now, that at the very center of that dead body was a piece of paper. Like a pit in a peach.

Was this the motive?

"None of the monks noticed anything odd this morning?" Gamache asked.

"Nothing. Everyone seemed to be doing what they were meant to do."

The Chief nodded and thought. "And Frère Mathieu? What was he meant to be doing?"

"Be here, in his study. Working on the music," said Beauvoir. "And that's the only interesting thing that came up. Frère Simon, the abbot's secretary, says he returned to the abbot's office right after Lauds, then he had to go to his work at the *animalerie*. But on his way he stopped by here."

"Why?" Gamache sat forward and removed his glasses.

"To deliver a message. The abbot apparently wanted to meet with the prior this morning after the eleven A.M. mass." The words sounded strange on Beauvoir's tongue. Abbots and priors and monks, oh my.

They weren't part of the vocabulary of Québec anymore. Not part of daily life. In just a generation those words had gone from respected to ludicrous. And soon they'd disappear completely.

God might be on the side of the monks,

thought Beauvoir, but time wasn't.

"Frère Simon says when he came to make the appointment, no one was in."

"That would've been at about twenty past eight," said the Chief, making a note. "I wonder why the abbot wanted to see the prior?"

"*Pardon?*" asked Inspector Beauvoir.

"The victim was the abbot's right-hand man. It seems likely he and the abbot had regularly scheduled meetings, like we do."

Beauvoir nodded. He and the Chief met every morning at eight, to go over the previous day and to review all the homicide cases currently being investigated by Gamache's department.

But it was just possible a monastery wasn't quite the same as the homicide department of the Sûreté. And it was just possible the abbot wasn't quite the same as the Chief Inspector.

Still, it seemed a good bet the abbot and prior would have held regular meetings.

"That would mean," said Beauvoir, "that the abbot wanted to talk to the prior about something other than normal monastery business."

"It could. Or that it was urgent. Unexpected. Something had suddenly come up."

"Then why not ask to see the prior right

away?" asked Beauvoir. "Why wait until after the eleven o'clock mass?"

Gamache thought about that. "Good question."

"So, if the prior didn't return to his office after Lauds, where did he go?"

"Maybe he went straight to the garden," said Charbonneau.

"Possibly," the Chief said.

"Then wouldn't Frère Simon, the abbot's secretary, have seen him?" asked Beauvoir. "Or passed him in the corridor?"

"Maybe he did," said the Chief. He lowered his voice and stage-whispered to Beauvoir. "Maybe he lied to you."

Beauvoir stage-whispered back, "A religious? Lie? Someone's going to Hell." He looked at Gamache with exaggerated concern, then smiled.

Gamache smiled back and rubbed his face. They were collecting a lot of facts. And probably more than a few lies.

"Frère Simon's name keeps coming up," said Gamache. "What do we know about his movements this morning?"

"Well, this is what he says," Beauvoir flipped a few pages in his notebook and stopped. "Right after Lauds, at quarter past eight, he returned to the abbot's office. There the abbot asked him to make an appointment for after the eleven o'clock mass with the prior. The abbot left to look at the geothermal and Frère Simon left to do his job at the animal place. On his way he stopped by here, looked in. No prior. So he went away."

"Was he surprised?" asked Gamache.

"Didn't seem surprised or concerned. The prior, like the abbot, pretty much came and went as he liked."

Gamache thought about that for a moment. "What did Frère Simon do then?"

"He worked for twenty minutes or so with the animals, then returned to the abbot's office to work in the garden. That's when he found the body."

"Do we know for sure Frère Simon went to the *animalerie?*" asked the Chief.

Beauvoir nodded. "His story checks. Other monks saw him there."

"Could he have left earlier?" asked Gamache. "Say at half past eight?"

"I wondered the same thing," Beauvoir smiled. "The other monks working there say it's possible. They were all busy with their own chores. But it'd be hard for Brother Simon to do what he had to do in so short a time. And all his chores were done."

"What were they?" asked Gamache.

"He let the chickens out of their cages and gave them all fresh food and water. Then he cleaned the cages. Not the sort of thing you can pretend to do."

Gamache made a few notes, nodding to himself. "The door to the abbot's office was locked when we arrived. Is it usually?"

The men looked at each other. "I don't know, *patron*," said Beauvoir, making a note. "I'll find out."

"Good."

It was clearly important. If it was usually locked then someone had had to let the prior in.

"Anything else?" asked Gamache, looking from Beauvoir to Charbonneau and back again.

"Nothing," said Beauvoir, "except that I tried to hook up this piece of shit and of course, it doesn't work." He waved a disgusted hand at the satellite dish they'd lugged all that way from Montréal.

Gamache took a deep breath. That was always a blow to a remote investigation. They brought state-of-the-art equipment into primitive surroundings, and then were surprised when it didn't work.

"I'll keep trying," said Beauvoir. "There's no telecommunication tower, so our cell phones won't work either, but we can still get text on our BlackBerrys."

Gamache looked at the time. It was just after four. They had an hour before the boatman left. A murder investigation was never a leisurely pursuit, but there was even more urgency about this one. They were chasing daylight and the boatman's deadline.

Once the sun set, they would all be trapped in the monastery. Along with the evidence and the body. And Chief Inspector Gamache didn't want that.

Dom Philippe made the sign of the cross over his community. They crossed themselves.

And then he sat. And they sat. Like shadows, mimicking his every move. Or children, he thought. More charitable, and perhaps more accurate.

Though some of the monks were considerably older than the abbot, he was their father. Their leader.

He was far from convinced he was a very good one. Certainly not as good as Mathieu. But he was all they had right now.

"As you know, Frère Mathieu has died," began the abbot. "Unexpectedly."

But it got worse. More words were appearing. Lining up. Crushing forward.

"He was killed."

Dom Philippe paused before that last word.

"Murdered."

Let us pray, he thought. *Let us pray. Let us chant. Let us close our eyes and chant the psalms and lose ourselves. Let us retreat to our songs and our cells, and let that police officer worry about this mess.*

But this was not the time for retreating. Nor was it the time for plainchant. It was the time for plain speech.

"The police are here. Most of you have been interviewed by them. We must cooperate. We must have no secrets. That means letting them not only into our cells and our workplaces, but into our thoughts and hearts."

As he spoke these unfamiliar words he noticed a few nods. And then a few more. And the flat faces of concealed panic began to give way to understanding. To agreement even.

Should he go further? *Dear Lord,* he silently pleaded, *should I go further? Surely this was far enough. Did the rest really need to be said? And done?*

"I'm lifting the rule of silence."

There was a sharp intake of breath. His brother monks looked as though he'd just stripped them of their clothing. Left them naked, exposed.

"It must be done. You're free to talk. Not idle chatter. Not gossip. But to help those officers get at the truth."

Now their faces were filled with anxiety. Their eyes holding his. Trying to grab his glance.

And while their fear was painful for him to see, he knew it was far more natural than the guarded, empty expressions he'd seen before.

And then the abbot took that last, irrevocable step.

"Someone in this monastery killed Brother Mathieu," said Dom Philippe, feeling himself plunging. The problem with words, he knew, was that they could never be taken back. "Someone in this room killed Brother Mathieu."

He'd wanted to comfort them, but all he'd managed to do was strip them naked and terrify them.

"One of us has a confession to make."

EIGHT

It was time to go.

"You have everything?" Gamache asked Captain Charbonneau.

"Everything except the body."

"Best not to forget that," agreed the Chief.

Five minutes later the two Sûreté agents were carrying the covered body of Frère Mathieu on a stretcher from the infirmary. Gamache had looked for the doctor, Frère Charles, to let him know. But there was no sign of the *médecin*. Nor was there any sign of Dom Philippe.

He'd disappeared.

As had the abbot's secretary, the taciturn Frère Simon.

As had all the dark-robed monks.

All gone.

The monastery of Saint-Gilbert-Entre-les-Loups felt not simply quiet, but empty.

As they carried Frère Mathieu through the Blessed Chapel, Gamache scanned the large room. The pews were empty. The long choir benches were empty.

Even the playful light had left. No more rainbows. No more prisms.

The absence of light wasn't simply darkness. There was a gloom about the place, as though something else was gathering at the edges of the day. As cheerful as the light had been, something equally foreboding was waiting to fill the void.

Balance, thought Gamache, as their feet echoed on the slate floors. As they escorted a murdered monk across the church. *Équilibre.* Yin and yang. Heaven and Hell. Every faith had them. Opposites. Providing balance.

They'd had the daylight. And now the night was coming.

They passed out of the church and into the final, long corridor. Gamache could see the heavy wooden door at the far end. He could see the wrought-iron deadbolt rammed in place.

The door was locked. But against what?

They arrived and the Chief looked into the porter's small office. But it too was empty. No sign of the young monk, Frère Luc. Only a thick book which proved to be more, what else? Chants.

Music, but no monk.

"It's locked, *patron,*" said Beauvoir, look-ing into the office. "The front door. Is there a key?"

Both men searched, but there was noth-ing.

Charbonneau opened the peephole and looked out. "I can see the boatman," he reported, smushing his face against the wooden door. Trying for a better look. "He's at the dock. Waiting. He's looking at his watch."

All three officers looked at their watches.

Twenty to five.

Beauvoir and Charbonneau looked at Ga-mache.

"Find the monks," he said. "I'll stay here with the body, in case Frère Luc returns. You split up. We haven't much time."

What had seemed an oddity, the sudden absence of monks, was now verging on a crisis. If the boatman left, they'd be stuck there.

"D'accord," said Beauvoir, but he looked uneasy.

Instead of moving off down the corridor Beauvoir stepped toward the Chief and whispered, "Would you like my gun?"

Gamache shook his head. "I'm afraid my monk is already dead. Not much of a threat."

"There are others, though," said Beauvoir, deadly serious. "Including the one who did this. And the one who locked us in. You'll be alone here. You might need it. Please."

"Then what would you do, *mon vieux*," asked Gamache. "If you run into trouble?"

Beauvoir was silent.

"I'd rather you keep it. But remember, Jean-Guy, you're looking for the monks, not hunting them."

"Looking not hunting," Beauvoir repeated in mock earnestness. "Got it."

Gamache accompanied them to the end of the corridor, walking briskly to the door into the church. Opening it he looked in. No longer filled with light, it was now filled with long, and growing, shadows.

"Père Abbé!" Gamache stood at the door and shouted.

It felt as though he'd lobbed a bomb into the building. The Chief's commanding voice bounded off the stone walls, magnifying and echoing. But instead of recoiling from it, Gamache yelled again.

"Dom Philippe!"

Still nothing. He stepped aside and Beauvoir and Charbonneau hurried in.

"Quickly, Jean-Guy," Gamache said as Beauvoir passed. "Carefully."

"Oui, patron."

The Chief watched as the two men peeled off in different directions. Beauvoir to the right, and Charbonneau to the left. Gamache stood at the door, watching, until both men disappeared.

"Allô!" called Gamache again, and listened. But the only response he got was his own voice.

Chief Inspector Gamache propped open the door to the church, then started down the long corridor, to the closed and locked and bolted door. And the body that lay before it like an offering.

It was counterintuitive to walk deliberately into a dead end. A *cul-de-sac*. Every training, every instinct, went against it. If anything came at him down this corridor, there was no way out. He knew that was why Beauvoir had offered him his firearm. So that he'd at least have a chance.

How often had he, in classes at the academy, in sessions with new recruits, ordered them never, ever to get caught in a dead end?

And yet here he was, walking back down. He'd have to give himself a stern talking to, he thought with a smile. And a failing grade.

Jean-Guy Beauvoir stepped into the long

corridor. It was exactly like all the others. Long, with tall ceilings and a door at the far end.

Emboldened by Gamache, Beauvoir yelled, *"Bonjour! Allô?"*

Just before the door had closed he'd heard the Chief's and Charbonneau's voices mix together. Calling out, in unison, a single word. *"Allô?"*

Then the door closed, and with it the familiar voices disappeared. All sound disappeared. There was silence. Except for the beating of Beauvoir's heart.

"Hello?" he repeated, less loudly.

There were doors down either side. Beauvoir hurried along the corridor, looking into rooms. The dining room. The pantry. The kitchen. All empty. The only sign of life a huge vat of pea soup simmering on a stove.

Beauvoir opened the last door on the left, before the final door. And there he stopped. Staring. Then he stepped inside and the door softly closed behind him.

Captain Charbonneau opened the doors all the way down the hallway. One after another. All were alike.

Thirty of them. Fifteen down one side. Fifteen down the other.

Cells. He'd started off yelling into them,

"Hello?" but soon realized there was no need.

This was obviously the bedroom wing. With the toilets and showers in the middle and the prior's office at the very beginning of the corridor.

A large wooden door at the far end was closed.

The rooms were empty. He'd known that as soon as he'd stepped into the hallway. Not a living soul. But that didn't mean there weren't some dead ones.

And so he'd stooped to look under the first few beds. Dreading what he might find, but needing to look anyway.

Twenty years he'd been on the force. He'd seen some terrible things. Horrific accidents. Appalling deaths. Kidnappings, assaults, suicides. The disappearance of two dozen monks was far from the most frightening thing he'd experienced.

But it was the eeriest.

Saint-Gilbert-Entre-les-Loups.

Saint-Gilbert-Among-the-Wolves.

Who names a monastery that?

"Père Abbé?" he called, tentatively. *"Allô?"*

The sound of his own voice at first calmed him. It was natural, familiar. But the hard, stone walls changed his voice. So that what came back to his ears wasn't exactly what had left his lips. Close. But not the same.

The monastery had twisted it. Taking his words and magnifying the feelings. The fear. Making his own voice grotesque.

Beauvoir stepped into the small room. Like the kitchen, there was a vat bubbling away on a stove. But unlike the kitchen, this one wasn't pea soup.

It smelled bitter. Heavy. Not a pleasant aroma at all.

Beauvoir peered into the vat.

Then he dipped his finger into the thick, warm liquid. And smelled it. Looking around, to see if anyone was watching, he put his finger into his mouth.

He was relieved.

It was chocolate. Dark chocolate.

Beauvoir had never liked dark chocolate. It seemed unfriendly.

He looked around the empty room. No, not just empty. It was abandoned. The unattended vat glugged gently, like a volcano considering whether to explode.

And on the wooden counter sat small mounds of very dark chocolate. Long rows of them, like tiny monks. He picked one up, turning it this way and that.

Then he ate it.

■ ■ ■ ■

Armand Gamache had spent the past few minutes looking around. Perhaps the monks had hidden a key? But there was no potted palm and certainly no welcome mat to look under.

It was, he had to admit, one of the strangest occurrences he'd had in the hundreds of murders his department had investigated. Granted, every homicide had its share of strange behavior. Indeed, normal behavior would be considered among the oddest.

Still, he'd never had an entire community vanish.

He'd had suspects hide. He'd had many people try to run away. But never all of them. The only monk left lay at his feet. The Chief Inspector hoped Frère Mathieu was still the only dead monk in the monastery of Saint-Gilbert-Entre-les-Loups.

Gamache gave up the search for a key and looked at his watch. It was almost five. With a sinking heart he slid open the slit in the door and looked out. The sun was low on the horizon, just touching to tops of the woods. He could smell the fresh air, the fragrant pine forest. But what he sought, he found.

The boatman was still at the dock.

"Etienne!" Gamache called, putting his mouth close to the small opening. "Monsieur Legault!"

Then he looked out. The boatman hadn't moved.

Gamache tried a few more times and wished he could whistle, that shrill, piercing sound some people achieved.

The Chief watched the boatman, sitting in his boat. And he realized the man was fishing. Casting. Reeling in. Casting. Reeling in.

With endless patience.

Or at least, Gamache hoped it was endless.

Leaving the small slit open, he turned back to the corridor and stood very still. Listening. He heard nothing. It was some comfort, he told himself, that he didn't hear an outboard motor.

Still he stared. Wondering where the monks were. Wondering where his agents were. He pushed away the image that came into his head, created by the small but mighty factory deep within him that produced terrible thoughts.

The monster under the bed. The monster in the closet. The monster in the shadows.

The monster in the silence.

With an effort, the Chief Inspector banished those horrors. Let them glide right past, as though they were water and he a rock.

To occupy himself, he went into the porter's room. It was really just a recess in the stone wall, with a small window to the corridor, a narrow desk and a single wooden stool.

The Spartans looked positively bourgeois next to these monks. There were no decorations, no calendars on the wall, no photos of the pope or the archbishop. Or Christ. Or the Virgin Mary.

Just stone. And a single thick book.

Gamache could barely turn around and wondered if he'd have to back out. He was hardly *petit* and when this monastery was built the monks had been considerably smaller. It would be embarrassing if when the others returned they found him wedged into the porter's room.

But it didn't come to that, and the Chief finally sat on the stool, adjusting himself to try to find a comfortable position. His back was against one wall, his knees against the other. This was not a place for the claustrophobic. Jean-Guy, for instance, would hate it. As he himself hated heights. Everyone had something they were afraid of.

Gamache picked up the old book on the narrow desk. It was heavy, and bound in soft, frayed leather. There was no date written into the first pages, and the lettering was gray. Faded. And written with a quill pen.

The Chief pulled a book of Christian meditations from his satchel, and from that he withdrew the vellum they'd found on the body. Placed in the slim volume for safekeeping.

Was this page torn from the huge book on his knees?

He put on his reading glasses and for what felt like the hundredth time that day, Gamache examined the page. The edges, while worn, didn't appear to be torn from a larger volume.

His eyes moved from the book to the page. Back and forth. Slowly. Trying to find similarities. Trying to find differences.

Every now and then he looked up, and down the empty corridor. And listened. At this stage he wanted to see his men more than the monks. Gamache no longer bothered to look at his watch. It didn't matter.

When Etienne decided to leave, Gamache couldn't stop him. But so far, no outboard motor.

Gamache turned over the brittle pages of

the book.

It appeared to be a collection of Gregorian chants, written in Latin with the neumes above the words. A handwriting analyst could tell far more, but Gamache had examined enough letters to have some expertise.

On first glance, the writing on the page and in the book seemed exactly the same. A simple form of calligraphy. Not the florid swirls of subsequent generations, these were clear, neat, graceful.

But some things didn't match. Tiny things. A swirl here, a tail on a letter there.

The chants in the book and the one on the torn page weren't written by the same hand. He was sure of it.

Gamache closed the large book and turned to the yellowed page. But now, instead of looking at the words, he examined the squiggles above them.

The abbot had called them neumes. Musical notations used a thousand years ago. Before there were notes and staffs, trebles and octaves, there were neumes.

But what did they mean?

He wasn't sure why he was looking at them again. It wasn't as though he'd suddenly be able to understand them.

As he stared, completely focused, willing

the ancient markings to make sense, he imagined he heard the music. He'd listened to the recording of the monks singing their plainchant so often the sound was imprinted on his brain.

As he stared at the neumes he could hear their soft, masculine voices.

Gamache lowered the paper, slowly, and removed his reading glasses.

He stared down the long, long, darkening corridor. And still he heard it.

Low, monotonous. And getting closer.

NINE

Gamache left the body and the book and walked swiftly toward the music.

He entered the Blessed Chapel. The chanting was all about him now. Emanating from the walls and floor and rafters. As though the building was built of neumes.

The Chief quickly scanned the church as he walked, his eyes sweeping into corners, rapidly absorbing everything there was to see. He was almost at the very center before he saw them. And stopped.

The monks had returned. They were filing through a hole in the wall at the side of the church. Their white hoods were up, hiding their bowed heads. Their arms were across their bodies, hands buried in their flowing black sleeves.

Identical. Anonymous.

Not a patch of skin or hair visible. Nothing to prove they were flesh and blood.

As they walked, single file, the monks sang.

This was what neumes sounded like, when lifted from the page.

This was the world-famous choir of the abbey of Saint-Gilbert-Entre-les-Loups, singing their prayers. Singing Gregorian chants. While it was a sound millions had heard, it was a sight few had ever witnessed. Indeed, as far as the Chief Inspector knew, this was unique. He was the first person to ever actually see the monks in their chapel, singing.

"Found 'em," said a voice behind Gamache. When the Chief turned, Beauvoir smiled and nodded toward the altar and the monks. "No need to thank me."

Beauvoir looked relieved and Gamache smiled, relieved himself.

Jean-Guy stopped beside the Chief Inspector and looked at his watch. "Five o'clock service."

Gamache shook his head and almost groaned. He'd been a fool. Any Québécois who'd been born before the Church fell from favor knew there was a service at five in the afternoon and that any monk alive would make his way there.

It didn't explain where the monks had been, but it did explain why they'd returned.

"Where's Captain Charbonneau?" Gamache asked.

"Down there." Beauvoir pointed across the chapel, through the monks and to the far end.

"Stay here," said the Chief and began to move in that direction when the far door opened and the Sûreté officer appeared. Charbonneau looked, thought Gamache, exactly as he must have looked when he'd arrived in the chapel.

Perplexed, alert, suspicious.

And finally, amazed.

Captain Charbonneau saw Gamache and nodded, then briskly made his way along the wall, skirting the monks but keeping his eyes on them.

They were taking their places along the wooden benches, two rows on either side of the altar.

The last man took his place.

The abbot, thought Gamache. He looked like all the others, in simple robes with a rope around his slender middle, but still the Chief knew it was Dom Philippe. Some mannerism, some movement. Something distinguished him from the rest.

"Chief," said Charbonneau quietly when he arrived at Gamache's side. "Where did they come from?"

"Over there," said Gamache, pointing off to the side. There was no door visible, just a stone wall, and the Captain looked back to Gamache, who didn't explain. Couldn't explain.

"We need to get out of here," said Beauvoir. He took a step toward the monks, but the Chief stopped him.

"Wait a moment."

As the abbot took his place the singing died. The monks continued standing. Absolutely motionless. Facing each other.

The Sûreté agents also stood, facing the monks. Waiting for a signal from Gamache. He was staring at the monks, at the abbot. His eyes sharp. Then he made up his mind.

"Get the body of Frère Mathieu, please."

Beauvoir looked confused, but left with Charbonneau and returned with the stretcher.

The monks remained motionless, apparently oblivious to the men standing together in the aisle. Staring at them.

Then the monks, in a single synchronized movement, removed their hoods but continued to stare straight ahead.

No, Gamache realized. They weren't staring. Their eyes were closed.

They were praying. Silently.

"Come with me," Gamache whispered, and led them down the very center of the chapel. He walked slowly.

The monks, even in a trance, could not fail to hear them approaching. Their feet on the floor. How disconcerting this must be for them, the Chief Inspector thought.

Since the walls were raised more than three hundred years ago, their services had been undisturbed. The same ritual, the same routine. Familiar, comfortable. Predictable. Private. They had never heard a sound during a service they themselves had not produced.

Until this very moment.

The world had found them, and slipped through a crack in their thick walls. A crack produced by a crime. But Gamache knew he was not the one violating the sanctity and privacy of their lives. The murderer had done that.

That vicious act in the garden this morning had summoned up a whole host of things. Including a Chief Inspector of homicide.

He took the two stone steps up and stood between the rows.

The Chief gestured to Beauvoir and Charbonneau to lower the body to the slate floor, in front of the altar.

Then silence again descended.

Gamache studied the rows of monks, to see if any of them were peeking. Sure enough, one was.

The abbot's secretary. Frère Simon. His heavy face stern, even in repose. And his eyes not quite shut. This man's mind was not entirely on prayer, not entirely with God. As Gamache watched, Brother Simon's eyes closed completely.

A mistake, Gamache knew. Had Frère Simon stayed as he was, Gamache might have had his suspicions but could not have been certain.

But that tiny flutter had betrayed him, as surely as if Frère Simon had screamed.

Here was a community of men who communicated all day, every day. Just not with words. The smallest gesture took on a meaning and significance that would be lost in the hurly-burly of the outside world.

Would be lost on him, Gamache knew, if he wasn't careful. How much had he already missed?

At that moment all the monks opened their eyes. At once. And stared. At him.

Gamache suddenly felt both very exposed and a little foolish. Like being caught where he shouldn't be. On the altar during a service, for instance. Beside a dead man.

He looked over to the abbot. Dom Philippe was the only monk not staring at him. Instead his cool, blue eyes rested on Gamache's offering.

Frère Mathieu.

For the next twenty-five minutes the Sûreté officers sat in a pew, side by side, while the monks held Vespers. They, along with the monks, sat, and stood, and bowed and sat. Then stood. And sat, then kneeled.

"I should've carbed up," murmured Beauvoir, standing again.

When not silent, the monks sang their Gregorian chants.

Jean-Guy Beauvoir sat back down on the hard wooden pew. He went to church as rarely as possible. Some weddings, though the Québécois now preferred to simply live together. Funerals mostly. And even those were becoming rarer, at least in churches. Even the elderly Québécois, when they died, now preferred a funeral home send-off.

It might not have nurtured them, the funeral home. But neither had it betrayed them.

The monks had been silent for a few moments.

Please, dear Lord, Beauvoir prayed, *let this be over.*

Then they stood, and started another chant.

Tabernac, thought Beauvoir, getting to his

feet. Beside him, the Chief was also standing, and resting his large hands on the wooden pew in front. His right hand trembled slightly. It was subtle, barely there, but in a man so still, so self-possessed, it was remarkable. Impossible to miss. The Chief didn't bother to hide the tremor. But Beauvoir noticed Captain Charbonneau glancing at the Chief. And the tell-tale tremble.

And Beauvoir wondered if he knew the tale it told.

He wanted to take him aside and scold Charbonneau for staring. He wanted to make it clear that slight quiver wasn't a sign of weakness. Just the opposite.

But he didn't. Taking his cue from Gamache, he said nothing.

"Jean-Guy," Gamache whispered, his eyes straight ahead, never leaving the monks, "Frère Mathieu was the choir director, right?"

"Oui."

"So who's directing them now?"

Beauvoir was quiet for a moment. Now, instead of just biding his time while this interminable, intolerable, tedious chanting droned on and on, he started to pay attention.

There was an obvious empty spot on the

benches. Directly across from the abbot.

That must have been where the man now laid at their feet had stood, and sat, had bowed and prayed. And led the choir in these dull chants.

Beauvoir had earlier amused himself by wondering if the prior had possibly done it to himself. Stoned himself to death rather than have to live through yet another mind-numbing mass.

It was all the Inspector could do to not run shrieking into one of the stone columns, hoping to knock himself out.

But now he had a puzzle to occupy his active mind.

It was a good question.

Who was leading this choir of men, now that their director was dead?

"Maybe no one is," he whispered, after studying the monks for a minute or two. "They must know the songs by heart. Don't they do the same ones over and over?"

They sure sounded the same to him.

Gamache shook his head. "I don't think so. I think they change from mass to mass and from day to day. Feast days, saints' days, that sort of thing."

"Don't you mean, et cetera?"

Beauvoir saw the Chief smile slightly and shoot him a glance.

"And so on," said Gamache. "Ad infinitum."

"That's better." Beauvoir paused before whispering, "Do you know what you're talking about?"

"I know a little, but not much," admitted the Chief. "I know enough about choirs to know they don't direct themselves, any more than a symphony orchestra can conduct itself, no matter how often they perform a work. They still need their leader."

"Isn't the abbot their leader?" asked Beauvoir, watching Dom Philippe.

The Chief also watched the tall, slender man. Who really led these monks? both men wondered, as they bowed and sat again. Who was leading them now?

The Angelus bell rang out, its deep, rich notes pealing over the trees and across the lake.

Vespers was over. The monks bowed to the crucifix and filed back off the altar while Gamache and the others stood in their pew and watched.

"Should I get the key from that young monk?" Beauvoir waved to Frère Luc, who was leaving the altar.

"In a moment, Jean-Guy."

"But the boatman?"

"If he hasn't left by now, he'll still be waiting."

"How d'you know?"

"Because he'll be curious," said Gamache, studying the monks. "Wouldn't you wait?"

They watched the monks leave the altar and pool on either side of the church. *Yes,* thought Beauvoir, shooting a glance at the Chief, *I'd wait.*

With their hoods down and heads up Gamache could see their faces. Some looked as though they'd been crying, some looked wary, some weary and anxious. Some just looked interested. As though they were watching a play.

It was difficult for Gamache to trust what he was sensing from these men. So many strong emotions masqueraded as something else. Anxiety could look like guilt. Relief could look like amusement. Grief, deep-felt and inconsolable, often looked like nothing at all. The deepest passions could appear dispassionate, the face a smooth plain while something mammoth roiled away underneath.

The Chief scanned the faces, and came back to two.

The young gatekeeper, who'd met them at the dock. Frère Luc. Gamache could see the large key dangling from the rope about his waist.

Luc looked the most blank. And yet, when they'd first met him, he'd clearly been very upset.

Then Gamache turned his gaze on the abbot's glum secretary. Brother Simon.

Sadness. Waves of it washed off the man.

Not guilt, not sorrow, not wrath or mourning. Not *irae* or *illa.*

But pure sadness.

Brother Simon was staring at the altar. At the two men still there.

The prior. And the abbot.

Who was this profound sadness for? Which man? Or, the Chief wondered, maybe it was for the monastery itself. Sadness that Saint-Gilbert-Entre-les-Loups had lost more than a man. It had lost its way.

Dom Philippe paused before the large wooden cross and bowed deeply. He was alone now, on the raised altar. Except for the body of his prior. His friend.

The abbot held his bow.

Was it longer, Gamache wondered, than usual? Was the effort of getting back up, of turning around, of facing the evening, the next day, the next year, the rest of life too much? Was the gravity too much?

Slowly the abbot raised himself to a standing position. He even seemed to square his shoulders, standing as tall as he could.

Then he turned and saw something he'd never seen before.

People in the pews.

The abbot had no idea why there were even pews in the Blessed Chapel. They'd been there when he'd arrived, forty years earlier, and they'd be there long after he was buried.

He'd never questioned why a cloistered order needed pews.

In his pocket Dom Philippe felt the rosary beads, his fingers running over them without conscious thought. They offered a comfort that he also never questioned.

"Chief Inspector," he said as he stepped off the altar and approached the men.

"Dom Philippe." Gamache bowed slightly. "I'm afraid we're going to have to take him away now." Gamache gestured toward the prior, then turned and nodded to Beauvoir.

"I understand," said Dom Philippe, though he privately realized he understood none of this. "Follow me."

Dom Philippe signaled Frère Luc, who hurried over, and the three men made for the corridor that led to the locked door. Beauvoir and Captain Charbonneau followed, carrying the stretcher with Frère Mathieu.

Beauvoir heard something behind him, a shuffling, and looked.

The monks had formed two rows and were following them like a long, black tail.

"We tried to find you earlier, *Père Abbé,*" said the Chief, "but couldn't. Where were you?"

"In Chapter."

"And where is Chapter?"

"It's both a place and an event, Chief Inspector. The room is just over there," the abbot waved toward the wall of the Blessed Chapel, just as they walked through the door and into the long corridor.

"I saw you coming out of there," said Gamache, "but when we looked earlier we didn't find a door."

"No. It's behind a plaque commemorating Saint Gilbert."

"It's a hidden door?"

The abbot, even in profile, looked puzzled and a little surprised by the question.

"Not from us," he finally said. "Everyone knows it's there. It's no secret."

"Then why not just have a door?"

"Because anyone who needs to know about it does," he said, not looking at Gamache, but looking toward the closed door ahead of them. "And anyone who doesn't need to know should not find it."

"So it is meant to be hidden," said Gamache, pressing the point.

"The option is meant to be there," admitted the abbot. They'd arrived at the locked door to the outside world. He finally turned to look directly at Gamache. "If we need to hide, the room exists."

"But why would you need to hide?"

The abbot smiled a little. It was just this side of condescending. "I'd have thought you of all people would know why, Chief Inspector. It's because the world is not always kind. We all need a safe place, sometimes."

"And yet the threat, finally, didn't come from the world," said Gamache.

"True."

Gamache considered for a moment. "So you concealed the door to your Chapter room in the wall of the chapel?"

"I didn't put it there. All this was done long before I came. The men who built the monastery did it. It was a different time. A brutal time. When monks really did need to hide."

Gamache nodded, and looked at the thick wooden door in front of them. The gateway to the outside world. That was still locked, even after the passage of centuries.

He knew the abbot was right. Back when

the massive tree was cut down for this door, hundreds of years ago, it wasn't tradition but necessity that turned the key in the lock. The Reformation, the Inquisition, the internecine battles. It was a dangerous time to be a Catholic. And, as with recent events, the threat often came from within.

And so, in Europe priest's holes were built into homes. Tunnels dug for escape.

Some had escaped so far they popped up in the New World. And even that wasn't far enough. The Gilbertines had gone even further. They disappeared into the blank spot on the map.

Vanished.

To reappear more than three hundred years later. On the radio.

The voices of an order everyone had thought was extinct were heard first by a few, then by hundreds, then by thousands and hundreds of thousands. Then, thanks to the Internet, finally millions of people listened to the odd little recording.

Of monks chanting.

The recording had become a sensation. Suddenly their Gregorian chants were everywhere. *De rigueur.* Deemed a "must listen" by the intelligentsia, by the cognoscenti, and finally, by the masses.

While their voices were everywhere, the

monks themselves were nowhere to be seen. Eventually they'd been found. Gamache remembered his own astonishment when it was discovered where the monks lived. He'd assumed it was some remote hilltop in Italy or France or Spain. Some tiny, ancient, crumbling monastery. But no. The recording was made by an order of monks living right there, in Québec. And it wasn't just any order. The Trappists, the Benedictines, the Dominicans. No. Their discovery seemed to astonish even the Catholic Church. The recording had been made by an order of monks the Church seemed to think had died out. The Gilbertines.

But there they were, in the wilderness, on the shores of this far-flung lake. Very much alive, and singing chants so ancient and so beautiful they awakened something primal in millions worldwide.

The world had come calling. Some curious. Some desperate for the peace these men seemed to have found. But this "gate," made from trees felled hundreds of years ago, held firm. It did not open for strangers.

Until today.

It had opened to let them in, and now it was about to open again, to let them out.

The *portier* came forward, the large black

key in his hand. At a small sign from the abbot he inserted it in the lock. It turned easily, and the door swung open.

Through the rectangle the men saw the setting sun, its reds and oranges reflected in the calm, fresh lake. The forests now were dark, and birds swooped low over the water, calling to each other.

But by far the most glorious sight was the oil-stained boatman, smoking a cigarette and sitting on the dock. Fishing.

He waved as the door swung open, and the Chief Inspector waved back. Then the boatman struggled to his feet, his considerable bottom all but mooning the monks. Gamache motioned Beauvoir and Charbonneau, with the body, to leave first. Then he and the abbot followed them to the dock.

The rest of the monks stayed inside, clustered around the open door. Craning to see out.

The abbot tipped his head to the red-streaked sky and closed his eyes. Not in prayer, Gamache thought, but in a sort of bliss. Enjoying the meager light on his pale face. Enjoying the pine-scented air. Enjoying his feet on the uneven, unpredictable ground.

Then his eyes opened.

"Thank you for not interrupting Vespers,"

he said, not looking at Gamache, but continuing to soak in the natural world around him.

"You're welcome."

They took a few more steps.

"Thank you too for bringing Mathieu to the altar."

"You're welcome."

"I don't know if you realized it, but it gave us a chance to offer special prayers. For the dead."

"I wasn't sure," admitted the Chief Inspector, also looking ahead at the mirror lake. "But I thought I heard *Dies irae.*"

The abbot nodded, "And *Dies illa.*"

Day of wrath. Day of mourning.

"Are the monks mourning?" asked Gamache. Their gait had slowed almost to a halt.

The Chief had expected an immediate answer, a shocked reply. But instead the abbot seemed to consider.

"Mathieu wasn't always an easy man." He smiled a little as he spoke. "No one is, I suppose. One thing we learn early when committing to a monastic life is that we have to accept each other."

"And what happens if you don't?"

The abbot paused again. It had been a simple question, but Gamache could see the answer wasn't simple.

"That can be very bad," said the abbot. He didn't meet Gamache's eyes. "It happens. But we learn to set aside our own feelings for the greater good. We learn to get along."

"But not necessarily to like each other," said Gamache. It wasn't a question. He knew the Sûreté was much the same. There were a few colleagues he didn't like, and he knew the feeling was mutual. Indeed, "didn't like" was a euphemism. The feeling had gone from disagreement, to dislike, to distrust. And was growing still. It had settled, for now, on mutual loathing. Gamache didn't know where it would stop, but he could imagine. The fact these people were his superiors made it simply more uncomfortable. It meant, at least for now, they had to figure out how to exist together. Either that, or tear each other and the service apart. And Gamache, as he tilted his own face to the glorious sunset, knew that was a possibility. In the calm of the early evening it seemed far away, but he knew this peaceful time wouldn't last. Night was coming. And it was a fool who met it unprepared.

"Who could have done this, *mon père?*"

Now they were stopped on the dock,

watching as the boatman and the officers secured Frère Mathieu's covered body to the boat, beside the catch of bass and trout and the writhing worms.

Again the abbot considered. "I don't know. I should know, but I don't."

He looked behind him. The monks had ventured out and were standing in a semi-circle, watching them. Frère Simon, the abbot's secretary, was standing a step or two forward.

"Poor one," said Dom Philippe under his breath.

"Who do you mean?"

"Pardon?"

"You said, 'Poor one.' Who did you mean?" asked Gamache.

"Whoever did this."

"And who is that, Dom Philippe?" He'd had the impression the abbot had been looking at one monk as he'd spoken. Brother Simon. The sad monk. The one who'd separated himself from the rest.

There was a moment's tense silence as the abbot looked at his community, and Gamache looked at the abbot. Finally the abbot turned back to the Chief Inspector.

"I don't know who killed Mathieu."

He shook his head. A weary smile appeared on the abbot's face. "I actually believed I could look at them just now and tell. That there'd be something different about him. Or me. That I'd just know."

The abbot gave a small grunt of laughter. "Ego. Hubris."

"And?" asked Gamache.

"It didn't work."

"Don't feel badly, I do the same thing. I have yet to look at anyone and know immediately that they're the killer, but I still try."

"And what would you do if it worked?"

"I'm sorry?"

"Suppose you did look at someone, and just knew?"

Gamache smiled. "I'm not sure I'd trust myself. Probably think it was all in my imagination. Besides, it wouldn't impress a judge if on the stand I said, 'I just knew.' "

"That's the difference between us, Chief Inspector. You need proof in your line of work. I don't."

The abbot glanced behind them again and Gamache wondered if this was idle conversation, or something more. The semi-circle of monks continued to watch.

One of them had killed Brother Mathieu.

"What're you looking for, *mon père?* You might not need proof, but you need a sign.

157

What sign in their faces are you looking for? Guilt?"

The abbot shook his head. "I wasn't looking for guilt. I was looking for pain. Can you imagine the pain he must have been in, to do this? And the pain he still feels?"

The Chief scanned their faces again, and finally came to rest on the man right beside him. Gamache did see pain in the face of one of the monks. Dom Philippe. The abbot.

"Do you know who did this?" Gamache asked again, quietly. So that it was only audible to the abbot and the sweet autumn air around them. "If you do, you must tell me. I'll find him eventually, you know. It's what I do. But it's a terrible, terrible process. You have no idea what's about to be unleashed. And once it starts, it won't stop until the murderer is found. If you can spare the innocent, I'm begging you to do it. Tell me who did this, if you know."

That brought the abbot's full attention back to the large, quiet man in front of him. The slight breeze tugged at the graying hair just curling by the Chief Inspector's ears. But the rest of the man was still. Firm.

And his eyes, deep brown like the earth, were thoughtful.

And kind.

And Dom Philippe believed Armand Gamache. The Chief Inspector had been brought to the monastery, admitted to their abbey, to find the murderer. It was what this man was always meant to do. And he was almost certainly very good at it.

"I would tell you if I knew."

"We're ready," Beauvoir called from the boat.

"Bon." Gamache held the abbot's eyes for another moment then turned to see the boatman's large hand resting on the outboard motor, ready to pull the cord.

"Captain Charbonneau?" Gamache invited the Sûreté inspector to take a seat.

"Is it possible to keep this quiet?" asked Dom Philippe.

"I'm afraid not, *mon père.* The news will get out, it always does," said Gamache. "You might consider issuing a statement yourself."

He saw the distaste on the abbot's face and suspected that wouldn't happen.

"Au revoir, Chief Inspector," said Dom Philippe, extending his hand. "Thank you for your help."

"You're welcome," said Gamache, taking the hand. "But it isn't over yet." At a nod from Gamache, the boatman yanked the cord and the motor leapt into life. Beauvoir dropped the rope into the boat and it drifted away. Leaving Gamache and Beauvoir standing on the dock.

"You're staying?" asked the abbot, bewildered.

"Yes. We're staying. I leave with the murderer, or not at all."

Beauvoir stood beside Gamache and together they watched the small boat chug down the sunset bay, and around the corner. Out of sight.

The two Sûreté investigators remained there until the sound had disappeared.

And then they turned their backs on the natural world and followed the robed figures back into the monastery of Saint-Gilbert-Entre-les-Loups.

Ten

Beauvoir spent the early evening setting up their Incident Room in the prior's study while Chief Inspector Gamache read the interviews with the monks, and spoke to some in more depth.

A picture was emerging. How accurate it was was impossible to say, but it was clear and surprisingly consistent from man to man.

After Vigils at five in the morning, the monks had had breakfast and prepared for the day. There was another service at seven thirty, Lauds. It ended at eight fifteen. Then their workday began.

Work was any number of things, but for each man it was much the same each day.

They worked in the garden, or with the animals. They cleaned the abbey, did the archives, did repairs. Cooked the meals.

Each man was, it turned out, quite expert in his field. Whether it was as a chef or gardener, engineer or historian.

And they were all, without exception, exceptional musicians.

"How does this happen, Jean-Guy?" Gamache asked, looking up from his notes. "That they're all remarkable musicians?"

"You're asking me?" Beauvoir's voice came from beneath the desk, where he was trying to reconnect the laptop. "Dumb luck?"

"Dumb luck would be you getting that thing to work," said the Chief. "I think there's another agency at work here."

"I hope you don't mean divine."

"Not entirely, though I wouldn't rule it out. No, I think they must have been recruited."

Beauvoir looked out from beneath the desk, his dark hair disheveled. "Like hockey players are recruited?"

"Like you were recruited. I found you lording it over the evidence locker in that Sûreté outpost, remember?"

Beauvoir would never forget. Banished to the basement, because no one wanted to work with him. Not because he was incompetent, but because he was an asshole. Though Beauvoir preferred to believe they were just jealous of him.

He'd been assigned to the evidence locker

since he was only fit for things not actually alive.

They'd wanted him to quit. Expected him to quit. And, to be honest, he'd been about to quit, when Chief Inspector Gamache had come calling on a murder investigation. He'd come to the locker looking for a piece of evidence. And found Agent Jean-Guy Beauvoir.

And had invited him to join the investigation.

It was a moment Beauvoir would never forget. Looking into those eyes, a smart-ass remark dying on his lips. He'd been fucked with so often, jerked around, insulted, bullied. He barely dared hope this wasn't another trick. A new bit of cruelty. Kicking a dead man. Because Beauvoir could feel himself dying down there. All he'd ever wanted was to be a Sûreté officer. And every day he came closer to losing it.

But now this large man with the quiet demeanor had offered to take him away.

To save him. Even though they were strangers.

And Agent Beauvoir, who had sworn to never trust again, had trusted Armand Gamache. That was fifteen years ago.

Had these monks also been recruited? Found? Saved, even? And brought here?

"So," said Beauvoir, getting up from the floor and dusting off his slacks, "you think someone lured these monks to the abbey?"

Gamache smiled and looked at Beauvoir over the top of his reading glasses. "You have a gift for making everything sound suspicious, even ominous."

"Merci." Beauvoir sat down with a thump on one of the hard wooden chairs.

"Does it work?" Gamache nodded toward the laptop.

Beauvoir pressed some buttons. "The laptop works, but we can't connect to the Internet." Beauvoir continued to pound the connect button as though that would help.

"Perhaps you should pray," suggested the Chief.

"If I was going to pray for anything it'd be food." He gave up trying to connect. "When's dinner, do you think?"

Then Beauvoir remembered something and brought a small wax paper packet from his pocket. He placed it on the desk between them and opened it up.

"What are those?" asked the Chief, leaning closer.

"Try one."

Gamache picked up a chocolate and held it between his large fingers. It looked microscopic there. Then he ate it. And Beauvoir smiled to see the astonishment, and delight, on Gamache's face.

"Blueberry?"

Beauvoir nodded. "Those tiny wild ones. Chocolate covered. They make them by the bucketload here. I found the *chocolaterie* when I was looking for the monks. Seems like the better find."

Gamache laughed, and together they ate the few chocolates. They were, the Chief had to admit, without a doubt the best he'd ever tasted, and he'd tasted a few chocolates in his life.

"What're the chances, Jean-Guy, that all two dozen monks here, all of them, would have good voices?"

"Pretty small."

"And not just good voices, but great voices. And ones that work together, that fit together."

"Maybe they were trained," suggested Beauvoir. "Isn't that what the choir director, the dead man, would've done?"

"But he had to have something to work with. I'm far from an expert on music but even I know a great choir isn't just a collection of great voices. They have to be the right voices, complementary. Harmonious. I think these monks are here by design. I think they were specially chosen, to sing the

165

chants."

"Maybe they were specially bred for this," said Beauvoir, his voice low and his eyes mock-mad. "Maybe this is some Vatican plot. Maybe there's some mind control in the music. To lure people back to the Church. Produce a zombie army."

"My God, man, that's brilliant! It's so obvious." Gamache looked at Beauvoir with awe.

Beauvoir laughed. "You think the monks were specially chosen?"

"I think it's a possibility." The Chief got to his feet. "Keep working at that. It would be nice to be able to contact the outside world. I'm going to speak to the *portier*."

"Why him?" asked Beauvoir as Gamache made for the door.

"He's the youngest here, probably the most recent arrival."

"And a murder happens because something changes," said Beauvoir. "Something provoked the murder of Frère Mathieu."

"It was almost certainly building for a while, most murders take years to actually happen. But finally something, or someone, tips the balance."

That was what Gamache and his team did. They sieved for that often tiny event. A word. A look. A slight. That final wound that released the monster. Something had made a man into a murderer. Had made a monk into a murderer, surely a longer journey than most.

"And what was the most recent change?" asked Gamache. "Perhaps the arrival of Frère Luc. Maybe that somehow upset the balance, the harmony, of the abbey."

The Chief closed the door behind him and Beauvoir went back to work. As he tried to figure out what was wrong with the connection, his mind went back to the evidence locker. His hell. But he also thought about the door with the word *"Porterie"* stamped on it.

And the young man relegated to it.

Was he hated? Surely you had to be, to be stuck there. Every other job made sense in the abbey. Except his. After all, why have a porter for a door that never opened?

Gamache walked through the halls, meeting a monk here and there. He was beginning to recognize them, though he couldn't yet put names to all the faces.

Frère Alphonse? Frère Felicien?

The monks' faces were almost always in repose, their hands thrust up their drooping sleeves in a mannerism the Chief realized was just something monks did. When he

167

passed, they always caught his eye and nodded. Some ventured small smiles.

All looked, at a distance, calm. Contained.

But up close, at that moment when they
passed, to a man Gamache saw anxiety in
their eyes. A plea.

For him to leave? To stay? To help? Or to
go away?

When he'd arrived, not that many hours
ago, the abbey of Saint-Gilbert had seemed
peaceful. Restful. It was surprisingly beautiful. Its austere walls not cold, but soothing.
The daylight refracted by the imperfect
glass, broken into reds and purples and yel-
lows. Apart they were individual colors, but
together they made giddy light.

Like the abbey. Made up of individuals.
Alone they were no doubt exceptional, but
together they were brilliant.

Except for one. The shadow. Necessary,
perhaps, to prove the light.

Gamache approached another monk as he
made his way through the Blessed Chapel.

Frère Timothé? Frère Guillaume?

They passed and nodded and again Gamache caught something in this anonymous
monk's passing glance.

Perhaps each man had a private plea, different from the rest, depending who he was
and what was his nature.

This man — Frère Joel? — clearly wanted Gamache to go away. Not because the monk was afraid, but because Gamache had become a walking billboard, advertising the murder of the prior. And their failure as a community.

They were supposed to do only one thing. Serve God. But instead, this abbey had gone in the opposite direction. And Gamache was the exclamation mark that drove that truth home.

The Chief turned right and walked down the long corridor toward the closed door. He was growing familiar with the abbey, comfortable even.

It was in the form of a cross, with the Blessed Chapel in the middle and arms out four sides.

It was now dark outside. The halls were dimly lit. It felt like midnight, but when he glanced at his watch the Chief saw it wasn't yet six thirty.

The door marked *"Porterie"* was closed. Gamache knocked.

And waited.

Inside he heard a small sound. A paper, a page turned. Then silence again.

"I know you're in there, Frère Luc," said Gamache, lowering his voice. Trying to make himself sound less like the Big Bad

Wolf. He heard more paper shuffling, and then the door opened.

Frère Luc was young, in his early twenties, perhaps?

"Oui?" the monk asked.

And Gamache realized it was the first time he'd heard this boy speak directly to him. Even in that short word, Gamache could hear that Frère Luc's voice was full and rich. A lovely tenor almost certainly. While the man was reedy the voice was not.

"May we talk?" Gamache asked. His own voice was deeper than this boy's.

Frère Luc's brown eyes flicked this way and that, over Gamache's shoulder.

"I believe we're alone," said the Chief.

"Oui," he repeated, folding his hands in front of him.

It was a parody of the composure of the other monks. There was no calm here. This young man seemed torn between being afraid of Gamache and being relieved to see him. Wanting him to both leave and stay.

"I've already been interviewed, monsieur."

It was, even in simple speech, a beautiful voice. A shame to hide it in a vow of silence.

"I know," said Gamache. "I read the report. You were here when Frère Mathieu was found."

Luc nodded.

"Do you sing?" the Chief asked.

In any other setting it would be a preposterous first question to a suspect. But not here.

"We all do."

"How long have you been at Saint-Gilbert-Entre-les-Loups?"

"Ten months."

There was a hesitation and Gamache felt this young man could have told him the days, hours and exact minutes since he'd walked past that heavy door.

"Why did you come here?"

"The music."

Gamache didn't know if Frère Luc was being deliberately unhelpful by giving terse answers, or if the rule of silence came naturally to him and words did not.

"I wonder if you could be a little fuller in your answers, *mon frère?*"

Frère Luc looked petulant.

A young man trying to hide a temper beneath monks' robes, thought Gamache. *So much can hide in silence. Or at least try.* Gamache knew most emotions eventually found their way out, especially anger.

"I'd heard the recording," said Luc. "The chants. I was a postulant in another monastery, down south, by the border. They also do chants, but this was different."

171

"How?"

"It's hard to say what's different." Frère Luc's face changed as soon as he thought about the music. That calm he'd only pretended to became genuine. "As soon as I heard the monks from Saint-Gilbert I knew I'd never heard anything like it."

Luc actually smiled. "I suppose I should say I came here to be closer to God, but the truth is, I think I can find God in any abbey. But I can't find the chants just anywhere. Only here."

"The death of Frère Mathieu must be a great loss."

The boy opened his mouth, then shut it. His chin dimpled just a bit, his emotions almost breaking through.

"You have no idea."

And Gamache suspected that might be right.

"Was the prior one of the reasons you came here?"

Frère Luc nodded.

"Will you stay?" Gamache asked.

Frère Luc dropped his eyes to his hands, and kneaded his robe. "I'm not sure where else I'd go."

"This is your home now?"

"The chants are my home. They happen to be here."

"The music means that much to you?"

Frère Luc cocked his head to one side and examined the Chief Inspector.

"Have you ever been in love?"

"I have," said Gamache. "I still am."

"Then you'll understand. When I heard that first recording I fell in love. One of the monks at my old monastery had a recording. This was a couple of years ago, when it first came out. He came into my cell and played it for me. We were both in the choir at the abbey and he wanted to know what I thought."

"And what did you think?"

"Nothing. For the first time in my life I had no thoughts. Just feelings. I listened to the recording over and over, in all my spare time."

"What did it do for you?"

"What did falling in love do for you? Can you ever really explain it? It filled empty spaces I never knew were empty. It cured a loneliness I never knew I had. It gave me joy. And freedom. I think that was the most amazing part. I suddenly felt both embraced and freed at the same time."

"Is that ecstasy?" Gamache asked, after thinking about what the monk had said for a few moments. "Was it a spiritual experience?"

Again, Frère Luc regarded the Chief Inspector.

"It wasn't having 'a' spiritual experience. I'd had them before. We all have here, otherwise we wouldn't be monks. This was 'the' spiritual experience. Completely separate from religion. From the Church."

"What do you mean?"

"I met God."

Gamache let that sit for a moment.

"In the music?" he asked.

Frère Luc nodded. Lost for words.

Jean-Guy stared at the laptop screen saver. Then at the portable satellite dish they took with them into remote areas.

Sometimes it worked. Sometimes it didn't.

Why it would work and why it would fail were mysteries to Beauvoir. He made the same connections every time. Made the same adjustments. Did the same thing at every investigation.

Then waited for the inexplicable to happen. Or not.

"Merde," he mumbled. Still, all was not completely lost. He had his BlackBerry.

Opening the door to the prior's office, he looked out. No one coming.

Then he sat and, using his thumbs, laboriously typed a message. Where once his emails had been single words and symbols, now they were whole sentences. He wrote "you" instead of "u." He never used the punctuation for a smile or a wink, preferring to make it clear, in language, how he felt.

It wasn't hard. With Annie. His feelings were always clear, and very simple.

He was happy. He loved her. He missed her.

Besides, even had he wanted to use contractions and symbols, none had yet been invented to convey his feelings. Even words couldn't do it. But they were the best Jean-Guy had.

Every letter, every space, brought him closer to her and gave him not just pleasure, but joy.

Annie would see what he'd created, for her. What he'd written.

He loved her, he wrote. He missed her, he wrote.

And she wrote to him. Not simply in reply, but her own messages. About her day. So full. But still empty, without him.

She was having dinner with her mother, but would wait until he and her father returned so they could tell them together.

Hurry home, she wrote. *I miss you,* she wrote. *I love you,* she wrote.

And he felt her presence. And he felt her absence.

"So you came to the monastery of Saint-Gilbert," said Gamache.

"Well, that's the short version," said Frère Luc. "Nothing with the Church is ever short."

He was relaxed, but having, with that question, strayed slightly from the discussion of music, Luc appeared to grow more guarded.

"And the long version?"

"It actually took a while to find out who'd produced the recording. I thought they must have been an order somewhere in Europe."

"And even so, you'd have been willing to go there?"

"If the woman you loved lived in France, would you have gone?"

Gamache laughed. The young monk had got him. A direct and accurate hit.

"My wife," said the Chief. "And I'd have gone to Hell to get her."

"I hope that wasn't necessary."

"Well, Hochelaga-Maisonneuve. But you had to search?"

"All I had was the CD, but it doesn't say anything on it. I have it in my cell still, somewhere."

Gamache had the CD. He'd bought it over a year ago. And he too had searched for the liner notes, to find out who the monks were. But there were none. Just a list of the chants. The CD cover showed simply monks in profile. Walking. It was stylized, seeming at once very abstract and very traditional. There were no credits. The CD didn't even have a name.

It looked, and was, amateurish. The sound echoey and tinny.

"So how did you find out who it was?"

"Like everyone else, I found out on the radio, when those reporters tracked them down. I couldn't believe it. Everyone in my monastery was shocked. Not just because they were Québécois, but mostly because they were Gilbertines. They're not listed among the living orders. According to Church records, they died out, or were killed off, four hundred years ago. There are no more Gilbertine monasteries. Or so everyone thought."

"But how did you come to join them?" Gamache persisted. He could get the history lesson later.

"Father Abbot visited my monastery and heard me sing. . . ." Frère Luc suddenly looked quite bashful.

"Go on," said Gamache.

"Well, I have an unusual singing voice. A strange timber."

"And what effect does that have?"

"It means I can sing with virtually any choir, and fit in."

"You harmonize well?"

"We sing in plainchant, which means we all sing the same note at the same time. But with different voices. We don't actually harmonize, but we need to be in harmony when we sing."

Gamache thought about that distinction for a moment, then nodded.

"I am the harmony."

It was such an extraordinary thing to say that the Chief merely stared at this young monk, with the simple robes. And the grandiose statement.

"*Pardon?* I don't understand what that means."

"Don't get me wrong, the choir doesn't need me. The CD proves that."

"Then what did you mean?" It seemed to the Chief a little late for humility.

"Any choir would be better with me in it."

The two men stared at each other. It now struck Gamache that this might not be pride or bragging. It might be a simple statement

178

of fact. Just as monks might learn to accept their failings, maybe they also learned to accept their gifts. And not pretend, for the sake of a false humility, not to have them.

This man didn't hide his gift. And yet, he did hide his voice. In a vow of silence. In a monastery far, far away from people. From an audience.

Unless.

"So, you weren't on this first disk —"

Luc shook his head.

"— but were there more recordings planned?"

Frère Luc paused. "*Oui*. Frère Mathieu was excited about it. He had all the pieces chosen."

Gamache pulled the paper from his satchel. "Is this one of them?"

Luc took it from the Chief. He was totally focused. Completely still. His brows drew together and he shook his head, handing the paper back.

"I can't tell you what this is, monsieur. But I can tell you what it isn't. It's not a Gregorian chant."

"How can you tell?"

Luc smiled. "There're very clear rules to a chant. Like a sonnet, or haiku. Things you must do, and things you mustn't. A Gregorian chant is about discipline, and simplicity. The humility to submit to the rules, and the inspiration to rise above them. The challenge is to use the rules and transcend them at the same time. To sing to God, and not impose your own ego. That," he gestured to the paper, now back in Gamache's hand, "is nonsense."

"You mean the words?"

"I don't understand the words. What I mean is the rhythm, the meter. It's way off. Too fast. Not even close to a Gregorian chant."

"But it has these things." Gamache pointed to the squiggles above the words. "Neumes, right?"

"Right. That's what's so troubling about it."

"Troubling, Frère Luc?"

"It's meant to look like a Gregorian chant. It's masquerading as one. But it's an imposter. Where did you find it?"

"On the body of Frère Mathieu."

Luc blanched. Gamache knew that there were two things a person could not create, no matter how much they willed it. A blanch and a blush.

"What does that tell you, Frère Luc?"

"That the prior died trying to protect what he loved."

"This?" Gamache lifted the page.

"No, not that at all. He must have taken that from someone here. Someone who was trying to turn the chants into a joke. Trying to make them an abomination. And the prior wanted to stop it."

"You think this was done as an insult?"

"Someone knew Gregorian chants and neumes enough to mock them. Yes, it was done on purpose, as an insult."

"Someone here, you said. Who?" Gamache watched the young monk.

Frère Luc was quiet.

Gamache waited. Then he spoke, recognizing that sometimes silence was a useful tactic. Much more oppressive and threatening than hurled insults. But here silence was their comfort. It was the spoken word that seemed to frighten the monks.

"Who hated Frère Mathieu enough to mock his life's work?" Gamache persisted. "Who hated him enough to kill him?"

Luc remained silent.

"If every monk here loves the chants, why would one mock them? Create what you call an abomination?" Gamache held the vellum up and leaned forward very slightly. Luc backed away very slightly, but he had nowhere to go.

"I don't know," said Luc. "I'd tell you if I did."

The Chief studied Frère Luc, and thought he probably would. He loved the chants and clearly admired and respected the prior. Frère Luc would not protect any man who was out to kill both. But while this monk might not know who did it, he might have suspicions. As the abbot had said earlier, Gamache needed proof, but a monk only needed his beliefs. Did Frère Luc believe he knew who'd killed the prior, and mocked the chants? And was he arrogant enough to think he could deal with them on his own?

The Chief Inspector held the monk's eyes and when he spoke his voice was stern.

"You must help me find out who did this."

"I don't know anything."

"But you suspect."

"No. That's not true."

"A murderer is walking these halls, young man. A killer is trapped in here with us. With you."

Gamache saw the fear in Luc's eyes. A young man who sat alone all day, the only key to the outside world attached to a rope around his waist. The only way out was through him. If the murderer ever wanted to escape it might literally be over this young man's dead body. Did Luc appreciate that?

The Chief Inspector leaned away, but not

by much. "Tell me what you know."

"All I know is that not everyone was happy about the recording."

"The new one? The one the prior was about to make?"

Frère Luc paused then shook his head.

"The old one? The first one?"

Frère Luc nodded.

"Who was unhappy?"

Now Frère Luc looked miserable.

"You must tell me, son," said Gamache.

Luc leaned forward. To whisper. His eyes darting into the dim corridor. Gamache also leaned forward. To hear.

But before he could say anything, Frère Luc's eyes widened.

"There you are, Monsieur Gamache. Your Inspector said you'd be here. I've come to take you to dinner."

Frère Simon, the abbot's secretary, stood in the hallway, a few feet from the porter's door. His hands up his sleeves, his head humbly bowed.

Had he heard their conversation? Gamache wondered.

This was the monk whose eyes never seemed to quite close. Who watched everything, and who, Gamache suspected, heard everything.

Eleven

Two monks came out of the kitchens carrying bowls of small new potatoes, drizzled with butter and chives. Broccoli and sweet squash and casseroles followed. Cutting boards with warm baguettes dotted the long refectory table and platters of cheeses and butter were silently passed up and down the long benches of monks.

The monks, though, took very little. Passing the bowls and bread, but only taking enough to be symbolic.

They had no appetite.

This left Beauvoir in a quandary. He wanted to drop huge spoonfuls of everything onto his plate until he could no longer see above it. He wanted to make an altar of the food, then eat it. All.

When the first casserole, a fragrant cheese and leek dish with a crunchy crumble top, came by he paused, looking at the modest amounts everyone else had taken.

Then he took the biggest scoop he could manage and plopped it onto his plate.

Bite me, he thought. And the monks looked like they might.

The abbot broke the silence with grace. And then another monk rose after the meal had been served, and walked to a lectern. There he read from a prayer book.

Not a word was said in conversation.

Not a word was said about the hole in their ranks. The missing monk.

But Frère Mathieu was very much present, hanging over them like a haunting. Taking advantage of the silence to grow until he finally filled the room.

Gamache and Beauvoir were not seated together. Like children who couldn't be trusted, they were at opposite ends of the table.

Near the end of the meal, the Chief folded his cloth napkin and rose.

Frère Simon, across from him, motioned, at first subtly then with more vigor, for the Chief to sit back down.

Gamache met the man's eyes, and also motioned. That he'd received the message, but was going to do what he needed to do anyway.

Down the bench, Beauvoir, seeing the Chief rise, also got to his feet.

There was perfect silence now. Not even the discreet clink of cutlery. All forks and knives were either put down, or suspended. All eyes were on the Chief.

He walked slowly to the lectern and looked down the table. Twelve monks on one side. Eleven monks on the other. The room, the community, out of balance.

"My name is Armand Gamache," he said into the shocked silence. "Some of you I've already met. I'm the Chief Inspector of homicide for the Sûreté du Québec. This is my second in command, Inspector Beauvoir."

The monks looked anxious. And angry. At him.

Gamache was used to this transference. They couldn't yet blame the killer, so they blamed the police for turning their lives upside down. He felt a rush of sympathy.

If they only knew how bad it would get.

"We're here to investigate what happened this morning. The death of Frère Mathieu. We're grateful for your hospitality, but we need more than that. We need your help. I suspect whoever killed your prior had no intention of hurting others." Gamache paused. Then his voice grew more intimate. More personal. "But others will be hurt, very badly, before this is over. Things that you want to remain private will be made public. Relationships, quarrels. All your secrets will come out as Inspector Beauvoir and I hunt for the truth. I wish it wasn't so, but it is. Just as you wish Frère Mathieu wasn't dead."

But even as he said it, Gamache wondered if it was true.

Did they wish Frère Mathieu was still among them? Or did they wish him dead? There was real pain here. The monks of this monastery were devastated. Deeply upset.

But what were they really mourning?

"We all know that the murderer is among us right now. He's shared our table, eaten the bread. Listened to the prayers and even joined in. I want to speak with him for a moment." Gamache paused. Not, he hoped, to be melodramatic, but to let his words sink through the armor these monks wore. Cloaks of silence and piety and routine. He needed to break through those, to get to the man inside. The soft center.

"I think you love this abbey and don't want to hurt your fellow monks. That was never your intention. But as careful as Inspector Beauvoir and I might be, more damage will be done. A murder investigation is catastrophic for all involved. If you thought the worst was the murder, wait for it."

His voice was quiet but commanding, authoritative. There could be no doubt he was speaking the truth.

"There is one way to stop it, though. Only one." Gamache let that hang in the air. "You must give yourself up."

He waited, and they waited.

A throat cleared and all eyes swung to the abbot, who rose to his feet. Eyes widened in shock. Frère Simon also made to get up, but the abbot, in a move barely visible, motioned him down.

Dom Philippe turned to his community. If the tension had been great before, it sizzled now, the room crackling with it.

"No," said the abbot, "I'm not about to confess. I join the Chief Inspector in asking, begging, whoever did this to come forward."

No one moved, no one spoke. The abbot addressed Gamache.

"We will cooperate, Chief Inspector. I've lifted the vow of silence. There might be a tendency toward silence now, but it's no longer an obligation."

He looked at the monks. "If any of you has information, you must not keep it to yourself. There's no moral or spiritual value in protecting whoever did this. You must tell

Chief Inspector Gamache everything you know, and trust him and Inspector Beauvoir to sort out what matters and what doesn't. That's what they do. We pray, and work, and contemplate God. And sing to the glory of God. And these men," he nodded to Gamache and Beauvoir, "find killers."

His voice was calm, matter-of-fact. This man, who didn't speak often, now found himself saying words like "killers." He pressed on.

"Our order has been tested over the centuries. And this is another test. Do we really believe in God? Do we believe all the things we say and sing? Or has it become a faith of convenience? Has it, in splendid isolation, grown weak? When challenged we simply do whatever is easiest. Do we sin by silence? If we have real faith then we must have the courage to speak up. We must not protect the killer."

One of the monks rose and bowed to the abbot.

"You say, *mon père,* that our order has been tested over the centuries, and that's true. We've been persecuted, driven out of our monasteries. Imprisoned and burned. Driven to the brink of extinction. Driven into hiding. All by the authorities, by men like these," he waved toward Gamache and

189

Beauvoir, "who also claimed to be acting in the interest of so-called truth. This man has even admitted he'll violate our abbey to get at that truth. And you're asking us to help? You invited them in. Gave them a bed. Share our food. Courage has never been our weakness, *Père Abbé*. Judgment has."

The monk was one of the younger men. Late thirties, Gamache guessed. His voice was assured, reasonable, sensible. A few of the other monks were nodding. And more than a few were averting their eyes.

"You ask us to trust them," he continued. "Why should we?"

The monk sat down.

The brothers who weren't busy studying the table in front of them moved their eyes from the monk who just spoke, to the abbot, and finally to Gamache.

"Because, *mon frère,* you have no choice," said the Chief. "As you say, we're already in. The door has locked behind us and the outcome is not in doubt. Inspector Beauvoir and I will find whoever killed Brother Mathieu and we'll bring him to justice."

There was a small, anonymous snort of derision.

"Not divine justice, but the best this world has to offer for now," continued Gamache. "The justice decided by your fellow Québécois. Because, like it or not, you are not citizens of some higher plane of existence, some greater dominion. You, like me, like the abbot, like the boatman who brought us here, are all citizens of Québec. And will abide by the laws of the land. You may, of course, also abide by the moral laws of your beliefs. But I pray to God they're the same thing."

Gamache was annoyed. That much was obvious. Not at being challenged, but by the arrogance, the haughty assumption of both superiority and martyrdom this monk had taken. And the others had supported.

Not all the others, Gamache could see. And Gamache saw something else with sudden clarity. This arrogant monk had done him a huge favor. And shown him something only vaguely hinted at before.

Here was a community divided, a fissure running through them. And this tragedy, rather than bridging it, was simply widening the gap. Something lived in that dark crevice, Gamache knew. And when he and Jean-Guy found it it would almost certainly have nothing to do with faith. Or God.

They left the monks to their stunned, and convenient, silence and walked toward the Blessed Chapel.

"You're pissed," said Beauvoir, almost

running to catch up to Gamache's long strides.

"Pissed off, perhaps, but not pissed," said the Chief, with a smile. "Seems, Jean-Guy, we've landed in the only monastery on earth that doesn't make liquor."

Beauvoir touched the Chief's arm to slow him down and Gamache stopped in the middle of the corridor.

"You old . . ."

At a look from Gamache, Beauvoir stopped what he was about to say, but also smiled.

"That was all an act," Beauvoir lowered his voice, "you storming out. You wanted to show that asshole monk you wouldn't be pushed around, unlike the abbot."

"It wasn't entirely an act, but yes. I wanted the others to know it was possible to challenge that monk. What's his name anyway?"

"Frère Dominic? Frère Donat? Something like that."

"You don't know, do you."

"Not a clue. They all look the same to me."

"Well, find out, please."

They'd started walking again, more slowly this time. When they reached the Blessed Chapel the Chief paused, glanced behind him to see the empty corridor, then walked through the center of the church, Beauvoir at his side.

Passing the pews, the two men mounted the steps, crossed the altar and Gamache took a seat on the front choir bench. The prior's place. Gamache knew that because it had been empty at Vespers. It was directly across from where the abbot sat. Beauvoir sat down next to the Chief.

"Do you feel a song coming on?" he whispered, and Gamache smiled.

"The main reason I pushed was to see what would happen. Their reaction was interesting, Jean-Guy, didn't you find?"

"Interesting that monks would be so self-satisfied? I'll alert the press."

Like many Québécois of his generation, he had no use for the Church. It just wasn't part of his life. Unlike previous generations. The Catholic Church wasn't just a part of his parents' lives, and his grandparents', it ruled their lives. The priests told them what to eat, what to do, who to vote for, what to think. What to believe.

Told them to have more and more babies. Kept them pregnant and poor and ignorant.

They'd been beaten in school, scolded in church, abused in the back rooms.

And when, after generations of this, they'd

finally walked away, the Church had accused them of being unfaithful. And threatened them with eternal damnation.

No, Beauvoir was not surprised that monks, when scratched, bled hypocrisy.

"What I found interesting was the divide," said the Chief. His voice was quiet, but it echoed through the chapel. This was the sweet spot, he realized. Right here. Where the benches were. The Blessed Chapel had been designed for voices. To pick them up, and bounce them off the perfect angles. So that a whisper here would become clear anywhere else in the church.

Transmutation, thought Gamache. Not water into wine, but a whisper into an audible word.

How curious, again, that a silent order would create an acoustic marvel.

This was not the place for a private conversation. But then, the Chief didn't care who overheard.

"Yes, that was pretty clear," agreed Beauvoir. "They all look so calm and peaceful, but there was real anger there. That monk doesn't like the abbot."

"Worse," said Gamache. "He doesn't respect him. It's possible to have a leader you wouldn't choose as a friend. But you need to at least respect them. Trust them.

That was quite a body-shot. Publicly accusing the abbot of bad judgment."

"Maybe it's true," said Beauvoir.

"Maybe."

"And the abbot let him get away with it. Would you?"

"Let someone insult me? Clearly you're not paying attention. It happens all the time."

"But one of your subordinates?"

"That too has happened, as you know. And I don't automatically fire them. I want to know where it's coming from. Get at the root. That's far more important."

"So where's this coming from, do you think?"

It was a good question. One Gamache had been asking himself as he'd left the dining hall, and walked through the church.

That this was an abbey divided was obvious. The murder wasn't, in fact, an isolated event, but the latest in probably an escalating series of blows.

The prior had been attacked with a stone.

And the abbot had also just been attacked. With words.

One killed instantly, the other slowly. Were they both victims of the same person? Were the abbot and the prior on the same side of the divide? Or opposite sides? Gamache looked across the slate floor, past the altar, to the far side. Where the abbot sat.

Two men, of an age, staring at each other for decades.

One in charge of the abbey, the other in charge of the choir.

When they'd been in the garden that morning and Gamache had taken the abbot aside for a talk, he'd had the impression that the abbot and the prior were very close.

Closer, perhaps, than the Church would officially condone.

Gamache had no problem with that. Indeed, he completely understood and would find it surprising if some of these men didn't find comfort in each other. It seemed perfectly natural to him. What he wanted to know, though, was what had started the rift. Where did the crack begin? What blow, minor or otherwise, had started it all?

And he wanted to know where the abbot and the prior stood. Together? Or apart?

The Chief's mind went to what the young monk had said, just before Frère Simon had arrived to announce dinner. Gamache told Beauvoir about their conversation.

"So not everyone was happy about the recording," said Beauvoir. "Why not, I wonder. It was a huge hit. Must have made a fortune for the abbey. And you can tell. New roof, new plumbing. Geothermal system. It's incredible. As great as those chocolate-covered blueberries are, I can bet they didn't pay for the heating system."

"And Frère Mathieu was apparently planning a new recording," said Gamache.

"Do you think he was killed to stop him?"

Gamache was quiet for a moment. And then he slowly turned his head. Beauvoir, sensing a new awareness in the Chief, also looked into the gloom. The only lights in the Blessed Chapel were sconces on the walls behind the altar. The rest was in darkness.

But in that darkness they could just make out small, white shapes. Like tiny vessels.

Slowly the armada took shape. They were cowls. The white hoods of the monks.

They'd come back into the chapel and were standing in the darkness. Watching.

And listening.

Beauvoir turned to Gamache. There was a very small smile on his face, only noticeable to someone very close. And in his keen eyes there was a gleam.

He's not surprised, thought Beauvoir. No, it was more than that. He'd wanted them to come. To hear their conversation.

"You old . . ." Beauvoir whispered, and wondered if the monks had heard that too.

TWELVE

Beauvoir lay in bed. It was surprisingly comfortable. A firm single mattress. Soft flannel sheets. A warm duvet. Fresh air came in through the open window and he could smell the forest and hear the lapping of the lake on the rocky shore.

And in his hand he held his BlackBerry. He'd had to unplug the reading lamp in order to charge up the BlackBerry. It was a fair trade. Light for words.

He could have left the device in the prior's office, plugged into a power bar.

He could have. But he didn't.

Beauvoir wondered what time it was. He hit the space bar and the snoozing Black-Berry woke up and told him he had one message and that it was 9:33.

The message was from Annie.

Back from dinner with her mother. It was a chatty, happy message and Jean-Guy found himself falling into the words. Joining her. Sitting beside her as Annie and Madame Gamache had their omelette and salad. As they'd talked about their days. Reine-Marie telling Annie that her father had been called away on a case. In a remote abbey. The one with the chants.

And Annie having to pretend this was news.

She felt horrible, but also confessed to finding their clandestine relationship thrilling. But mostly, she longed to tell her mother.

Beauvoir had written Annie earlier, when he'd gotten back to his bedroom. His cell. And told her everything. About the abbey, the music, the recording, the dead prior, the insulted abbot. He'd been careful not to make it all sound easy or fun.

He wanted her to know what it was really like. How he felt.

He told her about the interminable prayers. There'd been another service at a quarter to eight that night. After dinner. After the monks had overheard them in the Blessed Chapel.

Her father had gotten up, bowed slightly, acknowledging the monks, then left. Walking with measured pace off the altar and through the back door, to the prior's office. Beauvoir beside him.

All the way, until they got through the closed door to the corridor, Beauvoir could feel their eyes on him.

Jean-Guy told Annie how that felt. And about getting back to the office and spending the next half hour wrestling with the laptop, while her father continued to go through the prior's papers.

And then they'd heard the singing.

When they'd first arrived in the abbey that afternoon, the chanting had merely bored Beauvoir. Now, he told Annie, it gave him the willies.

"And then," Gamache typed, "Jean-Guy and I went back into the Chapel. Another service. Compline they call it. I need to get a schedule of these things. Did I tell you about the blueberries? My God, Reine-Marie, you'd love them. The monks cover them in handmade dark chocolate. I'll bring you some back, if there are any left. Jean-Guy's in danger of finishing them off. I, of course, am my normal, reticent self. Self-denial, *c'est moi.*"

He smiled and imagined his wife's delight at a small batch of the chocolates. He also imagined her in their home. She wouldn't be in bed yet. Annie had gone over for dinner, he knew. She had dinner with them every Saturday, since her separation from David. She'd have left by now and Reine-Marie would probably be sitting in the living room, by the fireplace, reading. Or in the television room at the back of their apartment, set up in Daniel's old room. It now had a bookcase, a comfortable sofa strewn with newspapers and magazines, and the television.

"Off to watch TV5," she'd say. "A documentary on literacy." But a few minutes later he'd hear laughter and wander down the hall to find her snorting at some ridiculous Québécois sitcom. He'd get sucked in and before long they would both be laughing at the broad and contagious humor.

Yes, she'd be in there, laughing.

He smiled at the thought.

"I swear to God," Jean-Guy wrote, "the service went on forever. And they sing every word. Droning on and on. And we can't even nap. It's up and down, up and down. Your father is right there with them. I think he almost enjoys it. Is that possible? Maybe he's just trying to mess with me. Oh, speaking of that, I have to tell you what he did with the monks. . . ."

"Compline was beautiful, Reine-Marie.

They sang the whole thing. All in Gregorian chant. Think of Saint-Benoit-du-lac, and then some. Very peaceful. I think part of it's because of the chapel. Simple. No adornments at all. Only one large plaque describing Saint Gilbert. There's a room hidden behind it."

Gamache paused in his typing. Thinking of that wall plaque, and the Chapter House hidden behind it. He'd have to get a schematic of the abbey.

Then he went back to his message.

"The chapel was in almost total darkness for the last service of the day, except for a few low lights on the walls behind the altar. Where candles or torches once were, I suppose. Jean-Guy and I sat in the pews, in darkness. You can imagine how much fun Jean-Guy was having. I could barely hear the chanting for all his snorting and huffing.

"There's clearly something very wrong here, among the monks. An enmity. But when they sing it's like all of that never happened. They seem to go to another place. A deeper place. Where no quarrels exist. A place of contentment and peace. Not even joy, I think. But freedom. They seem free from the cares of the world. That young monk, Frère Luc, described it as letting go of all thought. I wonder if that's what freedom is?

"Either way, it was very beautiful. To hear those remarkable chants performed live, Reine-Marie. Amazing. And then, near the end, they slowly dimmed the lights until we were in complete darkness. But out of it, like a light we could only feel, came their voices.

"It was magical. I wish you were here."

"Then, Annie, it was finally over. When the lights came up the monks were gone. But that sneaky one, Frère Simon, came and told us it was bedtime. That we could do whatever we wanted, but they were all going to their cells.

"Your father didn't seem displeased. In fact, I think he wanted them to have the long hours of the night to think about the murder. To worry.

"I found some more chocolate-covered blueberries and brought them back to my cell. I'll save some for you."

"I miss you," Armand wrote. "Sleep tight, *mon coeur*."

"I miss you," Jean-Guy wrote. "*Merde!* All

the chocolates are gone! How did that happen?"

Then he rolled over, the BlackBerry held lightly in his hand. But not before typing, in the darkness, his final message of the day.

"Je t'aime."

He carefully wrapped the chocolates and put them in the nightstand drawer. For Annie. He closed his eyes, and slept soundly.

"Je t'aime," Gamache typed and placed the BlackBerry on the table by the bed.

Chief Inspector Gamache woke up. It was still dark, and not even the predawn birds were singing. His bed was warm around his body, but if he moved his legs even a millimeter they were in frigid territory.

His nose felt chilled. But the rest of him was toasty warm.

He checked the time.

Ten past four.

Had something awoken him? Some sound?

He lay there, listening. Imagining the monks in their tiny cells, all around him. Like bees in a honeycomb.

Were they asleep? Or was at least one of them awake? Lying only feet from Gamache. Not allowed to sleep. The noise too

205

great in his head. The sounds and sights of a murder too disturbing.

For one of the monks, there would almost certainly never again be a quiet night's sleep.

Unless . . .

Gamache sat up in bed. He knew only two things could give a killer a good night's sleep. If he had no conscience. Or if he had a conscience, and that conscience had been an accomplice. Whispering to the killer, giving him the idea.

How could a man, a monk, convince himself that murder wasn't a crime, and wasn't even a sin? How could he be asleep, while the Chief Inspector was awake? There was only one answer. If this was a justified death.

An Old Testament death.

By stoning.

An eye for an eye.

Perhaps the murderer had believed he was doing the right thing. If not in the eyes of man, then in the eyes of God. Perhaps that was the tension Gamache was feeling in the abbey. Not that a murder had happened, but that the police might discover who did it.

Over dinner, that monk had accused the abbot of poor judgment. Not in failing to prevent a murder, but in calling in the

Sûreté. Was there both a vow and a conspiracy of silence?

The Chief Inspector was wide awake now. Alert.

He swung his legs out of bed and found his slippers, then putting on his dressing gown he grabbed a flashlight and reading glasses and left his cell. He paused for a moment in the middle of the long corridor. Looking this way and that. Keeping the flashlight off.

The hall was lined with doors on either side, each into a cell. No light shone under the cracks. And no sound escaped either.

It was dark and silent.

Gamache had been in fun houses with his kids, many times. Seen the hall of distorted mirrors, seen the optical illusions, where a room appeared tilted but wasn't. He'd also been in those deprivation rooms in the fun houses, where neither light nor sound penetrated.

He remembered Annie holding tight to his hand, and Daniel, invisible in the dark, calling for his daddy, until Gamache had found his little boy and held him. That, more than any of the other fun house effects, had terrified his children and they'd clung to him until he'd gotten them out.

That's what the abbey of Saint-Gilbert-

207

Entre-les-Loups felt like. A place of distortion and even deprivation. Of great silence and greater darkness. Where whispers became shouts. Where monks murdered, and the natural world was locked out, as though it was at fault.

The brothers had lived in the abbey so long they'd grown used to it. Accepted the distortion as normal.

The Chief took a deep breath and cautioned himself. It was equally possible he was imagining things, allowing the darkness and silence to get under his skin. It was completely possible the monks weren't the ones with the distorted perception, but that he was.

After a moment Gamache grew used to the lack of light and sight and sounds.

It's not threatening, he said to himself as he made his way toward the Blessed Chapel. *It's not threatening. It's just extreme peace.*

He smiled at the thought. Had peace and quiet become so rare that when finally found they could be mistaken for something grotesque and unnatural? It would appear so.

The Chief felt along the stone wall until he reached the door into the Blessed Chapel. He opened it, then gently closed the heavy wooden door behind him.

Here the darkness and silence were so deep he had the unpleasant sensation of both floating and falling.

Gamache switched on his powerful flashlight. The beam cut through the darkness and rested on the altar, on the benches, on the stone columns. This wasn't simply an early morning stroll by a sleepless man. There was a goal. And he found it easily, on the eastern wall of the chapel.

His light shone on the huge plaque, illuminating the story of Saint Gilbert.

Gamache smoothed his free hand over the plaque. Looking for the catch, the handle, into the Chapter House. Finally he found it by depressing the illustration of two sleeping wolves, etched into the top left corner of the plaque. The stone door opened and Gamache shone his flashlight in.

It was a small, rectangular room, with neither windows nor chairs, though a stone bench ran around the wall. The room was completely bare, barren.

After shining the flashlight into the corners to be certain, Gamache left and replaced the door. As the sleeping wolves popped back into place, the Chief put on his glasses and leaned forward, to read the inscription on the plaque. The life of Gilbert of Sempringham.

Saint Gilbert did not seem to be the patron saint of anything. Nor were any miracles mentioned. The only thing this man seemed to have done was create an order, name it after himself, and die at the staggering age of 106, in 1189.

One hundred and six years of age. Gamache wondered if that could possibly be true, but suspected it probably was. After all, if whoever made this plaque had wanted to lie, or exaggerate, surely they'd choose something more worthy than Gilbert's age. His accomplishments, for example.

If anything was going to put the Chief Inspector to sleep it would be reading about the life of Saint Gilbert.

Why, he wondered, would anyone choose to join this order?

Then he remembered the music, the Gregorian chants. Frère Luc had described them as unique. And yet this plaque mentioned nothing at all about music or chanting. It didn't appear to be a vocation of Saint Gilbert's. In 106 years, not once did Gilbert of Sempringham feel a song coming on.

Gamache scanned the plaque again, for something subtle. Something he might have missed.

He moved the bright circle of light slowly

over the engraved words, squinting, looking at the plaque this way and that. In case some symbol was etched lightly into the bronze. Or worn down over the centuries. A staff. A treble clef. A neume.

But there was nothing, absolutely nothing, to suggest the Gilbertines were renowned for anything, including Gregorian chants.

But there was one illustration. The sleeping wolves, curled together, intertwined.

Wolves, thought the Chief, stepping back from the wall and slipping his glasses back into his dressing gown pocket. *Wolves.* What did he know about wolves in the bible? What was their symbolism?

There were Romulus and Remus. They were saved by a she-wolf. Suckled. But that was Roman mythology, not the bible.

Wolves.

Most biblical imagery was more benign. Sheep, fish. But, of course, "benign" depended on your perspective. The sheep and fish were generally killed. No, wolves were more aggressive. If anything, they did the killing.

It was a strange image to have not only on this plaque but in the very name of the monastery. Saint-Gilbert-Entre-les-Loups. Saint Gilbert-Among-the-Wolves.

Especially odd given the banal, though interminable, life of Saint Gilbert. How could he possibly be associated with wolves?

The only thing that came to mind was "a wolf in sheep's clothing." But was that even from the bible? Gamache thought it was, but now he wondered.

A wolf in sheep's clothing.

Perhaps the monks of this abbey were sheep. A humble role. Just following the rules. Just following the shepherd. Working and praying and singing. Hoping for peace and quiet, to be left alone behind their locked door. To go about the business of praising God.

Except for one. Was there a wolf in the fold? Wearing a long black robe, with a white cowl and a rope around his middle. Was he the murderer, or the victim? Had the wolf killed the monk, or had the monk killed the wolf?

Gamache turned back to the plaque. He realized he hadn't actually read it all. He'd skimmed over the footnote at the very bottom. How important, after all, could a footnote be, to a man whose entire life was a footnote? He'd read it quickly. Something about an archbishop. But now he knelt, almost getting onto his hands and knees, to get a better look at the words. Taking out his reading glasses once again, he leaned toward the bronze afterthought.

It explained that Gilbert had been a friend to the archbishop of Canterbury, and had come to his aid. Gamache stared at it, trying to find the significance. After all, why mention this?

Finally he got to his feet.

Gilbert of Sempringham had died in 1189. He'd been an active member of the Church for sixty years. Gamache did the math.

That meant . . .

Gamache looked back at the plaque and the words almost scraping the floor. That meant his friend, the archbishop, the one he'd helped, was Thomas Becket.

Thomas à Becket.

Gamache turned his back to the plaque, and faced the Blessed Chapel.

Thomas à Becket.

Gamache stepped forward, picking his way slowly between the pews, lost in thought. He stepped onto the altar, and swung the flashlight in a slow arc around him until it came back to where it began. And then he turned it off. And let the night, and the silence, close back in.

Saint Thomas Becket.

Who was murdered in his cathedral.

Wolf in sheep's clothing. It was from the bible, but was famously quoted by Thomas à Becket, who'd called his killers "wolves in sheep's clothing."

T. S. Eliot had written a play about those events. *Murder in the Cathedral.*

"Some malady is coming upon us," Gamache quoted under his breath. *"We wait. We wait."*

But the Chief Inspector didn't have long to wait. Within moments the silence was broken.

Chanting. Getting closer.

The Chief took a few steps, but couldn't get all the way off the altar before he saw the monks, hoods up, filing toward him. Each carrying a candle. They walked right by him as though he wasn't there, and took their accustomed places at the benches.

Their chanting stopped and as a man they removed their hoods.

And twenty-three pairs of eyes stared at him. A man in pajamas and dressing gown, standing in the middle of their altar.

THIRTEEN

"What did you say?" asked Beauvoir, not even bothering to hide his amusement. They were in the prior's office, before heading for breakfast.

"What could I say?" asked Gamache, looking up from making a few notes. "I said, *'Bonjour,'* bowed to the abbot, and took a seat in one of the pews."

"You stayed? In your pajamas?"

"It seemed a bit late to leave," smiled Gamache. "Besides, I was wearing a robe. Like them."

"You were wearing a bathrobe."

"Still . . ." said the Chief.

"I think I'm going to need therapy," mumbled Beauvoir.

Gamache went back to his reading. He had to admit, this wasn't how anyone had expected to start the day. The monks by finding a man in pajamas on their altar at five A.M. Vigils, and Gamache by being that man.

And Beauvoir could not have expected such a gift of a story to land in his lap first thing in the morning. His only regret was not seeing it for himself. And possibly taking a picture. If the Chief cut up rough about his relationship with Annie that photo would surely silence him.

"You asked me to find out who that monk was who insulted the abbot at dinner last night," said Beauvoir. "His name's Frère Antoine. Been here since he was twenty-three. Fifteen years."

Beauvoir had done the math. He and Frère Antoine were exactly the same age.

"And get this," Beauvoir leaned across the desk, "he was the soloist on that recording."

The Chief also leaned forward. "How d'you know?"

"Those bells woke me up early. I assumed it was some sort of alarm. Apparently the monks found a man in his pajamas on their altar this morning."

"I don't believe it."

"Anyway, once those damned bells woke me up, I headed to the showers. That young monk who stays in the porter's office, Frère Luc, had the stall next to mine. We were alone, so I asked him who that monk was who'd challenged the abbot. Guess what else Frère Luc told me."

"What?"

"He said the prior planned to replace Frère Antoine and make him the soloist on the new recording." Beauvoir watched the Chief's eyes widen.

"Him, Luc?"

"Him, Luc. Me, Beauvoir."

Gamache leaned back in his chair and thought for a moment. "Do you think Frère Antoine knew that was the plan?"

"I don't know. More monks arrived and I didn't have a chance to ask."

Gamache glanced at his watch. It was almost seven. He and Beauvoir must have just missed each other in the showers.

If it was slightly unorthodox to eat at the same table with all the suspects, it was definitely unorthodox to shower with them. But there were private stalls, and no option.

Gamache had also had a shower conversation that morning, after Vigils. A few of the monks had come in while he was washing and shaving. Gamache had struck up polite, apparently pointless, conversation, asking each monk why he'd joined the Gilbertines. To a man they answered, "For the music."

And everyone he'd spoken with had been recruited. Specially chosen. For their voices, primarily, but also for their expertise. As the

217

Chief had discovered reading over their interviews the day before, each monk had a discipline. One was a plumber. Another a master electrician. One was an architect and another a stonemason. There were chefs and farmers and gardeners. A doctor, Frère Charles. An engineer.

They were like a Noah's Ark, or a fallout shelter. Able to rebuild the world in case of disaster. Every major element present. With one exception.

No womb.

So, in the event of a catastrophe that only the monastery of Saint-Gilbert-Entre-les-Loups survived, there'd be buildings and running water and electricity. But no life.

But there would be music. Glorious music. For a while.

"How were you recruited?" the Chief had asked his companion in the next stall, after all the other monks had dressed and left.

"By the abbot," said the monk. "Dom Philippe goes out once a year, looking for new monks. We don't always need one. But he keeps track of brothers with the qualities we need."

"And what would those be?"

"Well, Frère Alexandre, for instance, is in charge of the animals, but he's getting beyond it, so *Père Abbé* will keep an eye out

218

for a monk from the outside who has an expertise in that area."

"Another Gilbertine?"

The monk had laughed. "There are no other Gilbertines. We're it. The last of our kind. All of us came from other orders, and were recruited here."

"Is it a hard sell?" asked Gamache.

"A little, but when Dom Philippe explained that the vocation at Saint-Gilbert is Gregorian chant, well, that's all we needed to hear."

"The music is a fair exchange for all you give up? The isolation. You must never see your families or friends."

The monk stared at Gamache. "We would give up everything for the music. It's all that matters to us." Then he smiled. "Gregorian chants aren't just music and they're not just prayer. They're both, together. The word of God sung in the voice of God. We'd give up our lives for that."

"And do," said Gamache.

"Not at all. The lives we have here are richer, more meaningful, than anything we could ever have anywhere else. We love God and we love the chants. In Saint-Gilbert we get both. Like a fix." He laughed.

"Did you ever regret your decision to come here?"

"That first day, those first moments, yes. It seemed a very long boat ride, down the bay. Approaching Saint-Gilbert. I was already missing my old monastery. My abbot and friends there. Then I heard the music. The plainchant."

The monk seemed to leave Gamache, leave the shower room with its steam and fragrance of lavender and bee balm. Leave his body. And go to a better place. A blissful place.

"Within five or six notes I knew there was something different about it." His voice was strong, but his eyes were glazed. It was the same expression Gamache had noticed on the faces of the monks at the services. When they sang.

Peaceful. Calm.

"What was different?" Gamache asked.

"I wish I knew. They're just as simple as every chant I've ever sung, but there's something else there. A depth. A richness. The way the voices blend. It felt whole. I felt whole."

"You said Dom Philippe recruits new monks with the qualities you need here. That would obviously include a good singing voice."

"It doesn't just include," said the monk. "It's the first quality he looks for. Though not just any voice. Frère Mathieu would tell the abbot what kind of voice he needed, and the abbot would go to monasteries in search of it."

"But the recruit would also have to be good with animals, or a chef, or whatever other expertise you need," said Gamache.

"True, which is why it can take years to replace a monk and why the abbot goes out looking. He's like a hockey scout, keeping tabs even on the young guys. The abbot knows about prospects even before they take their final vows, when they're just entering the seminary."

"Is personality important?" asked Gamache.

"Most monks learn to live in community," explained the monk, putting on his robes. "That means accepting each other."

"And the authority of the abbot."

"Oui."

It was, Gamache knew, the most curt answer he'd received so far. The monk bent down to put on his socks, breaking eye contact with the Chief, who was himself already dressed.

When the monk straightened up he smiled again. "We're actually given very thorough personality tests. Evaluated."

Gamache had thought his expression was

neutral, but apparently his skepticism showed.

"Oui," said the monk with a sigh. "Given the Church's recent history it might be a good idea to reevaluate the evaluations. Seems the chosen few might not be so choice. But the fact is, most of us are good people. Sane and stable. We just want to serve God."

"By singing."

The monk examined Gamache. "You seem to believe, monsieur, that the music and the men can be separated. But they can't. The community of Saint-Gilbert-Entre-les-Loups is like a living chant. Each of us individual notes. On our own, nothing. But together? Divine. We don't just sing, we are the song."

Gamache could see he believed it. Believed that on their own they were nothing, but together the monks of Saint-Gilbert formed a plainchant. The Chief had a vision of the halls of the monastery filled not with monks in black robes, but with musical notes. Black notes bobbing through the halls. Waiting to come together in sacred song.

"How much does the prior's death diminish that?" asked Gamache.

The monk inhaled sharply, as though the

222

Chief had jabbed him with a pointy stick.

"We must thank God we had Frère Mathieu at all, and not be upset that he was taken from us."

This sounded less convincing.

"But will the music suffer?" Gamache had chosen his words deliberately and he saw the result. The monk broke eye contact again and fell silent.

Gamache wondered if an equally important part of a chant wasn't just the notes, but the space between them. The silence.

The two men stood in the silence.

"We need so little," said the monk at last. "Music and our faith. Both will survive."

"I'm sorry," said the Chief. "I don't know your name."

"Bernard. Brother Bernard."

"Armand Gamache."

The two men shook hands. Bernard held the Chief's for a moment longer than was necessary.

It was another one of the hundreds of unspoken messages that darted around the monastery. But what was the message? They were two men who had practically showered together. There did seem one obvious invitation. But Gamache instinctively knew that wasn't what Frère Bernard was trying to say.

"But something changed," said Gamache, and Frère Bernard released his hand.

The Chief had realized there were plenty of empty shower stalls. Bernard needn't have chosen the one right next to the Sûreté officer.

Bernard wanted to talk. Had something to say.

"You were right last night," said the monk. "We heard you in the Blessed Chapel. The recording changed everything. Not at first. At first it brought us even closer. It was a common mission. The point wasn't really to share the chants with the world. We were realistic enough to know that a CD of Gregorian chants might not get on the *Billboard* charts."

"Then why do it?"

"It was Frère Mathieu's idea," said Bernard. "The monastery needed repairs and as much as we tried to keep up with things, eventually what was needed wasn't effort or even expertise. It was money. The one thing we didn't have and couldn't make. We make those chocolate-covered blueberries. Have you tried them?"

Gamache nodded.

"I help look after the animals but I also work in the chocolate factory. They're very popular. We trade them to other monasteries in exchange for cheese and cider. And we sell them to friends and family. At a huge markup. Everyone knows that, but they also know we need the money."

"The chocolates are fabulous," agreed Gamache. "But you'd have to sell thousands of boxes to make enough money."

"Or sell each box for a thousand dollars. Our families support us a lot, but that seemed a little much to ask. Believe me, Monsieur Gamache, we tried everything. And finally Frère Mathieu came up with selling the one thing we never run out of."

"Gregorian chants."

"Exactly. We sing all the time and don't have to compete with bears or wolves for the blueberries and we don't have to milk goats for the notes."

Gamache smiled at the image of squirting Gregorian chants from the teats of goats and sheep.

"But you had no great hopes?"

"We always have hope. That's another thing we never run out of. What we didn't have were high expectations. The plan was to make the recording and sell it at extortionary rates to family and friends. And through the shops in some of the other monasteries. Our friends and families would play the CD once, just to say they'd done it, then put it away and forget about it."

"But something happened."

Bernard nodded. "It took a while. We sold a few hundred. Got enough to buy materials to repair the roof. But then about a year after the CDs went out we started getting money into our account. I remember being in Chapter when the abbot told us that more than a hundred thousand dollars had appeared in our account. He'd had the brother who does our accounting double-check and sure enough, it came from the recordings. More had been made, with our permission, but we didn't know how many. And then there were the electronic versions. The downloads."

"How did the brothers react?"

"Well, it seemed a miracle. On so many levels. We suddenly had more money than we could use, and more coming all the time. But money aside, it was as if God had given His blessing. Smiled on the project."

"And not just God, but the outside world," said Gamache.

"True. It seemed everyone all at once discovered how beautiful our music was."

"Validation?"

Frère Bernard colored and nodded. "I'm embarrassed to admit, but that's what it felt like. It seemed to matter after all. What the

226

world thought."

"The world loved you."

Bernard took a deep breath and lowered his gaze to his hands, now resting on the lap of his robe. Cradling the ends of the rope around his waist.

"And for a while that felt wonderful," said Frère Bernard.

"What happened?"

"The world not only discovered our music, they discovered us. Planes started buzzing overhead, people arrived by the boatload. Reporters, sightseers. Self-proclaimed pilgrims came to worship us. It was terrible."

"The price of fame."

"All we wanted was heat in the winter," said Frère Bernard. "And a roof that didn't leak."

"But still, you managed to hold them all off."

"That was Dom Philippe. He made it clear to other monasteries, and to the public, that we're a reclusive order. With a rule of silence. He even went on television, just the once. Radio Canada."

"I saw the interview." Though it could hardly be called an interview. It was Dom Philippe standing in an anonymous location, in his robes. Looking at the camera,

227

and imploring people to please leave his monastery alone. He was glad everyone was enjoying the chants, but said it was all they had to offer. They could give nothing more. But the world could give them, the monks of Saint-Gilbert, a great gift. Peace and quiet.

"And did they leave the monks alone?" asked Gamache.

"Eventually."

"But peace wasn't restored, was it?"

They left the shower rooms and Gamache followed Frère Bernard down the quiet corridor. Toward the closed door at the end. Not the one into the Blessed Chapel. But the other end.

Frère Bernard pulled on the handle and they stepped into a bright new day.

They were, in fact, in a huge walled enclosure. With goats and sheep, chickens and ducks. Frère Bernard took a reed basket for himself and handed one to Gamache.

The air was fresh, cool, and felt good after the heat of the shower. Over the high wall he could see pine trees, and hear birds and the soft lapping of water on rocks.

"Excusez-moi," said Bernard to the chicken before taking her egg. *"Merci."*

Gamache also burrowed his large hand under the chickens, and found the warm eggs. He placed them carefully in his basket.

"Merci," he said to each chicken.

"Peace appeared to have been restored, Chief Inspector," said Bernard as he moved from hen to hen. "But Saint-Gilbert didn't feel the same. There was tension. Some of the monks wanted to capitalize on our popularity. Arguing it was clearly God's will, and it would be wicked to turn our backs on such an opportunity."

"And others?"

"They argued that God had been generous enough, and we needed to accept what He'd given with humility. That this was a test. That fame was a serpent, masquerading as a friend. This was our temptation and we needed to reject it."

"Where did Frère Mathieu stand?"

Bernard came to a large duck and stroked her head, whispering words Gamache couldn't hear but recognized as endearments. Then Frère Bernard kissed the top of her head and moved on. Without taking away any of her eggs.

"With the abbot. They were best friends, two halves of a whole. Dom Philippe the aesthetic, the prior a man of action. Together they led the monastery. Without the abbot there would never have been a recording. He supported it completely. Helped with the connections with the outside world. Was as joyful about it as the rest."

"And the prior?"

"It was his baby. He was the undisputed leader of the choir and the recording. He chose the music, the arrangements, the soloists, the order in which they'd be recorded. It was all done in a single morning, in the Blessed Chapel, using an old tape machine the abbot borrowed on a trip to the abbey at Saint-Benoit-du-lac."

It was, Gamache knew from listening to the CD many times, not of good quality. But that added a sort of sheen to it, a legitimacy. No digital editing, no multiple tracks. No tricks or fakery. It was real.

And it was beautiful. It had captured what Frère Bernard had described. When people listened it was as though they too belonged. Were less alone. Were still individuals, but part of a community. Part of everything. People, animals, trees, rocks. There was suddenly no distinction.

It felt as though the Gregorian chants entered people's bodies and rearranged their DNA, so that they were part of everything around them. There was no anger, no competition, no winners or losers. Everything was splendid and everything was equal.

And everyone was at peace.

No wonder people wanted more. Cried for more. Demanded more. Showed up at the monastery, and pounded on the door, almost hysterical to be let in. And given more.

And the monks had refused.

Bernard had been quiet for a few moments, walking slowly around the perimeter of the enclosure.

"Tell me," said Gamache. There was more, he knew. There was always more. Bernard had followed him into the showers, with one purpose. To tell Gamache something, and so far while interesting, this wasn't it.

There was more.

"It was the vow of silence."

Gamache waited, then finally prodded. "Go on."

Frère Bernard hesitated, trying to find the words to explain something that didn't exist in the outside world. "Our vow of silence isn't absolute. It's also known as a rule of silence. We're allowed to talk to each other sometimes, but it disturbs the peace of the abbey, and the peace of the monk. Silence is seen as both voluntary and deeply spiritual."

"But you are allowed to talk?"

"Our tongues aren't cut out when we sign up," said the monk with a smile. "But it isn't encouraged. A chatty man would never make a monk. There're times of the day where quiet is more important. Night, for instance. That's called the Great Silence. Some monasteries have relaxed the vow of silence, but here at Saint-Gilbert we try to maintain a great silence most of the day."

Great silence, thought Gamache. That was what he'd experienced a few hours ago, when he'd risen and walked into the corridor. It had felt like a void into which he might fall. And if he had, what would he have met there?

"The greater the silence the louder the voice of God?" asked Gamache.

"Well, the better chance we have of hearing it. Some of the monks wanted the vow lifted so that we could go into the world and speak to people about the music. Maybe do concerts. We were getting all sorts of invitations. There was even a rumor that we'd been invited to the Vatican, but the abbot had declined."

"How did people feel about that?"

"Some were angry. Some were relieved."

"Some supported the abbot, and some didn't?"

Bernard nodded. "You have to understand, an abbot is more than a boss. Our allegiance isn't to the bishop or archbishop. It's to the abbot. And the abbey. We elect him and he keeps that job until he either dies or steps down. He's our pope."

"And is he considered infallible?"

Bernard stopped walking and crossed his arms, laying his free hand protectively and instinctively on the eggs.

"No. But the happiest abbeys are where the monks don't question their abbot. And the best abbots are open to suggestions. Discuss everything in Chapter. Then they make a decision. And everyone accepts. It's seen as an act of humility and of grace. It's not about winning or losing, but voicing your opinion. And letting God and the community decide."

"But that stopped happening here."

Bernard nodded.

"Was there someone who started this campaign to end the vow of silence? A voice for the dissenters?"

Again, Bernard nodded. This was what he'd wanted to say.

"Frère Mathieu," said Bernard, at last. He looked miserable. "The prior wanted the vow of silence lifted. It led to terrible rows. He was a forceful man. Used to getting what he wanted. Up until then what he wanted and what the abbot wanted were the same thing. But not anymore."

"And Frère Mathieu didn't submit?" asked Gamache.

"Not at all. And slowly other monks saw that the walls didn't crumble if they too didn't submit. If they continued to fight, and even disobeyed. The arguments escalated, became more vocal."

"In a silent community?"

Bernard smiled. "You'd be surprised how many ways there are to get your message across. Far more powerful, and insulting, than words. A turned back in a monastery is like dropping the f-bomb. A rolled eye is a nuclear attack."

"And by yesterday morning?" asked Gamache.

"By yesterday morning the monastery had been laid to waste. Except that the bodies were still walking and the walls still standing. But Saint-Gilbert-Entre-les-Loups was dead in every other way."

Gamache thought about that for a moment, then thanking Frère Bernard he handed him his basket of eggs and left the enclosure, returning to the dim monastery.

The peace had been not simply shattered, but murdered. Something precious had been destroyed. And then a rock had landed on Frère Mathieu's head. Shattering it too.

As he'd left Frère Bernard, Gamache had paused at the door to ask one last question.

"And you, *mon frère?* Where did you stand?"

"With Dom Philippe," he said without hesitation. "I'm one of the abbot's men."

The abbot's men, thought the Chief as he and Beauvoir entered the silent breakfast hall a few minutes later. Many of the monks were already there, but none looked in their direction.

The abbot's men. The prior's men.

A civil war, fought with glances and small gestures. And silence.

FOURTEEN

After a breakfast of eggs and fruit, fresh bread and cheese the monks left and the Chief and Beauvoir lingered over their herbal teas.

"This is disgusting." Beauvoir took a sip and made a face. "It's dirt tea. I'm drinking mud."

"It's mint. I think," said Gamache.

"Mint mud," said Beauvoir, putting his tea down and pushing the mug away. "So, who do you think did it?"

Gamache shook his head. "I honestly don't know. It seems likely to be someone who sided with the abbot."

"Or the abbot himself."

Gamache nodded. "If the prior was killed over the power struggle."

"Whoever won the struggle got to control a monastery that was suddenly extremely rich, and powerful. And not just because of the money."

"Go on," said Gamache. He always preferred to listen than to talk.

"Well, think about it. These Gilbertines disappear for four centuries, then suddenly, and apparently miraculously, walk out of the wilderness. And as though that wasn't biblical enough, they come bearing a gift. Sacred music. A New York marketing guru couldn't have come up with a better gimmick."

"Only it isn't a gimmick."

"Are you so sure, *patron?*"

Gamache put his mug on the table and leaned toward his second in command, his deep brown eyes thoughtful.

"Are you saying this was all manipulated? By these monks? Four hundred years of silence, then a recording of obscure Gregorian chants? All to put themselves in a position of wealth and influence. Quite a long-range plan. A good thing they didn't have shareholders."

Beauvoir laughed. "But it worked."

"But it was hardly a slam-dunk. The chances that this remote monastery filled with singing monks would become a sensation is minuscule."

"I agree. A bunch of things had to come together. The music had to grab people. But that probably wasn't enough. What really ignited it was when everyone found out who they were. A supposedly extinct order of monks who've taken a vow of silence. That's what grabbed people."

The Chief nodded. It added to the mystery of the music, and the monks.

But was it manipulated? It was all true, after all. But wasn't that what good marketing was? Not lying, but choosing what truths to tell?

"These humble monks become superstars," said Beauvoir. "Not only rich, but way more than that. They're powerful. People love them. If the abbot of Saint-Gilbert-Entre-les-Loups got on CNN tomorrow and announced he was the second coming, you can't tell me millions wouldn't believe it."

"Millions will believe anything," said Gamache. "They see Christ in a pancake and start worshipping it."

"But this is different, *patron,* and you know it. You even felt it yourself. The music does nothing for me, but I can see that it does something to you."

"True again, *mon vieux,*" Gamache smiled. "But it doesn't drive me to murder. Just the opposite. It's very calming. Like the tea." He picked up his mug again, and toasted Beauvoir, then relaxed back into his chair.

"What are you saying, Jean-Guy?"

"I'm saying there was more at stake than another recording. And there was way more at stake than petty squabbles and the right to boss around two dozen singing monks. Whether the monks like it or not, they're very influential now. People want to hear what they have to say. That must be pretty intoxicating."

"Or sobering."

"And all they have to do is get rid of an inconvenient vow of silence," said Beauvoir, his voice low and intense. "Go on tour. Do concerts. Do interviews. People would hang on their every word. They'd be more powerful than the pope."

"And the only one standing in the way is the abbot," said the Chief, then shook his head. "But if that was true then the wrong man was killed. Your argument would make sense, Jean-Guy, if Dom Philippe was dead, but he isn't."

"Ahhh, but you're wrong. Sir. I'm not saying that the murder happened to lift the vow of silence, I'm just saying there's a whole lot at stake. For the prior's camp it's power and influence, but for the other? There's a motive just as potent."

Now Gamache smiled, and nodded.

"To keep their peaceful, quiet life. To

protect their home."

"And who wouldn't kill to protect their home?" asked Beauvoir.

Gamache thought about that, and remembered collecting the eggs that morning, in the soft light of dawn, with Frère Bernard. And the monk's description of the planes overhead, and the pilgrims pounding on the door.

And the abbey laid to waste.

"If Frère Mathieu had won the battle he'd have made another recording, ended the vow of silence and changed the monastery forever," said the Chief. He smiled at Beauvoir and got to his feet. "Well done. Though there's one thing you're forgetting."

"I can't see how that can possibly be true," said Beauvoir, also getting up.

The two men left the dining hall and walked down the deserted corridor. Gamache opened the book he'd carried everywhere. The slim volume of Christian meditations. From it he drew the piece of yellowed paper found on the body, and handed it to his second in command.

"How do you explain this?"

"Maybe it's meaningless."

The Chief made a not very encouraging face. "The prior died curled around it. It sure meant something to him."

Beauvoir opened the large door for the Chief and both men entered the Blessed Chapel. They stopped while Beauvoir studied the page.

He'd glanced at it when it was first found, but hadn't spent the time with it the Chief had. Gamache waited, hoping maybe fresh, young, cynical eyes might see something he'd missed.

"We don't know anything about it, do we," said Beauvoir, concentrating on the script and the strange markings above the words. "We don't know if it's old, or who wrote it. And we sure don't know what it means."

"Or why the prior had it. Was he trying to protect it when he died, or was he trying to hide it? Was it precious to him, or was it blasphemy?"

"That's interesting," said Beauvoir, examining the page. "I think I've figured out what one of the words is. I think this," he pointed to a Latin word written in script and Gamache leaned toward it, "means 'ass.' "

Beauvoir handed the page back.

"Merci." Gamache returned it for safekeeping, and snapped the book shut. "Very enlightening."

"Frankly, *patron,* if you have a monastery full of monks and you come to me for enlightenment, you deserve what you get."

Gamache laughed. *"C'est vrai.* Well, I'm off to find Dom Philippe and see if there's a plan of the abbey."

"And I want a word with the soloist, Frère Antoine."

"The one who challenged the abbot?"

"That's him," said Beauvoir. "Must be one of the prior's men. What is it?"

Gamache had grown very still. Listening. The monastery, always quiet, seemed to be holding its breath.

But with the first notes of the chant, it breathed.

"Not again," sighed Beauvoir. "Didn't we just have one? Honestly, they're worse than crackheads."

Up and down. Bow. Sit. Stand.

The postbreakfast service called Lauds went on and on. But now Beauvoir found himself less bored. Probably, he told himself, because he knew some members of the band. He was also paying more attention. Seeing it as more than just a waste of time between interrogations and collecting evidence.

The prayer service itself was evidence.

The Gregorian chants. All the suspects lined up, facing each other.

Was the rift obvious? Could he see it, now

242

that he knew? Beauvoir found himself fascinated by the ritual. And the monks.

"This was the prior's last service," whispered Gamache, as they bowed then straightened. Beauvoir noticed the Chief's right hand was steady, no tremor today. "He was killed almost immediately after Lauds, yesterday."

"We still don't know for sure where he went after Lauds," whispered Beauvoir as they briefly sat. It was, he'd grown to realize, a tease. Within moments they were back on their feet.

"True. When this is over we need to watch which monks go where."

The Chief kept his eyes on the rows of monks. The sun was rising and, as Lauds went on, more and more light descended from the windows high up in the central tower. It hit the imperfect old glass and refracted. Split. Into all the colors ever created. And those tumbled to the altar and lit the monks and their music. So that it seemed that the notes and the cheerful light mixed and merged. Playing together on the altar.

Most of Gamache's experience with the Church had been fairly grim, so he'd sought, and found, his God elsewhere.

But this was different. There was delight

here. And not by pure chance. Gamache took his eyes off the monks for a moment and looked to the ceiling. The beams and buttresses. And the windows. The original architect of Saint-Gilbert-Entre-les-Loups had deliberately created an abbey that was a vessel for light and sound.

Perfect acoustics married playful light.

He lowered his gaze. The monks' voices seemed even more beautiful than yesterday. Tinged with sorrow now, but there was also a levity to the notes, a lift. The chants were both solemn and joyous. Grounded and winged.

And Gamache thought again about the page with the old neumes that he'd slipped for safekeeping into the book of meditations. The neumes looked, at times, like wings in flight. Was that what the composer of the ancient chants had tried to get across? That this music wasn't really of this earth?

Beauvoir had been right, of course. The music both touched Gamache and transported him. He was tempted to lose himself in the gentle, calming voices. So in tune with each other. To drop the worries he carried and drift away. To forget why he was there.

It was infectious, insidious.

Gamache smiled and realized to blame

the music was ludicrous. If he drifted away, lost focus, it was his fault. Not the monks'. Not the music's.

He doubled his efforts and scanned the rows. Like a game, but not a game.

Find the leader.

With the prior gone, who now led this world-famous choir? Because someone did. As he'd said to Beauvoir, choirs don't direct themselves. One of the monks, with movements so subtle as to be lost on even a trained investigator, had taken charge.

When Lauds ended the Chief and Beauvoir stood in their pew, watching.

It was, thought Beauvoir, a bit like taking the break in a game of pool. Balls heading off in all different directions. That's what this looked like. Monks going here, there and everywhere. Scattering, though not actually bouncing off the walls.

Beauvoir turned to say something sarcastic to Gamache, but changed his mind when he saw the Chief's face. It was stern, thoughtful.

Jean-Guy followed the Chief's gaze and saw Frère Luc walking slowly, perhaps reluctantly, toward the wooden door that would take him down the long, long corridor. To the locked door. The gate. And the tiny room marked *"Porterie."*

He was all alone, and looked it.

Beauvoir turned back to the Chief and saw in his eyes a look that was both sharp, and concerned. And he wondered if the Chief was seeing Frère Luc, but thinking about other young men. Who'd gone through a door. And not returned.

Who'd followed Gamache's orders. Followed Gamache. But while the Chief had come back, with a deep scar near his temple and a tremor in his hand, they hadn't.

Was the Chief looking at Frère Luc, but thinking about them?

Gamache seemed worried.

"OK, *patron?*" whispered Beauvoir.

The acoustics in the Blessed Chapel picked up the words and magnified them. Chief Inspector Gamache didn't answer. Instead he continued to stare. At the now-closed door. Where Frère Luc had gone, and disappeared.

Alone.

The other black-robed monks went through all the other doors.

Finally they were alone in the Blessed Chapel and Gamache turned back to Beauvoir.

"I know you want to speak with Frère Antoine —"

"The soloist," said Beauvoir. "Yes."

"That's a good idea, but I wonder if you'd mind joining Frère Luc first?"

"Sure, but what'll I ask him? You've already spoken to him. So have I, in the shower this morning."

"Find out if Frère Antoine knew he was about to be replaced as soloist on the next album. Just keep Frère Luc company for a while. See if anyone else shows up at the porter's door in the next half hour."

Beauvoir looked at his watch. The service had started bang on seven thirty, and ended exactly forty-five minutes later.

"Oui, patron," he said.

Gamache's eyes hadn't left that dim part of the church.

Beauvoir willingly followed Frère Luc, just as he willingly followed all of Gamache's orders. He knew it was a waste of time, of course. The Chief might make it sound like more interrogation, but Beauvoir knew what it really was.

Babysitting.

He was happy to do it, if it gave the Chief some peace. Beauvoir would have burped and diapered the monk, had Gamache asked. And had it helped ease the Chief's mind.

■ ■ ■ ■

"Would you mind having a look, Simon?"

The abbot smiled at his taciturn secretary, then turned to his guest.

"Shall we?" The abbot raised an arm and pointed, like a good host, to the two comfortable armchairs by the fireplace. The chairs were covered in a faded chintz and seemed to be stuffed with feathers.

The abbot was about ten years older than Gamache. Mid-sixties, the Chief guessed. But he seemed sort of ageless. The shaved head and robes, Gamache supposed, did that. Though there was no disguising the lines in Dom Philippe's face. And no attempt to disguise them.

"Brother Simon will find you a plan of the monastery. I'm sure we have one somewhere."

"You don't use one?"

"Good heavens, no. I know every stone, every crack."

Like a commander of a ship, thought Gamache. Coming up through the ranks. Intimately aware of every corner of his vessel.

The abbot seemed comfortable in command. Apparently unaware a mutiny was under way.

Or probably supremely aware there had been one, and it had been thwarted. The challenge to his authority had died with the prior.

Dom Philippe smoothed his long, pale hands over the arms of his chair. "When I first joined Saint-Gilbert one of the monks was an upholsterer. Self-taught. He'd ask the abbot to get the ends of bolts and bring them back. This's his work."

The abbot's hand stopped moving and rested on the arm, as though it was the arm of the monk himself.

"That was almost forty years ago now. He was elderly then, and died a few years after I arrived. Frère Roland was his name. A gentle, quiet man."

"Do you remember all the monks?"

"I do, Chief Inspector. Do you remember all your brothers?"

"I'm an only child, I'm afraid."

"I put it badly. I meant your other brothers, your brothers-in-arms."

The Chief felt himself grow still. "I remember every name, every face."

The abbot held his gaze. It wasn't challenging, it wasn't even searching. It felt, to Gamache, more like a hand to the elbow, helping him keep his balance.

"I thought you probably did."

"Unfortunately none of my agents is quite this handy." Gamache also smoothed the faded chintz.

"If you lived and worked here, believe me, they'd become handy even if they didn't start that way."

"You recruit everyone?"

The abbot nodded. "I have to go get them. Because of our history, we've taken not just a vow of silence but a vow of invisibility. A pledge to keep our monastery . . ."

He searched for a word. It was clearly not something Dom Philippe had had to explain very often. If ever.

". . . secret?" offered Gamache.

The abbot smiled. "I was trying to avoid that word, but I suppose it's accurate. The Gilbertines had a happy, uneventful life for many centuries, in England. And then with the Reformation all the monasteries were closed. That's when we first started fading. We packed up everything we could carry and disappeared from sight. We found a fairly remote plot of land and rebuilt in France. Then, with the Inquisitions, we again came under scrutiny. The Holy Office interpreted our desire for seclusion as a desire for secrecy, and judged us badly."

"And you don't want to be judged badly

by the Inquisition," said Gamache.

"You don't want to be judged at all by the Inquisition. Ask the Waldensians."

"The who?"

"Exactly. They lived not far from us in France, a few valleys over. We saw the smoke, inhaled the smoke. Heard the screams."

Dom Philippe paused, then looked down at his hands clasping each other in his lap. He spoke, Gamache realized, as though he'd been there himself. Breathing in his brother monks.

"So we packed up again," said the abbot.

"Faded further."

The abbot nodded. "As far as we could get. We came over to the New World with some of the first settlers. The Jesuits were the ones chosen to convert the natives and head out with the explorers."

"While the Gilbertines did what?"

"While we paddled north." The abbot paused then. "When I say we came across with the first settlers, I meant that we came across as settlers. Not as monks. We hid our robes. Hid our holy orders."

"Why?"

"Because we were worried."

"Does that explain the thick walls and hidden rooms and locked doors?" asked Gamache.

"So you've noticed those?" asked the abbot with a smile.

"I'm a trained observer, *mon père,*" and Gamache. "Hardly anything gets by my keen eye."

The abbot gave a soft laugh. He, like the chants themselves, seemed lighter this morning. Less burdened. "We appear to be an order of worriers."

"I notice that Saint Gilbert doesn't seem to have a calling," said Gamache. "Perhaps he can become the Patron Saint of Fretters."

"It would certainly fit. I'll alert the Holy Father," said the abbot.

While recognizing the joke, the Chief Inspector suspected this abbot wanted little, if anything, to do with bishops, archbishops or popes.

The Gilbertines, more than anything, just wanted to be left alone.

Dom Philippe moved his hand back to the arm of his chair, his finger probing a hole worn in the fabric. It seemed new to him. A surprise.

"We're used to solving our own problems," he said, looking at the Chief. "From roof repairs, to broken heating, to cancer and broken bones. Every single monk who lives here will die here too. We leave everything up to God. From holes in the fabric to harvests to how and when we die."

"Was what happened in your garden yesterday God's work?"

The abbot shook his head. "That's why I decided to call you in. We can handle God's will, no matter how harsh it can sometimes appear. But this was something else. It was man's will. And we needed help."

"Not everyone in your community agrees."

"You're thinking of Brother Antoine last night at dinner?"

"I am, and he was clearly not alone."

"No." The abbot shook his head, but held Gamache's eyes. "I've learned in more than two decades as abbot that not everyone will agree with my decisions. I can't worry about that."

"What do you worry about, *mon père?*"

"I worry about telling the difference."

"I'm sorry?"

"Between God's will and my will. And right now, I'm worried about who killed Mathieu, and why." He paused, worrying the hole in the upholstery. Making it worse. "And how I could've missed it."

Frère Simon arrived with a scroll and

unrolled it on the low pine table in front of the men.

"*Merci,* Simon," said the abbot, and leaned forward. Frère Simon made to leave but Gamache stopped him.

"I have another request, I'm afraid. It would be helpful to have a schedule of the services and meals and anything else we should be aware of."

"An horarium," said the abbot. "Simon, would you mind?"

It seemed Simon, while looking as though he minded breathing, in fact was willing to do anything the abbot asked of him. One of the abbot's men, without a doubt, thought Gamache.

Simon withdrew and the two men leaned over the plan.

"So," said Beauvoir, leaning against the doorjamb. "Do you spend all day here?"

"All day, every day."

"And what do you do?"

Even to his ears it sounded like a lame pickup line in a dingy bar. "Come here often, sweet cheeks?" Next he'd be asking this young monk what his sign was.

Beauvoir was Cancer, which always annoyed him. He wanted to be Scorpio, or Leo. Or even that ram thing. Anything other

254

than the crab that, according to the descriptions, was nurturing, nesting, and sensitive.

Fucking horoscopes.

"I read this."

Frère Luc lifted the huge book an inch off his lap then dropped it again.

"What is it?"

Frère Luc gave him a suspicious look, as though trying to assess the motives of the man he met in the shower that morning. Beauvoir had to admit, he'd be suspicious of himself too.

"It's the book of Gregorian chants. I study it. Learn my parts."

It was the perfect "in."

"You told me this morning that the prior had chosen you to be the new soloist in the next recording. You'd be replacing Frère Antoine. Did Frère Antoine know that?"

"Must have," said Luc.

"Why do you say that?"

"Because if Frère Antoine thought he was the soloist, he'd be studying the chants. Not me."

"All the chants are in that one book?" Looking at it, balanced on Frère Luc's thin knees, Beauvoir had an idea. "Who else knows about that?" Beauvoir nodded toward the old volume.

If knowledge was power, thought Beauvoir, that book was all-powerful. It held the key to their vocation. And now, it was also the key to all their wealth and influence. Whoever possessed this book had everything. It was their Holy Grail.

"Everyone. It's kept on a lectern in the Blessed Chapel. We look at it all the time. Take it to our cells, sometimes. No big deal."

Merde, thought Beauvoir. So much for the Holy Grail.

"We also copy out the chants ourselves," Frère Luc pointed to a workbook on the narrow table. "So we all have our own copies."

"It's not a secret, then?" asked Beauvoir, to be sure.

"This?" The young monk laid his hand on it. "Many monasteries have one. Most have two or three, and far more impressive ones than ours. I guess because this is such a poor order we only have one. So we have to be careful with it."

"Not read it in the bath?" asked Beauvoir.

Luc smiled. It was the first one Beauvoir had seen from the grim young monk.

"When were you supposed to do the new recording?"

"It wasn't decided yet."

Beauvoir thought about that for a moment. "What wasn't decided? The timing of the recording, or if there'd even be one?"

"It wasn't absolutely decided if there'd be another recording, but I don't think there was much doubt."

"But you led the Chief to believe the recording was going ahead, a *fait accompli*. Now you're saying it wasn't?"

"It was just a matter of time," said Luc. "If the prior wanted something, it happened."

"And Frère Antoine?" asked Beauvoir. "How do you think he took the news?"

"He'd have accepted it. He'd have to."

Not because Frère Antoine was humble, thought Beauvoir. Not as a reflection of his faith, but because it was useless to argue with the prior. Easier, probably, to just kill the man.

Was that the motive? Had Frère Antoine smashed the prior's head in because he was about to be replaced as soloist? In an order dedicated to Gregorian chant, the soloist would hold a special place.

More equal, as Orwell had it, than others. And people killed for that all the time.

Fifteen

The sunshine through the leaded-glass windows fell on the plan of the abbey of Saint-Gilbert-Entre-les-Loups. It was drawn on very old, very thick paper and showed the cruciform design of the abbey. Walled enclosures jutted off the two arms and the abbot's garden hung off the bottom of the cross.

The Chief Inspector put on his reading glasses and leaned closer to the scroll. He studied the drawing in silence. He'd been in the abbot's garden, of course. And had collected eggs with Frère Bernard a few hours ago in the walled enclosure with the goats and sheep and chickens, off the right arm of the cross.

His eyes shifted across the plan, to the opposite arm. With the chocolate factory, the dining hall, the kitchens. And another walled enclosure.

"What's this, *mon père?*" The Chief

pointed.

"That's our vegetable and herb garden. We grow our own, of course."

"Enough to feed all of you?"

"That's why we've never had more than two dozen monks. It was judged by the founders to be the perfect number. Enough to do the work, and not too many to feed. They were right."

"And yet you have thirty cells. Room for more. Why?"

"Just in case," said Dom Philippe. "As you so rightly said, Chief Inspector, we're an order of fretters. Suppose we needed more space? Suppose someone came? We're prepared for the unexpected. Though the perfect number is twenty-four."

"But now you're down to twenty-three. A spot has opened up."

"I suppose it has. I hadn't thought that far ahead."

The Chief Inspector wondered if that was true, and wondered if that might make a motive. If the abbot did the recruiting, could he have found another monk he wanted to invite to join the Gilbertines?

But someone would have to go before the new person could come. And who better than the troublesome prior?

Gamache tucked that possibility away, but

without any great enthusiasm. Even in the cutthroat world of universities, or New York co-ops, where there were finite places, people rarely actually cut throats. Or bashed in skulls.

He could see many reasons this abbot might kill his prior, but to open up a space for someone else seemed among the least likely.

"Who was the last person you recruited?"

"Brother Luc. He came just under a year ago, from an order close to the American border. They're also a musical order. Benedictines. Make wonderful cheese. We trade chocolate for their cheese. You had some at breakfast."

"Delicious," agreed the Chief, who wanted to get off cheese and back to the murder. "Why did you choose him?"

"I'd had my eye on him since he entered the seminary. Beautiful voice. Extraordinary voice."

"And what else does he bring?"

"Pardon?"

"I understand that singing might be what you look for first —"

"I look for piety first," said the abbot. His voice was still pleasant, but there was no mistaking his tone. He wanted to make that clear. "First I must believe that a brother

260

will fit in with the goal of Saint-Gilbert, to live with God through Christ. If that's satisfied, then I look at other things."

"Like his voice," said Gamache. "But there has to be more, *non?* Another skill he brings. As you say, you need to be self-sufficient."

For the first time, the abbot hesitated. Looked uncomfortable.

"Frère Luc has the advantage of youth. He can be taught."

But Gamache had seen the crack, the chink. The fret. And he moved in.

"And yet, every other monk came with a discipline. For instance, I understand Frère Alexandre is getting old, perhaps too old to look after the animals. Wouldn't it make more sense to find a replacement for him?"

"Are you questioning my judgment?"

"I certainly am. I'm questioning everything. Why did you recruit Frère Luc when all he could bring was his voice?"

"I judged that his voice was enough at this stage. As I said, he can be taught other things, like animal husbandry from Frère Alexandre, if he shows an aptitude for it. We're fortunate now."

"How so?"

"We don't need to beg other monks to come. Younger monks are interested. That was one of the great gifts of the recording. We now have a choice. And when they arrive we can train them. An older monk can mentor a younger, as Frère Roland was mentored and learned the trade of upholstering."

"Perhaps Frère Luc can learn it too," said Gamache, and saw the abbot smile.

"That's not a bad idea, Chief Inspector. *Merci.*"

Still, thought Gamache, it didn't quite explain the *volte-face* the abbot had made in recruiting. From choosing skilled and trained men, to choosing a novice. With only one outstanding skill. His extraordinary voice.

Gamache stared at the plan on the table in front of them. There was something wrong with it. Some sense he had, like in the fun house. A slight queasiness when he looked at it.

"Is there just the one hidden room?" he asked, his finger hovering over the Chapter House.

"As far as I know. There're always rumors of long-forgotten tunnels and vaults with treasure, but no one's ever found them. At least, not that I know of."

"And what did the rumors say the treasure was?"

"That was conveniently unclear," said the abbot with a smile. "Couldn't have been much, since the original two dozen monks would have had to paddle it up the river all the way from Québec City. And I can tell you, if you couldn't eat it or wear it, it probably didn't come on the voyage."

Since those were pretty much his own packing rules, Gamache accepted the abbot's explanation. Besides, what could men who'd taken vows of silence, poverty and isolation possibly treasure? Though even as he asked himself that question he knew the answer. People always found things to treasure. For little boys it was arrowheads and cat's-eye marbles. For adolescents it was a cool T-shirt and a signed baseball. And for big boys? Just because they were monks didn't mean they had no treasures. It simply might not be what others found valuable.

He rested his hand on the end of the plan to keep the paper from curling up. Then looked over to where his fingers touched.

"It's the same paper," he said, caressing the plan.

"Same as what?" asked the abbot.

"As this." Once again, the Chief brought the page from the book and laid it on top of the plan. "The chant is written on exactly the same paper as the plan for the monastery. Is it possible this," he touched the chant, "is as old as that?" He nodded to the plan of the monastery. "Were they written at the same time?"

The drawing was dated 1634 and signed Dom Clément, Abbot of Saint-Gilbert-Entre-les-Loups. Below the signature were two figures Gamache had grown to recognize. Wolves, intertwined, apparently sleeping.

Entre les loups. Among the wolves. It suggested coming to an agreement, finding peace rather than banishment or massacre. Perhaps when you flee an Inquisition you're less likely to visit those horrors on others. Even wolves.

Gamache compared the lettering. Both were simple, the letters not so much written as drawn. Calligraphied. They looked to be done by a similar hand. He'd need an expert to say if the plan and the chant were written by the same man. In 1634.

Dom Philippe shook his head. "It's certainly the same type of paper. But is it the same vintage? I think the chant was written much more recently, and whoever did it used vellum to make it look old. We have sheets of vellum still, made by monks centuries ago. Before paper."

"Where do you keep them?"

"Simon?" the abbot called and the monk appeared. "Can you show the Chief Inspector our vellum?"

Frère Simon looked put out, as though this was far too much effort. But he nodded and walked across the room, followed by Gamache. He pulled out a drawer filled with sheets of yellowed paper.

"Are any missing?" asked Gamache.

"Don't know," said Simon. "I never counted."

"What do you use them for?"

"Nothing. They just sit here. In case."

In case of what? Gamache wondered. Or just, in case.

"Who could've taken one?" he asked, feeling he was caught in a perpetual game of Twenty Questions.

"Anyone," said Frère Simon, closing the drawer. "It's never locked."

"But is your office locked?" Gamache turned back to the abbot.

"Never."

"It was locked when we arrived," said the Chief.

"I did that," said Frère Simon. "Wanted to make sure nothing was disturbed when I came to get you."

"Did you also lock it when you went to

find the doctor and the abbot?"

"*Oui.*"

"Why?"

"I didn't want anyone to come across the body." The monk was getting defensive, his eyes darting from Gamache to the abbot, who sat quietly listening.

"Did you know it was murder at the time?"

"I knew it wasn't natural."

"How many people use the abbot's garden?" the Chief asked and again saw the monk's eyes shoot off to the abbot, then back again.

"No one," said Dom Philippe, getting up and coming over. To the rescue? Gamache wondered. It had that feel. But he wasn't clear why Frère Simon needed rescuing.

"As I believe I mentioned earlier, Chief Inspector, this is my private garden. A sort of sanctuary. Mathieu used to visit, and Frère Simon does the gardening, but beyond that it's used only by me."

"Why?" Gamache asked. "Most other spaces in the abbey are communal. Why's your garden private?"

"You'd have to ask Dom Clément," said the abbot. "He designed the abbey. He put in the garden and the hidden Chapter House and everything else. He was a master architect you know. Renowned in his time. You can see his brilliance."

Gamache nodded. He could. And brilliance was exactly the right word. Not only in the simple, elegant lines, but in the placement of the windows.

Every stone was there for a reason. Nothing superfluous. Nothing ornate. All had a reason for being. And there was a reason the abbot's garden was private, if not secret.

Gamache turned back to Frère Simon. "If no one else used the garden, why did you think one of the monks might stumble across the body of Frère Mathieu?"

"I hadn't expected to find the prior there," said Simon. "I didn't know what else to expect."

There was silence then, as Gamache studied the guarded monk.

Then the Chief nodded and turned back to the abbot.

"We were talking about the sheet of paper found on the body of the prior. You think the paper's old, but the writing isn't. Why do you say that?"

The two men returned to their chairs, while Frère Simon hovered in the background, tidying, shifting papers. Watching. Listening.

"The ink's too dark, for one thing," said

Dom Philippe, as they studied the page. "Vellum soaks up liquid, over time, so that what's left on the surface isn't really ink anymore, but a stain, in the shape of the words. You can see that in the plan of the monastery."

Gamache leaned over the scroll. The abbot was right. He'd thought with the passage of time and exposure to the sun the black ink had faded slightly, but it hadn't. It had been absorbed into the vellum. The color was now trapped inside the page, not resting on top.

"But that," the abbot waved to the yellowed paper, "hasn't sunk in yet."

Gamache frowned, impressed. He'd still consult a forensics expert, but he suspected the abbot might be right. The yellowed chant wasn't old at all, just made to look that way. Made to deceive.

"Who would have done this?" Gamache asked.

"I can't know."

"Let me rephrase that, then. Who could have done this? I can tell you, not many people can sing a Gregorian chant, never mind write one, even a mockery of one, using these."

He placed his index finger firmly over one of the neumes.

"We live in different realities, Chief Inspector. What's obvious to you, isn't to me."

He left and returned a moment later with a workbook, clearly modern, and opened it. Inside, on the left page, were Latin text and the squiggled neumes. On the right was the same text, but this time instead of neumes there were musical notes.

"This is the same chant," Dom Philippe explained. "One side's in the old form, with neumes, and the other's in modern notes."

"Who did this?"

"I did. An early attempt to transcribe the old chants. Not very good, or accurate, I'm afraid. The later ones are better."

"Where did you get the old chant?" Gamache pointed to the neume side.

"From our Book of Chants. Before you get excited, Chief Inspector —"

Yet again Gamache realized even slight shifts in his expression were readable by these monks. And a tiny ripple of interest was considered "excited" in this placid place.

"— let me tell you that many monasteries have at least one, often many books, of chants. Ours is among the least interesting. No illuminated script. No illustrations. Pretty dull, by church standards. All the impoverished Gilbertines could afford at the time, I suspect."

"Where's your Book of Chants kept?"

Was this the treasure? Gamache wondered. Kept hidden. Was one monk assigned to guard it? Perhaps even the dead prior. How powerful would that make Frère Mathieu?

"It's kept on a lectern in the Blessed Chapel," said the abbot. "It's a huge book, left open. Though I think Frère Luc has it now in the *porterie*. Studying it."

The abbot gave an infinitesimal smile. He could see the slight disappointment on the Chief's face.

It was disconcerting, Gamache realized, to be so easily read. It also took away any assumed advantage an investigator had. That suspects didn't know what the police were thinking. But it seemed this abbot knew, or could guess, just about everything.

Though Dom Philippe wasn't all-seeing, all-knowing. After all, he hadn't known he had a murderer among them. Or perhaps he had.

"You must read neumes well," said the Chief, returning to the abbot's workbook, "to have transcribed them into musical notes."

"I wish that was true. I'm not the worst, but I'm far from the best. We all do it. When a monk arrives in Saint-Gilbert, it's the first task he's given. Like Frère Luc. To start transcribing the Gregorian chants from our old book into modern musical notes."

"Why?"

"As a sort of test, first off. See how dedicated the monk really is. For someone not truly passionate about Gregorian chant it's a long and tedious chore. It's a good way to weed out any dilettantes."

"And for those who are passionate?"

"It's heaven. We can hardly wait to get at the book. Since it sits on the lectern we can consult it whenever we want."

The abbot dropped his eyes to the workbook and flipped through it, smiling, sometimes shaking his head and even tsking over some mistake. Gamache was reminded of his children, Daniel and Annie, looking through albums of photos taken when they were kids. Laughing and sometimes cringing. At hairstyle and clothing choices.

These monks had no photo albums. No family pictures. Instead, they had workbooks with neumes and notes. Chants had replaced family.

"How long does it take to do the whole Book of Chants?"

"A lifetime. It can take a year to transcribe a single chant. It becomes a surprisingly beautiful relationship, very intimate."

The abbot seemed to detach, just for a moment. Go someplace else. A place without walls, and murder, and a Sûreté officer asking questions.

And then he came back. "Since the work is so long and complex, most of us die before we're finished."

"What happened just now?" asked Gamache.

"Pardon?"

"As you spoke about the music your eyes seemed to become unfocused. It felt as though you drifted off."

The abbot turned his full attention, and very alert eyes, on the Chief. But said nothing.

"I've seen that look before," said Gamache. "When you sing. Not just you, but all of you."

"It's joy, I suppose," said the abbot. "When I even think of the chants I feel freed of cares. It's as close to God as I can get."

But Gamache had seen that look on other faces. In stinking, filthy, squalid rooms. Under bridges and in cold back alleys. On the faces of the living, and sometimes on the dead. It was ecstasy. Of sorts.

Those people got there not through chants, but through needles in the arm, crack pipes and little pills. And sometimes they never came back.

If religion was the opiate of the masses, what did that make chants?

"If you're all transcribing the same chants," said the Chief, thinking about what the abbot had been saying before he drifted off, "can't you just copy off each other?"

"Cheat? You do live in a different world."

"It was a question," said Gamache with a smile, "not a suggestion."

"I suppose we could, but this isn't a chore. The point isn't to transcribe the chants, it's to get to know them, live inside the music, to see the voice of God in each note, each word, each breath. Anyone who'd want to take a shortcut wouldn't want to dedicate his life to Gregorian chant, and spend it here in Saint-Gilbert."

"Has anyone ever finished the whole Book of Chants?"

"A few monks, to my knowledge. No one in my lifetime."

"And what happens to their workbooks, after they die?"

"They're burned, in a ceremony."

"You burn books?" The shock on Gamache's face didn't need much interpretation.

"We do. Just as Tibetan monks spend

years and years creating their intricate works of art in sand, and then destroy them the moment they're finished. The point is not to grow attached to things. The gift is the music, not the workbook."

"But it must be painful."

"It is. But faith is often painful. And often joyous. Two halves of a whole."

"So," Gamache turned his attention back to the yellowed page lying on the plan of the monastery. "You don't think this is actually all that old?"

"I don't."

"What else can you tell me about it?"

"What's clear, and why I showed you my workbook, is the difference between the chants."

The abbot placed the yellowed page on his workbook so that it covered the modern translation. The two chants with neumes faced each other. The Chief Inspector studied them. He spent almost a minute in complete silence, staring. Looking from one to the other. At the words, and at the marks flitting all over the pages.

Then his eyes slowed and he stared longer at one. Then the other.

When he lifted his eyes there was the spark of discovery in them, and the abbot smiled, as he might to a bright postulant.

"The neumes are different," said Gamache. "No, not different. But there're more of them on the page we found on the prior. Far more. Now that I see the two examples side-by-side it seems obvious. The one in your notebook, copied from the original, has just a few neumes per line. But the one we found on the prior is thick with them."

"Exactly."

"So, what does it mean?"

"Again, I can't be sure," the abbot leaned over the yellowed page. "Neumes serve only one purpose, Chief Inspector. To give direction. Up, down, fast, slow. They're signs, signals. Like the hands of a conductor. I think whoever wrote this means for there to be many voices, going in different directions. This isn't plainchant. This is complex chant, multi-layered chant. It's also quite fast, a strong tempo. And . . ."

Now the abbot hesitated.

"Yes?"

"As I say, I'm not exactly the resident expert. Mathieu was that. But I think this was also meant to have music. I think one of the lines of neumes is for an instrument."

"And that would be different from Gregorian chants?"

"It would make it a new creature. Something never heard before."

Gamache studied the yellowed page.

How odd, he thought, that monks never seen should possess something never heard.

And one of them, their prior, had been found dead, curled around it in the fetal position. Like a mother, protecting an unborn child. Or a brother-in-arms, curled around a grenade.

He wished he knew which it was. Divine or damned?

"Is there an instrument here?"

"There's a piano."

"A piano? Were you planning to eat it, or wear it?"

The abbot laughed. "One of the monks arrived with it years ago and we hadn't the heart to send it back." The abbot smiled. "We're dedicated to Gregorian chants, passionate about them, but the fact is, we love all church music. Many of the brothers are fine musicians. We have recorders and violins. Or are they fiddles? I'm never sure what the difference is."

"One sings, the other dances," said Gamache.

The abbot looked at him with interest. "What a nice way of putting it."

"A colleague told me that. I learned a great deal from him."

"Would he like to become a monk?"

"I'm afraid he's beyond that now."

The abbot again correctly interpreted the look on Gamache's face, and didn't press.

Gamache picked up the page. "I don't suppose you have a photocopy machine?"

"No. But we have twenty-three monks."

Gamache smiled and handed it over to the abbot. "Can you have it transcribed? If you can make a copy that would be helpful, so I don't need to keep carrying around the original. And perhaps one of you could transcribe the neumes into musical notes? Is that possible?"

"We can try." Dom Philippe called his secretary over and explained what was needed.

"Transcribe it to musical notes?" Simon asked. He looked not very optimistic. The Eeyore of the monastery.

"Eventually. Just copy it for now so we can give the original back to the Chief Inspector. As accurately as possible, of course."

"Of course," said Simon. The abbot turned away, but Gamache caught the flash of a sour look on Simon's face. Aimed at the abbot's back.

Was he the abbot's man after all? the Chief wondered.

Gamache glanced through the leaded-glass window. It made the world outside look slightly distorted. But still he yearned to step into it. And stand in the sunshine. Away, even briefly, from this interior world of subtle glances and vague alliances. Of notes and veiled expressions.

Of vacant looks, and ecstasy.

Gamache longed to walk around the abbot's garden. No matter how tilled and weeded and pruned it was, that control was an illusion. There was no taming nature.

And then he realized what had made him uncomfortable earlier, when he'd first seen the plan of the monastery.

He looked at it again.

The walled gardens. On the plan they were all the same size. But in reality, they weren't. The abbot's garden was much smaller than the *animalerie.* But on the plan they appeared exactly the same size.

The original architects had distorted the drawing. The perspectives were off.

Things appeared equal that weren't.

SIXTEEN

Inspector Beauvoir left Frère Luc to the massive book resting on his skinny knees. He'd arrived thinking the poor bastard must want company, and left realizing he'd been simply an intrusion. All the young monk really wanted was to be left alone with his book.

Jean-Guy went off in search of Frère Antoine, but paused in the Blessed Chapel to check his BlackBerry.

Sure enough, there were two messages from Annie. Both short. Responding to his email from early that morning, and a more recent one, describing her day so far. Beauvoir leaned against the cool stones of the chapel and smiled as he wrote back.

Something rude and suggestive.

He was tempted to tell her about her father's adventures that morning, in his pajamas and bathrobe, being found by the monks on their altar. But it was too good a story to waste in an email. He'd take her to one of the *terrasses* not far from her home and tell her over a glass of wine.

When he'd finished his vaguely erotic message to Annie he turned right and looked in the chocolate factory. Brother Bernard was there, fishing tiny wild blueberries out of a vat of dark chocolate.

"Frère Antoine?" said Bernard, responding to the Sûreté officer's question. "Try either the kitchen or the garden."

"The garden?"

"Through the door at the end of the hall." He waved a wooden spoon and dribbled chocolate on his apron. He looked like he wanted to swear and Beauvoir paused, wondering how monks cursed. Like the rest of the Québécois? Like Beauvoir himself? Did they curse the Church? *Câlice! Tabernac! Hostie!* The Québécois had turned religious words into dirty words.

But the monk remained silent and Beauvoir left, glancing into the gleaming stainless-steel kitchen next door. It was easy to see where some of the music money had been spent. There was no Frère Antoine. Only the aroma of a soup simmering, and bread baking. Finally Beauvoir reached the large wooden door at the very end of the corridor. And opened it.

He felt a rush of autumn air, cool and fresh. And the sunshine on his face.

He'd had no idea how much he missed the sun, until it was back. And now he took a deep breath and stepped into the garden.

The abbot's bookcase swung open to reveal to Gamache a bright, fresh world. Of green grass and the last of the blooms, of neat shrubs and the huge maple in the middle, losing its autumn leaves. As the Chief watched, a single bright orange leaf lost its grip and wafted back and forth, gently falling to the ground.

This was a walled world. With a pretense of control, without the reality of it.

Gamache felt his foot sink into the soft grass and smelled musky autumn in the morning air. Insects buzzed and droned, almost drunk on the mid-September nectar. It was chilly, but milder than the Chief had expected. The walls, he supposed, acted as a wind barrier and a sun trap. Creating their own environment.

Gamache had asked to come into the garden not simply because he yearned for fresh air and sunshine, but because this was almost the exact moment, twenty-four hours earlier, when two other men had stood here.

Frère Mathieu and his killer.

And now the Chief Inspector of homicide and the abbot of Saint-Gilbert stood there.

Gamache looked at his watch. Just after half past eight in the morning.

When exactly had the prior's companion known what he was going to do? Had he come into the garden, stood where the Chief now stood, with murder in mind? Had he stooped and picked up a stone, and bashed in the prior's skull, on impulse? Or had that been his plan all along?

When was the decision made to murder?

And when did Frère Mathieu know he was about to be killed? Had been killed, in fact. It had clearly taken him a few minutes, after the blow was struck, to die. He'd crawled to the far wall. Away from the abbey. Away from the bright and warm sunshine. Into the darkness.

Was it simply instinct, as someone had suggested? An animal wanting to die alone. Or was something else at work? Had the prior one last service to perform?

To protect the yellowed page against the monks. Or the monks from the yellowed page?

"You were inspecting the new geothermal system yesterday morning at this time," said Gamache. "Alone?"

The abbot nodded. "The morning's a busy time in the abbey. The brothers are in the garden, or tending the animals, doing all sorts of chores. It takes near constant work to keep the abbey up."

"Is one of your monks in charge of the physical plant?"

The abbot nodded. "Frère Raymond. He looks after the infrastructure. The plumbing and heating and electrics. That sort of thing."

"So you met with him."

"Well, no." The abbot turned and started strolling slowly around the garden, and Gamache joined him.

"What do you mean, 'no'?"

"Brother Raymond wasn't there. He works in the garden every morning after Lauds."

"And that's when you chose to inspect the geothermal?" asked Gamache, perplexed. "Wouldn't you want him there, to go over it together?"

The abbot smiled. "Have you met Brother Raymond?"

Gamache shook his head.

"Lovely man. Gentle man. An explainer."

"A what?"

"He loves to explain how things work, and why. It doesn't matter that he's told me every day for fourteen years how an artesian

283

well works, he'll still tell me again."

The whimsical, affectionate look remained on Dom Philippe's face.

"Some days I'm very bad," he confided in the Chief, "and sneak down to do my rounds when I know he won't be there."

The Chief smiled. He had a few agents and inspectors like that. Who literally followed him through the halls explaining the intricacies of fingerprints. He'd hidden in his office more than once, to avoid them.

"And your secretary, Brother Simon? He tried to find the prior, but when he couldn't he went to work in the *animalerie,* I understand."

"That's right. He's very fond of chickens."

Gamache studied the abbot to see if he was joking, but he seemed perfectly serious.

Jean-Guy looked at the garden. It was huge. Much, much bigger than the abbot's garden. This was clearly a vegetable garden, whose main crop seemed to be massive mushrooms.

A dozen monks, in their black robes, were kneeling down or bending over. On their heads they wore large, extravagant straw hats. With wide floppy brims. One man wearing it would look ridiculous but since all of them were it looked normal. And

Beauvoir, bare-headed, became the abnormal one.

Plants were staked up, vines were trained along trellises, neat rows were being weeded by some of the mushrooms, while others gathered vegetables in baskets.

Beauvoir was reminded of his grandmother, who'd lived all her life on a farm. Short and stocky, she'd spent half her life loving the Church and the other half loathing it. When Jean-Guy had visited they'd collect little new peas together and shell them, sitting on the porch.

He now knew his grandmother must have been very busy, but she never gave that impression. Just as these monks now gave the impression of working steadily, working hard even, but working at their own pace.

Beauvoir found himself almost mesmerized by the rhythm of their movements. Standing, bowing, kneeling.

It reminded him of something. And then he had it. Had they been singing, this would be a mass.

Did this explain his grandmother's love of her garden? As she stood, and bowed, and knelt, had it become her mass? Her devotion? Had she found in her garden the peace and solace she'd sought in the Church?

One of the monks noticed him and smiled.

Motioning him over.

Their vow of silence had been lifted, but clearly it was also a choice. These men liked silence. Beauvoir was beginning to see why.

As he arrived, the monk lifted his hat in an old-fashioned greeting. Beauvoir knelt beside him.

"I'm looking for Frère Antoine," he whispered.

The monk pointed a trowel toward the far wall then went back to work.

Picking his way along the orderly rows, past the weeding and harvesting monks, Beauvoir approached Frère Antoine. Weeding. Alone.

The soloist.

"Poor Mathieu," said Dom Philippe. "I wonder why he was here."

"Didn't you invite him? You sent Frère Simon to request a meeting."

"Yes, after the eleven o'clock mass. Not after Lauds. He was three hours early, if that's why he came."

"Perhaps he misunderstood."

"You didn't know Mathieu. He was rarely wrong. And never early."

"Then maybe Frère Simon gave him the wrong time."

The abbot smiled. "Simon is wrong even

less of the time. Though more punctual."

"And you, Dom Philippe? Are you ever wrong?"

"Always and perpetually. One of the perks of the position."

Gamache smiled. He knew that perk too. But then he remembered that while Frère Simon had headed off to give the prior the message, he hadn't found him. The message hadn't been delivered.

So if it wasn't to meet the abbot, then why had the prior been here? Who was he meeting?

His killer, obviously. Though equally obviously, the prior couldn't have known that was on the agenda. So what had brought Frère Mathieu to this garden?

"Why did you want to see the prior yesterday?"

"Abbey business."

"An argument could be made that everything is abbey business," said Gamache. The two men continued their stroll around the garden. "But I'd rather you didn't waste my time making that argument. I understand that you and Frère Mathieu met twice a week to discuss abbey issues. The meeting you wanted to set up yesterday was extraordinary."

Gamache's voice was reasonable, but firm.

He was tired of this abbot, of all the monks, giving them facile answers. It was like copying someone else's neumes. It might be easier, but it got them no closer to their goal. If their goal was the truth.

"What was so important, Dom Philippe, that it couldn't wait until your next scheduled meeting?"

The abbot took another few steps in silence, except for the slight swish as his long black robe brushed the grass and dried leaves.

"Mathieu wanted to talk about making another recording." The abbot was grim-faced.

"The prior wanted to talk about it?"

"I'm sorry?"

"You said Mathieu wanted to talk about it. Was the meeting his idea, or yours?"

"The topic was his idea. The timing was mine. We needed to resolve the issue before the community met again in Chapter."

"So it wasn't yet decided if there'd be another recording?"

"He'd decided, but I hadn't. We'd discussed it in Chapter, but the outcome was —" The abbot searched for the right word. "Inconclusive."

"There was no consensus?"

Dom Philippe took a few paces and

slipped his hands into his sleeves. It made him look contemplative, though his face was anything but thoughtful. It was bleak. An autumn face, after all the leaves had fallen.

"I can ask others, you know," said the Chief.

"I suspect you already have." The abbot took a deep breath then exhaled with a puff in the early morning chill. "As with most things in the monastery, some were for it, some against."

"You make it sound as though this was just one more issue to be resolved. But it was more than that, wasn't it?" said Gamache. His words pressed but his tone was gentle. He didn't want the abbot to put up his defenses. At least, not any higher than they already were. Here was a guarded man. But what was he guarding?

Gamache was determined to find out.

"The recording was changing the abbey," the Chief pressed further, "wasn't it?"

The abbot stopped then, and cast his eyes over the wall, to the forest beyond and a single, magnificent tree in full autumn color. It shone in the sunlight, made all the brighter for the dark evergreens surrounding it. A living stained-glass window. More magnificent, surely, than anything found in a great cathedral.

The abbot marveled at it. And he marveled at something else.

How he'd actually forgotten what Saint-Gilbert had been like just a few years ago. Before the recording. Everything now seemed measured by that. Before and after.

Saint-Gilbert-Entre-les-Loups had been poor, and getting poorer. Before the recording. The roof leaked and pots and pans were put out by hurrying monks every time it rained. The woodstoves barely gave off enough heat. They had to put extra blankets on their cots in winter and wear their robes to bed. Sometimes, on the bitterest of nights, they'd stay up. In the dining hall. Gathered around the woodstove. Feeding it logs. Drinking tea. Toasting bread.

Warmed by the stove, and by each other. Their bodies.

And sometimes, waiting for the sun to rise, they'd pray. Their voices a low rumble of plainchant. Not because some bell had tolled and told them they had to. Not because they were afraid, of the cold, or the night.

They'd prayed because it gave them pleasure. For the fun of it.

Mathieu was always beside him. And as they sang Dom Philippe would notice the slight movement of Mathieu's hand. Privately conducting. As though the notes and words were part of him. Fused.

Dom Philippe had wanted to hold that hand. To be a part of it. To feel what Mathieu felt. But, of course, he never took Mathieu's hand. And never would now.

That was before the recording.

Now, all that was gone. Killed. Not by a stone to Mathieu's head. It had, in fact, been killed before that.

By that damned recording.

The abbot chose his words, even the ones he kept to himself, carefully. It was a damned recording. And he wished with all his heart it had never happened.

This large, quiet, quite frightening man from the police had asked if he was ever wrong. He'd answered glibly that he was always wrong.

What he should have said was that he was wrong many times, but one mistake over-shadowed all the rest. His error had been so spectacular, so stunning it had become a permanent wrong. In indelible ink. Like the plan of the abbey. His error had soaked into the very fabric of the monastery. It now defined the abbey and had become per-petual.

What had appeared so right, so good, on so many levels, had turned into a travesty.

The Gilbertines had survived the Reformation, survived the Inquisition. Survived almost four hundred years in the wilderness of Québec. But they'd finally been found. And felled.

And the weapon had been the very thing they'd wanted to protect. The Gregorian chants themselves.

Dom Philippe would die before he'd make that mistake again.

Jean-Guy Beauvoir stared at Frère Antoine.

It was like peeking into an alternate universe. The monk was thirty-eight years old. Beauvoir's age. He was Beauvoir's height. Beauvoir's coloring. They even shared the same lean and athletic build.

And when he spoke, Frère Antoine's voice had the same Québécois accent. From the same region. The streets of east end Montréal. Imperfectly hidden under layers of education and effort.

The two men stared, neither sure what to make of the other.

"Bonjour," said Frère Antoine.

"Salut," said Beauvoir.

The only difference was that one was a monk and the other a Sûreté officer. It was as though they'd grown up in the same home, but in different rooms.

Beauvoir could understand the other monks. Most were older. They seemed of an intellectual, contemplative nature. But this lean man?

Beauvoir felt a slight vertigo. What could possibly have led Antoine to become Frère Antoine? Why not a cop, like Beauvoir. Or a teacher. Or work for Hydro-Québec. Or a bum, or a vagrant, or a burden to society?

Beauvoir could understand the path to all those things.

But a religious? A man of his own age? From the same streets?

No one Beauvoir knew even went to church, never mind dedicated his life to it.

"I understand you're the soloist for the choir," said Beauvoir. He stood as tall as he could, but still felt dwarfed by Frère Antoine. It was the robes, Beauvoir decided. They were an unfair advantage. Gave the impression of height and authority.

Perhaps the Sûreté should consider it, if they ever redesigned the uniforms. He'd have to put it in the suggestion box, and sign Inspector Lacoste's name to it.

"That's true. I'm the soloist."

Beauvoir was relieved this monk hadn't called him "my son." He wasn't sure what he'd do if that happened, but he suspected it wouldn't reflect well on the Sûreté.

"I also understand you were about to be replaced."

That got a reaction, though not the one Beauvoir expected and hoped for.

Frère Antoine smiled.

"You've been talking to Frère Luc, I see. I'm afraid he's mistaken."

"He seems quite certain."

"Frère Luc is having difficulty separating what he hopes will happen from what actually will. Expectations from reality. He's young."

"I don't think he's much younger than Christ."

"You're not suggesting we have the second coming in the porter's room?"

Beauvoir, who had a tenuous hold on anything biblical, gave the point to the monk.

"Frère Luc must have misunderstood the prior," said Frère Antoine.

"Was that an easy thing to do?"

Frère Antoine hesitated then shook his head. "No," he admitted. "The prior was quite a definite man."

"Then why does Frère Luc believe the prior wanted him to be the soloist?"

"I can't explain what people believe, Inspector Beauvoir. Can you?"

"No," admitted Beauvoir. He was looking

at a man his own age, in a gown and floppy hat, head shaved, in a community of men in the woods. They'd dedicated their lives to a church most in Québec had renounced and they found meaning in singing songs in a dead language with squiggles for notes.

No, he couldn't explain it.

But Beauvoir knew one thing, after years of kneeling beside dead bodies. It was very, very dangerous to come between a person and their beliefs.

Frère Antoine handed Beauvoir a basket. The monk bent down and searched through thick elephant ear leaves.

"Why do you think Frère Luc is the *portier?*" the monk asked, not looking at Beauvoir.

"Punishment? Some sort of hazing ritual?"

Frère Antoine shook his head. "Every single one of us is assigned that little room when we first arrive."

"Why?"

"So we can leave."

Frère Antoine picked a plump squash and put it in Beauvoir's basket.

"Religious life is hard, Inspector. And this is the hardest. Not many can cut it."

He made it sound like the marines of religious orders. There's no life like it. And Beauvoir discovered a small stirring of understanding. Of attraction even. This was a tough life. And only the tough made it. The few. The proud. The monks.

"Those of us who stay at Saint-Gilbert have been called here. But that means it's voluntary. And we have to be sure."

"So you test each new monk?"

"We don't test him, the test is between himself and God. And there's no wrong answer. Just the truth. He's given the door to guard and the key to leave."

"Free choice?" asked Beauvoir, and saw the monk smile again.

"Might as well make use of it."

"Has anyone ever left?"

"Lots. More leave than stay."

"And Brother Luc? He's been here almost a year now. When's his test over?"

"When he decides it's over. When he asks to be taken out of the porter's room and comes to join the rest of us. Or he uses the key and leaves."

Another heavy gourd landed in Beauvoir's basket.

Frère Antoine moved down the row.

"He's in a sort of purgatory there," said the monk, searching among the huge leaves for more squash. "Of his own making. It must be very painful. He seems paralyzed."

"By what?"

"You tell me, Inspector. What generally paralyzes people?"

Beauvoir knew that answer. "Fear."

Frère Antoine nodded. "Frère Luc is gifted. By far the best voice we have here, and that's saying something. But he's frozen with fear."

"Of what?"

"Of everything. Of belonging. And not belonging. He's afraid of the sun and afraid of shadows. He's afraid of creaks in the night and afraid of the morning dew. That's why I know Frère Mathieu wouldn't have chosen him to be the soloist. Because his voice, while beautiful, is full of fear. When that fear is replaced by faith he'll be the soloist. But not before."

Beauvoir thought about that as they inched down the row, his basket growing heavy with produce.

"But suppose the prior had chosen him? Suppose he decided most people wouldn't hear the fear, or care. Maybe it even made the music more attractive, richer, more human. I don't know. But suppose Frère Mathieu had chosen Luc. How would you've felt?"

The monk took the straw hat from his head and wiped his brow. "You think I'd care?"

Beauvoir met the stare. It really was like looking into a mirror. "I think you'd care very deeply."

"Would you? If a man you admired, respected, revered even passed you up in favor of someone else, what would you do?"

"Is that how you felt about the prior? You revered him?"

"I did. He was a great man. He saved the monastery. And if he wanted a monkey to sing solo I'd happily plant bananas."

Beauvoir found himself wanting to believe this man. Perhaps because he wanted to believe he'd react the same way himself.

But he had his doubts.

And Jean-Guy Beauvoir also doubted this monk. Beneath that robe, beneath that ridiculous hat, wasn't the son of God but the son of man. And the son of man, Beauvoir knew, was capable of almost anything. If pushed. If betrayed. Especially by a man he revered.

Beauvoir knew that the root of all evil wasn't money. No, what created and drove evil was fear. Fear of not having enough money, enough food, enough land, enough power, enough security, enough love. Fear of not getting what you want, or losing what you have.

Beauvoir watched Brother Antoine collect

hidden squash. What drove a healthy, smart young man to become a monk? Was it faith or was it fear?

"Who's leading the choir now that the prior is gone?" Gamache asked. They'd walked to the end of the garden and were wandering back. Their cheeks were red from the cold morning air.

"I've asked Brother Antoine to take over the choir."

"The soloist? The one who challenged you last night?"

"The one who is by far the most accomplished musician, after Mathieu."

"You weren't tempted to take over?"

"I was tempted, and still am," said the abbot with a smile. "But I passed up that fruit. Antoine is the man for the job. Not me."

"And yet, he was one of the prior's men."

"What do you mean by that?" The abbot's smile faded.

Gamache cocked his head slightly and examined his companion. "I mean that this abbey, this order, is divided. The prior's men on one side, the abbot's men on the other."

"That's preposterous," the abbot snapped. Then snapped back into place. But it was too late. Gamache had had a glimpse of what hid beneath the face. A serpent's tongue had lashed out, and retreated just as quickly.

"It's the truth, *mon père,*" said Gamache.

"You're mistaking dissent for dissension," said the abbot.

"I'm not. I do know the difference. What's happening here, and has probably been going on for quite a while, is far more than healthy disagreement. And you know it."

The two men had stopped walking and now stared at each other.

"I don't know what you mean, Monsieur Gamache. There's no such creature as an abbot's man. Or a prior's man. Mathieu and I worked together for decades. He looked after the music, I looked after their spiritual life —"

"But weren't they one and the same? Frère Luc described the chants as both a bridge to God and God himself."

"Frère Luc is young and tends to simplify."

"Frère Luc is one of the prior's men."

The abbot bristled. "The chants are important, but only one aspect of our spiritual lives here at Saint-Gilbert."

"Does the split cut along those lines?" asked Gamache. His voice was calm but unrelenting. "Those for whom the music was paramount joined with the prior. Those whose faith came first joined with you?"

"There was no joining," said the abbot, his voice raised in exasperation. Desperation, even, thought Gamache. "We're united. We can sometimes disagree, but that's all."

"And did you disagree about the direction of the abbey? Did you disagree about something as fundamental as the vow of silence?"

"I lifted that."

"Yes, but only after the prior was dead, and only to answer our questions, not to allow the monks to go into the world. Do concerts, give interviews."

"The vow of silence will never be permanently lifted. Never."

"Do you think the second recording'll go ahead?" Beauvoir asked.

Now, finally, he saw a reaction in Frère Antoine. A flash of anger, then suppressed. Like the root vegetables beneath their feet. Buried, but still growing.

"I have no idea. If the prior was alive I'm sure it would have. The abbot was against it, of course. But Frère Mathieu would've won."

There was no uncertainty in the monk's voice. And Beauvoir finally had his button.

301

It had taken him awhile to find it. He could push and insult and harangue Frère Antoine all day, and he'd remain composed, good-humored even. But mention the abbot?

Kaboom.

"Why do you say, 'of course'? Why would the abbot be against it?"

As long as he could keep pushing the "abbot button" this monk would be off-balance. And there was a better chance something unexpected would come out of that mouth.

"Because it wasn't under his control."

The monk leaned closer to Beauvoir. Jean-Guy felt the force of this monk's personality. And his physical vitality. Here was a strong man, in every way.

Why are you a monk? was really the question Beauvoir was longing to ask. But didn't. And he knew, deep down, why not. He too was afraid. Of the answer.

"Look, the abbot decides everything within these walls. In a monastic life the abbot is all-powerful," said Frère Antoine, his hazel eyes focused on Beauvoir. "But he let something slip through his fingers. The music. In allowing the first recording he let the music out into the world and lost control of it. The chants took on a life of their own. He's spent the past year trying to undo all that. To contain them again." A malicious smile appeared on that handsome face. "But he can't. It's God's will. And he hates it. And he hated the prior. We all knew that."

"Why would he hate the prior? I thought they were friends."

"Because the prior was everything he isn't. Brilliant, gifted, passionate. The abbot's a dry old stick. A decent enough administrator, but no leader. He could quote the bible front and back, in English and French and Latin. But with the Gregorian chants? The center of our life here? Well, some know it and some feel it. The abbot knows the chants. The prior felt them. And that made Frère Mathieu a far more powerful man in the monastery. And the abbot knew it."

"But it must have always been like that, why would the recording change anything?"

"Because as long as it was just us, they worked it out. Made a good team, in fact. But with the success of the recording, the power shifted. Suddenly the prior was getting recognition from the outside."

"And with that came influence," said Beauvoir.

"The abbot felt threatened. Then Frère Mathieu decided we should not only do another recording but go out into the world. Respond to the invitations. He felt strongly

303

that those invitations came as much from God as from the people. It was, in essence, a literal 'calling.' Suppose Moses had kept the tablets? Or Jesus had remained a carpenter, privately communing with God? No. These gifts are meant to be shared. The prior wanted to share them. But the abbot didn't."

The words tumbled over themselves to leave Frère Antoine's body. He couldn't condemn Dom Philippe fast enough.

"The prior wanted the vow of silence lifted, so that we could go into the world."

"And the abbot refused," said Beauvoir. "Did he have much support?"

"Some of the brothers were loyal to him, more out of habit than anything. Habit and training. We're taught to always bend our will to the abbot."

"Then why didn't you?"

"Because Dom Philippe would've destroyed Saint-Gilbert. Taken it back to the Dark Ages. He wanted nothing to change. But it was too late. The recording changed everything. It was a gift of God. But the abbot refused to see it that way. He said the recording was like the serpent in the garden, trying to lure us away, seduce us with promises of power and money."

"Maybe he was right," Beauvoir suggested

and was rewarded with a look of fury.

"He's a frightened old man, clinging to the past."

Frère Antoine was leaning toward Beauvoir, practically spitting the words. Then he paused, and a perplexed look crossed his face. The monk cocked his head to one side.

Beauvoir also paused to listen.

Something was coming.

Armand Gamache looked into the sky.

Something was coming.

He and the abbot had been discussing the garden. He wanted to bring the interview back to a more conversational tone. It was like fishing. Reel in, let go. Reel in, let go. Give the suspect the impression of freedom. That they were off the hook. Then reel them in again.

It was exhausting. For everyone. But mostly, Gamache knew, for whoever was on the hook and writhing.

The abbot had clearly interpreted this shift of tone and subject as Gamache relenting.

"Why do you think Dom Clément built this garden?" the Chief had asked.

"What do people who live close together value most?"

Gamache thought about that. Was it

companionship? Peace and quiet? Tolerance?

"Privacy?"

The abbot nodded. "*Oui. C'est ça.* Dom
Clément gave himself the one thing no one
else in Saint-Gilbert had. Privacy."

"Another division," said Gamache, and
the abbot looked at him. Dom Philippe had
felt the slight tug on the line and realized
what he'd taken for freedom wasn't that at
all.

Gamache considered what the abbot had
just said. Maybe their legendary treasure
wasn't a thing, but nothing. An empty room
no one knew about. And a lock.

Privacy. And with privacy, of course, came
something else.

Safety.

That was, Gamache knew, what people
valued most of all.

Then he heard it.

He scanned the clear blue sky. Nothing.

But something was there. And it was getting closer.

A roar shattered the peace. It seemed to be
coming from all around them, as though
the sky had opened its mouth and was
shrieking at them.

All the mushroom monks, and Beauvoir,

looked up.

Then, as a man, they ducked.

Gamache ducked and pulled Dom Philippe down with him.

The plane zoomed overhead and was gone in an instant. But Gamache heard it bank, and turn back.

Both men stood stock-still, staring into the sky, Gamache still clasping the abbot's robes.

"It's coming back," Dom Philippe shouted.

"Shit," yelled Beauvoir, above the straining engines.

"Christ," yelled Frère Antoine.

The straw hats had been blown from the monks' heads and lay on the plants, breaking some of the vines.

"It's coming back," shouted Frère Antoine.

Beauvoir stared into the sky. It was maddening, only being able to see the patch of blue directly over their heads. They could hear the plane banking, straining, approaching. But couldn't see it.

And then it was upon them again, even lower this time. Apparently heading straight for the bell tower.

"Oh, shit," said Frère Antoine.

Dom Philippe grabbed at Gamache's jacket and the two men ducked again.

"Damn."

Gamache heard the abbot, even above the straining engines.

"They almost hit the monastery," screamed Dom Philippe. "It's the press. I'd hoped we'd have more time."

Beauvoir slowly stood but remained alert, listening.

The sound grew momentarily louder, disappeared, then there was a mighty splash.

"Christ," said Beauvoir.

"Merde," said Frère Antoine.

The monks and Beavoir ran to the door, back into the monastery. Their floppy hats abandoned in the garden.

Damn, thought Gamache, leaving the garden with the abbot.

He'd scanned the plane as it zoomed over the garden within feet, it seemed, of their heads. At the last moment it banked to miss the bell tower.

In that moment, before it disappeared again, he'd seen an insignia on the door of the plane.

They joined the parade of monks walking quickly down the corridors, picking up more monks and more speed as they progressed through the halls, across the Blessed Chapel, and into the final corridor. Gamache could see Beauvoir just ahead, walking rapidly beside Frère Antoine.

Young Frère Luc stood in front of the locked door holding the wrought-iron key in his hand. He stared at them.

Gamache, alone among the men, knew exactly what was on the other side of that door. He'd recognized the insignia on the plane. It wasn't the press. Nor was it curiosity seekers, come to gawk at the famous monastery, made infamous by a terrible crime.

No, this was another creature entirely.

Smelling blood.

SEVENTEEN

At a nod from the abbot, Frère Luc put the
key in the lock. It turned easily and the door
opened, letting in a breeze of pine-scented
air, and sunshine, and the sound of a float
plane taxiing to the dock.

The monks clustered around the open
door. Then the abbot stepped forward.

"I'll ask them to leave," he said, his voice
determined.

"Perhaps I should come along," said Gamache.

Dom Philippe studied the Chief, then
nodded.

Beauvoir made to join them but was
stopped by a subtle wave of Gamache's
hand. "It would be better if you stayed
here."

"What is it?" Beauvoir asked, seeing the
look on the Chief's face.

"I'm not really sure."

Gamache turned back to the abbot and

motioned toward the wharf. "Shall we?"

The plane had almost reached the dock. The pilot cut power, the props slowed, and the plane, on its pontoons, drifted the last few feet to the dock. Gamache and the abbot grabbed the struts and steadied the plane. Then the Chief reached for the ropes dangling in the cold lake.

"I wouldn't bother," said the abbot. "They won't be staying long."

The Chief turned, the wet line in his hand. "I think they might."

"You forget who's in charge here."

Gamache knelt and made a couple of quick knots, securing the float plane to the dock, then he stood back up.

"I don't forget. It's just that I think I know who's in the plane. It's not the press, you know."

"No?"

"I wasn't completely sure I'd seen it right, when the plane flew over. That's why I wanted to come with you."

The Chief pointed to the crest on the door. It showed four fleurs-de-lys. And above them was stenciled MJQ.

"MJQ?" asked the abbot.

The small door opened.

"Ministère de la Justice du Québec," said Gamache and stepped forward, offering his

hand to steady the visitor as he squeezed out of the float plane.

The Chief Inspector's offer was either not noticed or ignored. A fine black leather shoe appeared, then a second, and a man stood for a moment on the pontoon, then strolled casually onto the dock, as though into an opera house or an art gallery.

He looked around, taking in his surroundings.

Not an explorer, landed in a new world, but a conqueror.

He was in late middle age, sixty perhaps. His hair was gray, his face was clean-shaven, handsome and assured. No weakness there. Neither was it the face of a bully. He appeared to be completely at home, composed and comfortable. While most men would look slightly ridiculous arriving in the wilderness in a fine suit and tie, this man made it seem perfectly natural. Even enviable.

And Gamache suspected, if the visitor stayed long enough, the monks would eventually be in suits and ties themselves. And thanking the visitor.

He had that effect on people. Not adjusting to the world, but having the world adjust to him. Which it did. With few, but notable, exceptions.

The man stood on the dock and looked around, his eyes sweeping over Gamache. Over and through and by him. And came to rest on the abbot.

"Dom Philippe?"

The abbot bowed, but didn't take his blue eyes off the stranger.

"My name is Sylvain Francoeur." The man put out his hand. "I'm the Chief Superintendent of the Sûreté du Québec."

The abbot's eyes shifted, for a moment. To Gamache. Then back again.

Armand Gamache knew his own expression was relaxed, attentive. Respectful.

But had Dom Philippe, so good at neumes, read the tiny lines on the Chief Inspector's face, and seen how Gamache really felt?

"What the fuck is this about?" whispered Beauvoir, as they walked back down the corridor a few feet behind the abbot and Chief Superintendent Francoeur.

Gamache shot Beauvoir a warning. Not a slight visual reprimand, but a club to the head. *Shut up,* said the stern expression. *Hold your tongue now, if you've never held it before.*

Beauvoir shut up. But that didn't stop him from watching, and listening. As they progressed they walked through the clouds of conversation created by the two men ahead.

"A terrible shame, *mon père,*" the Chief Superintendent was saying. "The prior's death is a national tragedy. I can assure you, though, that we'll solve this quickly and you'll have your privacy to grieve. I've ordered my people to keep Frère Mathieu's death quiet for as long as possible."

"Chief Inspector Gamache said that wouldn't be possible."

"And he was quite correct, of course. He couldn't do it. I have the highest respect for Monsieur Gamache, but his powers are limited."

"And yours are not?" asked the abbot.

Beauvoir smiled and wondered if the abbot knew who he was dealing with.

Superintendent Francoeur laughed. It was relaxed and good-humored.

"By your measurement, Dom Philippe, my powers are pretty puny. But measured in mortal terms they're substantial. And are at your disposal."

"*Merci, mon fils.* I'm most grateful."

Beauvoir turned a disgusted face to Gamache and opened his mouth, but shut it again upon seeing the Chief's expression. It wasn't angry. It wasn't even upset.

Chief Inspector Gamache was puzzled. As

though trying to work out some complex mathematical formula that didn't add up.

Beauvoir had a question of his own.

What the fuck is this about?

"Can I say it now?" Beauvoir leaned against the closed door.

"No need," said the Chief, taking a chair in the prior's cramped office. "I know the question, but not the answer."

"Like *Jeopardy,*" said Beauvoir, crossing his arms over his chest and continuing to lean against the door. A human deadbolt. "I'll take 'What the Fuck' for two hundred, Alex."

Gamache laughed. "It is puzzling," he admitted.

And, thought Beauvoir, it might also be jeopardy.

They'd last seen Superintendent Francoeur walking through the Blessed Chapel, deep in conversation with the abbot. The homicide agents and the monks had been dismissed but had, for a moment, stood together watching these two men progress through the church and down the long corridor toward the abbot's office.

Francoeur's head, with its distinguished gray hair, was bent toward the abbot's shaved head. Two extremes. One finely dressed, the other in austere robes. One forceful, the other a study in humility.

But both in charge. Apparently.

Beauvoir wondered if the two men would form an alliance, or start another war.

He looked at Gamache, who'd put his reading glasses on and was making notes.

And where did this leave the Chief? The appearance of Sylvain Francoeur seemed to have left Gamache perplexed but unconcerned. Beauvoir hoped he genuinely was, and there was no need to worry.

But it was too late for that. Worry had taken root in Beauvoir's belly. An old and familiar ache.

Gamache looked up and met Beauvoir's eyes. The Chief smiled reassuringly.

"It's no use speculating, Jean-Guy. We'll know why Superintendent Francoeur's here soon enough."

They spent the next half hour discussing their conversations that morning, Beauvoir with Frère Antoine and Gamache with the abbot.

"So the abbot made Frère Antoine the new choir director?" Beauvoir's surprise was obvious. "He didn't tell me that."

"Perhaps it made the abbot look too good, and Frère Antoine wouldn't want that."

"Yeah, maybe. But do you think that's why

316

the abbot did it?"

"What do you mean?" Gamache leaned forward.

"He could've appointed anyone. Could've taken the job himself. But maybe he gave it to Frère Antoine just to screw with the prior's men. A mind fuck. Do the opposite of what they expect. Prove he's above their stupid little fights by making Frère Antoine the choir director. Maybe the abbot wanted to show he's better than them. It's a smart move, if you think about it."

Gamache thought about it. He thought about the two dozen monks. Messing with each other's minds. Trying to keep each other off-balance. Is that what was going on here, perhaps for years? A form of psychological terrorism?

Subtle, invisible. A glance, a smile, a turned back.

In a silent order a single word, a sound, could be devastating. A tsk, a sniff, a chuckle.

Had the gentle abbot perfected those weapons?

Promoting Frère Antoine was the right thing to do. He was the best musician, a clear successor to the prior as choirmaster. But did the abbot do it for the wrong reason?

To screw with the prior's men?

And the vow of silence? Had the abbot fought to keep it because of the spiritual significance to the community? Or, again, to screw with the prior? To deny the prior what he most wanted?

And why was the prior so determined to lift a vow in place for nearly a thousand years? Was it for the good of the order, or the good of the prior?

"What're you thinking?" asked Beauvoir.

"A phrase popped into my mind and I was just trying to remember where it came from."

"Is it poetry?" asked Beauvoir, a little nervously. It didn't take much for the Chief to start quoting some unintelligible poem.

"As a matter of fact, I was thinking of an epic work by Homer." Gamache opened his mouth as though to start reciting then laughed at the distress on Beauvoir's face. "No. It's just a line. *To do the right deed for the wrong reason.*"

Beauvoir thought about that. "I wonder if the opposite is ever true."

"What do you mean?"

"Well, can you do the wrong thing for the right reason?"

Gamache took off his glasses. "Go on." He listened closely, his calm brown eyes not

318

straying from his Inspector.

"Like murder," said Beauvoir. "Killing someone is wrong. But can the reason ever be right?"

"Justifiable homicide," said Gamache. "It's a defense, but a shaky one."

"Do you think this might be justifiable?"

"Why do you ask?"

Beauvoir thought for a moment. "Something went wrong here. The monastery was falling apart. Imploding. Suppose it was the prior's fault. So . . ."

"He was killed to save the rest of the community?" asked Gamache.

"Maybe."

They both knew it was a hideous argument. One made by many a madman. That the killing was for the "greater good."

But was it ever true?

Gamache had wondered about that himself. Suppose the prior was that one bad apple, spreading dissent, rotting this peaceful community, one monk at a time.

People killed in war all the time. If there was a quiet but devastating war going on at Saint-Gilbert, maybe one of the monks convinced himself this was the only way to end it. Before the entire abbey was rotted out from the inside.

Banishing the prior wouldn't be possible.

He'd done nothing overtly wrong.

That was the thing with the bad apple. It was insidious. Slow. It looked just fine, from the outside, until the rot spread. And by then it was too late.

"Maybe," said Gamache. "But maybe the bad apple is still here."

"The murderer?"

"Or maybe it was someone whispering in the murderer's ear." On that thought he leaned back. *"Will no one rid me of this troublesome priest?"*

"You think that's what was said?" asked Beauvoir. "Seems a little flowery to me. I'd probably say, 'Fucking die already.'"

Gamache laughed. "You should write to Hallmark with that one."

"Not a bad idea. There're lots of people I'd send it to."

"Will no one rid me of this troublesome priest," Gamache repeated. "It's what Henry the Second said about Thomas à Becket."

"Is that supposed to mean something to me?"

Gamache grinned. "Hang in there, young man. This story ends in murder."

"Better."

"This was almost nine hundred years ago," the Chief continued. "In England."

"I'm already asleep."

"King Henry promoted his good friend Thomas to be archbishop, thinking that would give him control of the Church. But it backfired."

Despite himself, Beauvoir leaned forward.

"The king was worried that there was too much crime in England. He wanted to crack down on it —" As Gamache spoke Beauvoir nodded. Sympathizing with the king. "— but he felt all his efforts were undermined by the Church since it was pretty lenient with criminals."

"So this king —"

"Henry," said Gamache.

"Henry. He sees his chance and makes his friend Thomas an archbishop. What went wrong?"

"Well, to begin with, Thomas didn't want the job. He even wrote to Henry saying that if he took the job their friendship would turn to hate."

"And he was right."

Gamache nodded. "The king passed a law saying that anyone found guilty in a Church court would be punished by the royal court. Thomas refused to sign it."

"So he was killed?"

"Not immediately. It took six years, the animosity growing every day. Then one day King Henry muttered those words and four knights took it to be an order."

"What happened?"

"They killed the archbishop. In Canterbury Cathedral. *Murder in the Cathedral.*"

"*Will no one . . .*" Beauvoir struggled to remember the quote.

"*. . . rid me of this troublesome priest.*" Gamache finished it.

"You think the abbot said something like that, and someone took it as an order?"

"Maybe. In a place like this the abbot might not even need to speak. A look would be enough. A raised brow, a grimace."

"What happened after the archbishop was killed?"

"He was sainted."

Beauvoir laughed. "That must've pissed off the king."

Gamache smiled. "Henry spent the rest of his life regretting the murder, and said he'd never meant for that to happen."

"Do you think that's true?"

"I think it was easy to say, after the fact."

"So, you think the abbot here might have said something like that, and one of his monks killed the prior?"

"It's possible."

"And knowing what happened, Dom Philippe turns around and does the unexpected. He appoints one of the prior's men to lead the choir." Beauvoir was picking his way through it. "Guilty mind?"

"Penance? Amends?" Gamache frowned, thinking. "Could be."

It was so difficult to know why these monks did anything, thought Gamache. They were so different from anyone he'd ever met, or investigated.

But finally, he had to tell himself, they were just men. With the same motives as anyone else, only theirs were hidden behind black robes and angelic voices. And silence.

"The abbot denies there's a split," said Gamache, leaning back in his chair and lacing his fingers together.

"Wow." Beauvoir shook his head. "The things these monks can believe without evidence. But give them proof of something, and they don't believe it. The split's so obvious. Half want to record more chants, half don't. Half want the vow of silence lifted, half don't."

"I'm not sure it's half and half," said Gamache. "I suspect the balance had shifted, in the prior's favor."

"And that's why he was killed?"

"I think it's possible."

Beauvoir considered what the Chief had said. "So the abbot's kinda screwed. Frère Antoine called him a frightened old man.

323

Do you think he killed Frère Mathieu?"

"I honestly don't know. But if Dom Philippe's filled with fear, he isn't the only
one," said Gamache. "I think most of them
are."

"Because of the murder?"

"No. I'm not sure these men are really
afraid of death. I think they're afraid of life.
But here, in Saint-Gilbert, they finally found
where they belonged."

Beauvoir thought of the field of giant
mushrooms, with the floppy hats. And how
he'd felt the odd one out, in his pressed
slacks and merino wool sweater.

"So if they finally found where they be-
long, what're they afraid of?"

"Losing it," said the Chief. "They'd been
in purgatory. Many have probably been in
Hell. And once you've been there, you sure
don't want to go back."

Gamache paused and the two men held
each other's eyes. Beauvoir could see the
deep scar by the Chief's temple. And could
feel the ache gnawing his own gut. He saw
the bottle of tiny pills he kept hidden in his
apartment. Just in case.

Yes, thought Beauvoir. *You sure don't want
to slip back into Hell.*

The Chief leaned forward, put on his
glasses, and unrolled a large cylinder of

paper on the desk.

Beauvoir watched Gamache, but saw something else. Superintendent Francoeur stepping from the plane that had descended so quickly from the sky. The Chief had offered his hand, but Francoeur had turned his back on Gamache, for all to see. For Beauvoir to see.

The sick feeling sat like a fist in Beauvoir's stomach. It had found a home there. Was settling in. And growing.

"The abbot gave us a plan of the monastery." Gamache stood and leaned over the desk.

Beauvoir joined him.

The drawing looked exactly as Beauvoir imagined the abbey in his mind, after walking the halls for twenty-four hours. Shaped like a cross, with the chapel in the very center and the bell tower above that.

"Here's the Chapter House," said Gamache. The room was shown on the drawing, attached to the side of the chapel. There was no attempt to hide it in the design. But in real life it was hidden, behind the plaque to Saint Gilbert.

The abbot's garden was also on the plan, plain to see in ink, but not in real life. It too was hidden but not secret.

"Are there other hidden rooms?" Beauvoir asked.

"The abbot doesn't know of any, but he admits there're rumors of secret rooms, and something else."

"What?" asked Beauvoir.

"Well, it's almost embarrassing to say," admitted Gamache, taking off his glasses and looking at Beauvoir.

"I would have thought a man caught in his pajamas on a church altar would have a high tolerance for embarrassment."

"You make a good point." The Chief smiled. "Treasure."

"Treasure? Are you kidding? The abbot says there's a treasure hidden here?"

"He doesn't say it," said Gamache, "he says those are the rumors."

"Have they looked?"

"Unofficially. I think monks aren't supposed to care about such things."

"But men do," said Beauvoir, looking back down at the plan.

An old abbey with a hidden treasure, thought Beauvoir. It was too ridiculous. No wonder the Chief was embarrassed to say it. But while he ridiculed the idea, Beauvoir's eyes were bright as he scanned the drawing.

What child, boy or girl, hadn't dreamed of hidden treasure? Hadn't lapped up stories of derring-do, of galleons and pirates and fleeing princes and princesses, burying something precious. Or, better yet, finding something precious.

As ridiculous and far-fetched as a hidden room with treasure almost certainly was, Beauvoir couldn't help but be sucked into the fantasy. In an instant he found himself wondering what the treasure could be. The riches of the medieval Church? Chalices, paintings, coins. Priceless jewels brought back by Crusaders.

Then Jean-Guy imagined finding it.

Not for the sake of the fortune. Or, at least, not entirely for that. But for the fun of finding it.

Instantly he saw himself telling Annie. He could see her watching him, listening. Hanging on his every word. Reacting to each twist in the tale. Her face expressive as he told her about the search. Gasping. Laughing.

They'd talk about it for the rest of their lives. Tell their children and grandchildren. About the time Grandpapa found the treasure. And returned it to the Church.

"So," said Gamache, rolling the plan back up. "I can leave this with you?"

He handed it to Beauvoir.

"I'll split everything with you, *patron.*

Fifty-fifty."

"I already have my treasure, thank you very much," said Gamache.

"I don't think a bag of chocolate-covered blueberries could be considered a treasure."

"Non?" asked Gamache. "To each his own."

A deep bell started ringing. Not a joyous celebration, but a solemn toll.

"Again?" said Beauvoir. "Can't I just stay here?"

"Of course you can." Gamache took from his breast pocket the horarium the abbot's secretary had given him and examined it. Then he looked at his watch.

"Eleven A.M. mass," he said and walked toward the closed door.

"Is it only eleven? Feels like bedtime."

For a place that ran like clockwork, time seemed to stand still.

Beauvoir opened the door for the Chief and after the smallest hesitation, and a whispered curse, he followed him down the corridor and back into the Blessed Chapel.

Gamache slipped into the pew, Beauvoir beside him. They sat quietly, waiting for the service to begin. Again, the Chief marveled at the light falling through the high windows. Split into all different colors. It spilled onto the altar and the benches and seemed

328

to dance there. Waiting happily for the company of the monks.

The Chief glanced around the now familiar space. It felt as though he'd been there a very long time, and it came as a surprise he and Beauvoir hadn't yet spent a full day at Saint-Gilbert-Entre-les-Loups.

The Blessed Chapel, Gamache now knew, was built to honor a saint so dull the Church couldn't find some equally dull complaint to let him patronize.

Few prayed to Saint Gilbert.

And yet in his excruciatingly long life, Gilbert had done one spectacular thing. He'd stood up to a king. He'd defended his archbishop. Thomas had been killed, but Gilbert had stood up to tyranny, and survived.

Gamache remembered joking with the abbot that maybe Gilbert could become the Patron Saint of Fretters, since his monastery had such strong defenses and locked doors.

And so many places to hide.

But maybe he'd been wrong, done Gilbert a disservice. He might have fretted, but Gilbert had finally found more courage than anyone else. Sitting quietly in the refracted light, Gamache wondered if he'd have the same courage.

He spent a moment thinking about the

new visitor, and praying to Saint Gilbert.

As the last note of the solemn bell resonated the monks entered. They appeared in single file. Singing. White hoods hid their faces. Hands were buried up to the elbows in their loose black sleeves. The singing grew as more voices entered the Blessed Chapel, until the empty space was filled with the plainchant. And the light.

And then someone else entered.

Chief Superintendent Francoeur bobbed, crossed himself, then, despite all sorts of empty pews, he slipped into the one directly in front of Gamache and Beauvoir, obscuring their view.

And once again the Chief Inspector tilted his head slightly to the side. Hoping to see more clearly. The monks. But also the motives of the man in front of him. Who'd dropped so precipitously from the skies, with a purpose.

As Beauvoir huffed and snorted beside him, Gamache closed his eyes and listened to the beautiful music.

And thought about tyranny, and murder.

And whether it was ever right to kill one for the sake of the many.

Eighteen

"Are you lost?"

Beauvoir spun around to confront the voice.

"I only ask because it's unusual to find someone here."

A monk was standing in the thick forest, a few feet from Beauvoir. It was as though he'd suddenly materialized. Beauvoir recognized him. It was the monk from the chocolate factory, who'd been covered in dribbled dark chocolate the last time Beauvoir had seen him. Now he had on a clean cassock and was carrying a basket. Like Little Red Riding Hood. *Entre-les-Loups,* thought Beauvoir. Among the wolves.

"No, I'm not lost," he said, and tried to quickly roll up the plan of Saint-Gilbert. But it was way too late for that. The monk was standing very still, just watching. It made Beauvoir feel foolish and wary. It was disconcerting to be around people who were so still and so quiet. And so stealthy.

"Can I help you with something?" asked the monk.

"I was just . . ." Beauvoir waved the semi-rolled plan.

"Looking?" he smiled. Beauvoir half expected to see long canine teeth, but instead it was a small, almost tentative grin. "I'm looking too," said the monk, "but probably not for the same thing."

It was the kind of vaguely patronizing remark Beauvoir expected from a *religieux*. He was probably on some spiritual quest, so much more worthy than whatever the bumbling human in front of him might be about. The monk was strolling the forest looking for inspiration or salvation, or God. Praying or meditating. While Beauvoir was looking for treasure.

"Ah," said the monk. "Found some."

He stooped, then stood back up and offered his palm to Beauvoir. Tiny wild blueberries rolled together in the valley of the man's hand.

"They're perfect," said the monk.

Beauvoir looked at them. They looked like every other wild blueberry he'd ever seen.

"Please." The monk moved his palm closer and Beauvoir took a single tiny berry. It was like trying to pick up an atom.

He popped it in his mouth and there was an immediate wallop of flavor far out of proportion to the portion. It tasted, not surprisingly, of blueberry. But it also tasted like autumn in Québec. Sweet and musky.

This monk was right. It really was perfect.

He took another, as did the monk.

The two men stood in the shadow of the tall wall of the abbot's garden, eating berries. Just a few feet away, over the wall, was a manicured garden, beautifully planted and cared for. With lawns and flower beds, clipped bushes and benches.

But here, on this side of the wall, there were tiny perfect blueberries.

There was also a tangle of undergrowth so thick it had scratched Beauvoir's legs through his slacks as he'd plowed his way through the thickets. He'd been following the line of the monastery, on foot, and on paper. He'd borrowed rubber boots from the monks, and found himself stepping into muck, climbing over downed tree trunks and scrambling over rocks. Trying to figure out if the lines on the page matched the walls of the actual abbey.

"How'd you sneak up on me?"

"Sneak?" the monk laughed. "I'm just doing my rounds. There's a path over there. Why didn't you take that?"

"Well, I would have had I known," said Beauvoir, not altogether sure they were talking about the same thing. He'd worked long enough with Chief Inspector Gamache to smell an allegory.

"My name's Bernard," said the monk, sticking out his purple-stained hand.

"Beauvoir." The handshake surprised Beauvoir. He'd expected a soft, doughy hand, but instead it was firm and assured, the skin far tougher than his own.

"Wow, look at that." Frère Bernard stooped again and stayed there, kneeling and plucking berries. Beauvoir knelt as well, and peered at the ground. Slowly, instead of seeing just a riot of twigs and moss and dried leaves, he began to see what Frère Bernard had been looking for.

Not salvation, but the tiniest of wild fruit.

"My God," laughed Bernard. "It's the mother lode. I've been along that path every fall for years and never knew this was here."

"You can't be suggesting it's sometimes good to wander from the path." Beauvoir was pleased with himself. He could give good allegory too.

The monk laughed again. *"Touché."*

They spent the next few minutes crawling around the undergrowth, collecting blueberries.

"Well," said Frère Bernard at last, standing and stretching and brushing twigs from his cassock. "This must be a record." He looked at his basket, piled high with berries. "You're my good-luck charm. *Merci*."

Beauvoir felt quite pleased with himself.

"Now," said Bernard, pointing to a couple of flat rocks. "It's my turn to help you."

Beauvoir hesitated. He'd stuck the plan of the monastery in a bush, where it would be safe while they picked the berries. Now he looked over at it. Bernard followed his gaze, but said nothing.

Beauvoir retrieved the plan and the two men sat facing each other on the rocks.

"What're you looking for?" asked the monk.

Still Beauvoir hesitated. Then made up his mind and unrolled the plan.

Frère Bernard lowered his gaze from Beauvoir's face to the vellum. His eyes widened slightly. "Dom Clément's plan of the monastery," he said. "We'd heard he'd made one. He was a famous architect in his day, you know. Then he joined the Gilbertines and disappeared along with the other twenty-three monks. No one knew where they went. No one much cared, actually. The Gilbertines were never a rich or powerful order. Just the opposite. So when the

335

monastery in France was abandoned everyone just assumed the order had disbanded or died out."

"But they hadn't," said Beauvoir, also staring at the plan.

"No. They came here. Might as well have been the moon, in those days."

"Why'd they come?"

"They were afraid of the Inquisition."

"But if they were so poor and marginal, why were they afraid?"

"Why is anyone afraid? Most of the time it's all in their heads. Has nothing to do with reality. I imagine the Inquisition couldn't have cared less about the Gilbertines, but they took off anyway. Just in case. That could be our motto. Just in case. *Exsisto paratus.*"

"You've never seen this before?" Beauvoir pointed to the drawing.

Frère Bernard shook his head. He seemed lost in the lines on the page. "It's fascinating," said the monk, leaning closer, "seeing Dom Clément's actual plans. I wonder if this was made before or after Saint-Gilbert was built."

"Would it matter?"

"Maybe not, but one would be the ideal, the other would be the reality. If it was made after, then this shows what's really here. Not what they might have wanted then changed their minds."

"You know the monastery," said Beauvoir. "What do you think?"

For a few minutes Frère Bernard bowed his head over the vellum, sometimes tracing the ink with his blueberry finger. He gave a few grunts. Hummed a bit. Shook his head, then backed up his finger to follow another line, another corridor.

Finally he looked up and met Beauvoir's eyes.

"There's something wrong with this drawing."

Beauvoir felt a thrill, a *frisson.* "What?"

"The scale's off. You see here and here —"

"The vegetable garden and the place for the animals."

"Right. They're shown as the same size as the abbot's garden. But they're not. In reality, they're at least twice the size."

It was true. Beauvoir remembered picking the squash that morning with Frère Antoine. The vegetable garden had been huge. But the abbot's garden, the murder scene, was much smaller.

"But how do you know?" asked Beauvoir. "Have you ever been in the abbot's garden?" He glanced to the tall wall.

"Never, but I've been around it. Looking for berries. I've also been around the other gardens. This plan," he looked back down, "is wrong."

"So what does that mean?" asked Beauvoir. "Why would Dom Clément do that?"

Bernard considered, then shook his head. "Hard to say. The Church had a way of exaggerating things. If you see some of the old paintings, the baby Jesus looks about ten years old when he was born. And old maps of cities show cathedrals much bigger than they actually were. Dominating their surroundings."

"So you think Dom Clément exaggerated the size of the abbot's garden? But why?"

Again the monk shook his head. "Vanity, maybe. To make the drawing look more to scale. Church architecture has little tolerance for anything unusual, out of balance. This looks better on paper," again the monk gestured toward the drawing, "than the real thing. Though the real thing functions better in reality."

Again Beauvoir was taken by the clash of perception and reality in this monastery. And the choice to reflect what looked good rather than what was truthful.

Frère Bernard continued to study the drawing. "If Dom Clément had drawn it exactly as it is, the monastery wouldn't look like a crucifix anymore. It'd look like a bird. Two big wings and a shorter body."

"So he cheated?"

"I suppose that's one way of putting it."

"Could he have cheated in other areas of the plan?" asked Beauvoir. Though he knew the answer to that. When someone deceived once, they'd do it again.

"I suppose." The monk looked as though one of the angels had fallen. "But I can't see anything else wrong. Why does it matter?"

"It might not." Beauvoir rolled the plan back up. "You asked what I was looking for. I'm looking for a hidden room."

"Like the Chapter House?"

"We know about that one. I'm looking for another."

"So there is one."

"We don't know. We've just heard rumors, and obviously you have too."

For the first time in their conversation Beauvoir sensed a hesitation in the monk. As though a door had slowly swung shut. As though Frère Bernard had his own hidden room.

Of course, everyone had one. And it was his job, and the Chief's, to find those too. Unfortunately for them those rooms almost never hid treasure. What they invariably found were mountains of crap.

"If there really is a secret room in the monastery, you need to tell me," Beauvoir pressed.

"I don't know of any."

"But you've heard rumors?"

"There're always rumors. I heard that one the first day I arrived."

"For a silent order you seem to do a lot of talking."

Bernard smiled. "We're not completely silent, you know. We're allowed to talk at certain times of the day."

"And one of the things you talk about is secret rooms?"

"If you're only allowed a few minutes' conversation a day, what do you think you'd talk about? The weather? Politics?"

"Secrets?"

Frère Bernard smiled. "Sometimes the divine mystery, and sometimes just mysteries. Like hidden rooms. And treasure."

He gave Beauvoir a knowing look. A sharp look. This monk, thought Beauvoir, might be calm and even gentle. But he was no fool.

"Do you think they exist?"

"A room and some treasure lugged here by Dom Clément and the other monks centuries ago?" Frère Bernard shook his

340

head. "It's fun to think about. Passes the time on cold winter nights. But no one really believes it exists. Someone would've found it ages ago. The abbey's been renovated, updated, repaired. If there was a secret room we'd have found it."

"Maybe someone did." Beauvoir stood. "So, how often are you allowed to leave?"

The monk laughed. "It's not a prison, you know."

But even Frère Bernard had to admit, from that angle, Saint-Gilbert sure looked like one.

"We leave whenever we want, though we don't go far. Walks, mostly. We look for berries and firewood. We fish. In the winter we play hockey on the ice. Frère Antoine organizes that."

Beauvoir felt again that vertigo. Frère Antoine played hockey. Was probably the captain and the center. The same position Beauvoir played.

"In the summer some of us jog and do tai chi. You're welcome to join us after Vigils."

"Is that the early morning service?"

"Five A.M." He smiled. "Your Chief was there this morning."

Beauvoir was about to say something sharp, to shut down any ridiculing of Gamache, when he saw that Frère Bernard seemed simply amused. Not mocking.

"Yes, he mentioned it to me," said Beauvoir.

"We talked later, you know."

"Oh, really?" But Beauvoir knew perfectly well it was Frère Bernard the Chief had spoken to that morning in the showers and that they'd then collected eggs together. Brother Bernard had told the Chief about the rift in the community. In fact, Chief Inspector Gamache had the impression the monk had sought him out specifically to tell him that.

And only then did it occur to Beauvoir to wonder if the same thing was happening here. Had this monk simply been out collecting blueberries and stumbled upon him? Or was this no accident? Had Frère Bernard seen Beauvoir leave, with the scroll, and followed him?

"Your Chief's a good listener," said the monk. "He'd fit in well here."

"He does look good in a robe," said Beauvoir.

Frère Bernard laughed. "I was afraid to say it." The monk looked at Beauvoir, examining the younger man. "I think you'd also enjoy it here."

Enjoy? thought Beauvoir. *Enjoy? Does anyone actually enjoy it here?*

He'd presumed they tolerated it, like a hair shirt. It never occurred to him living in Saint-Gilbert-Entre-les-Loups actually made them happy.

Frère Bernard picked up his basket of blueberries and they walked a few paces before he spoke again. He seemed to be choosing his words carefully.

"I was surprised to see someone else arrive. We all were. Including your boss, I think. Who was that man who flew in?"

"His name's Francoeur. He's the Chief Superintendent."

"Of the Sûreté?"

Beauvoir nodded. "The big boss."

"Your pope," said Bernard.

"Only if the pope's a moron with a gun."

Frère Bernard snorted then fought to wipe the smile from his face.

"You don't like him?"

"Years of contemplation have sharpened your instincts, Frère Bernard."

Again Bernard laughed. "People come from miles around to hear my insights." Then his smile disappeared completely. "For instance, this Francoeur, he doesn't like your boss, does he?"

This too, they both knew, wasn't exactly an incredible feat of perception.

Beauvoir wondered what to say. His impulse was always to lie. He'd have made, he thought, a good medieval architect. He immediately wanted to deny there was a problem, to cover the truth. To at the very least hide the scale of it. But he could see that would be useless. This man had seen clearly, as had everyone else, Francoeur's easy dismissal of Gamache on the dock.

"It goes back a few years. They had a disagreement over a fellow officer."

Frère Bernard didn't say anything. He simply listened. His face calm, his eyes noncommittal and attentive. They walked slowly through the forest, their feet crackling on the twigs and leaves, fallen to the well-trodden path. The sun broke through the trees in patches and every now and then they heard the scrambling of a chipmunk or a bird or some other wild creature.

Beauvoir waited a moment, then went on. Might as well, he thought. It was all public knowledge anyway. Unless you lived in a monastery in the middle of nowhere.

What the monks knew and what everyone else knew seemed two very different things.

"The Chief arrested one of the superintendents of the Sûreté, even though Francoeur and the others had ordered him not to. His name was Arnot. He was actually the Chief Superintendent at the time."

And now there was a small reaction on the monk's placid face. A tiny lifting of the brows. And then they settled back into place. It was almost invisible. Almost.

"Arrested him for what?"

"Murder. Sedition. It came out that Arnot was encouraging officers on reserves to kill any native who made trouble. Or, at the very least, when a young native was shot or beaten to death, Arnot didn't discipline the officers who did it. It was a short step from turning a blind eye, to actively encouraging the killings. It became, apparently —" Beauvoir spoke haltingly, finding it difficult to talk about something so shameful. "— almost a sport. An elderly Cree woman asked Gamache for help finding her missing son. That's when he discovered what was going on."

"And the rest of the Sûreté leadership wanted your boss to stay quiet about it?"

Beauvoir nodded. "They agreed to fire Arnot and the other officers, but they didn't want a scandal. Didn't want to lose the trust of the public."

Frère Bernard didn't drop his eyes, but Beauvoir had the impression they wavered.

"Chief Inspector Gamache arrested Arnot anyway," said Frère Bernard. "He disobeyed orders."

"It never occurred to him not to. He thought the mothers and fathers and loved ones of those who were killed deserved an answer. And a public trial. And an apology. It all came out. It was a mess."

Bernard nodded. The Church knew from scandals, and knew from cover-ups and knew from messes.

"What happened?" the monk asked.

"Arnot and the others were convicted. They're serving life sentences."

"And the Chief Inspector?"

Beauvoir smiled. "He's still Chief. But he'll never make Superintendent and he knows it."

"But he kept his job."

"They couldn't fire him. Even before this happened he was one of the most respected officers in the Sûreté. The trial made him hated by the big bosses, but adored by the rank and file. He restored their pride. And, ironically, the public trust. Francoeur couldn't fire him. Though he wanted to. He and Arnot were friends. Good friends."

Frère Bernard thought about that for a moment. "So did this Francoeur know what his friend was doing? They were both super-intendents."

"The Chief could never prove it."

"But he tried?"

"He wanted to get all the rot out," said Beauvoir.

"And did he?"

"I hope so."

Both men thought back to that moment on the dock. Gamache's extended hand, to help Francoeur from the plane. And Francoeur's look. A glance.

There wasn't just enmity there. There was hatred.

"Why's the Chief Superintendent here?" asked Frère Bernard.

"I don't know." Beauvoir tried to keep his voice light. And it was the truth. He really didn't know. But again he felt the worry in his stomach roll over and scrape his insides.

Frère Bernard frowned as he thought. "Must be difficult for them to work together. Do they have to often?"

"Not often."

He'd go no further. He certainly wouldn't tell this monk about the last time Gamache and Francoeur had been thrown together on a case. The raid on the factory. Almost a year ago now. And the disastrous results.

He saw again the Chief gripping the sides of his desk and leaning toward Francoeur in a manner so threatening the Chief Superintendent had paled and stepped back. Beauvoir could count on one hand the number of times he'd heard Gamache yell. But he'd yelled that day. Right into Francoeur's face.

The ferocity of it had frightened even Beauvoir.

And the Chief Superintendent had shouted back.

Gamache had prevailed. But only by stepping back. By apologizing. By begging Francoeur to see reason. Gamache had begged. That was the price he'd paid, to get Francoeur to act.

Beauvoir had never seen the Chief beg before. But he'd done it that day.

Gamache and Francoeur had barely spoken since. Perhaps a word at the state funeral for the officers killed in that raid on the factory, though Beauvoir doubted it. And maybe something at the ceremony, when Francoeur had pinned a medal of bravery on Gamache's chest. Against Gamache's wishes.

But Francoeur had insisted. Knowing that to the rest of the world it would appear he was rewarding the Chief Inspector. But the two men, privately, knew the truth.

Beauvoir had been in the audience for that ceremony. Had seen his Chief's face when the medal had been placed on his chest. It might as well have pierced his heart.

It was the right deed. For the wrong reason.

Beauvoir knew his Chief deserved that medal, but Francoeur had done it to humiliate. Publicly rewarding Gamache for an action that had left so many Sûreté agents dead and wounded. Francoeur had given it to him not as recognition for all the lives Gamache had saved that terrible day, but as an accusation. A permanent reminder. Of all the young lives lost.

Beauvoir could have killed Francoeur at that moment.

Again he felt a clawing in the pit of his stomach. Something was trying to rip its way out. He wanted desperately to change the subject. To wipe away the memories. Of the ceremony, but mostly of that horrific day. In the factory.

When one of the lives lost had almost been his own.

When one of the lives lost had almost been the Chief's.

Beauvoir thought about the tiny pills the size of wild blueberries. The ones still hidden in his apartment. And the burst they brought. Not of musky flavor, but of blessed oblivion.

Numbing what hid in Beauvoir's secret room.

349

He hadn't had an OxyContin or a Percocet in months, not since the Chief had
confronted him. Taken the pills away. Gotten him help.

He might make a good Gilbertine after
all. Like them, he lived in fear. Not of what
would come at him from the outside, but
what was patiently lying in wait inside his
own walls.

"Are you all right?"

Beauvoir followed the soft voice back. Like
candies along a path. Leading him out of
the forest.

"Can I help?"

Frère Bernard had put out his rough hand
and was touching Beauvoir's arm.

"No, I'm fine. Just thinking about the
case."

The monk continued to examine his
companion. Far from convinced he was
hearing the truth.

Beauvoir scrambled around in his
memory, picking up bits and pieces, desperate to find something useful. The case. The
case. The prior. The murder. The scene. The
garden.

The garden.

"We were talking about the abbot's garden," said Beauvoir. His voice was gruff,
not inviting any more confidences. He'd

already gone too far.

"Were we?" asked Frère Bernard.

"You said everyone knows about it. But you haven't actually been in the garden yourself."

"That's right."

"Who had?"

"Anyone Dom Philippe invited."

Beauvoir realized he wasn't listening as closely as he should. He was still distracted by his memories, and the feelings they awakened.

Had there been resentment in Frère Bernard's voice just now?

Beauvoir didn't think so, but with his attention frayed he couldn't be sure. And again he cursed Francoeur. For being where he wasn't wanted. In the monastery. And in Beauvoir's head. Rattling around in there. Poking awake things better left sleeping.

He remembered what one of his counselors had advised when he felt anxious.

Breathe. Just breathe.

Deep breath in. Deep breath out.

"What do you think of the abbot?" he asked. He was feeling light-headed.

"What do you mean?"

Beauvoir wasn't sure what he meant.

Deep breath in. Deep breath out.

"You're one of the abbot's men, aren't

351

you?" he asked. Grabbing at whatever questions surfaced.

"I am."

"Why? Why not join with the prior?"

The monk starting kicking a stone and Beauvoir focused on that as it danced and jumped along the dirt path. The door into the monastery seemed a long way off. And suddenly he wished he was back in the Blessed Chapel. Where it was calm and peaceful. Listening to the monotone chants. Clinging to the chants.

No chaos there. No thoughts, no decisions. No raw emotions.

Deep breath in. Deep breath out.

"Frère Mathieu was a gifted musician," Frère Bernard was saying. "He turned our vocation of singing chants into something sublime. He was a great teacher and a natural leader. He gave our lives new meaning and purpose. He breathed life into the abbey."

"Then why wasn't he abbot?"

It was working. Beauvoir followed his breath, and the monk's quiet voice, back into his own body.

"Perhaps he should have been. But Dom Philippe was elected."

"Over Frère Mathieu?"

"No. Frère Mathieu didn't run."

"Did Dom Philippe get in by acclamation?"

"No. The prior at the time ran. Most expected him to win since it was a natural progression. The prior almost always became the abbot."

"And who was the prior at the time?" Beauvoir's mind was working again. Taking things in, and churning rational questions back out. But the fist in his belly remained.

"I was."

Beauvoir wasn't sure he heard right. "You were the prior?"

"Yes. And Dom Philippe was just plain old Frère Philippe. A regular monk."

"It must have been humiliating."

Frère Bernard smiled. "We try not to personalize these things. It was God's will."

"And that makes it better? I'd rather be humiliated by men than God himself."

Bernard chose not to answer.

"So you go back to being a regular monk, and the abbot appoints his friend as prior. Frère Mathieu."

Bernard nodded, and absently took a handful of blueberries from his basket.

"Did you resent the new prior?" asked Beauvoir, helping himself to some of the berries.

"Not at all. It turned out to be an inspired

choice. The former abbot and I were a good team. But I wouldn't have been as good a prior to Dom Philippe as Frère Mathieu proved. It worked well for many years."

"So you had to suck it up."

"You have a singular way of putting things."

"You should hear what I'm not saying," Beauvoir said and saw Frère Bernard smile. "Have you heard that the prior was considering replacing Frère Antoine as soloist?"

"With Frère Luc? Yes. It was a rumor spread by Frère Luc, and apparently believed by him, but no one else."

"Are you sure it wasn't true?"

"The prior could be difficult. I think," Frère Bernard shot Beauvoir a glance, "you might call him an asshole."

"I'm hurt."

"But he knew music. Gregorian chant was more than just music to him. It was his path to the Divine. He would rather die than do anything to undermine the choir or the chants."

Frère Bernard walked on, apparently unaware of what he'd said. But Beauvoir tucked it away.

"Frère Antoine should be soloist," said the monk, nibbling at more berries. "He has a magnificent voice."

"Better than Luc's?"

"Far better. Frère Luc's is better technically. He can control it. It has a beautiful tone but there's nothing divine there. It's like seeing a painting of a person, instead of the real thing. It's missing a dimension."

Frère Bernard's opinion of Luc's voice was almost exactly the same as Frère Antoine's.

Still, the young monk had been convinced and convincing.

"If Luc was right," ventured Beauvoir, "what would the reaction have been?"

Bernard thought about that for a moment.

"I think people would have wondered."

"Wondered what?"

Now Frère Bernard was distinctly uncomfortable. He popped more berries into his mouth. The basket, once overflowing, had been reduced to a puddle of blueberries.

"Just wondered."

"You're not telling me everything, Frère Bernard."

Bernard remained silent. Swallowing his thoughts and opinions and words along with the berries.

But Beauvoir had a pretty good idea what he meant.

"You'd have wondered at their relationship."

Bernard's mouth clamped shut, the muscles around his jaw bulging with the effort of keeping the words in.

"You'd have wondered," Beauvoir pressed, "what was going on between the older prior and the new recruit."

"That's not what I meant."

"Of course it is. You and the other monks would have wondered what happened after choir practice. When the rest of you went back to your cells."

"No. You're wrong."

"Is that how Antoine got his job? Was he more than just a soloist, and Frère Mathieu more than just the choirmaster?"

"Stop," snapped Frère Bernard. "It wasn't like that."

"Then what was it like?"

"You're making the chants, the choir, sordid. Mathieu was a deeply unpleasant man. I didn't like him at all. But even I know that never," Bernard hissed the words, "never would he have chosen a soloist in exchange for sex. Frère Mathieu loved the chants. Above all else."

"But still," said Beauvoir, his voice very quiet now. "You would have wondered."

Frère Bernard stared at Beauvoir, his eyes wide. His hand around the handle of the basket showed a strip of white knuckles.

"Did you know that the abbot has made Frère Antoine the new choirmaster?"

Beauvoir's voice was friendly. Conversational. As though the confrontation hadn't just happened. It was a trick he'd learned from Gamache. Don't keep attacking. Move forward, back, sideways. Stand still.

Be unpredictable.

Slowly Frère Bernard gathered himself. And took a deep breath in.

A deep breath out.

"It doesn't surprise me," he finally said. "It's the sort of thing the abbot would do."

"Go on."

"A few minutes ago you asked why I'm the abbot's man. This is why. Only a saint or a fool would promote an adversary. Dom Philippe's no fool."

"You think he's a saint?"

Frère Bernard shrugged. "I don't know. But I think he's the closest we have. Why do you think he was elected abbot? What did he have to offer? He was just a quiet little monk going about his day. He wasn't a leader. He wasn't a great administrator. He wasn't a fine musician. He brought almost no actual skills to the community. He wasn't a plumber or carpenter or stonemason."

"Then what is he?"

"He's a man of God. The real deal. He

believes with all his heart and soul. And he inspires that in others. If people hear the Divine when we sing, Dom Philippe put it there. He makes us better men and better monks. He believes in God and he believes in the power of love and forgiveness. And not just a faith of convenience. If you ever needed proof, look at what he just did. He made Frère Antoine choirmaster. Because it was the right thing to do. For the choir, for the chants and for the peace of the community."

"That just makes him a savvy politician, not a saint."

"You're a skeptic, Monsieur Beauvoir."

"And for good reason, Frère Bernard. Someone killed your prior. Bashed his head in in the abbot's pretty little garden. You talk of saints. Where was the saint then? Where was God then?"

Bernard said nothing.

"Oui," snapped Beauvoir. "I'm a skeptic."

Will no one rid me of this troublesome priest?

Someone had.

"And your precious abbot wasn't simply elected out of the blue," Beauvoir reminded him. "He chose to run. He wanted the job. Does a saint seek power? I thought they were supposed to be humble."

358

They were within sight of the gate now. Inside were the long, light hallways. And small cells. And silent, gliding monks. And Chief Inspector Gamache. And Francoeur. Together. Beauvoir was a little surprised the walls and foundations of the monastery weren't shaking.

They approached the door, made of thick wood, cut from this forest four hundred years ago. And then hinges were forged. And a deadbolt. And a lock.

On the rolled paper in Beauvoir's hand Saint-Gilbert-Entre-les-Loups looked like a crucifix. But in reality?

It looked like a prison.

Beauvoir stopped.

"Why is the door locked?" he asked Frère Bernard.

"Tradition, nothing more. I expect lots of what we do seems senseless, but our rules and traditions make sense to us."

Still Beauvoir stared.

"A door is locked as protection," he finally said. "But who's being protected?"

"Pardon?"

"You said your slogan could be 'Just in case.' "

"Exsisto paratus, yes. It was a joke."

Beauvoir nodded. "Lots of truth is said in jest, or so I've heard. Just in case of what, *mon frère?* What're the locked doors for? To keep the world out, or the monks in? To protect you, or protect us?"

"I don't understand," said Frère Bernard. But Beauvoir could see by his expression that he understood perfectly well. He could also see that the monk's basket, with its mother lode of berries, was now empty. The perfect offering gone.

"Maybe your precious abbot was neither a savvy politician nor a saint. But a jailer. Maybe that's why he was so against another recording. So adamant about keeping the vow of silence. Was he just enforcing a long tradition of silence? Or was the abbot afraid of loosing some monster into the world?"

"I can't believe you just said that," said Bernard, trembling with the effort to contain himself. "Are you talking about pedophilia? Do you think we're here because we violated little boys? Do you think Brother Charles, Brother Simon, the abbot —" he sputtered. "— I . . . You can't possibly . . ."

He could go no further. His face was red with rage and Beauvoir wondered if his head might explode.

But still, the homicide inspector said nothing. He waited. And waited.

Finally silence was his friend. And this monk's enemy. Because in that silence sat a

360

specter. Fully grown. Fully fleshed. Of all the little boys. All the choirboys. The schoolboys. The altar boys. The trusting boys. And their parents.

That lived forever, in the silence of the Church.

When given a choice, given free will, the Church had chosen to protect the priests. And how better to protect those clerics than to send them into the wilderness. To an order all but extinct. And build a wall around them.

Where they could sing, but not speak.

Was Dom Philippe as much guard as abbot? A saint who kept watch over sinners?

NINETEEN

"Do you know why the Gilbertines have black robes and white hoods? It's unique, you know. No other order wears it."

Chief Superintendent Sylvain Francoeur was sitting behind the prior's desk, leaning back casually in the hard chair, his long legs crossed.

Chief Inspector Gamache was now in the visitor's chair, on the other side of the desk. He was trying to read the coroner's report and the other papers Francoeur had brought with him. He looked up and saw the Superintendent smiling.

It was an attractive smile. Not slimy, not condescending. It was warm and confident. The smile of a man you could trust.

"No, sir. Why do they?"

Francoeur had arrived at the office twenty minutes earlier and given the reports to Gamache. He'd then proceeded to interrupt the Chief's reading with trivial statements.

362

Gamache recognized it as a twist on an old interrogation technique. Designed to irritate, to annoy. Interrupt, interrupt, interrupt, until the subject finally exploded and said far more than they normally would have, out of frustration at not being allowed to say anything at all.

It was subtle and time consuming, this wearing away at a person's patience. Not used by the brash young agents of today. But the older officers knew it. And knew, if they waited long enough, it was almost always effective.

The Chief Superintendent of the Sûreté was using it on his head of homicide.

Gamache, as he listened politely to Francoeur's mundane observations, wondered why. Was it just for fun, to toy with him? Or was there, as there always was with the Chief Superintendent, some deeper purpose?

Gamache looked into that charming face and wondered what was going on inches from the smile. In that rotting brain. In that Byzantine mind.

As much as Jean-Guy might consider this man an idiot, Gamache knew he wasn't. No one rose to be the most senior police officer in Québec, in one of the most respected forces in the world, without having skills.

To dismiss Francoeur as a fool would be a grave mistake. Though Gamache could never totally shake the impression Beauvoir was partly right. While Francoeur wasn't an idiot, he wasn't as clever as he appeared. And certainly not as clever as he thought he was. After all, Francoeur was skilled enough to use an old and subtle interrogation technique, but arrogant enough to use it on someone who'd almost certainly recognize what it was. He was really more cunning than clever.

But that didn't make him less dangerous.

Gamache looked down at the coroner's report in his hand. In twenty minutes he'd only managed to read a single page. It showed the prior to be a healthy man in his early sixties. The usual wear and tear on a sixty-year-old body. Some slight arthritis, some hardening of the arteries.

"I looked up the Gilbertines as soon as I'd heard about the prior's murder." Francoeur's voice was agreeable, authoritative. People not only trusted this man, they believed him.

Gamache lifted his eyes from the page and put a politely interested look on his face.

"Is that right?"

"I'd read some of the newspaper articles, of course," said the Superintendent, moving his eyes from Gamache to gaze out the narrow slat of the window. "The news coverage when their recording was such a hit. Do you have it?"

"I do."

"So do I. Don't understand the attraction myself. Dull. But lots liked it. Do you?"

"I do."

Francoeur gave him a small smile. "I thought you might."

Gamache waited, quietly watching the Superintendent. As though he had all the time in the world and the paper in his hand was far less interesting than whatever his boss was saying.

"Caused a sensation. Amazing to think these monks have been here for hundreds of years and no one seemed to notice. And then they do one little recording and *voilà*. World famous. That's the problem, of course."

"How so?"

"There's going to be an uproar when news of Frère Mathieu's murder gets out. He's more famous than Frère Jacques." Francoeur smiled and, to Gamache's surprise, the Superintendent sang, *"Frère Jacques, Frère Jacques, dormez-vous? Dormez-vous?"*

But he sang the cheerful child's song like a dirge. Slowly, sonorously. As though there was some meaning hidden in the nonsense verse. Then Francoeur stared for a long, cold moment at Gamache.

"There's going to be hell to pay, Armand. Even you must have figured that out."

"Yes, I had. *Merci.*"

Gamache leaned forward and placed the coroner's report on the desk between them. He stared directly at Francoeur, who stared back. Not blinking. His eyes cold and hard. Daring the Chief Inspector to speak. Which he did.

"Why are you here?"

"I've come to help."

"Forgive me, Superintendent," said Gamache. "But I'm still not sure why you came. You've never felt the need to help before."

The two men glared at each other. The air between them throbbed with enmity.

"In a murder investigation, I mean," said Gamache, with a smile.

"Of course."

Francoeur looked at Gamache with barely disguised loathing.

"With communications down," the Superintendent looked at the laptop on the desk, "and only one phone in the monastery, it was clear someone would need to bring those."

He waved at the dossiers on the desk. The coroner's report and the findings of the forensics team.

"That is extremely helpful," said Gamache. And meant it. But he knew, and Francoeur knew, that it didn't take the Chief Superintendent of the Sûreté to act as courier. In fact, it would have been far more helpful, if that really was the goal, to have one of Gamache's homicide investigators bring it.

"Since you're here to help, perhaps you'd like me to give you the facts of the case," Gamache offered.

"Please."

Gamache spent the next few minutes trying to give Superintendent Francoeur the facts, while the Superintendent continually interrupted with meaningless questions and comments. Most suggesting Gamache might have missed something, or failed to ask something, or failed to investigate something.

But, haltingly, Gamache managed to tell the story of the murder of Frère Mathieu.

The body, curled around the yellowed paper, with the neumes and Latin gibberish. The three monks praying over the dead prior in the garden. The abbot, Dom Philippe, his secretary, Frère Simon, and the doctor, Frère Charles.

The evidence of an increasingly bitter rift in Saint-Gilbert. Between those who wanted the vow of silence lifted and another recording of Gregorian chants made, and those who wanted neither. Between the prior's men and the abbot's men.

Through constant interruptions, Gamache told the Superintendent about the hidden Chapter House and the abbot's secret garden. The rumors of more hidden rooms, and even a treasure.

At that the Superintendent looked at Gamache as though at a credulous child.

Gamache simply continued, giving concise character sketches of the monks.

"It seems you're no closer to solving the murder than when you arrived," said Francoeur. "Everyone's still a suspect."

"It's a good thing that you're here, then," Gamache paused. "To help."

"It is. For instance, you don't even have the murder weapon."

"That's true."

"Or even know what it was."

Gamache opened his mouth to say they suspected a rock from the garden had crushed the prior's skull, then was tossed over the wall and into the woods. But instinct, and perhaps a slight gleam of satisfaction in Francoeur's eyes, told him to stop. Instead he looked at the Superintendent, then down at the mostly unread coroner's report.

He turned the page and scanned. Then looked up, meeting Francoeur's eyes. The gleam had become a glow, of triumph.

Gamache cupped his right hand in his left. Holding it steady. So that Francoeur wouldn't see the slight tremble and believe he'd caused it.

"You read the reports?" Gamache asked.

Francoeur nodded. "On the flight. You've been looking for a rock, I understand."

He made it sound ridiculous.

"That's true. Clearly we were wrong. It wasn't a rock at all."

"No," Francoeur uncrossed his legs and leaned forward. "No dirt or residue in the wound. Nothing at all. As you see, the coroner thinks it was a long metal object like a pipe or a poker."

"You knew this when you arrived and didn't tell me?" Gamache's voice was calm, but the censure was clear.

"What? Me presume to tell the great Gamache how to do his job? I wouldn't dream of it."

"Then why are you here, if not to pass on valuable information?"

"Because, Armand," Francoeur spat the name out as though it was *merde* in his mouth, "one of us cares for the service and one of us cares about his career. I'm here so that when news of the murder gets out and all hell breaks loose, and the world's media descends, we don't look like complete imbeciles. I can at least give the impression the Sûreté is competent. That we're doing all we can to solve the brutal killing of one of the most beloved *religieux* in the world. You know what the world will want to know when his murder is made public?"

Gamache remained quiet. He knew that while continually interrupting could cause an explosion of information, silence could too. A man like Francoeur, so tightly restraining his rage, needed simply to be given space. And, perhaps, a well-timed shove.

"Why, with only two dozen suspects in a cloistered abbey, the famed Sûreté du Québec still couldn't make an arrest," Francoeur sneered. "What could possibly be taking so long, they'll ask."

"And what will you tell them, Sylvain? That it's difficult to get at the truth when your own people are withholding information?"

"The truth, Armand? You want me to tell them that an arrogant, smug, incompetent

370

asshole is in charge of the investigation?"

Gamache raised his brows and faintly gestured toward where Francoeur was sitting. Behind the desk.

And Gamache saw Francoeur slip over the edge. The Superintendent stood and the stone floor screamed as the chair scraped against it. Francoeur's handsome face was livid.

Gamache remained seated, but after a moment he slowly, slowly got to his feet, so that they faced each other across the desk. Gamache's hands were behind his back, clasping each other. His chest was exposed, as though inviting Francoeur to take his best shot.

There was a soft tapping on the door.

Neither man responded.

Then it came again, and a tentative "Chief?"

The door opened a crack.

"You need to treat your people with more respect, Armand," snapped Francoeur, his voice loud. Then he turned to the door. "Come."

Beauvoir stepped in and looked from man to man. It was near impossible to enter the prior's office, so thick was the atmosphere. But Beauvoir did. He stepped in, and stood shoulder to shoulder with Gamache.

Francoeur dragged his stare from the Chief Inspector over to Beauvoir and took a deep breath. And even managed a coy smile.

"You've come at a good time, Inspector. I think your Chief and I have said enough. Perhaps even more than enough."

He gave a disarming little laugh and put out his hand.

"I didn't get a chance to say hello when I arrived. My apologies, Inspector Beauvoir."

Jean-Guy hesitated, then took it.

A bell rang and Beauvoir made a face. "Not again."

Superintendent Francoeur laughed. "My feelings exactly. But perhaps while the monks go about their business of praying we can go about ours. At least we'll know where they are."

He all but winked at Beauvoir, then turned back to Gamache.

"Think about what I said, Chief Inspector." His voice was warm, almost cordial. "That's all I ask."

He made to leave and Gamache called after him.

"I think, Chief Superintendent, you'll find that bell isn't for prayers but for lunch."

"Well," Francoeur smiled fully, "then my prayers are answered. I hear the food here is excellent. Is it?" he asked Beauvoir.

"Not bad."

"*Bon.* Then, I'll see you at lunch. I'll be staying a few days, of course. The abbot has been good enough to give me one of the rooms. If you'll excuse me, I'll just freshen up and meet you there."

He nodded to both of them, then walked off confidently. A man in complete command of himself, of the situation, of the monastery.

Beauvoir turned to Gamache.

"What was that about?"

"I honestly haven't a clue."

"You all right?"

"Just fine, thank you."

"Fucked up, insecure, neurotic and egotistical? F.I.N.E.?"

"I think that would be the Chief Superintendent's assessment," Gamache smiled and they walked down the corridor toward the Blessed Chapel, and the dining hall.

"He came here to tell you that?"

"No, according to him he came to help. He also brought with him the coroner's report and the findings of the forensics team."

Gamache told Beauvoir what the reports said. Beauvoir listened as they walked. Then stopped and turned to Gamache in anger.

"He knew that's what the report said, that

373

the weapon wasn't a rock at all, and he didn't tell us right away? What's he playing at?"

"I don't know. But we need to focus on the murder, not be distracted by the Superintendent."

"D'accord," agreed Beauvoir, begrudgingly. "So where's the damned murder weapon? We searched outside the wall and didn't find anything."

Except, he thought, wild blueberries. And they probably weren't lethal, until dipped in dark chocolate.

"I know one thing," said the Chief. "The report tells us something crucial."

"What?"

"The murder of Frère Mathieu was almost certainly premeditated. If you're in a garden you might pick up a rock in a moment of overwhelming emotion, and kill someone —"

"But not a piece of metal," said Beauvoir, following the Chief's thoughts. "That had to be brought with the murderer. There's no way a pipe or a poker would just be lying around the abbot's garden."

Gamache nodded.

One of the monks hadn't just lashed out at the prior, killing him in a fit of rage. It was planned.

Mens rea.

The Latin legal phrase came to Gamache.

Mens rea. A guilty mind. Intent.

One of these monks had met the prior in the garden, already armed with a metal pipe and a guilty mind. The thought and the act collided, and the result was murder.

"I can't believe Francoeur's staying," said Beauvoir as they crossed the Blessed Chapel. "I'll admit to the crime myself if it means that stupid shit'll leave."

Gamache stopped. They were dead in the center of the chapel.

"Be careful, Jean-Guy." Gamache kept his voice low. "Superintendent Francoeur's no fool."

"Are you kidding? As soon as he stepped off the plane he should have handed you the dossiers. But instead he ignores you, in front of everyone, and sucks up to the abbot."

"Lower your voice," cautioned Gamache.

Beauvoir gave a furtive glance around then spoke in an urgent whisper. "The man's a menace."

He glanced toward the door from the corridor, for Francoeur. Gamache turned and they resumed their walk to the dining hall.

"Look," Beauvoir hurried to catch up to the Chief's long strides. "He's undermining you here. You must see that. Everyone saw what happened on the dock, and they now think Francoeur's in charge."

Gamache opened the door and motioned Beauvoir through to the next corridor. The aroma of fresh baked bread and soup met them. Then, with a swift glance behind him into the dimness of the Blessed Chapel, Gamache closed the door.

"He is in charge, Jean-Guy."

"Oh, come on."

But the laughter died on Beauvoir's lips. The Chief was serious.

"He's the Chief Superintendent of the Sûreté," said Gamache. "I'm . . . not. He's my boss. He'll always be in charge."

At the thunderous look on Beauvoir's face Gamache smiled. "It'll be all right."

"I know it will, *patron.* After all, nothing bad ever happens when a senior Sûreté officer starts abusing his power."

"Exactly, *mon vieux,*" the Chief grinned and caught Beauvoir's eye. "Please, Jean-Guy. Stay out of it."

Beauvoir didn't need to ask "Out of what?" Chief Inspector Gamache's calm brown eyes held his. There was a plea in them. Not for help, but for the opposite. To be left alone to deal with Francoeur.

Beauvoir nodded. *"Oui, patron."*
But he knew he'd just lied.

TWENTY

Most of the monks were already in the dining hall by the time Gamache and Beauvoir arrived. The Chief Inspector nodded to the abbot, who sat at the head of the long table, an empty chair beside him. The abbot lifted his hand in greeting, but didn't offer the seat. Neither did the Chief offer to join him. Both men had other agendas.

Baskets of fresh baguettes, rounds of cheeses, pitchers of water and bottles of cider sat on the wooden table, and monks sat around it in their black robes, white hoods hanging down their backs. Gamache realized Superintendent Francoeur hadn't told him why Gilbert of Sempringham had chosen this unique design nine hundred years ago.

"That's Brother Raymond," whispered the Chief, nodding toward a space on the bench between the doctor, Frère Charles, and another monk. "He's in charge of maintenance."

"Got it," said Beauvoir, and walked quickly to the other side of the table.

"Do you mind?" Beauvoir asked the monks.

"Not at all," said Frère Charles. He looked happy, indeed almost hysterically so, to see the Sûreté agent. It was a welcome Beauvoir rarely received while on a murder investigation.

Gamache's lunch companion, on the other hand, looked far from pleased to see him. He looked far from pleased to see the bread, or the cheese. Or the sun in the sky, or the birds outside the window.

"*Bonjour,* Frère Simon," said the Chief, taking his seat. But apparently the abbot's secretary was maintaining his own strict personal vow of silence. He also seemed to have taken a vow of annoyance.

Across the table, and a little way down, Gamache could see that Beauvoir was already engaged in conversation with Brother Raymond.

"The first brothers knew what they were doing," said Raymond in answer to Beauvoir's question about the original plans for the abbey. His answer surprised Beauvoir. Not for the content, but for the monk's voice.

He spoke in a broad, almost unintelligible, country accent. A twang yanked from the woods and mountains and tiny villages of Québec. It had been planted by the first settlers and *voyageurs* from France, hundreds of years ago. Rugged men, schooled in what mattered here. Not *politesse,* but survival. The aristocrats, the learned administrators and mariners might have found the New World, but the hardy peasants had settled it. Their voices had taken deep root in Québec, like some ancient oak. Unchanged, for centuries. So that a historian speaking to these Québécois might feel she'd traveled in time back to medieval France.

Over the generations most Québécois had lost the accent. But every now and then this voice emerged from a valley, from a village.

It had become popular to mock such accents, thinking if the voice was rustic the thinking must be backward too. But Beauvoir knew different.

His grandmother spoke like this, as they'd shelled peas on the rickety old verandah. As she'd talked about her garden. And the seasons. And patience. And nature.

His gruff grandfather, when he chose to speak, also sounded like a peasant. But he thought and acted like a nobleman. Never failing to help a neighbor. Never failing to share what little he had.

No, Beauvoir had no inclination to dismiss Frère Raymond. Just the opposite. He felt drawn to this monk.

Raymond's eyes were deep brown and despite the robe Beauvoir could see the monk's body was strappy. His hands were lean and sinewy, from a lifetime of hard work. He was, Beauvoir guessed, in his early fifties.

"They built Saint-Gilbert to last," said Frère Raymond, reaching for the cider bottle and pouring some for Beauvoir and himself. "Craftsmanship, that's what it was. And discipline. But after those first monks? Disaster."

What followed was a litany of how every generation of monks had screwed up the monastery in their own special way. Not spiritually. Frère Raymond didn't seem too concerned with that. But physically. Adding stuff, taking down stuff. Adding it again. Changing the roof. All disasters.

"And the toilets. Don't get me started on the toilets."

But it was too late. Frère Raymond was started. And Beauvoir began to understand why Frère Charles was almost maniacally pleased to have someone come between him and Brother Raymond. Not because of the voice, but what that voice was saying. Non-stop.

"They messed those up," said Brother Raymond. "The toilets were —"

"A disaster?" asked Beauvoir.

"Exactement." Raymond knew he was in the company of a kindred spirit.

The last few monks arrived and took their seats. Chief Superintendent Francoeur paused in the doorway. The room grew quiet, except for Frère Raymond, who couldn't seem to stop the locomotive of words.

"Shit. Great holes of it. I can show you if you like."

Brother Raymond looked at Beauvoir with enthusiasm, but Beauvoir shook his head and looked over at Francoeur.

"Merci, mon frère," he whispered. "But I've seen enough shits."

Frère Raymond snorted. "Me too."

And then he grew quiet.

Superintendent Francoeur had a way of dominating a room. Beauvoir watched as one by one the monks turned to the Superintendent.

He's fooled them too, thought Beauvoir. Surely men of God would see behind the fake front. They'd see the meanness, the pettiness. They'd see he was a nasty piece of

382

shit. A disaster.

But they didn't seem to. Just as many in the Sûreté didn't either. They were fooled by Francoeur's bravado. His manliness, his swagger.

Beauvoir could see the testosterone-filled world of the Sûreté being taken in. But not the quiet and thoughtful monks.

But they too seemed in awe of this man, who'd arrived so swiftly. Flying in and landing, almost on top of them. Nothing effete, nothing tentative about Francoeur. He'd practically fallen from the sky. Into their abbey. Into their laps.

And judging by the look on their faces, they seemed to admire him for that.

But not all of them, Beauvoir realized. His blueberry-picking companion from that morning, Frère Bernard, was looking at Francoeur with suspicion, as were a few others.

Perhaps these monks weren't quite as naïve as Beauvoir had feared. But then he had it. The abbot's men were looking at Francoeur with wariness. Their faces polite but veiled.

It was the prior's men who were practically swooning.

Francoeur's gaze swept the room and came to rest on the abbot. And the empty chair beside him. The air seemed to leave the room as all eyes swung from the Superintendent to the chair. Then back again.

Dom Philippe sat perfectly still at the head of the table. Neither inviting the Superintendent to join him, nor discouraging it.

Finally Francoeur gave a small, respectful bow to the monks and walked purposefully down the long table. To the head. And took his place, on the right-hand side of the abbot.

The prior's seat. Filled. The void filled, the vacuum filled.

Beauvoir returned his attention to Frère Raymond and was surprised to see a look of admiration on the lean and weathered face as he too watched the Superintendent.

"The prior's place, of course," said Raymond. "The king is dead. Long live the king."

"The prior was king? I thought the abbot would be considered that."

Frère Raymond gave Beauvoir a keen, assessing look. "In name only. The prior was our real leader."

"You're one of the prior's men?" asked Beauvoir, surprised. He'd have thought this man would be loyal to the abbot.

"Absolutely. I can only take incompetence so long. He," Frère Raymond jerked his

384

shaved head toward the abbot, "is ruining the abbey. The prior was going to save it."

"Ruining? How?"

"By doing nothing." Raymond kept his voice low, but his annoyance scraped out anyway. "The prior had handed him the means to make all the money we'd ever need, to finally fix the abbey, so that it'd stand a thousand years, and Dom Philippe turned it away."

"But I thought lots of work had been done. The kitchens, the roof, the geo. The abbot wasn't exactly doing nothing."

"But he wasn't doing what was really needed. We could've survived just fine for a while without a new kitchen, or geothermal."

Frère Raymond paused. It was as though a void had suddenly opened up in the flow of words. Beauvoir stared. And waited. As Frère Raymond teetered on the edge. Of silence. Or more words.

Beauvoir decided to give him a little push.

"What can't you survive without?"

The monk lowered his voice further. "The foundations are rotten."

Now Beauvoir wasn't sure if Frère Raymond was speaking metaphorically, as *les religieux* tended to do, or for real. But he thought this monk, with this accent, probably didn't go in for metaphors.

"What do you mean?" Beauvoir also whispered.

"How many ways are there to interpret that?" Raymond asked. "The foundations are rotten."

"Is that a big job?"

"Are you kidding? You've seen the monastery. If the foundations go, the monastery collapses."

Beauvoir stared at the intense monk, whose eyes were boring into him.

"Collapses? The monastery will fall down?"

"Completely. Not today. Not tomorrow. I'd say we have about ten years. But it'll take that long to repair. The foundations have supported the weight of the walls for hundreds of years," said Raymond. "It's amazing what those first monks did. Way ahead of their time. But they hadn't counted on the terrible winters. The cycles of freezing and thawing and what that does. And something else."

"What?"

"The forest. Saint-Gilbert-Entre-les-Loups is fixed in place, but the forest keeps moving. Toward us. Roots are breaking through the foundations. Cracking them, making them weak. Then water got in. The

386

foundations are crumbling and rotting."

Rotting, thought Beauvoir. It wasn't a metaphor, but it could be.

"When we arrived we noticed many of the trees around the monastery have been cut down recently," said Beauvoir. "Is this why?"

"Too little too late. The damage is done, the roots are already here. It'll take millions to repair. And all sorts of skilled workers. But he," now Raymond jerked his knife toward the abbot, "thinks two dozen aging monks can do the work. He's not only incompetent, he's delusional."

Beauvoir would have to agree. He watched the abbot in what appeared to be polite conversation with the Superintendent, and for the first time, wondered about his sanity.

"What does he say when you tell him it's impossible for you to fix the foundation yourselves?"

"He tells me I should do as he does. Pray for a miracle."

"And you don't believe there'll be one?"

Now Brother Raymond turned completely, to look at Beauvoir face on. The anger, so evident a moment earlier, all gone.

"Just the opposite. I told the abbot he could stop praying. That the miracle had happened. God gave us voices. And the most beautiful chants. And an age when they can be sent around the world. To inspire millions, while making millions. If that isn't a miracle, I don't know what is."

Beauvoir sat back and looked at this monk, who not only believed in prayer and miracles, but believed God had granted them one. The silent order would make money with their voices, and save the abbey.

But the abbot was too blind to see that what he prayed for he already had.

"Who else knows about the foundations?"

"No one. I only discovered the problem a couple of months ago. Did some tests, then told the abbot, expecting him to tell the community."

"But he didn't?"

Frère Raymond shook his head and lowered his voice further, glancing around at his brother monks. "He ordered the trees to be cut, but told the brothers it was for firewood, in case the geothermal ever fails."

"He lied?"

The monk shrugged. "It's a good idea to have an emergency supply of wood, in case. But it wasn't the real reason. None of them knows that. Only the abbot. And me. He had me promise not to tell anyone."

"Do you think the prior knew?"

"I wish he had. He'd have saved us. It

would be so easy. One more recording. And maybe a concert tour. We'd have enough to save Saint-Gilbert."

"But then Frère Mathieu was killed," said Beauvoir.

"Murdered," agreed the monk.

"By who?"

"Come on, son. You know as well as I do."

Beauvoir shot a look at the head of the table, where the abbot had risen to his feet. There was a shuffling as the other monks, and Sûreté officers, also got up.

The abbot gave the benediction over the food. When he'd finished, they all sat, and one of the monks walked to a podium, cleared his throat with a little cough, then began to sing.

Again, thought Beauvoir with a sigh, and looked longingly at the fresh bread and cheese, so tantalizingly close. But mostly, as the monk sang, Beauvoir thought about this straight-talking, no-crap monk beside him. Who was one of the prior's men. And who considered the abbot a disaster. And worse. A murderer.

When the monk finally stopped singing, other monks brought vats of warm soup to the table, made from the vegetables Beauvoir had helped harvest that morning.

Beauvoir took a hunk of warm baguette

and smoothed whipped butter onto it, and watched it melt. Then he cut a slab of blue and Brie from the cheese board making the rounds. As Brother Raymond continued his liturgy of the faults in the monastery, Beauvoir took a spoonful of soup, with carrots, peas, parsnips and potatoes bumping together in the fragrant broth.

While he found it difficult stopping the near biblical flood of words from his companion, Beauvoir noticed that the Chief was having difficulty coaxing just a few words out of Brother Simon.

Gamache had met many suspects who refused to speak. Mostly they sat cross-armed and belligerent across a hacked-up old table in some far-flung Sûreté outpost.

Eventually the Chief Inspector had gotten them all to talk. Some had confessed. But at the very least, most had finally said far more than they expected or certainly intended.

Armand Gamache was very good at coaxing indiscretions out of people.

But he wondered if he might have met his Waterloo with Frère Simon.

He'd brought up the subject of the weather. Then, thinking that might be too mundane for the abbot's secretary, he asked about Saint Cecilia.

"We found a statue to her in Frère Mathieu's cell."

"Patron saint of music," said Simon, concentrating on his soup.

It was at least a start, thought the Chief, as he cut a piece of Camembert and smoothed it onto a hunk of warm baguette. And one mystery solved. Frère Mathieu prayed every night to the patron saint of music.

Sensing a small opening, Gamache asked about Gilbert of Sempringham. And the design of the robes.

That brought a reaction. Frère Simon looked at him as though he'd lost his mind. Then went back to eating. As did Gamache.

The Chief took a sip of the cider.

"Nice drink," he said, replacing his glass. "I understand you trade blueberries for it from a monastery in the south."

He might as well have been speaking to the Camembert.

Had this been just a stunningly awkward social occasion, Gamache would have given up and probably turned to the monk on his other side, but this was a murder investigation. He didn't have that option. So the Chief Inspector turned back to Brother Simon, determined to breach his defenses.

391

"Rhode Island Red."

Frère Simon's spoon lowered into the broth, and his head slowly turned. To look at Gamache.

"Pardon?" he asked. His voice was beautiful, even in that single word. Rich. Melodic. Like a full-bodied coffee, or aged cognac. With all sorts of subtleties and depth.

Gamache realized, with surprise, that he hadn't heard more than a dozen words from the abbot's secretary their whole visit.

"Rhode Island Red," Gamache repeated. "A lovely breed."

"What do you know about them?"

"Well, they have fantastic plumage. And are, in my opinion, dismissed far too easily."

Gamache, of course, had no idea what he was saying except that it sounded good and might appeal to this man. For a small miracle had occurred. The Chief Inspector had remembered a single sentence from all the conversations he'd had with the abbot.

Frère Simon had a fondness for chickens.

Gamache, who did not have a fondness for chickens, could remember only one breed. He'd been about to say, "Foghorn Leghorn," when the first miracle occurred and he remembered just in time that that was a cartoon character not a breed of chicken.

Camptown racetrack's five miles long. To the Chief's horror the cartoon character's favorite song had insinuated itself into his head. *Doo-dah.* He fought it off. *Doo-dah.*

He turned to Frère Simon, hoping this conversational sally had worked. *Doo-dah, doo-dah.*

"It's true that they have nice temperaments, but be careful. They can get aggressive when annoyed," said Frère Simon. With those three magic words, "Rhode Island Red," Gamache hadn't simply breached the monk's defenses, the gates were now thrown wide open. And the Chief Inspector was marching in.

Gamache, though, did pause long enough to wonder what could possibly annoy a chicken. Perhaps the same things that annoyed Frère Simon and the other monks, pressed together in their tiny cells. Not exactly free range. More like battery monks.

"You have them here?" Gamache asked.

"Rhode Island Reds? No. They're hardy, but we find only one breed works well so far north."

The abbot's secretary had turned completely in his seat, toward Gamache. Far from being taciturn any longer, the monk was now almost begging Gamache to ask the question. The Chief, of course, obliged.

393

"And what breed is that?" Hoping, praying, Frère Simon wouldn't ask him to guess.

"You'll slap yourself for not knowing," said Frère Simon, almost giddy.

"I'm sure I will."

"It's the Chantecler."

Frère Simon said it with such triumph Gamache almost did slap himself for not guessing. Before realizing he'd never heard of the breed before.

"Of course," he said, "the Chantecler. What a fool I am. A fabulous chicken."

"You're right."

For the next ten minutes Gamache listened as Frère Simon gestured, drew pictures with his stubby finger on the wooden table, and spoke nonstop about the Chantecler. And his own prize rooster, Fernando.

"Fernando?" Gamache had to ask.

Simon actually laughed, to the surprise and near consternation of the monks directly around him. It was doubtful they'd ever heard that sound before.

"Truthfully?" asked Simon, leaning toward Gamache. "I had the Abba song in mind."

The monk sang the familiar tune, a single phrase about drums and guns. Gamache felt his heart leap, as though it wanted to attach itself to this monk. Here was an extraordinarily beautiful voice. Where others were glorious for their clarity, Simon's was beautiful for its tonality, its richness. It elevated the simple pop lyric into something splendid. The Chief found himself wishing Brother Simon also had a chicken named Mama Mia.

Here was a man filled with passion. Granted, it was for chickens. Whether he was passionate about music, or God, or monastic life was another question.

All the doo-dah day.

"Your boss seems to have made a conquest," said Frère Charles, leaning into Beauvoir.

"*Oui.* I wonder what they're talking about."

"I do too," said the doctor. "I've never been able to get more than a grunt out of Frère Simon. Though that makes him a great gatekeeper."

"I thought Frère Luc was the gatekeeper."

"He's the *portier,* the doorkeeper. Simon has another job. He's the abbot's guard dog. No one gets to Dom Philippe except through Frère Simon. He's devoted to the abbot."

"And you? Are you devoted?"

"He's the abbot, our leader."

"That's not an answer, *mon frère,*" said Beauvoir. He'd managed to turn away from

395

Frère Raymond toward the medical monk, when the maintenance monk had reached for more cider.

"Are you one of the abbot's men, or the prior's men?"

The doctor's gaze, friendly before, now sharpened, examining Beauvoir. Then he smiled again.

"I'm neutral, Inspector. Like the Red Cross. I just tend to the wounded."

"Are there many? Wounded, I mean."

The smile left Frère Charles's face. "Enough. A rift like that in a previously happy monastery hurts everyone."

"Including yourself?"

"*Oui,*" the doctor admitted. "But I really don't take sides. It wouldn't be appropriate."

"Was it appropriate for anyone?"

"It wasn't anyone's first choice," said the doctor, an edge of impatience in his friendly voice. "We didn't wake up one morning and pick teams. Like a game of Red Rover. This was excruciating and slow. Like being eviscerated. Gutted. A civil war is never civil."

Then the monk's gaze left Beauvoir and looked first at Francoeur, beside the abbot, then across the table to Gamache.

"As perhaps you know."

A denial was on Beauvoir's lips, but he stopped it. The monk knew. They all knew.

"Is he all right?" Frère Charles asked.

"Who?"

"The Chief Inspector."

"Why shouldn't he be?"

Brother Charles hesitated, searching Beauvoir's face. Then he looked down at his own steady hand. "The tremble. In his right hand." He returned his eyes to Beauvoir. "I'm sure you've noticed."

"I have and he's fine."

"I'm not asking just to be nosy, you know," Frère Charles persisted. "A tremble like that can be a sign of something seriously wrong. It comes and goes, I notice. For instance, his hand seems steady right now."

"It happens when the Chief is tired, or stressed."

The doctor nodded. "Has he had it long?"

"Not long," said Beauvoir, careful not to sound defensive. He knew the Chief didn't seem to care who saw the occasional quiver in his right hand.

"So it's not Parkinson's?"

"Not at all," said Beauvoir.

"Then what caused it?"

"An injury."

"Ahh," said Frère Charles, and again he

looked across at the Chief Inspector. "The scar near his left temple."

Beauvoir was silent. Regretting turning away from Frère Raymond and the long list of structural disasters, and other disasters, visited upon the abbey by incompetent abbots, Dom Philippe prominent among them. Now he wanted to turn back. To hear about artesian wells, and septic systems and load-bearing walls.

Anything was better than discussing the Chief's injuries. And, by association, that terrible day in the abandoned factory.

"If you think he needs anything, I have some things that might be helpful in the infirmary."

"He'll be fine."

"I'm sure he will." Frère Charles paused and his eyes held Beauvoir's. "But we all need help sometimes. Including your Chief. I have relaxants and painkillers. Just let him know."

"I will," said Beauvoir. *"Merci."*

Beauvoir turned his attention to his meal. But as he ate, the words drifted in through Beauvoir's own wounds. Sinking deeper and deeper.

Relaxants.

Until they finally hit bottom, and came to

rest in Beauvoir's hidden room.
And painkillers.

TWENTY-ONE

When lunch was over Chief Inspector Gamache and Beauvoir walked back to the prior's office, comparing notes.

Beauvoir on foundations and Gamache on chickens.

"These aren't ordinary chickens, but the Chantecler," said Gamache, with enthusiasm. Beauvoir was never sure if the Chief really was that interested, or just pretending, but he had his suspicions.

"Ahh, the noble Chantecler."

Gamache smiled. "Don't mock, Jean-Guy."

"Me, mock a monk?"

"It seems our Frère Simon is a world expert on the Chantecler. It was bred right here in Québec. By a monk."

"Really?" Despite himself, Beauvoir was interested. "Right here?"

"Well, no, not in Saint-Gilbert, but in a monastery just outside Montréal, about a hundred years ago. The climate was too harsh in Canada, he thought, for the regular chickens to survive, so he spent his lifetime developing a native Canadian breed. The Chantecler. They almost went extinct, but Frère Simon is bringing them back."

"Just our luck," said Beauvoir. "Every other monastery makes alcohol. Brandy and Bénédictine. Champagne. Cognac. Wines. Ours sings obscure chants and breeds near extinct chickens. No wonder they almost went the way of the dodo. But that brings me to my lunch table conversation with Frère Raymond. Thank you for that, by the way."

Gamache grinned. "Talkative, was he?"

"You couldn't get your monk started and I couldn't get mine to stop. But wait 'til you hear what he had to say."

They were in the Blessed Chapel now. The monks had dispersed, off to do more work, or read, or pray. The afternoons seemed less structured than the mornings.

"The foundations of Saint-Gilbert are crumbling," said Beauvoir. "Frère Raymond says he discovered it a couple of months ago. The abbey won't stand another ten years if something isn't done right away. The first recording made them lots of money, but not enough. They need more."

"You mean, the entire abbey might collapse?" asked Gamache, who stopped dead in his tracks.

"Boom, gone," said Beauvoir. "And he blames the abbot."

"How so? Surely the abbot hasn't been undermining the abbey, at least not literally."

"Frère Raymond says if they don't get the money from a second recording and a concert tour they can't save the monastery. And the abbot won't allow either."

"Dom Philippe knows about the foundations?"

Beauvoir nodded. "Frère Raymond says he told the abbot, but no one else. He's been begging Dom Philippe to take it seriously. To raise the money to repair the foundations."

"And no one else knows?" Gamache confirmed.

"Well, Brother Raymond didn't tell anyone. The abbot might've."

Gamache walked a few paces in silence, thinking. Then he stopped.

"The prior was the abbot's right hand. I wonder if Dom Philippe told him."

Beauvoir thought about that. "It seems the sort of thing you tell your second in command."

"Unless you were at war with him," said Gamache, lost in thought. Trying to see what might have happened. Did the abbot tell the prior that Saint-Gilbert was literally crumbling? But then continued to hold firm against another recording. And continued, even in the face of this news, to refuse to break the silence that would allow the monks to tour and give interviews. To make the millions and millions it would take to save the abbey.

Suddenly the second recording of Gregorian chants went from a possible vanity project on the part of the monks and Frère Mathieu, to something vital. It wouldn't simply put Saint-Gilbert-Entre-les-Loups on the map, it would save the entire abbey.

This had become no mere philosophical difference between the abbot and the prior. The very survival of the abbey was in the balance.

What would Frère Mathieu have done had he known?

"Their relationship was already strained," said Gamache, starting to walk again, but slowly. Thinking out loud. His voice low, to avoid being overheard. It gave them the appearance of conspirators in the Blessed Chapel.

"The prior would've been in a fff . . ." On

seeing Gamache's face, Beauvoir shifted his words. "In a rage."

"He was already in an effin' rage," agreed the Chief. "This would've propelled him right over the edge."

"And if, faced with all this, the abbot continued to refuse a second recording? I bet Frère Mathieu would've threatened to tell the other monks. And then the shhh . . . the . . ." But Beauvoir could think of no other way of putting it.

"It certainly would," agreed Gamache. "So . . ."

The Chief stopped again and stared into space. Putting the pieces together to form a similar, but different, image.

"So," he turned to Beauvoir, "maybe Dom Philippe didn't tell his prior that the foundations were crumbling. He's smart enough to know what Frère Mathieu would do with that. He'd be handing his adversary a nuclear bomb of information. The cracked and rotting foundations would be the last and most potent argument the prior and his men would need."

"You think the abbot kept the information to himself?"

"I think it's possible. And he swore Frère Raymond to secrecy."

"But if he told me," said Beauvoir,

"wouldn't he have told the other monks?"

"Perhaps he felt the promise he made to the abbot only extended to the community. Not to you."

"And maybe he's had enough of silence," said Beauvoir.

"And maybe," said Gamache, "maybe Frère Raymond lied to you, and he did tell one other person."

Beauvoir considered that for a moment. They heard the soft shuffling of monk feet in the Blessed Chapel and saw monks walking here and there, hugging the old walls. As though afraid to show themselves.

Gamache and Beauvoir had kept their voices low. Low enough, Beauvoir hoped. But if not, it was too late now.

"The prior," said Beauvoir. "If Frère Raymond was going to break his promise to the abbot, he'd have gone to Frère Mathieu. He'd have felt justified, if he thought the abbot wasn't going to act."

Gamache nodded. It made sense. In the logical little world they'd just created. But so much about the lives of the monks didn't seem logical. And the Chief Inspector had to remind himself not to confuse what should have been, what could have been, with what actually was.

They needed facts.

"If Frère Raymond told the prior, *patron,* what do you think would happen next?"

"I think we can guess. The prior would've been enraged —"

"— or maybe not," Beauvoir interrupted and the Chief looked at him. "Well maybe the abbot, in staying silent about something so vital, had finally given the prior the weapon he needed. The prior might have pretended to be angry, but in fact, he might have been ecstatic."

Gamache imagined the prior. Saw him getting the news about the crumbling foundations. The fact the abbot knew, and was apparently doing nothing. Except praying. What would the prior then do?

Would he tell anyone else?

Gamache thought not. At least, not right away.

In a silent order, information became a powerful currency, and Frère Mathieu was almost certainly a miser. He'd never have shared that information so quickly. He'd have hoarded it. Waited for the perfect moment.

Gamache couldn't be sure, but he thought the prior would probably ask for a meeting with the abbot. Someplace private. Not overlooked. Not overheard. With only the birds, and the old-growth maple, and the

406

black flies as witnesses. If you didn't count God.

Again, though, the Chief shook his head. It didn't fit all the facts. One fact, supported by witnesses, was that it was the abbot who had sought out the prior. Not the other way around.

Except.

Gamache thought back to one of his interviews with the abbot. In the garden. When the abbot admitted it was the prior's idea to meet. Only the timing was the abbot's.

So, the prior had asked for the meeting. Could it have been about the foundations?

And the scenario shifted again. To the abbot, sending his private secretary on a fool's errand. To find the prior and ask him to meet later that morning.

Frère Simon leaves.

And the abbot has his office, his cell, and his garden to himself. And there he waits, for Frère Mathieu, and the assignation he'd secretly set up. Not for after the 11 A.M. mass, but after Lauds.

They go into the garden. Dom Philippe doesn't know for sure why the prior wants to meet, but he suspects. He's brought a length of pipe out with him, hidden in the long black sleeves of his robe.

Frère Mathieu tells the abbot he knows about the foundations. Demands the second recording. Demands a lifting of the vow of silence. To save the monastery. Or in Chapter later that day he'll tell all the monks about the foundations. About the abbot's silence. About the abbot's paralysis in the face of crisis.

When Frère Mathieu brings out his bomb, the abbot brings out his pipe. One weapon is figurative, and the other isn't.

Within seconds the prior lies dying at the abbot's feet.

Yes, thought Gamache, imagining the scene. It fit.

Almost.

"What's wrong?" asked Beauvoir, seeing the unease on the Chief's face.

"It almost makes sense, but there's a problem."

"What?"

"The neumes. That piece of paper the prior had on him when he died."

"Well, maybe he just brought it with him. Maybe it's nothing."

"Maybe," said Gamache.

But neither man was convinced. There was a reason the prior had the paper. A reason he died curled around it.

Could it have something to do with the

rotting foundations of Saint-Gilbert-Entre-les-Loups? Gamache couldn't see how.

"I'm all confused," Beauvoir admitted.

"So am I. What's confusing you, *mon vieux?*"

"The abbot, Dom Philippe. I talk to Frère Bernard, who seems a good guy, and he thinks the abbot's almost a saint. Then I talk to Frère Raymond, who also seems pretty decent, and he thinks the abbot's first cousin to Satan."

Gamache was quiet for a moment. "Can you find Frère Raymond again? He's probably in the basement. I think that's where his office is. Ask him directly if he told the prior about the foundations."

"And if a pipe was the murder weapon the killer probably got it from the basement. And might've taken it back."

Which, Beauvoir knew, made the strappy, chatty Frère Raymond a pretty good suspect. The prior's man, who knew about the cracks, who loved the abbey and believed the abbot was about to destroy it. And who better than the maintenance monk to know where to find a length of pipe?

Except. Except. Yet again, Beauvoir came up against the fact that the wrong monk had been killed. All that fit. If the abbot had died. But he hadn't. The prior had.

"I'll also ask Frère Raymond about the hidden room," said Beauvoir.

"*Bon.* Take the plans. See what he thinks. And look at the foundations. If they're that bad, it should be easy to see. I wonder why no one noticed before?"

"You think he was lying?"

"Some people do, I'm told."

"It goes against my nature to be cynical, *patron,* but I'll try. And you?"

"Frère Simon must be finished copying the chant we found on the prior. I'll go and get it. I also have a few quiet questions for him. But first I want to finish reading the coroner's and the forensics reports in peace."

A sharp, determined footfall echoed in the chapel. Both men turned toward it, though each knew what they'd see. Not one of the soft-footed monks, that was certain.

Chief Superintendent Francoeur was walking toward them, his feet clacking on the stone floor.

"Gentlemen," said Francoeur. "Did you enjoy your lunch?" He turned to Gamache. "I could hear you and the other monk discussing poultry, was it?"

"Chickens," confirmed Gamache. "Chantecler, to be exact."

Beauvoir repressed a smile. Francoeur

hadn't meant for Gamache to be quite so enthusiastic. Asshole, thought Beauvoir. And then he caught sight of Francoeur's cold eyes, staring at the Chief, and his smile froze on his face.

"I hope you have something more useful planned for this afternoon," said the Superintendent, his voice casual.

"We do. Inspector Beauvoir is planning to tour the basement with Frère Raymond, looking for a possible hidden room. And maybe even the murder weapon," Gamache added. "And I'm off to speak further with the abbot's secretary, Frère Simon. The man I was talking to over lunch."

"About pigs perhaps, or goats?"

Beauvoir grew very still. And watched the two men, in the peaceful, cool chapel, glare at each other. For a beat.

And then Gamache smiled.

"If he'd like, but mostly about that chant I told you about."

"The one found on Frère Mathieu?" asked Francoeur. "Why talk to the abbot's secretary about that?"

"He's making a copy of it, by hand. I'm just going to get it."

Beauvoir noticed that Gamache was underplaying what he wanted to speak to Frère Simon about.

411

"You gave him the one piece of solid evidence we have?"

That Francoeur was incredulous was obvious. What wasn't obvious to Beauvoir was how Gamache managed to not snap back.

"I had no choice. I needed the monks' help in figuring out what it is. Since they don't have a photocopier, this seemed the only solution. If you have another I'd be happy to hear it, sir."

Francoeur barely pretended at civility anymore. Beauvoir could hear his breathing from feet away. He suspected the monks, silently moving along the edges of the Blessed Chapel, could also hear the deep and ragged breaths. Like bellows, fanning Francoeur's rage.

"Then I'll come with you," said the Superintendent. "To see this famous piece of paper."

"With pleasure," said Gamache, and pointed the way.

"Actually," said Beauvoir, thinking quickly. It felt a bit like leaping off a cliff. "I was wondering if the Superintendent would like to come with me."

Both men now stared at Beauvoir. And he could feel himself in free fall.

"Why?" they asked together.

"Well . . ." He couldn't possibly give them

the real reason. That he'd seen the murderous look in Francoeur's eyes. And he'd seen the Chief slip his right hand into his left. And hold it softly there.

"Well," Beauvoir repeated. "I thought the Superintendent might like a tour of the abbey, the places most people never see. And I could use his help."

Beauvoir saw Gamache's brows rise, ever so slightly, then lower. And Beauvoir looked away, unable to meet his Chief's eyes.

Gamache was annoyed at Beauvoir. It happened from time to time, of course, in the high-stress, high-stakes job they had. They'd sometimes clash. But never had he seen that look on Gamache's face.

It was annoyance, but it was more than that. The Chief knew perfectly well what Beauvoir was doing. And Gamache's feelings about it went way beyond mere disapproval, beyond anger even. Beauvoir knew the man enough to see that.

There was something else in the Chief's face, visible for just that instant, when he'd raised his brows.

It was fear.

TWENTY-TWO

Jean-Guy Beauvoir grabbed the rolled-up plans of the monastery off the desk in the prior's office. As he did he glanced at Gamache, who sat in the visitor's chair. On his lap were the coroner's and forensic reports.

Francoeur was waiting for Beauvoir in the Blessed Chapel and he had to hurry back. But still, he paused.

Gamache put his half-moon reading glasses on, then looked at Beauvoir.

"I'm sorry if I overstepped, Chief," said Beauvoir. "I just . . ."

"Yes, I know what you 'just.' " Gamache's voice was unyielding. Little warmth left in it. "He's no fool, you know, Jean-Guy. Don't treat him like that. And never treat me like that."

"Désolé," said Beauvoir, and meant it. When he'd offered to take the Superintendent off Gamache's hands he never dreamed this would be the Chief's reaction. He

thought the Chief would be relieved.

"This isn't a game," said Gamache.

"I know it isn't, *patron.*"

Chief Inspector Gamache continued to stare at Beauvoir.

"Do not engage with Superintendent Francoeur. If he taunts, don't respond. If he pushes you, don't push back. Just smile and keep your eye on the goal. To solve the murder. That's all. He's come here with some agenda, we both know that. We don't know what it is, and I for one don't care. All that matters is solving the crime and getting home. Right?"

"Oui," said Beauvoir. *"D'accord."*

He nodded to Gamache and left. If Francoeur had an agenda, so did Beauvoir. And it was simple. To just keep the Superintendent away from the Chief. Whatever Francoeur had in mind, it had something to do with Gamache. And Beauvoir was not going to let that happen.

"For God's sake, be careful."

The Chief's final words followed Beauvoir down the corridor and into the Blessed Chapel. As did his last view of Gamache, sitting in the chair, the dossiers on his lap. A paper in his hand.

And the slight tremor of the page as a draft caught it. Except that the air was completely still.

At first Beauvoir couldn't see the Superintendent, then he found him by the wall, reading the plaque.

"So this's the hidden door into the Chapter House," said Francoeur, not looking up as Beauvoir approached. "The life of Gilbert of Sempringham isn't interesting reading I'm afraid. Do you think that's why they hid the room behind here? Knowing any possible invader would die of boredom on this very spot?"

Now Chief Superintendent Francoeur did look up, right into Beauvoir's eyes.

There was humor there, Beauvoir saw. And confidence.

"I'm all yours, Inspector."

Beauvoir regarded the Chief Superintendent and wondered why the man was so friendly to him. Francoeur knew without a doubt that Beauvoir was loyal to Gamache. Was one of the Chief's men. And while Francoeur baited and goaded and insulted the Chief, he was only extremely pleasant, charming even, to Beauvoir.

Beauvoir grew even more guarded. A frontal attack was one thing, but this slimy attempt at camaraderie was something else. Still, the longer he could keep this man away from the Chief, the better.

"The stairs are over here." The two Sûreté men walked to the corner of the chapel, where Beauvoir opened a door. Worn stone steps led down. They were well lit and the men descended until finally they were in the basement. Beauvoir stood, not on dirt as he'd expected, but on huge slabs of slate.

The ceilings were high and vaulted.

"The Gilbertines don't seem to do anything half-assed," said Francoeur.

Beauvoir didn't answer, but it was exactly what he'd been thinking. It was cooler down there, though not cold, and he suspected the temperature would stay much the same even as the seasons above changed.

Large wrought-iron candleholders were bolted to the stone, but the light came from naked bulbs strung along the walls and ceiling.

"Where to?" Francoeur asked.

Beauvoir looked this way. Then that. Not at all sure. His plan, he realized, hadn't been thought all the way through. He'd expected to arrive in the basement and for some reason find Frère Raymond right there.

Now he felt a fool. If he'd been with Chief Inspector Gamache he'd have made a joke and they'd have gone looking for Frère Raymond together. But he wasn't with Gamache. He was with the Chief Superintendent of the Sûreté du Québec. And Francoeur was staring at Beauvoir. He wasn't angry. Instead he looked patient, as though working with a rookie agent who was just doing his bumbling best.

Beauvoir could have slapped that look right off his face.

Instead he smiled.

Deep breath in. Deep breath out.

He was the one who'd invited the Superintendent along, after all. He had to at least appear happy to have him. To cover his uncertainty, Beauvoir walked over to one of the stone walls and put his hand on it.

"Frère Raymond told me over lunch that the foundations are cracking," said Beauvoir, examining the stone, as though this was the plan all along. He mentally kicked himself for not making arrangements with the monk.

"*Vraiment?*" asked Francoeur, though he seemed less than interested. "What does that mean?"

"It means Saint-Gilbert is collapsing. He says it'll fall down completely within ten years."

Now he had Francoeur's attention. The Superintendent walked over to the wall across from Beauvoir and examined it.

"Looks fine to me," he said.

It looked fine to Beauvoir too. No gaping cracks, no roots breaking through. Both men peered around. It was magnificent. Another engineering marvel by Dom Clément.

The stone walls ran under the entire monastery. It reminded Beauvoir of the Montréal metro system, only without the humming subway trains. Four cavernous corridors, like tunnels, stretched away from them. All well lit. All swept clean. Nothing out of place.

No murder weapon lying around. And no pine forest growing out of the walls.

But if Frère Raymond was to be believed, Saint-Gilbert-Entre-les-Loups was falling in on itself. And while Beauvoir had no great fondness for monks or priests or churches or abbeys, he discovered he'd be sorry if this one disappeared.

And he'd be very sorry if it disappeared while they were standing in the basement.

The sound of a door closing echoed toward them, and Francoeur started walking in that direction, not waiting to see if Beauvoir followed. As though it didn't matter to him, so insignificant and incompetent was Inspector Beauvoir.

"Shithead," mumbled Beauvoir.

"Sound travels down here, you know,"

said Francoeur, without turning around.

Despite Gamache's warnings. Despite his own pledges, Beauvoir had already allowed himself to be goaded. Allowed his feelings to flare.

But maybe it was a good thing, thought Beauvoir, as he slowly followed Francoeur. Maybe Gamache was wrong, and Francoeur needed to know that Beauvoir wasn't afraid of him. Francoeur needed to know he was dealing with a grown man, not some kid out of the academy, in awe of the title of Chief Superintendent. Some kid he could manipulate.

Yes, thought Beauvoir as he walked a few steps behind the striding Superintendent, that wasn't a mistake at all.

They arrived at a closed door. Beauvoir knocked. There was a long pause. Francoeur reached for the handle just as the door opened. Frère Raymond stood there. He looked alarmed, but on seeing them his expression changed to one of exasperation.

"Are you trying to scare me to death? You could've been the murderer."

"They rarely knock," said Beauvoir.

He turned, and had the satisfaction of seeing the Superintendent looking at Frère Raymond, completely bewildered.

Francoeur appeared not just surprised but

stunned by this rough-hewn subterranean monk, who spoke with the ancient dialect. It was as though the door had opened and a monk from the first congregation, from Dom Clément's community, had stepped out.

"Where're you from, *mon frère?*" Francoeur finally asked.

And now it was Beauvoir's turn to be surprised. As was Frère Raymond.

Chief Superintendent Francoeur had asked the question in the same broad accent as the monk's. Beauvoir examined the Superintendent, to see if he was making fun of the monk, but he wasn't. In fact, his expression was one of delight.

"Saint-Felix-de-Beauce," said Frère Raymond. "You?"

"Saint-Gédéon-de-Beauce," said Francoeur. "Just down the road."

What followed was a rapid exchange between the men that was almost unintelligible to Beauvoir. Finally Frère Raymond turned to Beauvoir.

"This man's grandfather and my great-uncle rebuilt the church in Saint-Ephrem after the fire."

Frère Raymond motioned the men into the room. It too was huge. Wide and long, running the balance of the corridor. The monk gave them a tour, explaining the geothermal system, the ventilation system, the hot water system, the filtration system. The septic system. All the systems.

Beauvoir tried to remain focused, in case anything useful was said, but eventually his mind grew numb. At the end of the tour Frère Raymond walked to a cabinet and brought from it a bottle and three glasses.

"This calls for a celebration," he said. "It's not often I meet a neighbor. A friend of mine is a Benedictine and sends me this." Frère Raymond handed Beauvoir the dusty bottle. "Like a slug?"

Beauvoir examined the bottle. It was B&B. Brandy and Bénédictine. Not made, fortunately, from fermented monks, though he suspected there were enough of those. But by the Benedictines themselves, from a long-secret recipe.

The three men pulled chairs around a drafting table and sat.

Frère Raymond poured. *"Santé,"* he said, tipping the deep amber liquid toward his rare guests.

"Santé," Beauvoir said and brought it to his lips. He could smell it, rich and full, sweet but also medicinal. His eyes burned from the strength of it. The B&B seared his throat as he swallowed, then the alcohol

exploded into his gut, and brought tears to his eyes.

And it was good.

"So, *mon frère*," Superintendent Francoeur cleared his throat, then began again. His accent was back to where Beauvoir recognized it, as though the B&B had burned the ancient dialect away. "Inspector Beauvoir here has some questions."

Beauvoir shot him an annoyed look. It was a small dig. As though he needed Francoeur to pave the way. But Beauvoir simply smiled and thanked the Superintendent. Then he unfurled the scroll and watched Frère Raymond for a reaction. But there was none, beyond the polite nodding as the monk stood and bent over the old plan of the monastery.

"Have you seen this before?" asked Beauvoir.

"Many times." He looked into Beauvoir's face. "I consider this an old friend." His lean hand hovered over the vellum. "Practically memorized it when we were looking to put in the geothermal." He turned back to the plan, an affectionate look on his face. "It's beautiful."

"But is it accurate?"

"Well, not these bits." The monk pointed to the gardens. "But the rest is surprisingly precise."

Frère Raymond sat back down and launched into an explanation of how the first monks, back in the mid-1600s, would have built the monastery. How they did measurements. How they transported rocks. How they dug.

"It would've taken them years and years," said Raymond, warming to his topic. "Decades. Just to dig the basement. Imagine that."

Beauvoir found himself fascinated. It was indeed a feat of mammoth proportions. These men had fled the Inquisition to come here. Where they were met by a climate so savage it could kill within days. They were met by bears and wolves and all sorts of strange, feral beasts. By black flies so ravenous they'd strip a newborn moose. By deer flies so persistent they'd drive a saint to insanity.

How horrible was the Inquisition, that this was better?

And instead of building some modest wooden shelter, they'd built this.

It beggared belief.

Who had that sort of discipline? That sort of patience? Monks, that was who. But maybe, with Frère Raymond, it was also bred into him. Like Beauvoir's grandmother's patience. With blight, and drought, and hail, and floods. With unkindness. With encroaching towns, and clever new neighbors.

Beauvoir looked over at Superintendent Francoeur, a son of the same soil as the monk, and as Beauvoir's grandparents.

What patient plan was he working on, even now? Was it years in the making? Was he constructing it stone by stone? And what part of that plan had brought the Superintendent here?

Beauvoir knew he himself would have to be patient if he was to find out, though he was not exactly overflowing with that quality.

Frère Raymond droned on. And on.

After a while Beauvoir lost interest. Frère Raymond had the rare gift of turning a mesmerizing story into tedium. It was a sort of alchemy. Another transmutation.

Finally, as silence penetrated Beauvoir's now numb skull, he emerged from his reverie.

"Then," Beauvoir grasped at the last relevant thing he remembered, "the plan is accurate?"

"It's accurate enough so that I didn't need to draw another plan when the new system was going in. The thing with geothermal —"

"Yes, I know. *Merci.*" Beauvoir was damned if he was going to be provoked by one man and bored to death by another. "What I want to know is, is it possible there's a room hidden somewhere in the abbey —"

He was interrupted by a snort. "You don't believe that old wives' tale, do you?" asked Frère Raymond.

"It's an old monks' tale. One you've obviously heard."

"As I've heard of Atlantis and Santa Claus and unicorns. But I don't expect to find them in the abbey."

"But you do expect to find God," said Beauvoir.

Far from looking insulted, Frère Raymond smiled. "Believe me, Inspector, even you will find God here before you'll find any hidden room. Or a treasure. You think we could put in a geothermal system and not have found a hidden room? You think we could put in the solar panels, electricity, running water and plumbing, and not have found it?"

"No," said Jean-Guy. "I don't think that's possible. I think it would have been found."

The meaning in his voice wasn't lost on

the monk, but instead of being defensive he simply smiled.

"Listen, my son," said Frère Raymond, speaking slowly. Beauvoir was getting very tired of being spoken to as though he was their son. A child. "That was just a story the old monks told each other to pass the time on long winter nights. It was a bit of fun. Nothing more. There's no hidden room. No treasure."

Frère Raymond leaned forward, his hands together in front of him, his elbows resting on his thin knees. "What're you really looking for?"

"The man who killed your prior."

"Well, you won't find him down here."

There was a moment as the two men looked at each other, and the cool atmosphere crackled.

"I wonder if we'll find the murder weapon down here then," said Beauvoir.

"A rock?"

"Why do you think it was a rock?"

"Because that's what you told us. We all understood Frère Mathieu was killed by a rock to the head."

"Well, the coroner's report says the weapon was more likely a length of pipe, or something like it. Do you have any?"

Frère Raymond got up and led him to a

427

door. He switched on a light and they saw a room no larger than the monks' cells. There was shelving on the walls, and everything was neatly arranged. Boards, nails, screws, hammers, old pieces of broken wrought iron, all the miscellanies of any household, though considerably less than most.

And leaning up in the corner were lengths of piping. Beauvoir moved over there, but after a moment he turned back to Frère Raymond.

"Is this all you have?" Beauvoir asked.

"We try to reuse everything. That's it."

The Sûreté officer turned back to the corner. There were pipes there, all right, but none shorter than five feet, most considerably longer. The killer might have used one to pole vault over the wall, but not to actually brain the prior.

"Where could someone find another piece of pipe?" Beauvoir asked as they left the room and closed the door.

"I don't know. It's not the sort of thing we leave lying around."

Beauvoir nodded. He could see that. The basement was pristine. And he knew if there was a length of pipe to be found, Frère Raymond would know about it.

He was the abbot down here. The master of this underworld. And while the abbey above seemed filled with incense and mystery, music and odd, dancing light, down here everything felt organized and clean. And constant. The temperature, the light, all unchanging.

Beauvoir liked it. There was no creativity, nothing beautiful in this netherworld. But neither was there chaos.

"The abbot says he came down yesterday morning, after Lauds, but that you weren't here."

"After Lauds I work in the garden. The abbot knows that." Frère Raymond's voice was light and friendly.

"Which garden?"

"The vegetable garden. I saw you there this morning." He turned to Superintendent Francoeur. "And I saw you arrive. Very dramatic."

"You were there?" asked Beauvoir. "In the garden?"

Frère Raymond nodded. "Apparently all monks look alike."

"Did anyone see you?" Beauvoir asked.

"In the garden? Well, I didn't talk to anyone, but I wasn't exactly invisible."

"So it's possible you weren't there?"

"No, it's not possible. It's possible I wasn't seen, but I was there. What is possible is that the abbot wasn't here. There was no one at all to see him down here."

"He says he came to look at the geothermal system. Does that sound likely?"

"It does not."

"Why not?"

"The abbot knows nothing about all this."
Frère Raymond waved to the mechanics.
"And when I try to explain he loses interest."

"Then you think he wasn't here yesterday,
after your prayers?"

"Yes."

"Where do you think he was?"

The monk stood silent. They're like rocks,
thought Beauvoir. Big black rocks. Like
rocks, their natural state was to be silent.
And still. Speaking was unnatural to them.

Beauvoir knew of only one way to break a
rock.

"You think he was in the garden, don't
you?" said Beauvoir. His voice no longer
quite so friendly.

Still the monk stared.

"Not the vegetable garden, of course,"
Beauvoir continued, taking a step closer to
Frère Raymond, "but his own garden. The
abbot's private garden."

Frère Raymond made no sound. Made no
movement. Did not recoil as Beauvoir advanced.

"You think the abbot wasn't alone in his garden."

Beauvoir's voice was rising. Filling the cavern. Bouncing off the walls. In his peripheral vision he could see the Superintendent, and thought he heard a cough. A clearing of his throat. No doubt to stop this audacious and inappropriate agent.

To correct him. To get Beauvoir to back down, back away, back off this *religieux.*

But Beauvoir would not. Frère Raymond, for all his gentleness, all his passion for mechanical things, for all he sounded like Beauvoir's grandfather, was hiding something. In a convenient silence.

"You think the prior was there as well."

Beauvoir's words were clipped, hard. Like pelting the stone monk with pebbles. The words bounced off Frère Raymond, but they were having an effect. Beauvoir took another step forward. He was close enough now to see alarm in Frère Raymond's eyes.

"You've all but led us to this conclusion," said Beauvoir. "Have the guts to go all the way. To say what you really think."

The only way to break a stone, Beauvoir knew, was to pound it. And keep pounding.

"Or do you just insinuate, hint, gossip?" sneered Beauvoir. "And expect braver men to do your dirty work. You're willing to throw the abbot to the wolves, you just don't want it on your conscience. Instead you imply, suggest. You all but wink at us. But you don't have the guts to stand up and say what you really believe. Fucking hypocrite."

Frère Raymond took a step back. The pebbles had turned to stones. And Beauvoir was making direct hits.

"What a pathetic excuse for a man you are," Beauvoir continued. "Look at you. You pray and sprinkle holy water and light incense and pretend to believe in God. But you only stand up to run away. Just like the old monks ran away. They came to Québec, to hide, and you've come down here. Hiding in your basement. Organizing things, cleaning, tidying. Explaining. While up above the real work is happening. The messy work of finding God. The messy fucking work of finding a murderer."

Beauvoir was so close to Frère Raymond he could smell the brandy and Bénédictine on his breath.

"You think you know who did it? Well, tell us. Say the words." Beauvoir's voice was rising until he was shouting into Frère Raymond's face. "Say the words."

Now Frère Raymond looked frightened.

"You don't understand," he stammered.

"I've said too much."

"You haven't even begun. What do you know?"

"We're supposed to be loyal to our abbots," Raymond said, sliding away from Beauvoir. He turned to look at Francoeur, his voice pleading. "When we join a monastery, our loyalty isn't to Rome or even to the local archbishop or bishop. It's to the abbot. It's part of our vows, our devotion."

"Look at me," Beauvoir demanded. "Don't look at him. It's me you're answering to now."

Frère Raymond really did look frightened, and Beauvoir wondered if this monk actually believed in God. And he wondered if Frère Raymond believed God would strike him dead for speaking. And he wondered who could be loyal to a God like that.

"I never thought it would go this far," Frère Raymond whispered. "Who could've known?"

He was pleading with Beauvoir now. But for what? Understanding? Forgiveness.

He'd get neither from Beauvoir. The Inspector wanted only one thing. To solve the murder and get home, as Gamache said. Just get the fuck out of there. And away from Francoeur, who'd sat cross-legged and remotely interested throughout.

"What did you think would happen?" Beauvoir pushed.

"I thought the prior would win."

Frère Raymond had finally cracked. And now the words tumbled out.

"I thought after some debate the abbot would come to his senses. He'd finally see that doing another recording was the right thing to do. Even without the issue of the foundations." Frère Raymond sunk to his seat and looked stunned. "We'd already done one recording, you see. How much harm could another do? And it would save the monastery. It would save Saint-Gilbert. How could that possibly be wrong?"

He searched Beauvoir's eyes, as though expecting to find an answer there.

There was none.

In fact, Beauvoir was unexpectedly faced with a new mystery. When Frère Raymond had cracked more than just words had come out. A whole new voice had rushed out of the monk. One without the ancient dialect.

The thick accent was gone.

He spoke now in the cultured French of scholars and diplomats. The *lingua franca.*

Was he finally speaking the truth? Beauvoir wondered. Did Frère Raymond want to make sure, after all this struggle, he wasn't misunderstood? That Beauvoir would grasp each and every painful word?

But far from having the impression Frère Raymond had dropped the act, Beauvoir suspected the monk had just assumed one. This was the voice his grandmother had used when she spoke to the new neighbors. And the notary. And the priests.

It was not her real voice. That she kept for people she trusted.

"When did you decide to defy your abbot?" Beauvoir asked.

Frère Raymond hesitated. "I don't understand."

"Of course you do. When did you realize he wasn't going to change his mind and agree to the recordings?"

"I didn't know that."

"But you were afraid that's what he'd announce. In the Chapter House. That there'd be no second recording. And once the abbot pronounced, it was game over."

"I'm not his confidant," said Raymond. "I didn't know what the abbot was going to do."

"But you couldn't risk it," Beauvoir pushed. "You'd promised the abbot not to tell anyone else about the foundations, but you decided to break that promise. To defy the abbot."

"I didn't."

435

"Of course you did. You hated the abbot. And you love the abbey. You know it better than anyone, don't you? You know every stone, every inch, every chip. And every crack. You could save Saint-Gilbert. But you needed help. The abbot was a fool. Praying for a miracle that had already happened. You'd been given the means to repair the foundation. Your voices. The recordings. But the abbot wasn't listening. So you switched your loyalty to the prior. To the one man who might save Saint-Gilbert."

"No," Frère Raymond insisted.

"You told the prior."

"No."

"How many times are you going to deny it, *mon frère?*" Beauvoir growled.

"I never told the prior."

The monk was almost weeping now, and finally Beauvoir stepped back. He glanced at Superintendent Francoeur, who was looking grave. Then he looked back at Frère Raymond.

"You told the prior, hoping to save Saint-Gilbert, but instead you sent him to his death." Beauvoir's voice was matter-of-fact. "And now you hide down here and pretend that isn't true."

Beauvoir turned and picked up the old plans.

"Tell me what you believe happened in that garden, Frère Raymond."

The monk's lips were moving but no sound came out.

"Tell me."

He stared at the monk, whose eyes were now closed.

"Speak," demanded Beauvoir. Then he heard a soft murmur.

"Hail Mary, full of grace . . ."

Frère Raymond was praying. But for what? Beauvoir wondered. For the prior to rise up? For the cracks to close?

The monk's eyes opened and he looked at the Inspector with such gentleness, Beauvoir almost had to steady himself against the wall. They were his grandmother's eyes. Patient and kindly. And forgiving.

Beauvoir saw then that Frère Raymond was praying for him.

Armand Gamache slowly closed the last dossier. He'd read it twice, pausing each time over one phrase in the coroner's report.

The victim, Frère Mathieu, had not died immediately.

Of course, they already knew that. They could see that he'd crawled away, until there was no more "away" left. And there the dying man had curled into a ball. The very shape his mother had carried. Had comforted, when he'd entered this world, naked and crying.

And yesterday, Mathieu had curled up again, to leave this world.

Yes, it had been clear to Gamache and all the other investigators, and probably the abbot and the monks who'd prayed over the body, that Frère Mathieu had taken some time to die.

But they didn't know how long.

Until now.

Chief Inspector Gamache got up and, taking the dossier with him, he left the prior's office.

"Inspector Beauvoir," Superintendent Francoeur's voice was raised, "I need to speak with you."

Beauvoir took another few steps along the basement corridor, then turned around.

"What the fuck did you expect me to do?" he demanded. "Just let him lie? This is a murder investigation. If you don't like how messy it gets, then get out of the way."

"Oh, I can cope with the mess," said Francoeur, his voice hard but steady. "I just didn't expect you to handle it in quite that way."

"Is that right?" said Beauvoir, his voice

filled with contempt. No need to hide it now. "And how'd you expect me to handle it?"

"Like a man without balls."

This so surprised Beauvoir he didn't know what to say. Instead he stared as Francoeur walked past him and up the stairs.

"What the fuck is that supposed to mean?"

Francoeur stopped, his back to Beauvoir. Then he turned. His face was serious as he examined the man in front of him.

"You don't want to know."

"Tell me."

Francoeur smiled, shook his head, and continued up the stairs. After a moment Beauvoir ran after him, taking the worn stone steps two at a time until he'd caught up.

Francoeur opened the door just as Beauvoir arrived. They heard the sound of hard shoes on the stone floor of the Blessed Chapel, and saw Chief Inspector Gamache walking with purpose toward the corridor leading to the abbot's office and garden.

Both men, as though by mutual consent, stayed quiet until the door into the hallway had closed and the sound of steps vanished.

"Tell me," Beauvoir demanded.

"You're supposed to be a trained investigator with the Sûreté du Québec. You figure it out."

"Supposed to be?" Beauvoir called to the retreating back. "Supposed to be?"

The words echoed and grew and bounced back to Beauvoir without apparently ever reaching Francoeur.

Twenty-Three

"There you are, Chief Inspector."

Frère Simon came around the desk, his hand out.

Gamache took it and smiled. What a difference a chicken could make.

Doo-dah, doo-dah.

Gamache sighed to himself. Of all the literally divine music here, he had to have "Camptown Races" sung by a rooster stuck in his head.

"I was about to come looking for you," Simon continued. "I have your paper."

Frère Simon handed the yellowed page to the Chief Inspector and smiled. A smile would never, on that face, look completely at home. But it camped comfortably there for an instant.

Once again, in repose, the abbot's secretary slipped back to severe.

"Merci," said Gamache. "You were able to make a copy, obviously. Have you started

transcribing the neumes into musical notes?"

"Not yet. I was planning on working at it this afternoon. I might ask some of the other brothers for help, if that's all right with you."

"*Absolument,*" agreed Gamache. "The sooner the better."

Once again Frère Simon grinned. "I think your idea of time and ours is slightly different. We deal with millennia here, but I'll try to make it quicker than that."

"Believe me, *mon frère,* you don't want us hanging around for that long. Do you mind?" Gamache indicated a comfortable chair and the abbot's secretary nodded.

The two men sat facing each other.

"As you worked on this," Gamache raised the page slightly, "did you translate any of the Latin?"

Frère Simon looked uneasy. "I'm not exactly fluent, and I suspect whoever wrote it wasn't either."

"Why do you say that?"

"Because what little I could understand is ridiculous."

He went to the desk and returned with a notebook.

"I jotted down some thoughts as I went. Even if we manage to figure out the neumes and turn them into notes, I don't think we can possibly sing the words."

"So it's not a known hymn or chant or even a prayer?" Gamache glanced at the original.

"Not unless there was a prophet or apostle in need of medication." Frère Simon consulted his notebook. "The first phrase, there," Simon pointed to the top of the chant, "now I may be wrong but I translate it as saying, *I can't hear you. I have a banana in my ear.*"

He said it so solemnly Gamache had to laugh. When he tried to suppress it, it bubbled up again. He looked down at the page, to cover up his amusement.

"What else does it say?" he asked, his voice slightly squeaky from the effort of keeping the laughter in.

"This isn't funny, Chief Inspector."

"No, of course not. It's sacrilege." But a little snort betrayed him and when he dared look at the monk again, he was surprised to see on Frère Simon's face a slender grin.

"Were you able to understand anything else?" asked Gamache, regaining control of himself after a mighty effort.

Frère Simon sighed and leaned forward, pointing to a line further down the page. "This you probably know."

Dies irae.

Gamache nodded. He no longer felt like laughing and all the *doo-dah*s had gone away. "Yes, I had noticed that. Day of wrath. It's the one Latin phrase I recognize in this. The abbot and I talked about it."

"And what did he say?"

"He also thought the words were nonsense. He seemed as perplexed as you."

"Did he have a theory?"

"No particular one. But he found it odd, as do I, that while there is clearly in here a *dies irae,* a day of wrath, there's no accompanying *dies illa.*"

"Day of mourning. Yes, that struck me too. Even more strongly than the banana."

Gamache smiled again, but only briefly. "What do you think it means?"

"I think whoever wrote this did it as a joke," said Frère Simon. "He just tossed all sorts of Latin into it."

"But why not use more phrases or words from chants? Why is 'day of wrath' the only phrase from a prayer?"

Frère Simon shrugged. "I wish I knew. Maybe he was angry. Maybe that's what this is. A mockery. He wants to show his rage, and actually declares it. *Dies irae.* And then throws in all sorts of ridiculous Latin words and phrases, so that it looks like a chant, looks like something we'd sing to God."

"But is actually an insult," said Gamache, and Frère Simon nodded.

"Who here might be able to help with the translation?"

Frère Simon thought about that. "The only one who comes to mind is Frère Luc."

"The porter?"

"He's not long out of the seminary, so he's closer to having studied Latin than the rest of us. And he's just pompous enough to enjoy having us know it."

"You don't like him?"

The question seemed to surprise Frère Simon.

"Like him?" It was as though he'd never considered it before, and Gamache realized, a bit surprised himself, that Frère Simon probably hadn't. "It's not a matter of like or dislike here. It's a matter of accepting. Like can turn to dislike fairly easily in a closed environment. We learn here not to even think in those terms, but to accept as God's will that the monks who are here are meant to be. If it's good enough for God, it's good enough for us."

"But you just called him pompous."

"And he is. And he probably calls me morose, and I am. We all have flaws we're working on. Denying them doesn't help."

Gamache again held up the page. "Is it

possible Frère Luc wrote this?"

"I doubt it. Frère Luc doesn't like to make mistakes, or to be wrong. If he wrote a hymn in Latin it would be perfect."

"And might not have a lot of humor," said Gamache.

Frère Simon smiled a little. "Unlike the hilarity of the rest of us."

Gamache recognized the sarcasm, but thought Simon was wrong. The monks he'd met here seemed to have a good sense of humor and to be able to laugh at themselves and their world. It was quiet, and gentle, and fairly well hidden behind a solemn visage, but it was there.

Gamache studied the paper in his hand. He agreed with Simon, Frère Luc could not possibly have written this. But one of them had.

More than ever, Chief Inspector Gamache was convinced this slim paper in his hand was the key to the killing.

And Gamache knew he'd figure it out, if it took millennia.

"The neumes," he began, trying to work out what he wanted from Frère Simon. "You say you haven't started transcribing them into notes, but can you still read them?"

"Oh, yes. They're confused." Frère Simon

446

picked up his own copy. "No, that's the wrong word. They're complex. Most neumes for chants look confusing but once you know what you're looking at, they're really quite simple. That was the point of them. Simple directions for plainchants."

"But these aren't simple," said Gamache.

"Far from it."

"Can you give me an idea what it sounds like?"

Frère Simon looked up from the page, his face extremely stern, severe even. But Gamache didn't back down. The two men stared at each other for a moment until Simon finally broke contact and looked back down at the page.

After a minute or so of silence, Gamache heard a sound. It seemed quite far off, and he wondered if a plane was approaching again. It was a haunting sort of hum.

Then he realized it wasn't coming from outside at all. But inside.

The sound was coming from Frère Simon.

What started as a drone, a hum, a note hanging in the air, turned into something else. With a swoop, the note descended and seemed to play in the lower registers before leaping back up. Not a jagged leap, but a soft soar.

It seemed to sweep into Gamache's chest

and surround his heart, then take it along for the ride. Higher and higher. But never precipitous, never dangerous. Never did Gamache feel the music, or his heart, were about to come crashing down.

There was a certainty, a confidence. A lilting joy.

Words had replaced the hum, and now Frère Simon was singing. Gamache, of course, couldn't understand the Latin, and yet, he felt he understood completely.

Frère Simon's clear, calm, rich tenor held the notes, the nonsensical words, like a lover. There was no judgment there, just acceptance, in the voice and in the music.

And then, the final note descended to the earth. Softly, gently. A tender landing.

And the voice stopped. But the music stayed with Gamache. More a feeling than a memory. He wanted that feeling back. That levity. Wanted to ask Frère Simon to please keep going, to never stop.

The Chief realized there was no sign of "Camptown Races." It had been replaced by this brief, but glorious, burst of song.

Even Frère Simon seemed surprised by what he'd just produced.

Gamache knew he'd be humming this beautiful tune for a long time to come. The *doo-dah*s had been replaced with *I can't hear you. I have a banana in my ear.*

Beauvoir tossed a rock into the water, as far from the shore as he could heave it.

No skipping of flat stones. He chose another heavy rock, hefted it in his hand, then cocked his arm back and threw.

The rock arched away and landed in the water with a plop.

Beauvoir stood on the shore, strewn with water-rounded pebbles and stones and clamshells, and looked into the clear, clean lake. The waves he'd created washed ashore, breaking over the pebbles in tiny white caps. Like a miniature world, inundated by an unexpected tidal wave. Of Beauvoir's making.

After his encounter with Francoeur he needed fresh air.

Frère Bernard, the wild blueberry monk, had mentioned a path. Beauvoir found it and started walking, though he didn't take in much of his surroundings. Instead he was squirreling away in his head. Going over the few words he'd had with Francoeur.

And what he should have said. Could have said. The clever, cutting remarks he might have made.

But after a few minutes his furious think-

449

ing and his furious pace slowed, and he realized this path hugged the coastline. The shore here was strewn with boulders. And blueberry bushes.

He slowed to a normal walk, then a stroll, then finally he stopped on a small, stony peninsula that jutted into the remote lake. Huge birds swooped and glided overhead, never seeming to flap their wings.

Beauvoir removed his shoes and socks, rolled up his pant legs and put his big toe into the lake. Then quickly brought it out again. It was so cold it scalded. He tried again, until, millimeter by millimeter, both his feet were in the freezing water. They'd grown used to it. It constantly amazed him what you could get used to. Especially if you went numb.

He sat quietly for a minute, picking and eating tiny wild blueberries from a nearby bush, and trying not to think.

And when he did think, what came to mind was Annie. He took out his Black-Berry. There was a message from her. He read it, smiling.

It talked about her day at the law office. A funny little story about an Internet mix-up. Trivial, but Beauvoir read every word twice. Imagining her bafflement, the crossed communications, the happy resolution. She told him how much she missed him. And loved him.

Then he wrote back, describing where he was. Telling her they were making progress. He hesitated before hitting send, knowing while he hadn't exactly lied, neither had he told her the complete truth. Of how he was feeling. His confusion, his anger. It seemed both directed at Francoeur and undirected. He was mad at Frère Raymond, mad at the monks, mad at being in the monastery instead of with Annie. Mad at the silence, broken by interminable masses.

Mad at himself for letting Francoeur get under his skin.

Mostly he was mad at Superintendent Francoeur.

But he told Annie none of that. Instead, he ended his message with a smiley face and hit send.

Wiping his feet off with his sweater, he put his socks and shoes back on.

He should be heading back. But instead, he picked up another stone and threw it, watching the rings disturb the calm waters.

"The funny thing is," said Frère Simon, after he'd stopped singing. "The words actually fit."

"I thought you said they were ridiculous.

451

Nonsense," said Gamache.

"They are. What I mean is, they fit the meter of the music. Like lyrics, they have to fit with the rhythm."

"And these do?" Gamache looked back down at the yellowed page, though he didn't know what he expected. That some magic would have worked, and he'd suddenly understand? But he understood nothing. Not the words, not the neumes.

"I think whoever wrote this knew music," said Frère Simon. "But didn't know how to write lyrics."

"Like Lerner and Loewe" said Gamache.

"Simon and Garfunkel," said Frère Simon.

"Gilbert and Sullivan," said Gamache, smiling.

Simon actually laughed. "I heard they despised each other. Wouldn't be in the same room."

"So," said Gamache, working his way through his thoughts, "the music is beautiful, we agree on that. And the words are ridiculous. We agree on that."

Frère Simon nodded.

"You're thinking there was a writing team involved. Not one monk but two?"

"One wrote the music," said Simon, "and the other wrote the words."

They looked down at the papers in their hands. Then looked up into each other's eyes.

"But that doesn't explain why the words are so stupid," said Frère Simon.

"Unless whoever wrote the neumes didn't understand the Latin. Maybe he assumed his partner wrote lyrics as beautiful as the music deserved."

"And when he found out what the words really meant . . ." said Frère Simon.

"*Oui,*" said Gamache. "It led to murder."

"Do people really kill over something like this?" Simon asked.

"The Church castrated men to keep them sopranos," Gamache reminded the monk. "Emotions run high when it comes to sacred music. It might not be such a big step from maiming to killing."

Frère Simon thrust out his lower lip, thinking. It made him look suddenly quite young. A boy, working on a puzzle.

"The prior," said Gamache. "Which is he likely to have written? The words or the music?"

"The music, without a doubt. He was a world authority on neumes and Gregorian chants."

"But could he write original music using neumes?" asked the Chief.

"He certainly knew his neumes, so I suppose it's possible."

"Something's bothering you," said Gamache.

"It just seems unlikely, that's all. Frère Mathieu loved Gregorian chants. He didn't just like them, it was a form of adoration for him. A great religious passion."

Gamache understood what the monk was saying. If he adored the plainchants so much, had made them his life's work, why would he suddenly diverge from them, and create what the Chief held in his hands?

"Unless . . ." said Frère Simon.

"Unless he didn't write this," said Gamache, lifting the page slightly. "But found it in someone else's possession and confronted him. In the one place they wouldn't be seen."

Which brought the Chief Inspector to his next question. "When you found the prior, was he still alive?"

TWENTY-FOUR

The door to the prior's office was closed.

The last time Beauvoir had been in this position he'd walked in on what was clearly an argument between Gamache and Francoeur.

He leaned in and listened.

The wood was thick and dense. A hard wood, making it hard to hear. But he could just make out the Chief. The words were muffled, but he recognized the voice.

Beauvoir stood back, wondering what to do. That didn't take long. If the Chief was again arguing with that fuck-head Francoeur, Beauvoir wasn't going to let him fight it out alone.

He rapped twice and opened the door.

The sound inside abruptly stopped.

Beauvoir looked around. There was no Gamache.

Superintendent Francoeur sat behind the desk. Alone.

"What is it?" the Superintendent de-manded.

It was one of the few times Beauvoir had seen Francoeur rattled. Then Beauvoir noticed the computer. The laptop had been facing in the other direction, toward the visitor's chair. Now it was turned around, facing Francoeur. He appeared to have been using it when Beauvoir interrupted him.

Was he downloading something? Beauvoir couldn't see how. The satellite connection hadn't worked since they arrived. Unless Francoeur had gotten it to work, but Beau-voir doubted it. He wasn't that smart.

Francoeur had the guilty look of a teen-ager interrupted by Mom.

"Well?" The Superintendent glared at Beauvoir.

"I heard voices," he said and immediately regretted it.

Francoeur gave him a dismissive look and picking up a dossier he started to read. Ignoring Beauvoir completely. As though a hole in the atmosphere had just walked in. Nothing. No one. Beauvoir was empty air as far as the Superintendent was concerned.

"What did you mean earlier?" Beauvoir shut the door hard and Francoeur looked up.

Jean-Guy hadn't meant to ask, had promised himself not to. And had Gamache been there he certainly would never have asked. But the Chief wasn't there, and Francoeur was, and the question shot out, like lightning from a storm cloud.

Francoeur ignored him.

"Tell me," Beauvoir kicked the chair, then grabbed it from behind and leaned over it, toward the Superintendent.

"Or what?" asked Francoeur. He was amused, not afraid at all, and Beauvoir felt his cheeks burning. His knuckles turned white where he gripped the wooden chair.

"You going to beat me up?" the Superintendent asked. "Threaten me? That's what you do, isn't it? You're Gamache's dog." Now Francoeur put the dossier down and leaned toward Beauvoir. "You want to know what I meant when I said I thought you had no balls? That's what I meant. It's what all your colleagues say, Jean-Guy. Is it true?"

"What the fuck are you talking about?"

"That your only use is as Armand Gamache's puppy. They call you his bitch, because while you growl and sometimes bite, they don't think you actually have balls."

Francoeur looked at Beauvoir as if he was something soft and smelly real men wiped from the bottom of their shoes. The chair squeaked as the Superintendent leaned back, comfortably. His suit jacket opened and Beauvoir saw his gun there.

Through the howl of rage in his head Beauvoir had enough presence of mind to wonder why the Chief Superintendent, a bureaucrat, wore a gun.

And why he had brought it into the abbey.

Not even Gamache wore a gun, though Beauvoir did. And now he was glad.

"That's what I meant earlier," said Francoeur. "I went with you when you interviewed that monk not because you invited me, but because I was curious. How would this man who was the laughingstock of the Sûreté handle an interrogation? But you surprised me. I was actually impressed."

And Beauvoir surprised himself. Some small part of him was relieved to hear that. But it was deeply buried under the wrath, the rage, the near apocalyptic fury of the insult.

He opened his mouth but only stuttering came out. No words formed. Just empty air.

"You can't tell me you didn't know." Francoeur actually looked surprised. "Come on, man, only an idiot could miss that. You strut through headquarters, half a pace behind your master, practically sniveling, and you think the other agents and inspectors admire you? They admire the Chief Inspector, and fear him a little. If he could cut your balls off, maybe he could do it to them too. Look, no one blames you. You were this little agent in a little Sûreté outpost. You were about to be fired because no one wanted to work with you, and Gamache hired you. Right?"

Beauvoir stared at Francoeur, dumbfounded.

"Right," Francoeur leaned forward. "And why do you think he did that? Why do you think he's surrounded himself with agents no one else wanted? He just promoted Isabelle Lacoste to inspector. Your rank —" Francoeur gave Beauvoir a sharp look, "— I'd watch that if I were you. Not good when you're supposed to be the second in command but she's the one left at headquarters, in charge. What was I saying? *Oui*, the Chief Inspector's hiring practices. Have you looked around the homicide department? He's created a division of losers. He's taken the dregs. Why?"

Now Beauvoir's anger finally erupted. He lifted the chair and brought it down so hard the two back legs broke off. But he didn't care. He only had eyes for the man in front of him. He had Superintendent Francoeur in his sights.

"Losers?" Beauvoir rasped. "The Chief

Inspector surrounds himself with agents who think for themselves, who can act on their own. The rest of you shits are afraid of us. You toss us out, demote us, treat us like crap until we quit. And why?"

He was actually, literally, spitting his words across the desk.

"Because you're threatened by us. We won't play your corrupt little games. Chief Inspector Gamache picked up your garbage and gave us a chance. He believed in us when no one else did. And you, you fuck-head, you think I'm going to believe any of your crap? Let your weasels laugh at me. That's the biggest compliment I can think of. We have the best arrest record of the force. That's what matters. And if you and your assholes think that's laughable, then laugh."

"The best arrest record?" Francoeur was on his feet now. His voice glacial. "Like the Brulé case? Your Chief arrested him. Cost the province a fortune to try him, for murder. He was even convicted, the poor shit, and what happens? It turns out he didn't kill that guy. And what did your Gamache do? Did he go and clean up his own mess? No. He sent you to find the real murderer. And you did. That's when I began to think you might not be the complete waste of space you appear to be."

Francoeur gathered up some papers but paused at the desk. "You're wondering why I came here, aren't you?"

Beauvoir said nothing.

"Of course you are. Gamache is too. He even asked. I didn't tell him the truth, but I'll tell you. I had to catch him and you away from headquarters. Away from where he has some influence. So I could talk to you. I didn't need to come all this way to bring you some reports. I'm the Chief Superintendent, for chrissake. A homicide agent could've done that. But I saw the chance and I took it. I came here to save you. From him."

"You're insane."

"Think about what I said. Put it together. You're smarter than that. Think. And while you're at it, you might wonder why he promoted Isabelle Lacoste to inspector."

"Because she's a fine investigator. She earned it."

Francoeur gave him that look again, as though Beauvoir was spectacularly stupid. Then he walked to the door.

"What?" demanded Beauvoir. "What're you trying to say?"

"I've said far too much already, Inspector Beauvoir. Still, it's out there now." He gave

461

Beauvoir an appraising look. "You're actually a very good investigator. Use those skills. And feel free to tell Gamache exactly what I've just said. It's about time he realized someone was on to him."

The door closed and Beauvoir was alone with his anger. And the laptop.

Frère Simon gaped at Gamache.

"Do you think the prior was still alive when I found him?"

"I think it's possible. I think you knew he was dying and instead of going to get help, which would almost certainly mean he'd die alone, you stayed with him for the final moments. To comfort him. Give him last rites. It was an act of kindness. Of compassion."

"Then why wouldn't I say anything? The rest of the congregation would've been relieved to hear that even in this terrible situation, at least the prior was given last rites." He looked closely at the Chief Inspector. "You think I'd keep that quiet? Why?"

"Now, that was the question," Gamache crossed his legs and got comfortable, to Frère Simon's obvious discomfort. The Chief was prepared for a long visit.

"I haven't had all that long to think about it," the Chief admitted. "I only just read in the autopsy report that the coroner believes Frère Mathieu might have lived up to half an hour after the fatal blow."

"Could have doesn't mean he did."

"Absolutely true. But suppose he did? He was strong enough to crawl to the wall. Maybe he fought off death to the very last second. Grabbed every moment of life available. Does that sound like something the prior would do?"

"I didn't think the hour and time of our death was our choice," said Frère Simon, and Gamache smiled. "If it was," the monk continued, "I suspect the prior would've chosen not to die at all."

"I think Dom Clément would still be walking these familiar halls, if we really had a choice," agreed Gamache. "I'm not saying force of will can fight off a clearly lethal blow. But I am saying, from personal experience, a strong will can hold off death, by moments, sometimes minutes. And sometimes, in my job, those moments and minutes are crucial."

"Why?"

"Because it's that golden time, between this world and whatever you believe is the next. When the person knows they're dying. And if they've been murdered, what do they do?"

Frère Simon said nothing.

"They tell us who killed them, if at all possible."

The monk's cheeks reddened and his eyes narrowed slightly. "You think Frère Mathieu told me who killed him? And I've said nothing?"

Now it was Gamache's turn to be silent. He examined the monk. Taking in the full, round face. Not fat, but cheeks like chipmunks'. The shaved head. The short, pug nose. The near permanent scowl of disapproval. And hazel eyes, like the bark of a tree. Mottled. And rough. And unyielding.

And yet, the voice of an archangel. Not simply a member of the celestial choir, but one of the Chosen. A favorite of God. Gifted beyond all others.

Except the other men in this monastery. Two dozen of them.

Was this place, Saint-Gilbert-Entre-les-Loups, a golden moment? Between two worlds. It felt like it. Out of time, and place. A netherworld. Between the vibrant life of Québec. The bistros and brasseries, the festivals. The hardworking farmers and brilliant academics.

Between the mortal world, and Heaven. Or Hell. There was here.

Where quiet was king. And calm reigned.

And the only sounds were the birds in the trees and plainchant.

And where, a day ago, a monk was killed.

Did the prior, at the very end, his back to the wall, break his vow of silence?

Jean-Guy Beauvoir propped the broken chair against the door into the prior's office.

It wouldn't stop anyone, but it would slow them down just enough. And it would certainly give Beauvoir warning.

Then he walked around the desk and sat in the chair Francoeur had just left. It was still warm from the Superintendent. The thought made Beauvoir slightly queasy, but he ignored it and pulled the laptop toward him.

It too was warm. Francoeur had been on it, but had closed it down when Beauvoir entered.

After he'd rebooted the laptop, Beauvoir tried to connect to the Internet.

It wouldn't. There was still no satellite hookup.

So what was the Superintendent doing? And why had he shut it down so quickly?

Jean-Guy Beauvoir settled in to find the answer.

■ ■ ■ ■

"Shall I tell you my thinking?" asked Gamache.

Frère Simon's face screamed no. Gamache, of course, ignored it.

"It's unorthodox," admitted the Chief. "We generally like the people we're talking to to do all the talking. But I think it might be sensible to be flexible, in this case."

He looked, with some amusement, at the mule-like monk. Then his face grew solemn.

"This is what I think happened. I think Frère Mathieu was still alive when you went into the garden. He was curled against the wall, and it probably took you a minute or so to see him."

As Gamache spoke an image sprang up between the two men, a vision of Frère Simon entering the garden with his gardening gear. More bright autumn leaves had fallen since he'd last raked, and some of the flowers were in need of deadheading. The sun was out and the day was crisp and fresh and filled with the scent of wild crab apple trees in the forest, their fruit baking in the late-season sun.

Frère Simon walked down the lawn, scanning the flower beds, looking at what needed to be cut down and put to bed for the harsh winter so obviously approaching.

And then he stopped. The grass at the far end of the garden had been mussed up. Disturbed. It wasn't obvious. A casual visitor would have probably missed it. But the abbot's secretary was not a casual visitor. He knew every leaf, every blade of grass. He tended it as he would a child in his care.

Something was wrong.

He looked around. Was the abbot here? But he knew the abbot was going to the basement, to look at the geothermal.

Frère Simon stood very still in the late September sunlight, his eyes sharp, his senses alert.

"Am I right so far?" Gamache asked.

The Chief Inspector's voice had been so mesmerizing, his words so descriptive that Frère Simon had forgotten he was still sitting inside, in the office. He could almost feel the chill autumn air on his cheeks.

He looked at the Chief Inspector, sitting so composed across from him, and thought, not for the first time, that this was a very dangerous man.

"I'll take your silence as assent," said Gamache with a small smile, "though I realize that's often a mistake."

He continued his story, and once again

the image between the men sprang up and began to move.

"You walked a few steps, trying to make out the lump at the far end of the garden, not yet concerned, but curious. Then you noticed the grass wasn't just disturbed, but there was blood."

Both men saw Frère Simon bending over, looking at the bent blades, and here and there a smear of red, as though the fallen leaves had sprung a stigmata.

Then he stopped and looked ahead of him, in the direction of the trail.

At the end of the path lay a figure. Curled into a tight, black ball. With just a crest of distinctive white. Only it wasn't all white. There was deep red there too.

Frère Simon threw his gardening tools to the ground and leapt forward, wading through the bushes to get there. Stomping on his precious perennials. Killing the cheerful black-eyed Susans standing in his way.

A monk, one of his brothers, was hurt. Badly hurt.

"I thought," said Frère Simon, not looking into Gamache's eyes, but down at the rosary in his hands. His voice was low, not above a whisper, and the Chief leaned forward to grasp each rare word. "I thought . . ."

Now Frère Simon did look up. The memory alone was enough to frighten him.

Gamache said nothing. He kept his face neutral, interested. But his deep brown eyes never left the monk's.

"I thought it was Dom Philippe."

His eyes fell to the simple cross swinging from his rosary. Then Frère Simon brought his hands up, and dropped his head and held it there, so that the cross knocked softly against the monk's forehead. And then stopped.

"Oh, God, I thought he was dead. I thought something had happened to him." Frère Simon's voice was muffled. But while his words were obscured, his feelings couldn't have been clearer.

"What did you do?" asked Gamache, softly.

His head still in his hands, the monk spoke to the floor. "I hesitated. God help me, I hesitated."

He lifted his head to look at Gamache. His confessor. Hoping for understanding, if not absolution.

"Go on," said Gamache, his eyes never wavering.

"I didn't want to see. I was afraid."

"Of course you were. Anyone would be.

But you did go to him, finally," said the Chief. "You didn't run away."

"No."

"What happened?"

Now Frère Simon held on to Gamache's eyes as though they were a rope and he was dangling from a cliff.

"I knelt and turned him a little. I thought maybe he'd fallen from the wall or the tree. I know, it's ridiculous, but I couldn't see how else it could've happened. And if he'd broken his neck I didn't want to . . ."

"*Oui,*" said Gamache. "Go on."

"Then I saw who it was." The monk's voice had changed. It was still filled with stress, with anxiety, reliving those terrible moments. But the degree had changed. "It wasn't the abbot."

There was clearly relief.

"It was the prior."

And even more relief. What had started as a dreadful tragedy had ended as almost good news. Frère Simon couldn't hide it. Or chose not to.

Still, he held the Chief's gaze. Searching it for disapproval.

He found none. Only acceptance, that what he was hearing was almost certainly, finally, the truth.

"Was he alive?" Gamache asked.

"*Oui.* His eyes were open. He stared at me, and grabbed my hand. You're right. He knew he was dying. And I knew. I couldn't tell you how I knew, but I did. I couldn't just leave him."

"How long did it take?"

Frère Simon paused. It had obviously taken an eternity. Kneeling in the earth, holding the bloody hand of a dying man. A fellow monk. A man this man despised.

"I don't know. A minute, maybe slightly more. I gave him last rites, and it calmed him a bit."

"What are the last rites, can you repeat them for me?"

"Surely you've heard them?"

Gamache had heard them, and knew them. Had given them himself, swiftly, urgently, while holding one dying agent after another. But he wanted Frère Simon to say them now.

Simon closed his eyes. His right hand reached out just a little, and cupped just a little. Holding an invisible hand.

"O Lord Jesus Christ, most merciful lord of earth, we ask that you receive this child into your arms, that he might pass in safety from this crisis, as thou hast told us with infinite compassion."

His eyes still closed, Frère Simon lifted

471

his other hand and with his thumb he sketched a cross. On the dying monk's forehead.

Infinite compassion, thought Gamache, looking down at the young agent, his own specter in his own arms. In the heat of the moment, Gamache hadn't had time to give the full last rites, so he'd simply bent down and whispered, *"Take this child."*

But the agent was already gone. And Gamache himself had to go.

"This is where," the Chief said, "a dying man, if he's able, gives his confession."

Frère Simon was silent.

"What did he say?" Gamache asked.

"He made a noise," said Frère Simon, as though in a trance. "Trying to clear his throat and then he said 'homo.' "

Now Simon focused. He came back from far away. The two men stared at each other.

"Homo?" asked the Chief.

Frère Simon nodded. "You can see why I didn't say anything. It has nothing to do with his death."

But, thought Gamache, perhaps a lot to do with his life. The Chief considered for a moment.

"What do you think he meant?" he finally asked.

"I think we both know what he meant."

"Was he gay? Homosexual?"

For a moment Frère Simon tried on his disapproving look, then abandoned it. They were far beyond that.

"It's hard to explain," said Frère Simon. "We're two dozen men here alone. Our goal, our prayer, is to find divine love. Compassion. To be consumed by the love of God."

"That's the ideal," said Gamache. "But in the meantime, you're also human."

The need for physical comfort was, he knew, powerful and primal and didn't necessarily go away with a vow of chastity.

"But what we need isn't physical love," said Frère Simon, correctly interpreting Gamache's thoughts, and correcting him. The monk didn't sound at all defensive. He was simply struggling to find the right words. "I think most, if not all of us, have left that far behind. We're not highly sexed or sexual."

"What do you need then?"

"Kindness. Intimacy. Not sexual. But companionship. God should replace man in our affections, but the reality is, we all want a friend."

"Is that how you feel, with the abbot?" Gamache asked the question baldly, but his voice and his manner were gentle. "I saw how you reacted when you thought he was

473

the one hurt and dying."

"I love him, it's true. But I have no desire for physical relations. It's hard to explain a love that goes so far beyond that."

"And the prior? Did he love another?"

Frère Simon was silent. Not a mulish silence, but a contemplative one.

After a minute or so he spoke. "I wondered if he and the abbot . . ."

It was as far as he could go, for the moment. There was another pause.

"There were many years when they were inseparable. Besides myself, the prior was the only other person ever invited into the abbot's garden."

For the first time, Gamache began to wonder if the garden existed on different planes. It was both a place of grass and earth and flowers. But also an allegory. For that most private place inside each one of them. For some it was a dark, locked room. For others, a garden.

The secretary had been admitted. And so had the prior.

And the prior had died there.

"What do you think the prior meant?" asked Gamache.

"I think there's only one possible interpretation. He knew he was dying and he wanted absolution."

"For being a homosexual? I thought you just said he probably wasn't."

"I don't know what to think anymore. His relationships might've been platonic, but he might've privately yearned for more. He knew it. And God knew it."

"Is it the sort of thing God would condemn him for?" Gamache asked.

"For being gay? Maybe not. For breaking his vow of chastity, probably. It's the sort of thing that would need to be confessed."

"By saying 'homo'?" Gamache was far from convinced, though when a person was dying reason played a very small part, if any. When the end came and there was time for only one word, what would that be?

The Chief Inspector had no doubt what his last words would be. And were. When he'd thought he was dying he'd said two words, over and over until he could speak no more.

Reine-Marie.

It would never occur to him to say "hetero." But then, he carried no guilt about his relationships. And maybe the prior did.

"Do you have his personal records I might see?" asked Gamache.

"No."

" 'No,' you don't want to show me, or 'no,' you really don't have files."

"We really don't have files."

On seeing the Chief Inspector's expression, Frère Simon explained. "When we enter the religious life we're rigorously tested and screened. And our first abbey would've kept records. But not Dom Philippe, not here at Saint-Gilbert."

"Why not?"

"Because it can't possibly matter. We're like the French Foreign Legion. We leave the past behind."

Gamache stared at this *religieux*. Was he really that naïve?

"Just because you want to leave your past at the gate doesn't mean it stays there," said the Chief. "It has a way of creeping through the cracks."

"If it comes all this way, then I suppose it was meant to find us again," said Frère Simon.

By this logic, thought Gamache, the prior's death was also God's will. Meant to happen. God clearly had his hands full with the Gilbertines. The French Foreign Legion of religious orders.

It fit, Gamache thought. No retreat was possible. There was no past to go back to. Nothing outside the walls but wilderness.

"Speaking of cracks, do you know about the foundations?" Gamache asked.

"The foundations of what?"

"The abbey."

Frère Simon looked confused. "You need to speak to Frère Raymond about them. But give yourself half a day and be prepared to come away knowing more about our septic system than is probably healthy."

"So the abbot didn't say anything to you about the foundations of the abbey? And the prior didn't either?"

Now it dawned on Frère Simon. "Is there something wrong with them?"

"I was asking if you'd heard anything."

"No, nothing. Should I have?"

So the abbot had kept it to himself, as Gamache had suspected. Only the abbot and Frère Raymond knew that Saint-Gilbert was crumbling. Had, at best, a decade of life left.

And maybe the prior also knew. Maybe Frère Raymond, in desperation, had told him. If so, the prior had died before he could tell anyone else. Was that the motive? To shut him up?

Will no one rid me of this troublesome priest?

"You knew the prior had been murdered, didn't you?"

Frère Simon nodded.

"When did you realize?"

"When I saw his head. And . . ."

The monk's voice petered out. Gamache stayed completely quiet. Waiting.

". . . and then I saw something in the flower bed. Something that shouldn't be there."

Gamache stopped breathing. The two men became a *tableau vivant,* frozen in time. Gamache waited. And waited. His breathing now was shallow, quiet, not wanting to even disturb the air around them.

"It wasn't a stone, you know."

"I know," said the Chief. "What did you do with it?"

He almost closed his eyes to pray that this monk hadn't picked it up and thrown it over the wall. To disappear back into the world.

Frère Simon got up, opened the main door into the abbot's office, and stepped into the corridor. Gamache followed, presuming the monk was leading him to some hiding place.

But instead, Frère Simon stopped at the threshold and reached over, then presented Chief Inspector Gamache with the murder weapon. It was the old iron rod, used for hundreds of years to gain admittance to the abbot's most private rooms.

And used, yesterday, to crush the skull of the prior of Saint-Gilbert-Entre-les-Loups.

TWENTY-FIVE

Jean-Guy Beauvoir coursed through the corridors of Saint-Gilbert-Entre-les-Loups. Searching.

The monks who ran into him initially paused to greet him with their customary bow. But as he got closer they stepped back. Out of his way.

And were relieved when he passed them by.

Jean-Guy Beauvoir stalked the corridors of the monastery. Looking in the vegetable garden. Looking in the *animalerie*, with the grazing goats and Chantecler chickens.

Looking in the basement. Where Frère Raymond was invisible, but his voice echoed down the long, cool corridors. He was singing a chant. The words were slurred and his voice, while still beautiful, held little of the Divine and more of the brandy and Bénédictine.

Beauvoir raced back up the stone stairs

and stood in the Blessed Chapel, breathing heavily. Turning this way and that.

Monks in their long black robes stood away from the dancing light, watching him. But he paid no attention. They weren't his quarry. He was hunting someone else.

Then he turned and pushed his way through the closed door. The hallway was empty, and the door at the end was closed. And locked.

"Open it," he demanded.

Frère Luc didn't dawdle. The massive key was in the lock and turned, the deadbolt thrust back, and the door open within moments. And Beauvoir, robed in black as surely as if he'd been wearing a cassock, was out the door.

Luc closed it quickly. He was tempted to open the slat in the door and look out. To watch what was about to happen. But he didn't. Frère Luc didn't want to see, or hear, or know. He went back to his little room and put the big book on his knees, and lost himself in the chants.

Beauvoir saw what he was looking for immediately. Standing by the shore.

Not thinking, not caring, he was miles beyond either, Beauvoir ran with all his might.

Ran as though his life depended on it.

Ran as though lives depended on it.

Straight at the man in the mist.

As he ran he let out a terrible sound from deep in his belly. A sound he'd kept in for months and months. A sound he'd swallowed, and hid and locked away. But now it was out. And propelling him forward.

Chief Superintendent Francoeur turned just moments before Beauvoir crashed into him. He took half a step away, avoiding the brunt of the blow. Both men fell to the rocks, but Francoeur not as heavily as Beauvoir.

He scrambled out from underneath Beauvoir and reached for his gun, just as Beauvoir rolled over and sprang to his feet, also reaching for his weapon.

But it was too late. Francoeur had his gun out, and aimed at Beauvoir's chest.

"You shithead," Beauvoir screamed, barely noticing the weapon. "You fucker. I'll kill you."

"You just attacked a superior officer," snapped Francoeur, shaken.

"I attacked an asshole, and I'll do it again." Beauvoir was yelling at the top of his lungs, shrieking at the man.

"What the hell is this about?" Francoeur yelled back.

"You know damn well. I found what you

had on the laptop. What you were looking at when I came in."

"Oh, fuck," said Francoeur, looking at Beauvoir with uncertainty. "Did Gamache see it?"

"What the hell does that matter?" screamed Beauvoir, then he bent over, hands on his knees, trying to catch his breath. He looked up. "I saw it."

Deep breath in, he begged his body. Deep breath out.

Christ, don't pass out.

Deep breath in, deep breath out.

He felt light-headed.

Oh, dear God, don't let me pass out now.

Beauvoir released his knees and slowly straightened. He'd never be as tall as the man opposite. The man with the gun pointed at Beauvoir's chest. But Beauvoir stood as tall as he could. And stared at the creature.

"You leaked the video."

His voice had changed. It was raspy. Insubstantial. Each word rode out of his mouth on a deep, deep breath, from deep, deep down.

The door to his private place had blown off, and with it came the words.

And the intent.

He would kill Francoeur. Now.

Beauvoir kept his eyes locked on the Superintendent. In the blurry edge of vision he could see the gun. And he knew, when he leapt, Francoeur would get off at least two shots. Before Beauvoir covered the space between them.

And Beauvoir calculated that as long as he wasn't hit in the head or the heart, he'd make it there. And have just enough life left, enough will, to tackle this man to the ground. Grab a rock. And crush his skull.

He was reminded, for a mad moment, of the story his father had read to him, over and over. About the train.

I think I can. I think I can.

I think I can kill Francoeur before he kills me.

Though Beauvoir knew he'd die too. Just not first. Dear God, not first.

He tensed and leaned forward a fraction, but Francoeur, hyperalert, raised the gun a fraction. And Beauvoir stopped.

He would bide his time. Wait for that split second of distraction on Francoeur's part.

That's all I need.

I think I can. I think I can.

"What?" the Superintendent demanded. "You think I leaked the video?"

"Stop the fucking games. You betrayed my friends, your own people. They died." Beauvoir felt himself slipping into hysteria, nearly sobbing, and hauled himself back. "They died, and you leaked the fucking tape of it happening."

Beauvoir's throat was closing in, his voice just a squeal. His breathing came in wheezes as he hauled air through the shrinking passage.

"You turned what happened into a circus, you — you —"

He could go no further. He was overwhelmed by images, of the raid on the factory. Of Gamache leading them. Of the Sûreté officers surging in, following their leader. To save the kidnapped officer. To stop the gunmen.

Jean-Guy Beauvoir stood on the quiet shore, and could hear the explosions of gunfire. Hear the bullets strike the concrete, the floors, the walls. His friends. He could smell the acrid smoke mixed with concrete dust. And he felt his heart pound, with adrenaline. And fear.

But still he'd followed Gamache. Deeper and deeper into the factory. They'd all followed Gamache.

The raid had been captured on the cameras attached to each agent's headgear. And later, months later, it had been hacked and edited and released onto the Internet.

Beauvoir had become as addicted to that video as he had to painkillers. Two halves of a whole. First the pain, then the killers. Over and over and over. Until it had become his life. Watching his friends die. Over and over. And over.

But one question remained. Who had leaked that video? Beauvoir knew it was an inside job. And now he had his answer.

Now, all he wanted was to stay conscious long enough to kill the man in front of him.

For betraying his own people. Gamache's agents. Beauvoir's friends. To lose them was bad enough, but to have the tape of the attack released onto the Internet. For millions and millions worldwide to see. For all of Québec to see.

And they had.

Everyone had grabbed their popcorn and watched, over and over, as the Sûreté officers had been gunned down in that factory. They watched as though the deaths were entertainment.

And the families of the slain had seen it too. It had become an Internet sensation, replacing the box of kittens as the most watched video.

Beauvoir stared into Francoeur's eyes. He didn't need to look at the gun. He knew it was there. And he knew what it would feel like, any moment now, when the first bullet hit.

He'd felt it before. The thud, the shock, then the searing pain.

He'd seen so many war movies, so many westerns. He'd seen so many bodies. Real ones. Shot to death. He'd somehow fooled himself into thinking he knew what it would be like. To be shot.

He'd been wrong.

It wasn't just the pain, it was the terror. The blood. The frantic scrambling to get at the burning, but the hurt was too deep.

That had been less than a year ago. It'd taken him a long time to recover. Longer than the Chief. Gamache had thrown himself headlong into recovery. Into the physiotherapy. Into the weights, the walking, the exercises. The counseling.

Beauvoir knew that every sight, every scent, every sound that the Chief took in was keener now. It was as though he was living for five. Himself and four young agents.

It had somehow invigorated the Chief.

But the attack, the losses, had had the opposite effect on Beauvoir.

He'd tried. He really had. But the pain seemed too deep. And the agony too great. And the painkillers too effective.

486

And then the video had appeared, and the pain sizzled again. Burning even deeper. And more painkillers were needed. And more. And more. To dull the hurt. And the memories.

Until finally the Chief had intervened. Gamache had saved him that day in the factory. And had saved him again months later, when he'd insisted Beauvoir get help. For the pills and for the images that had wormed into his head. Forcing him to go into intense therapy. Into rehab. Forcing him to stop running and turn. And face what had happened.

Gamache had also forced a promise from him, to never again watch that video.

And Beauvoir had kept his promise.

"They'd give anything to be here now," Gamache had said one day in the spring, as he and Beauvoir strolled through the park across from the Gamaches' apartment in Outremont. Beauvoir knew who the Chief meant. He could see Gamache taking everything in, as though to share it with his dead agents. The Chief had stopped then, to admire a massive old lilac bush in full bloom. Then he turned to Beauvoir. "It's against the law to pick them, you know."

"Only if you get caught."

Beauvoir moved to the other side of the

bush and saw it shaking, as though with laughter, as Gamache tugged the spiky, fragrant flowers off.

"An interesting take on justice," called the Chief. "It's only wrong if you're caught."

"Would you prefer me to arrest you?" Beauvoir yanked some more flowers off.

He heard the Chief laugh.

Beauvoir knew the burden the Chief now carried. To live for so many. Gamache had staggered, at first, but had finally grown stronger, under that weight.

And Beauvoir felt better, every day he was clean. Away from the drugs and away from the hair shirt of images he'd inflicted on himself.

The Chief had given Madame Gamache his bouquet of stolen lilacs and she'd put them in a white jug and placed them on the table. Then she'd put Beauvoir's smaller bouquet in water, so they'd stay fresh to take back home after dinner. But of course, they didn't make it to his own small apartment.

He'd given them to Annie.

They'd just started their courtship, and these were the first flowers he'd offered.

"Stolen," he admitted as she'd opened the door and he'd held them out to her. "Your father's influence, I'm afraid."

"It's not the only thing you've stolen, monsieur," she'd said with a laugh, stepping aside to let him in.

It had taken him a moment to realize what she meant. He watched her place the lilacs in a vase on her kitchen table, and fluff them a bit, trying to arrange them. He'd stayed the night. For the first time. And woke in the morning to the suggestion of lilac, and the realization that he had Annie's heart in his chest. And she had his. And would keep it safe.

Beauvoir had kept his promise to Annie's father, to the Chief. To not watch that video again. Until now. Until he'd found out what Superintendent Francoeur had been doing in the prior's office. On the laptop.

Francoeur had brought the video with him. And was watching it.

Those were the voices Beauvoir had heard. The Chief's, issuing orders. Commanding. Leading his agents deeper and deeper into that damned factory. After the gunmen.

Beauvoir had found the file on the laptop.

As he'd hit play, he'd known what he'd see. And, God help him, he'd wanted to see it again. He'd missed his misery.

Beauvoir stared at Francoeur in front of him on the misty shore. He'd brought that monstrosity into the monastery. To contaminate the last place in Québec, the last place on earth, that hadn't seen the images.

And Beauvoir knew, at that moment, why despite the strangeness of the surroundings, the oddity of the monks, the mind-numbing dullness of the endless chants, he'd felt a kind of creeping calm here.

Because these men, unique in Québec, didn't know. Hadn't seen the video. Didn't look at him and Gamache as though at men forever wounded, damaged. Instead, the monks looked at them as though they were just men. Like themselves. Going about their jobs.

But Francoeur had fallen from the skies and brought this blight.

But it would stop here. Now. This man had done enough damage. To Gamache, to Beauvoir, to the memories of those who died, and their families.

"You think I leaked that video?" Francoeur repeated.

"I know you did," gasped Beauvoir. "Who else had access to the raw tape? Who else could influence that internal investigation? An entire Sûreté department devoted to cyber crime and all they came up with was that some unknown hacker had gotten lucky?"

"You don't believe it?" asked Francoeur.

"Of course I don't."

Beauvoir moved, but stopped when Francoeur jutted his gun forward.

There'd be a better time, thought Beauvoir. In a moment, or two. When Francoeur was distracted. Just a blink, that's all it'll take.

"Does Gamache believe it?"

"The hacker theory?" For the first time Beauvoir was thrown off. "I don't know."

"Of course you know, you little shit. Tell me. Does Gamache believe it?"

Beauvoir said nothing, just stared at Francoeur. His mind taken up with only one question.

Was now the time?

"Is Gamache investigating the leak?" Francoeur yelled. "Or has he accepted the official report? I need to know."

"Why? So you can kill him too?"

"Kill him?" Francoeur demanded. "Who do you think released that video?"

"You."

"Christ, you really are thick. Why do you think I brought it with me? To enjoy my handiwork? The thing's repulsive. It makes me sick just thinking about it. Watching it is . . ."

Francoeur was trembling now, almost erupting with rage.

"Of course I don't believe the findings of that goddamned investigation. It's ridiculous. Obviously a cover-up. Someone inside the Sûreté leaked the video, not some mythical hacker. One of us. I brought that fucking tape with me because I watch it every chance I get. So I don't forget. So that I remember why I'm still looking."

His voice had changed. The accent grew thicker, the sophistication fell off in hunks to reveal the man who'd grown up a village away from Beauvoir's own grandparents.

Francoeur had lowered the muzzle of his gun. Just a fraction.

Beauvoir saw this. Francoeur was distracted. Now was the time.

But he hesitated.

"What're you looking for?" Beauvoir asked.

"For evidence."

"Don't give me that crap," said Beauvoir. "You leaked it and now that you're caught you're bullshitting."

"Why would I leak it?"

"Because —"

"Why?" roared Francoeur, his face red with anger.

"Because . . ."

But Beauvoir didn't know why. Why would the Chief Superintendent of the Sûreté release a tape of his own agents being killed? It didn't make sense.

But Beauvoir knew there was a reason. Somewhere.

"I don't know," Beauvoir admitted. "And I don't have to know why. I just know you did it."

"Fucking great detective. You don't need evidence? Don't need motive? You just accuse and condemn? Is that what Gamache taught you? I'm not surprised."

Francoeur looked at Beauvoir as though at something profoundly, spectacularly stupid.

"But you're right about one thing, you damned fool. One of us here leaked that tape."

Beauvoir's eyes widened and his mouth all but fell open.

"You can't be serious." His arms dropped to his sides and all thought of attack vanished in the face of Francoeur's words. "Are you saying Chief Inspector Gamache leaked the tape?"

"Who else benefited?"

"Benefited?" Beauvoir whispered, shock muting his voice. "He almost died in the attacks. Those were his agents. He hired them, mentored them. He'd die —"

"But he didn't, did he? I saw that tape. I

know every frame. I saw the raw tape too. Even more telling."

"What're you saying?"

"Is Gamache investigating the leak of the video?" Francoeur demanded.

Beauvoir was silent.

"Is he?" Francoeur didn't just shout now, he screamed at Beauvoir. "I thought not," said Francoeur at last, his voice quiet now. "Why would he? He knows who released it. He wants all questions to die away."

"You're wrong." Beauvoir was confused and angry. This man had gotten him twisted around, so that up was down, and down was up, and nothing made sense. Francoeur sounded like his grandfather, but said terrible things.

The Superintendent lowered his gun completely, then looked at it as though wondering how it got into his hand. He replaced it in the leather holster attached to his belt.

"I know you admire him," he said quietly. "But Armand Gamache isn't the man you think he is. He made a hatchet job of that rescue. Four Sûreté agents were killed. You yourself almost died. You were left to bleed to death on the floor. The man you so respect and admire led you in there, then left you to die. I see it every time I watch the tape. He even kissed you good-bye. Like Judas."

Francoeur's voice was calm, reasonable. Comforting. Familiar.

"He had no choice." Beauvoir's voice was hoarse. There was nothing left. No impetus forward.

He wouldn't attack Francoeur now. Wouldn't smash a rock into his temple. Beauvoir hadn't the energy left. All he wanted to do was sag to the ground. To sit on the jagged shore, and let the mist swallow him up.

"We all have a choice," said Francoeur. "Why release that video? We both know what a mess that raid was. Four young agents died. That can't be considered a success by any standard —"

"Lives were saved," said Beauvoir, though he barely had the energy to speak. "Hundreds of thousands of lives. Because of the Chief. The deaths weren't his fault. He was given the wrong information —"

"He was in charge. It was his responsibility. And after all that mess, who comes out a hero? Because of the tape? It could've been edited any way. To show anything. To show the truth. Then why did it make Gamache look so good?"

"That wasn't his doing."

"Well, it sure wasn't mine. I know what really happened. And so do you." Francoeur's eyes held Beauvoir's. "God help me, I was even forced to give the man a medal of bravery, so strong was public sentiment. It makes me sick just thinking about it."

"He didn't want it," said Beauvoir. "He hated that whole thing."

"Then why did he accept it? We have a choice, Jean-Guy. We really do."

"He deserved that medal," said Beauvoir. "He saved more lives than —"

"Than he killed? Yes. Perhaps. But he didn't save you. He could have, but he ran off. You know it. I know it. He knows it."

"He had to."

"Yes, I know. He had no choice."

Francoeur examined Beauvoir, apparently trying to make up his mind about something.

"He probably likes you. Like he likes his car or a nice suit. You suit him. You're useful." Francoeur paused. "But that's all."

His voice was soft, reasonable.

"You'll never be his friend. You'll never be anything other than a convenient subordinate. He has you over to his home, treats you like a son. But then he leaves you to die. Don't be fooled, Inspector. You'll never be a member of his family. He comes from

Outremont. Where're you from? East end Montréal, right? Balconville? He went to Cambridge and Université Laval. You went to some grungy public school and played shinny on the streets. He quotes poetry and you don't understand it, do you?"

There was a gentleness in his tone.

"A lot of what he says you don't understand. Am I right?"

Despite himself, Beauvoir nodded.

"Neither do I," said Francoeur with a small smile. "I know after that raid you separated from your wife. I'm sorry to be so personal, but I wondered . . ."

Francoeur's voice petered out and he looked almost bashful. Then he met Beauvoir's eyes and held them for a moment.

"I wondered if you were in a new relationship."

On seeing Beauvoir's reaction Francoeur held up his hand. "I know, it's none of my business."

But still he held Beauvoir's eyes and now he lowered his voice still further.

"Be careful. You're a good officer. I think you can be a great officer, if given a chance. If you can just get out on your own. I've seen you texting, and making sure the Chief didn't see."

497

Now there was a long silence between them.

"Is it Annie Gamache?"

The silence was complete. Not a bird called, not a leaf quivered, not a wave came to shore. The world disappeared and all that was left were two men and a question.

Finally Francoeur sighed. "I hope I'm wrong."

He walked back to the door, took out the iron knocker, and hit.

It opened.

But Beauvoir saw none of this. He'd turned his back on Saint-Gilbert-Entre-les-Loups and looked out across where the tranquil lake would be, if it hadn't disappeared into the mist.

Jean-Guy Beauvoir's world was upside down. The clouds had descended, and the sky had become slate. And the only familiar thing was the ache too deep to grasp.

TWENTY-SIX

"Why did you hide the murder weapon?" Gamache asked. "And why didn't you tell us about the prior's last words?"

Frère Simon dropped his eyes to the stone floor of the abbot's rooms, then lifted them again.

"I think you can guess."

"I can always guess, *mon frère,*" said the Chief. "What I need from you is the truth."

Gamache looked around. They'd returned to the privacy of the abbot's office. The weak sun no longer lit the room, and his secretary had been too distracted to turn on the lamps, or to even notice they were needed.

"Can we speak in the garden?" Gamache asked, and Frère Simon nodded.

He seemed to have run out of words, as though he was allocated only so many, and he'd used enough for a lifetime.

But it was his actions that were being

called to account now.

The two men walked through the book-case, filled with volumes on early Christian mystics, like Julian of Norwich, Hildegard of Bingen, and the writings of other great Christian minds, from Erasmus to C. S. Lewis. Filled with books on prayer and meditation. On leading a spiritual life. On leading a Catholic life.

They swung aside the words, and walked into the world.

The hills outside the wall were thick with low-hanging cloud. Mist was sitting on the trees, and among the trees, turning the world from the brilliant colors of that morn-ing to shades of gray.

Far from diminishing the beauty, it seemed to add to it, giving the world a degree of softness, and subtlety, of comfort and intimacy.

Wrapped in a towel in the Chief's hand was the length of iron that, like a magic wand, had turned the living prior into a dead body.

Frère Simon walked to the center of the garden, and paused under the huge nearly bare maple tree.

"Why didn't you tell us that the prior spoke to you?" said Gamache.

"Because his words were in the form of a

confession. My sort, not yours. It was my moral obligation."

"You have convenient morals, *mon frère.* They seem to allow lying."

That brought Frère Simon up short, and again he reverted to silence.

He also, thought Gamache, *has a convenient vow of silence.*

"Why didn't you tell us the prior had said 'homo' just before he died?"

"Because I knew it'd be misunderstood."

"Because we're stupid, you mean? Not given to the nuance of mind so obvious in *les religieux?* Why did you hide the murder weapon?"

"I didn't hide it, it was in plain sight."

"Enough of this," snapped Gamache. "I know you're frightened. I know you're cornered. Stop playing these games and tell me the truth and let's end this. Have the decency and courage to do that. And trust us. We're not the fools you're afraid we are."

"*Désolé,*" said the monk, with a sigh. "I've been trying so hard to convince myself what I did wasn't wrong, I almost forgot that it was. I'm sorry. I should've told you. And God knows, I should never have taken the knocker away."

"Why did you?"

Frère Simon stared into Gamache's eyes.

"You suspect someone, don't you," said the Chief, holding that stare.

The monk's eyes held a plea. A desperate plea for this interrogation to stop. For the questions to stop.

But they both knew it couldn't. This conversation was destined to happen, from the moment the blow fell, and Frère Simon heard a dying man's last words, and took the murder weapon. He knew, one way or another, he'd have to answer for his actions.

"Who do you think did this?" Gamache asked.

"I can't tell you. I can't say the words."

And he looked as though, physically, he couldn't.

"We'll stand here for eternity, then, *mon frère*," said Gamache. "Until you say the words. And then we'll both be free."

"But not . . ."

"The man you suspect?" Gamache's eyes, and voice, softened. "You think I don't know?"

"Then why force me to say it?" The monk was almost in tears.

"Because you must. It's your burden, not mine." He looked at Frère Simon with sympathy, as one brother to another. "Believe me, I have my own."

Simon paused, and looked at Gamache.

"*Oui. C'est la vérité.*" He took a breath. "I didn't tell you that the prior said 'homo' just before he died, then I hid the murder weapon, because I was afraid the abbot had done it. I thought Dom Philippe had killed Frère Mathieu."

"*Merci,*" said Gamache. "And do you still think that?"

"I don't know what to think. I don't know what else to think."

The Chief nodded. He didn't know if Frère Simon was telling the truth, but he did know these words had cost the monk. Simon had, in effect, thrown the abbot to the Inquisition.

The question Gamache asked himself now, that the Inquisitors had failed to ask, was whether this was the truth. Or was this poor man so terrified he'd say anything? Did Frère Simon name the abbot to save himself?

Gamache didn't know. What he did know was that Frère Simon, the taciturn monk, had loved the abbot. Still did.

Will no one rid me of this troublesome priest?

Had Frère Simon rid the abbot of the troublesome prior? Had he taken some subtle look, a raised brow, a twitch of the hand, as a plea from the abbot? And acted

503

upon it? And now, consumed with guilt and flailed by his conscience, was Frère Simon trying to blame the abbot himself?

The prior might have been troublesome, but it was nothing compared to an aroused conscience. Or the trouble created when the head of homicide knocked at the door.

The monks' external lives in Saint-Gilbert might be simple, ruled by the bell and the chants and the changing seasons. But their internal life was a quagmire of emotions.

Emotions, Gamache knew from years of kneeling beside corpses, were what made the body. Not a gun, not a knife. Not a length of old iron.

Some emotion had slipped the leash and killed Frère Mathieu. And to find his killer, Armand Gamache needed to use his logic, but also, his own feelings.

The abbot had said, *Why didn't I see this coming?*

The question had seemed genuine, the angst certainly was. He hadn't seen that one of his community, his flock, wasn't a sheep at all. But a wolf.

But suppose the question, filled with wonder and shock, wasn't aimed at one of the brothers? Maybe the abbot was asking it of himself. *Why didn't I see this coming?* Not the murderous thoughts and actions of another, but of himself.

Maybe Dom Philippe was amazed that he himself could, and did, kill.

The Chief Inspector took half a step back. Physically, not much, but it was a signal to the monk that he had a little space, and time. To compose himself. To gather himself and his wits back up. It might have been a mistake, the Chief knew, to give Frère Simon this time. His colleagues, including Jean-Guy, would almost certainly have pressed on. Knowing the man was on his knees, they'd have forced him to the ground.

But Gamache knew that while that sort of thing might be effective in the short term, a man humiliated, emotionally raped, would never again open up.

Besides, while Gamache wanted very much to solve the crime, he didn't want to lose his soul in the process. He suspected there were enough lost souls already.

"Why would Dom Philippe kill the prior?" Gamache eventually asked.

The garden was quiet, all sound muffled by the mist. Not that there was much sound to begin with. Birds called every now and then, chipmunks and squirrels chattered at each other. Twigs and branches broke, as something larger moved through the thick Canadian forest.

All muffled now.

"You were right about the rift," said Frère Simon. "As soon as that first recording was a success things started falling apart. Ego, I suspect. And power. Suddenly there was something worth fighting over. Up until then we were all equal, just sort of meandering through our days in a rickety old monastery. We were quite happy, certainly content. But the recording brought so much attention, and so much money so quickly."

The monk raised his palms to the gray sky and gave a little shrug.

"The abbot wanted us to take it slowly. To not rush off and leave our vows behind. But the prior and others saw the success as a sign from God, that we needed to be out in the world more. To share our gifts."

"Each claimed to know God's will," said the Chief.

"We were having some difficulty interpreting it," Frère Simon admitted with a small smile.

"Perhaps not the first *religieux* to have that problem."

"You think?"

It was as Gamache had heard from everyone except the abbot. Before the recording the monastery was falling apart but the congregation was solid. After the recording

506

the monastery was being repaired but the congregation was falling apart.

Some malady is coming upon us.

The abbot was stuck trying to figure out the will of a God who seemed himself conflicted.

"The abbot and his prior were good friends, even loving friends, before the recording."

The monk nodded.

Gamache thought the Gilbertines could begin a new calendar. There was BR, before the recording. And AR.

Some malady is coming upon us. Disguised as a miracle.

They were now roughly two years AR. Plenty of time for a close friendship to turn to hate. As only a good friendship could. The conduit to the heart was already created.

"And the piece of paper," Gamache asked, indicating the yellowed chant he still held. "What part could this have played?"

Frère Simon thought about that. As did Gamache.

The two men stood in the garden, as the mist slipped over the wall.

"The abbot loves plainchant," said Frère Simon, speaking slowly, working his way through this. "And he has a wonderful voice. Very clear, very true."

"But?"

"But he isn't the most gifted musician in Saint-Gilbert. And he isn't fluent in Latin. Like the rest of us, he knows scripture and the Latin mass. But beyond that, he wasn't a Latin scholar. You might have noticed, all his books are in French, not Latin."

Gamache had noticed.

"I doubt he'd know the Latin word for 'banana,' for instance." Simon pointed to that silly phrase.

"But you did," said Gamache.

"I looked it up."

"As could the abbot."

"But why would he look up and use a string of nonsense words in Latin?" asked Frère Simon. "If he was going to put Latin words on paper he'd probably use bits of prayers or chants. I doubt he was Gilbert to the prior's Sullivan. Or the other way around."

Gamache nodded. That had been his reasoning as well. He could see the abbot braining the prior, in a fit of passion. Not sexual passion, but a much more dangerous kind. A religious fervor. Believing Frère Mathieu was going to kill the monastery, kill the order. And it was Dom Philippe's burden, given by God, to stop him.

It was also Dom Philippe's job, as father to his sons, to protect them. And that meant protecting their home. Defending their home. Gamache had looked into the eyes of too many grieving fathers not to know the force of that love.

He felt it himself, for his own son and daughter. He felt it, God help him, for his agents. He chose them, recruited them, trained them.

They were his sons and daughters, and every day he sent them after murderers.

And he'd crawled over to each and every mortally wounded one, and held them and whispered an urgent prayer.

Take this child.

As gunshots exploded into walls and floors, he'd held Jean-Guy, protecting him with his own body. He'd kissed his brow and whispered those words too. Believing this boy he loved was dying. And he could see in Jean-Guy's eyes, he believed it too.

And then he'd left him. To help the others. Gamache had killed that day. Coolly taken aim and seen men lose their lives. He'd killed deliberately, and he'd do it again. To save his agents.

Armand Gamache knew the power of a father's love. Whether it be a biological father or a father by choice. And fate.

If he could kill, why couldn't the abbot?

But Gamache couldn't, for the life of him, see what role the neumes might have played. It all made sense. Except for the mystery he held in his hand.

Like a father himself, the prior had died hugging it.

The Chief Inspector left Frère Simon and went in search of Beauvoir, to bring him up to speed and to give him the murder weapon for safekeeping.

Gamache doubted the iron knocker had much to tell them. Frère Simon had admitted washing it off, scrubbing it down, and replacing it by the door. So that anyone wanting admittance to the abbot's locked rooms yesterday morning would put their fingerprints and DNA on it. And many had. Including Gamache himself.

The prior's office was empty. A few monks were working in the *animalerie,* feeding and cleaning the goats and chickens. Down the other corridor, Gamache looked in the dining hall and then opened the door to the *chocolaterie.*

"Looking for someone?" Frère Charles asked.

"Inspector Beauvoir."

"I'm afraid he isn't here." The medical

monk put a scoop into the vat of melted chocolate and brought out a ladle filled with dripping blueberries. "Last batch of the day. Picked by Frère Bernard this morning. He had to go out twice, poor man. Apparently he ate the first harvest himself." Frère Charles laughed. "An occupational hazard. Like some?"

He gestured to the long rows of tiny, dark brown spheres already cooled and ready to be packaged and shipped south.

Gamache, feeling a bit like a child playing hooky, walked into the *chocolaterie* and closed the door.

"Please." Frère Charles motioned to a sturdy stool and pulled one up himself. "We take shifts working here. When the monks first started making chocolate-covered berries one monk was assigned the work, but then they noticed he was getting larger and the output was shrinking."

Gamache smiled and took the confection the monk was offering. *"Merci."*

If possible, the wildly flavorful berry covered in the musky chocolate was even tastier than before. Now, if a monk was murdered for these, Gamache could understand. *But then,* he thought, taking another chocolate, *we all have our drug of choice. For some it's chocolate, for others it's chants.*

"You told Inspector Beauvoir that you were neutral in the conflict within the monastery, *mon frère.* A sort of Red Cross, ministering to the wounded in the battle for control of Saint-Gilbert. Who would you say were the most hurt? By the fighting, but also by the prior's death."

"In the fighting I'd say not a man was left untouched. We all felt horrible about what was happening, but no one quite knew how to stop it. So much seemed at stake, and there didn't seem to be any middle ground. You couldn't make half a recording or remove half the vow of silence. There didn't seem a compromise possible."

"You say there was so much at stake, do you know about the foundations?"

"What foundations? Of the abbey?"

Gamache nodded, watching the cheerful doctor closely.

"What about them?"

"Do you know if they're solid?" asked Gamache.

"Are you talking literally or figuratively? Literally, nothing could knock these walls down. The original monks knew what they were doing. But figuratively? I'm afraid Saint-Gilbert is very shaky."

"Merci," said Gamache. Here was another who didn't seem to know anything about

cracked foundations. Was it possible Frère Raymond was wrong? Or lying? Did he make the whole thing up to help pressure the abbot into the second recording?

"And after the prior's death, *mon frère?* Which of the monks was most upset?"

"Well, we were all devastated. Even those brothers who bitterly opposed him were shocked."

"Bien sûr," said the Chief, shaking his head and refusing more chocolate. If he didn't stop now, he'd eat them all. "But can you separate them out? The community here isn't amorphous. You might sing with a single voice, but you don't react with a single emotion."

"True." The doctor sat back and thought about that for a moment. "I'd say two people were the most upset. Frère Luc. He's the youngest of us, the most impressionable. And the least connected to the community. His only connection seems to be the choir. And, of course, Frère Mathieu was the choirmaster. He adored Frère Mathieu. He was a big reason Luc joined the little old Gilbertines. To study under the prior, and to sing the Gregorian chants."

"Are the chants here that different? Dom Philippe says every monastery sings from the same book of plainchant."

"True. But strangely enough they sound different here. I don't know why. Maybe it's the prior. Or the acoustics. Or the specific combination of voices."

"I understand Frère Luc has a beautiful voice."

"He does. Technically the best of all of us. By far."

"But?"

"Oh, he'll get there. Once he learns to channel those emotions from his head and into his heart. One day he'll be the choir-master himself. And he'll be a magnificent one. He has all the passion, he just needs to direct it."

"But will he stay?"

The medical monk absently ate a few more blueberries. "Now that Frère Mathieu is dead? I don't know. Perhaps not. It was a huge loss to the whole community, but perhaps to Frère Luc most of all. I think there was some hero worship there. Not unusual in a mentor-pupil relationship."

"Was the prior Frère Luc's mentor?"

"He mentored all of us, but since Luc was the newest he needed the most guidance."

"Could Frère Luc have misread their relationship? Assumed it was more special? Unique even?"

"In what way?" Frère Charles, while still

cordial, was now guarded. They all became defensive, when there was any suggestion of a "special" friendship.

"Could he have thought the choir director was grooming him? That this was more than simply schooling him in the ways of this particular choir?"

"It's possible," admitted Frère Charles. "But the prior would have been sensitive to that and stopped it. Frère Luc wouldn't have been the first monk to fall under his spell."

"Had Frère Antoine? The soloist?" asked Gamache. "They must have been close."

"You're not suggesting Frère Antoine killed the prior in some fit of jealousy, when the prior turned his attentions to Luc?" The doctor all but snorted.

But Gamache knew laughter often covered up an uncomfortable truth.

"Is it so ludicrous?" asked the Chief.

The smile fell from the monk's face. "You mistake us for the cast of some soap opera. Frères Antoine and Mathieu were colleagues. They shared a love of Gregorian chant. That is the only love they shared."

"But that was quite a potent love, wouldn't you say?" asked Gamache. "All-consuming even."

The doctor remained silent now, just

watching the Chief. Not agreeing. But not disagreeing either.

"You said there were two people most affected by the prior's death." Gamache broke the silence. "One was Luc. Who was the other?"

"The abbot. He's trying to hold it together, but I can see what a strain it is. There're small signs. A slight inattention. Forgetting things. His appetite is off. I've ordered him to eat more. It's always the small things that give us away, isn't it?"

Brother Charles dropped his gaze, to the Chief Inspector's hands, one lightly clasping the other.

"Are you all right?"

"Me?" asked Gamache, surprised.

The doctor brought his hand up and grazed his finger along his left temple.

"Ah," said the Chief. "That. You noticed."

"I'm a medical man," said Brother Charles with a smile. "I almost never miss a deep scar on the temple." Then his face grew serious. "Or a trembling hand."

"An old issue," said Gamache. "In the past."

"A bleed?" asked the doctor, not letting it go.

"A bullet," said the Chief.

"Oh," said Brother Charles. "A hema-

516

toma. Is that the only effect? The tremble in your right hand?"

Gamache didn't quite know how to answer that. So he didn't. Instead he smiled and nodded. "It gets slightly more noticeable when I'm tired, or stressed."

"Yes, Inspector Beauvoir told me."

"Did he?" Gamache looked interested. And not particularly pleased.

"I asked." The doctor looked at Gamache for a moment, examining him. Seeing the friendly face. The lines from the corners of his eyes, and his mouth. Laugh lines. Here was a man who knew how to smile. But there were other lines too. On his forehead and between Gamache's brows. Lines that came with worry.

But more than this man's physical body, what struck Frère Charles about Gamache was his calm. Frère Charles knew this was the sort of peace a person found only after being at war.

"If that's your only symptom, you're a lucky man," the medical monk finally said.

"Yes."

Take this child.

"Though the arrival of your boss doesn't seem to have improved the situation."

Gamache said nothing. Not for the first time he realized these monks missed very little. Every breath, every look, every movement, every tremble told these monks something. This medical monk in particular.

"It was a surprise," Gamache admitted. "Who do you think killed the prior?"

"Changing the subject?" The doctor smiled, then thought before he answered. "I honestly don't know. I've thought of little else since his death. I can't believe any of us did it. But of course, one of us did."

He paused again and looked directly at Gamache. "One thing I know for sure, though."

"What's that?"

"Most people don't die at once."

It wasn't what Gamache was expecting the doctor to say, and he wondered if Brother Charles realized the prior was alive when Frère Simon found him.

"They die a bit at a time," said the doctor.

"Excusez-moi?"

"They don't teach this at medical school, but I've seen it in real life. People die in bits and pieces. A series of *petites morts*. Little deaths. They lose their sight, their hearing, their independence. Those are the physical ones. But there're others. Less obvious, but more fatal. They lose heart. They lose hope. They lose faith. They lose interest. And finally, they lose themselves."

"What are you telling me, Frère Charles?"

"That it's possible both the prior and his killer were well down the same path. Both might have suffered a series of *petites morts,* before the final blow."

"The *grande mort,*" said Gamache. "And who here fits that description?"

Now the doctor leaned forward, past the field of chocolate blueberries.

"How do you think we get here, Chief Inspector? To Saint-Gilbert-Entre-les-Loups? We didn't follow the yellow brick road. We were shoved along, by our own *petites morts.* There isn't a man in this monastery who didn't come through that door wounded. Damaged. Almost dead inside."

"And here you found what?"

"Healing. Our wounds were bound. The holes inside us were filled with faith. Our loneliness healed by the company of God. We thrived on simple work and healthy food. On routine and certainty. By no longer being alone. But more than anything, it's the joy of singing to God. The chants saved us, Chief Inspector. Plainchants. They resurrected each and every one of us."

"Well, maybe not all of you."

Both men sat with the knowledge that the

miracle hadn't been perfect. One man was missed.

"Eventually those chants destroyed your community."

"I can see how it would appear that way, but the chants weren't the problem. It was our own egos. Power struggles. It was terrible."

"Some malady is coming upon us," said Gamache.

The doctor looked puzzled, then nodded. Placing the quote.

"T. S. Eliot. *Murder in the Cathedral. Oui.* That's it. A malady," said the medical monk.

Gamache, as he made his way out the door, was left to wonder just how neutral this Red Cross really was. Had the good doctor found the malady and cured it, with a blow to the head?

Jean-Guy Beauvoir reentered the monastery and went in search of one private place. Just someplace he could be alone.

Finally he found it. The narrow walkway running above and around the Blessed Chapel. Beauvoir climbed the winding steps and sat on the narrow stone bench carved into the wall. He could stay there without being seen.

Once sitting, though, he felt he might

never get up. They'd find him decades from now, ossified. Turned to rock, up there. A gargoyle. Perched and permanently looking down on the bowing and genuflecting men in black and white.

Beauvoir longed at that moment to slip into a robe. To shave his head. To tighten the cord around his waist. And see the world in black and white.

Gamache was good. Francoeur was bad.

Annie loved him. He loved Annie.

The Gamaches would accept him as their son. As their son-in-law.

They'd be happy. He and Annie would be happy.

Simple. Clear.

Beauvoir closed his eyes and took deep breaths, smelling the incense. Years and years of it. Instead of bringing up bad memories, of hours wasted on hard pews, it actually smelled good. Comforting. Relaxing.

Deep breath in. Deep breath out.

In his hand he clasped a pill bottle he'd found on the table in his cell, a note scribbled beside it.

Take as needed. The signature was illegible, but it looked like Frère Charles's. He was a doctor, after all, thought Beauvoir. There could be no harm.

521

He'd stood in his cell, uncertain. The familiar bottle rested in his hand as though the small cavity in the center of his fist was designed for it. He knew what the bottle contained without even reading the label, but he read it anyway and felt both alarm and relief.

OxyContin.

Beauvoir was tempted to bolt down a pill right then and there, in his cell. Then lie down on the narrow cot. And feel the warmth spread and the pain ebb.

But he was afraid Gamache might walk in. Instead, he'd found a place he suspected the Chief, afraid of heights, wouldn't go, even if he knew it was there. The exposed catwalk above the Blessed Chapel.

Now Beauvoir looked at the bottle in his hand, clasped so tightly the cap had left a purple circle in his palm. It was, after all, from a doctor. And he was in pain.

"Oh, Christ," he whispered, and opened the bottle. A few moments later, in the Blessed Chapel, Jean-Guy Beauvoir found blessed relief.

The bells of Saint-Gilbert rang out. Not the thin call to prayers of earlier in the day, but all the bells pealed in a hearty, robust, full-bodied invitation.

Chief Inspector Gamache looked at his watch, out of habit. But he knew what the bells signaled. Five o'clock service.

Vespers.

The Blessed Chapel was empty when he slid into a pew. He put the murder weapon on the seat beside him, and closed his eyes. But not for long. Someone had joined him in the pew.

"Salut, mon vieux," said Gamache. "Where've you been? I was looking for you."

He'd known it was Jean-Guy without looking.

"Here and there," said Beauvoir. "Investigating a murder, you know."

"Are you all right?" Gamache asked. Beauvoir seemed dazed and his clothes were disheveled.

"Fine. I went for a walk and slipped on the path outside. I need to get out every now and then."

"I know what you mean. Any luck with Frère Raymond in the basement?"

Beauvoir looked lost for a moment. Frère Raymond? Then he remembered. Had that even happened? It seemed so long ago.

"The foundations look OK to me. And no sign of a steel pipe."

"Well, no need to look further. I've found the murder weapon."

Gamache handed the towel to his second in command. Above them the bells stopped ringing.

Beauvoir carefully unwrapped the package. There, in the folds, was the iron knocker. He looked at it, not touching, then up at Gamache.

"How d'you know this's what killed him?"

The Chief Inspector told him about his conversation with Frère Simon. The Blessed Chapel was very quiet now and Gamache kept his voice in the lowest register. When he looked up it was to see that the Chief Superintendent had arrived and was sitting in a pew across from them and down a row.

The gap between them, it seemed, was widening. This was fine with Gamache.

Beauvoir wrapped the length of iron back up. "I'll put it in an evidence bag. Not much hope of forensics, though."

"I agree," whispered the Chief.

From the wings of the chapel came a now familiar sound. A single voice. Frère Antoine, Gamache recognized, alone, came in first. The new choirmaster.

Then his rich tenor was joined by another voice. Frère Bernard, who collected eggs and wild blueberries. His voice was higher, less rich but more precise.

Then Brother Charles, the *médecin,*

walked in, his tenor filling in the gaps between the first two monks.

One after another the brothers filed in, their voices joining, mixing, complementing. Giving a plainchant depth and life. As beautiful as the music had been on CD, as wonderful as it had been yesterday, it was even more glorious now.

Gamache could feel himself both invigorated and relaxed. Calmed and enlivened. The Chief wondered if it was simply because he knew the monks now, or if it was something less tangible. Some shift in the monks that came with the death of their old choirmaster and the ascension of the new.

One after another, the monks walked in, singing. Frère Simon. Frère Raymond. And then, at last, Frère Luc.

And everything changed. His voice, not a tenor, not a baritone. Neither, yet both, joined the rest. And suddenly the individual voices, the individual notes were connected. Joined. Held in an embrace, as though the neumes had lengthened and become arms, and were holding each monk and each man listening.

It became whole. No more wounds. No more damage. The holes became whole. The damage repaired.

Frère Luc sang the simple chant, simply.

No histrionics. No hysteria. But with a passion and fullness of spirit that Gamache hadn't noticed before. It was as though the young monk was free. And being freed, he gave new life to the gliding, soaring neumes.

Gamache listened, struck dumb by the beauty of it. By the way the voices claimed not just his head, but his heart. His arms, his legs, his hands. The scar on his head, and his chest, and the tremble in his hand.

The music held him. Safe. And whole.

Frère Luc's voice had done that. The others, alone, were magnificent. But Frère Luc elevated them to the Divine. What had he told Gamache? *I am the harmony.* It seemed the simple truth.

Beside Gamache on the bench, Jean-Guy Beauvoir had closed his eyes, and felt himself slip away to that familiar world, where nothing mattered. There was no more pain, no more ache. No more uncertainty.

Everything would be fine.

And then, the music stopped. The last note died away. And there was silence.

The abbot stepped forward, made the sign of the cross, opened his mouth.

And stood there.

Stunned by another sound. One never heard during Vespers. Never before heard during any prayer service at Saint-Gilbert-

Entre-les-Loups.

It was a rod on wood.

Pounding.

Someone was at the door. Someone wanted in.

Or out.

Twenty-Seven

Dom Philippe tried not to notice.

He intoned a blessing. Heard the response. Gave the next call.

He'd become quite good, he realized, at not noticing. At shutting out unpleasantness.

His vow of silence had been expanded to include a vow of deafness. Much longer and he'd be completely senseless.

Standing perfectly still, he surrendered to God.

Then Dom Philippe sang, in a voice no longer young and vigorous but still filled with adoration, the next line of the prayer.

And heard the pounding on the gate, as though in response.

"Lord have mercy," he sang.

Pounding.

"Christ have mercy."

Pounding.

"Holy Trinity, have mercy on him."

528

Pounding.

The abbot's mind went blank. For the first time in decades, after hundreds, thousands of services, his mind went blank.

The peace of Christ, the grace of God had been replaced. By pounding.

Pounding.

Like a giant metronome.

Pounding at the gate.

The monks, lined up on either side of him, looked. At him.

For guidance.

Oh, God, help me, he prayed. *What should I do?*

The pounding wouldn't stop, he realized. It had taken on a rhythm. A dead, repetitive thumping. As though a machine was doing it.

Bang. Bang. Bang.

It would go on forever. Until . . .

Until it was answered.

The abbot did something he'd never, ever done before. Not as a novice, not in all his years as a monk, and now as abbot. The thousands of services he'd celebrated. He'd never once left.

But he did now. He bowed to the cross, then turning his back on his congregation, he walked off the altar.

His heart was pounding too, but much

faster than the banging at the gate. He could feel perspiration beneath his robes. They felt heavy as he walked down the long aisle.

Past that Superintendent of the Sûreté, with his clever eyes and clever face.

Past the young Inspector, who seemed so anxious to be anywhere other than where he was.

Past the Chief Inspector, who listened so closely, as though trying to find answers not just for the crime, but for himself.

Dom Philippe walked past them all. He tried not to rush. Told himself to be measured. To walk with purpose, but with containment.

The pounding continued. Not louder, not softer. Not faster, but neither did it slow. It kept an almost inhuman consistency.

And the abbot found himself rushing. Toward it. Desperate to make it stop. The noise that had shattered Vespers. And finally blown a hole through his determined calm.

Behind Dom Philippe the monks followed, in a long, thin line. Hands up sleeves, heads bowed. Feet hurrying along. Trying to keep up, while not appearing to run.

As the last monk left the altar, the Sûreté officers joined them, Gamache and Beauvoir a step behind Francoeur.

Dom Philippe exited the Blessed Chapel

and turned down the long, long corridor. With the door at the very end. He knew it was a trick of his imagination, but the wood seemed to strain forward with each thump.

Lord have mercy, he prayed as he approached the door. It was the last prayer he'd said on the altar and the only one that had stayed with him, clinging on when everything else had fled. *Lord have mercy. Oh, dear God, have mercy.*

At the door, the abbot stopped. Should he look through the slat, to see who was there? But would it matter? Whoever was there wouldn't stop, the abbot knew, until the heavy door had been opened.

He realized he didn't have a key.

Where was the *frère portier?* Would he have to go all the way back to the Blessed Chapel, to get the key?

The abbot turned and was surprised to see the other monks, in a semi-circle, behind him. Like a choir about to sing Christmas carols. All ye faithful had come, but they were hardly joyful and triumphant. They looked more glum and distressed.

But they were there. The abbot was not alone. God did have mercy.

Frère Luc appeared beside him, the key shaking slightly in his slender hand.

"Give it to me, my son," said the abbot.

"But it's my job, *mon père.*"

Bang.

Bang.

Bang on the door.

Dom Philippe kept his hand out. "This job falls to me," he said and smiled at the alarmed young monk. With trembling hands Frère Luc unclipped the heavy metal key and gave it to the abbot, then stepped back.

Dom Philippe, his own hand unsteady, thrust back the deadbolt. Then he tried to get the key in the lock.

Bang.

Bang.

He brought his other hand up, to steady the key, to help guide it.

Bang.

It slid into place, and he turned it.

The banging stopped. Whoever was on the other side had heard, through the banging, the thin metallic click as the door unlocked.

The gate opened.

It was twilight, the sun almost set. The mist was thicker now. Some light spilled out of the monastery, from the crack in the door, but no light came in.

"Oui?" said the abbot, wishing his voice sounded firmer, more authoritative.

"Dom Philippe?"

The voice was polite, respectful. Disembodied.

"Oui," said the abbot, his voice still not his own.

"May I come in? I've come a long way."

"Who are you?" asked the abbot. It seemed a reasonable question.

"Does it matter? Would you really turn a person away on a night like this?"

It seemed a reasonable answer.

But reason wasn't the Gilbertines' long suit. Passion, commitment, loyalty. Music. But not, perhaps, reason.

Still, Dom Philippe realized the voice was right. He couldn't possibly shut the door now. It was far too late. Once opened, whatever was out there had to come in.

He stepped back. Behind him he heard, as one, the rest of the congregation step back. But out of his peripheral vision he noticed two people holding their ground.

Chief Inspector Gamache and his Inspector, Beauvoir.

A foot stepped in. Well shod, in black leather, with mud and a piece of bright, dead leaf stuck to it. And then the man was in.

He was slender and of medium height, slightly shorter than the abbot. His eyes were light brown, as was his hair, and his skin was pale, except for a slight flush from the cold.

"Merci, mon père." He hauled in a duffel bag and turned to look at his hosts. He smiled then, fully and completely. Not with amusement, but with wonderment. "At last," he said. "I found you."

He wasn't handsome, nor was he hideous. He was unremarkable, except for one thing.

What he wore.

He was also in a monk's robes, but while the Gilbertines wore a white surplice on black, his robes were black on white.

"The hound of the Lord," one of the monks whispered.

When Gamache turned to see which of them had spoken he saw they all had their mouths slightly open.

"We don't use that term anymore," said the new arrival, scanning the men in front of him, his smile widening. "Puts people off."

His voice was pleasant as he continued to stare at them.

The Gilbertines stared back, not smiling.

Finally the stranger turned to Dom Philippe, and offered his hand. The abbot, silently, took it. The young man bowed, then straightened up.

"My name is Brother Sébastien. I've come

from Rome."

"Tonight?" asked the abbot and immediately regretted the stupidity of the question. But he'd heard no plane, nor had he heard the motorboat.

"I flew in from Rome this morning, and made my way here."

"But how?" the abbot asked.

"I paddled."

Now it was Dom Philippe's turn to stare, his mouth slightly open.

Frère Sébastien laughed. It was, like the rest of him, pleasant.

"I know. Not my most brilliant idea. A small plane got me to the local airfield but the fog was getting too thick and no one wanted to take me the rest of the way, so I decided to take myself." He turned to look at Gamache, paused, perplexed, then looked back at the abbot. "You were much farther away than I realized."

"You paddled all this way? From the village?"

"I did."

"But that's miles. How'd you even know where to go?" The abbot willed himself to be quiet, but he couldn't seem to stop the questions.

"The boatman directed me. Said to keep going past three bays and to turn right at the fourth." He seemed delighted by the directions. "But the mist got really heavy and I was afraid I'd made my last mistake. But then I heard your bells and followed the sound. When I got to the head of the bay I saw your lights. You have no idea how happy I am to find you."

And he looked happy, thought Gamache. In fact, he looked ecstatic. He kept staring at the monks as though he wasn't one himself. As though he'd never met a *religieux.*

"Have you come because of the prior?" asked Dom Philippe.

And Gamache had a sudden insight. He stepped forward, but it was too late.

"About his murder?" the abbot asked.

The abbot, a man who longed for great silence, had said too much.

Gamache took a deep breath and Frère Sébastien looked over at him, then his gaze shifted to Beauvoir, before finally resting on Superintendent Francoeur.

The smile slid from the young monk's face, to be replaced by a look of great sympathy. He crossed himself and kissed his thumb, then folded his long hands in front of himself, and bowed slightly, his eyes grave.

"That's why I was in such a rush. I came

as soon as I heard. God rest his soul."

Now all the monks crossed themselves, while Chief Inspector Gamache studied the newcomer. The man who'd paddled through the gathering darkness, through the gathering mist. Across an unfamiliar lake. And finally found the abbey by following the sound. And the light.

He'd traveled all the way from Rome.

Desperate, it would seem, to reach Saint-Gilbert-Entre-les-Loups. So desperate, he'd taken his life in his hands. This young man, while making a joke about his foolish decision making, looked extremely competent to Gamache. So why had he taken such a risk? What couldn't wait until morning?

It wasn't the prior's murder, Gamache was sure of that. He'd known in the instant Dom Philippe had asked that this stranger knew nothing about it. It was news to Frère Sébastien.

If he'd really come all the way from Rome because of the prior's death he'd have been more solemn. Would have offered his sympathies right away.

Instead he'd laughed at his own folly, talked of his travels, said how happy he was to see them. Marveled at the monks. But hadn't once mentioned Frère Mathieu.

No. Frère Sébastien had a reason to be

537

there. And an important one. But it had nothing to do with Frère Mathieu's death.

"Were those the Vesper bells?" Frère Sébastien asked. "I'm so sorry, *mon père,* to have interrupted. Please, continue."

The abbot hesitated then turned and walked back down the long corridor, the newcomer behind him, looking this way and that.

Gamache watched him closely. It was as though the visitor had never been in a monastery before.

The Chief signaled Brother Charles to stay at the back of the procession, with him. He waited until the others were a good distance ahead, then turned to the doctor.

"Was it you who called Frère Sébastien the hound of the Lord?"

"Well, I didn't mean him personally."

The doctor looked pale, shaken. Not his jovial self. In fact, he looked considerably more upset about the live stranger than the dead prior.

"Then what did you mean?" insisted Gamache.

They were almost in the Blessed Chapel, and he wanted to finish this conversation before entering the church. Not out of some sense of religious propriety, but because of the astonishing acoustics.

This conversation must remain private.

"He's a Dominican," said Brother Charles, his voice also low, his eyes never leaving the head of the procession. Frère Sébastien and the abbot.

"How'd you know?"

"His robes and belt. Dominican."

"But how does that make him the hound of the Lord?"

The head of the procession, like the head of a snake, had entered the Blessed Chapel and the rest were following.

"Dominican," Brother Charles repeated. "*Domini canis.* Hound of the Lord."

Then they too entered the Blessed Chapel and all conversation ended. Brother Charles gave Gamache a small nod and followed his fellow monks back onto the altar, where they took their places.

Frère Sébastien genuflected, crossed himself, then sat in a pew, craning his neck. Looking this way and that.

Beauvoir had returned to the pew and Gamache frowned as Superintendent Francoeur joined Jean-Guy. Gamache walked around and slid into the seat on the other side of Beauvoir, so that the Inspector was bracketed by his bosses.

But Beauvoir didn't care. As Vespers began again he closed his eyes and imagined

himself in Annie's apartment. Lying together on the sofa in front of the fireplace.

She'd be in the crook of his arm. He'd be
holding her secure.

Every other woman he'd dated, and Enid,
whom he'd married, had been tiny. Slender,
petite.

Annie Gamache was not. She was athletic,
full bodied. Strong. And when she lay with
him, clothed or not, they fit together perfectly.

"I never want this to end," Annie would
whisper.

"It won't," he'd assure her. "Never ever."

"It'll change, though, when people find
out."

"It'll be even better," he'd say.

"Oui," Annie would agree. "But I like it
like this. Just us."

And he liked it like that too.

Now, in the Blessed Chapel, with its scent
of incense and candles, he imagined he
heard the murmur of the fireplace. Smelled
the sweet maple logs. Tasted the red wine.
And could feel Annie on his chest.

The music began. At once, from some signal
invisible to Gamache, the monks went from
still and silent to full voice.

Their voices filled the chapel like air in

540

lungs. It seemed to emanate from the rocks of the walls. As though the Gregorian chants were as much a part of the abbey as the stones and slate and wooden beams.

In front of Gamache, Frère Sébastien stared. Transfixed. Unmoving.

His mouth was open slightly, and there was a glistening down his pale cheek.

Frère Sébastien listened to the Gilbertines sing their service, and wept, as though he'd never heard the voice of God before.

Dinner that night was an almost silent affair.

Since Vespers ended late, the brothers and their guests had gone directly to the dining hall. Tureens filled with brilliant pea and mint soup sat on the table, next to baskets of fresh, warm baguette.

A brother sang the prayer of thanksgiving for the meal, the monks crossed themselves, and then the only sound was of the soup being served and spoons against earthenware bowls.

And then, a low hum was heard. In any other environment it would've been inaudible, but here, in the silence, it sounded as loud as the boatman's engine.

And it got louder. And louder.

The monks, one by one, stopped eating

and soon the only sound in the long dining hall was the humming. Every head turned to see where it was coming from.

It came from Chief Inspector Gamache.

He sipped his soup, and he hummed. Looking down at his plate, apparently engrossed in the delicious meal. Then, perhaps sensing scrutiny, he looked up.

But the humming didn't stop.

Gamache smiled a little as he hummed, and looked at the faces of the monks.

Some looked scandalized. Some looked worried, as though a madman had appeared. Some looked angry, to have their peace disturbed.

Beauvoir looked blank, his soup untouched in front of him, his appetite gone. Francoeur shook his head slightly, as though ashamed.

One monk looked frightened. Frère Simon.

"What's that you're humming?"

The question came from the head of the table. But not from Dom Philippe. It was the Dominican who'd asked the question. His young face was interested, goodnatured. Not angry, not pained, not scandalized.

In fact, Frère Sébastien seemed sincerely interested.

"I'm sorry," said Gamache, "I didn't realize I was humming so loud. *Désolé.*"

But the Chief Inspector didn't look at all desolate.

"I think it's a Canadian folk song," said Frère Simon, his voice slightly higher than usual.

"Is that right? It's very pretty."

"Actually, *mon frère,*" said Gamache, and beside him Frère Simon was squirming and knocking his knee against Gamache beneath the table, "it's a chant. I have it stuck in my head. Can't seem to get it out."

"It's not a chant," said Simon quickly. "He thinks it is but I was trying to explain that a chant is much simpler."

"Whatever it is, it's very beautiful," said Frère Sébastien.

"Much better than the song it replaced in my head. 'Camptown Races.' "

"Camptown racetrack's five miles long. Doo-dah, doo-dah," Frère Sébastien sang. "That one?"

All eyes swung from the Chief Inspector to the newcomer. Even Gamache was speechless for a moment.

Frère Sébastien had made the silly old song sound like a work of genius. As though Mozart or Handel or Beethoven had written it. If the works of da Vinci could turn themselves into music, they'd have sounded like that.

"All the doo-dah day," Frère Sébastien concluded with a smile.

These monks, who sang so gloriously for God, looked at the Dominican as though at a brand-new creature.

"Who are you?"

It was Frère Antoine who asked. The new choirmaster. He wasn't demanding, not at all accusing. His face and voice held a note of wonderment Gamache hadn't heard before.

The Chief looked at the other monks.

The discomfort had disappeared. The anxiety gone. Frère Simon had forgotten to be taciturn, Brother Charles was no longer fearful.

What they did look was deeply curious.

"I'm Frère Sébastien. A simple Dominican friar."

"But who are you?" Frère Antoine persisted.

Frère Sébastien carefully folded his napkin and placed it in front of him. Then he looked down the long wooden table, worn and marked by hundreds and hundreds of years of Gilbertines sitting at it.

"I said I came from Rome," he began, "but I wasn't very specific. I come from the

Palace of the Holy Office at the Vatican. I work at the CDF."

Now the silence was profound.

"The CDF?" Gamache asked.

"The Congregation for the Doctrine of the Faith." Frère Sébastien turned to Gamache and clarified. He had an apologetic look on his nondescript face.

Fear had crept back into the room. Whereas before it seemed vague, without form, now it had a form and a focus. The pleasant young monk at the head of the table, sitting beside the abbot. The hound of the Lord.

As he looked at Frère Sébastien and Dom Philippe side by side, the Chief Inspector was reminded of the unlikely emblem of Saint-Gilbert-Entre-les-Loups. Two wolves, intertwined. One wore black on white, the other, the abbot, wore white on black. Polar opposites. Sébastien, young and vital. Dom Philippe, older and aging by the moment.

Entre les loups. Among the wolves.

"The Congregation for the Doctrine of the Faith?" asked Gamache.

"The Inquisition," said Frère Simon, in a very small voice.

TWENTY-EIGHT

Gamache and Beauvoir waited until they were back in the prior's office to talk. Superintendent Francoeur had corralled the newcomer right after dinner and the two had stayed in the dining hall.

Everyone else had left as soon as they politely could.

"Jeez," said Beauvoir. "The Inquisition. I didn't expect that."

"No one does," said Gamache. "There hasn't been an Inquisition in hundreds of years. I wonder why he's here?"

Beauvoir crossed his arms and leaned against the door while Gamache sat behind the desk. Only then did he notice the other chair was broken, and leaning, crooked, in a corner.

Gamache said nothing, but looked at Beauvoir and raised a brow.

"A slight disagreement."

"With the chair?"

"With the Superintendent. No one was hurt," he hurriedly added on seeing the Chief's face. But the assurance didn't seem to work. Gamache continued to look upset.

"What happened?"

"Nothing. He said some stupid things and I disagreed."

"I told you not to engage him, not to argue. It's what he does, he gets into people's heads —"

"And what was I supposed to do? Just nod and bow and take his shit? You might, but I won't."

The two men stared at each other for a moment.

"Sorry," said Beauvoir, and stood up straight. He wiped his tired face with his hands then looked at Gamache.

The Chief was no longer looking angry. Now he looked concerned.

"Has something happened? What did the Superintendent say?"

"Oh, just the usual crap. That you don't know what you're doing and I'm exactly like you."

"And that made you angry?"

"To be compared to you? Who wouldn't be?" Beauvoir laughed, but he could see the Chief wasn't amused. He continued to examine Beauvoir.

"Are you all right?"

"God, why do you always ask that, as soon as I get angry, or upset? You think I'm that fragile?"

"Are you all right?" Gamache repeated. And waited.

"Oh, fuck," said Beauvoir and leaned heavily against the wall. "I'm just tired, and this place is getting to me. And now this new monk, this Dominican. I feel like I've landed on another planet. They're speaking the same language as me, but I keep thinking they're saying more than I understand, you know?"

"I do." Gamache kept his gaze on Beauvoir, then looked away. Deciding to let it drop for the moment. But something had clearly crawled inside the younger man's skin. And Gamache could guess what. Or who.

Chief Superintendent Francoeur had many skills, Gamache knew. It was a terrible mistake to underestimate him. And in all the years they'd worked together, Gamache knew that Francoeur's greatest gift was bringing out the worst in people.

However well hidden that demon, Francoeur would find it. And Francoeur would free it. And feed it. Until it consumed its host, and became the man.

Gamache had seen decent young Sûreté officers turned into cynical, vicious, strutting thugs. Young men and women with little conscience and big guns. And a superior who modeled and rewarded their behavior.

Once again Gamache looked at Beauvoir, leaning exhausted against the wall. Somehow Francoeur had gotten into Jean-Guy. He'd found the entrance, found the wound, and was roaming around inside him. Looking to do even more damage.

And Gamache had allowed it.

He felt himself almost quaking with rage. In a flash it had claimed his core, and raced to his extremities, so that his hands closed into white-knuckled fists.

Rage was transforming him, and Gamache fought to regain control. To grip his humanity and haul himself back.

Francoeur wouldn't get this young man, Gamache vowed. It stops here.

He got up, excused himself and left the room.

Beauvoir waited for a few minutes, thinking the Chief must have just gone down the hall to the washrooms. But when he didn't return Beauvoir got up and went into the hallway, looking this way and that.

The halls were dim, the light low. He checked the washrooms. No Gamache. He knocked on the Chief's cell and when there was no answer poked his head in. No Gamache.

Beauvoir was at a loss. Now what?

He could text Annie.

Taking out his BlackBerry he checked. There was a message from her. She was having dinner with friends and would email him when she got home.

It was short and cheerful.

Too short, thought Beauvoir. Too cheerful? Was there, perhaps, just a hint of abruptness about the message? A dismissiveness. Not caring that he was still working well into the night? That he couldn't just drop everything and go for drinks and dinner with friends.

He stood in the murky hallway and imagined Annie at that *terrasse* she liked on Laurier. Young professionals, drinking microbrewery ales. Annie laughing. Having a good time. Without him.

"Would you like to see what's behind that?"

The voice, more than the question, made Francoeur jerk in a small spasm of surprise. The Superintendent had been looking at the plaque to Saint Gilbert when Gamache walked quietly across the Blessed Chapel.

Without waiting for a reply, Gamache reached over and depressed the two wolves. The door swung open to reveal the hidden Chapter House.

"I think we should go in, don't you?" Gamache placed a large, firm hand on Francoeur's shoulder and propelled him into the room. It wasn't a shove, exactly. A witness would never testify that there was any assault. But both men knew it was neither Francoeur's idea to enter the room, nor his own steam.

Gamache closed the door then turned to face his superior.

"What did you say to Inspector Beauvoir?"

"Let me out of here, Armand."

Gamache considered him for a moment. "Are you afraid of me?"

"Of course not." But Francoeur looked a little frightened.

"Would you like to leave?" Gamache's voice was friendly but his eyes were cold and hard. And his stance, in front of the door, unyielding.

Francoeur was silent for a moment, assessing the situation.

"Why don't you ask your Inspector what happened?"

"Stop the schoolyard games, Sylvain. You came here with an agenda. I thought it was to screw with me, but it wasn't, was it? You knew I wouldn't care. So you took off after Inspector Beauvoir. He's still recovering from his wounds —"

Francoeur made a gruff, dismissive noise.

"You don't believe that?" asked Gamache.

"Everyone else recovered. You recovered, for God's sake. You treat him like a child."

"I won't discuss the Inspector's health with you. He's still recovering, but he's not as vulnerable as you think. You've always underestimated people, Sylvain. That's your great weakness. You think others are weaker than they are. And that you're more powerful than you actually are."

"Which is it, Armand? Is Beauvoir still wounded? Or is he stronger than I think? You might've fooled your people, mesmerized them with your bullshit, but not me."

"No," said Gamache. "We know each other too well."

Francoeur had begun to roam the room, pacing it. But Gamache stayed put, in front of the door. His eyes never leaving the Chief Superintendent.

"What did you say to Inspector Beauvoir?" Gamache repeated.

"I told him what I told you. That you're

incompetent and he deserves better."

Gamache studied the prowling man. Then shook his head.

"It's more than that. Tell me."

Francoeur stopped and turned to face Gamache.

"My God, Beauvoir's said something to you, hasn't he?" Francoeur got within inches of the Chief, staring point-blank into his eyes. Neither man blinking. "If he's not recovered from his wounds, they're wounds you made. If he's weak, it's a weakness you created. If he's insecure it's because he knows he's not safe with you. And now you blame me?"

Francoeur laughed. The peppermint breath hot and moist on Gamache's face.

And again Gamache could feel his rage, so tightly contained, spill out. He fought with all his might to control it, knowing the enemy wasn't this leering, lying, vicious man. It was himself. And the rage that threatened to consume him.

"Jean-Guy Beauvoir is not to be harmed." Each word was said slowly. Clearly. Precisely. And in a voice few had heard from the Chief Inspector. A voice that made his superior step back. That sizzled the smile right off the handsome face.

"It's too late, Armand," said Francoeur.

"The harm's already done. And you're the one who did it. Not me."

"Inspector?"

Frère Antoine had been reading in his cell when he heard the footfall outside his door. He looked into the corridor and noticed the Sûreté officer standing there, looking confused.

"You look lost. Are you all right?"

"I'm fine," said Beauvoir, wishing people would stop asking him that.

Once again the two men stared at each other. The same man, in so many ways. The same age, height, build. The same neighborhood growing up.

But one had entered the Church and never left. The other had left the Church and never returned. Now they looked at each other across the dim corridor of Saint-Gilbert-Entre-les-Loups.

Beauvoir approached the monk. "That fellow who just arrived. The Dominican. What's the story there?"

Frère Antoine's eyes darted up and down the hallway. Then he stepped into his cell and Beauvoir followed.

It was exactly the same as the cell Beauvoir had been assigned, with a few personal tweaks. A sweatshirt and pants lay in a bundle in the corner. Books were stacked beside the bed. A biography of Maurice Richard. A hockey playbook, written by a former coach of the Montréal Canadiens. Beauvoir had those books too. Hockey had replaced religion for most Québécois.

But here they seemed to co-exist. On top of the pile was a history of a monastery in someplace called Solesmes. And a bible.

"Frère Sébastien," said Brother Antoine, his voice not exactly a whisper, but low enough so that Beauvoir had to concentrate to hear, "is from the office in the Vatican that used to be known as the Inquisition."

"I gathered that. But what's he doing here?"

"He said he came because of the prior's murder." Frère Antoine didn't look any too happy about that.

"But you don't believe it, do you?"

Frère Antoine grinned, just a little. "Is it that obvious?"

"No. I'm just that observant."

Antoine chuckled before growing serious again. "The Vatican might send a priest to investigate what happened in a monastery where there's been a murder. Not to find the killer, but to find out how the climate in an abbey got so bad there was a murder."

"But we know what went wrong," said

Beauvoir. "You were all fighting over the chants, the recording."

"But why were we fighting?" asked Frère Antoine. He seemed genuinely perplexed. "I've been praying over it for weeks, months. We should've been able to resolve this. So what went wrong? And why didn't we see that one of us was not only capable of murder, but actually contemplating it?"

Seeing the confusion, the pain, in the monk's eyes, Beauvoir wanted to tell him. To answer his question. But he hadn't a clue what the answer was. He didn't know why the monks had turned on each other. Just as he hadn't a clue why any of them were there in the first place. Why any of these men were even monks.

"You said the Vatican might send a priest, but you don't seem convinced. Do you think he's not who he says he is?"

"No, I believe he really is Frère Sébastien, and that he works for the Congregation for the Doctrine of the Faith in Rome. I just don't think he's here because of the murder of Frère Mathieu."

"Why not?" Beauvoir sat on the wooden chair and the monk sat on the side of his bed.

"Because he's a monk, not a priest. I think they'd send someone more senior for something this serious. But really," Frère Antoine tried to find the words to express what was mostly a feeling. An intuition. "The Vatican doesn't move this fast. Nothing in the Church moves quickly. It's mired in tradition. There are proper procedures for everything."

"Even murder?"

Antoine grinned again. "If you've studied the Borgias you know the Vatican has a tradition of that too. So yes, even murder. The CDF might send someone to investigate us, but not so quickly. It'd take months, maybe even years, for them to act. Frère Mathieu would be dust. It's inconceivable a Vatican man would arrive before the prior is even buried."

"Then what's your theory?"

The monk thought, then shook his head. "I've been trying to figure it out all evening."

"So're we," Beauvoir admitted, then regretted giving out that information. The less a suspect knew of the investigation, the better. Sometimes they planted information, to unnerve a suspect. But it was always deliberate. This was an unguarded slip.

"I have those books," he said, hoping to cover up his indiscretion.

"The hockey ones? You play?"

"Center. You?"

557

"Center too, but I have to admit there wasn't much competition for the position once Frère Eustache died of old age."

Beauvoir laughed, then sighed.

"Do you want to talk about it?" Frère Antoine asked.

"About what?"

"Whatever it is that's eating you."

"All that's eating me is trying to find the killer and getting out of here."

"You don't like the monastery?"

"Of course not. You do?"

"I wouldn't be here if I didn't," said Frère Antoine. "I love Saint-Gilbert."

It was such a simple statement it left Beauvoir dumbfounded. He'd said it in the same way Beauvoir might talk about Annie. No confusion, no ambiguity. It just was. Like the sky just was, and the stones just were. It was natural and absolute.

"Why?" Beauvoir leaned forward. It was one of the questions he'd been dying to ask this monk with the beautiful voice and the body so like his own.

"Why do I love it here? What's not to love?" Frère Antoine looked around his cell as though it was a suite at the Ritz in Montréal. "We play hockey in the winter, fish in the summer, swim in the lake and collect berries. I know what each day will bring, and yet each day feels like an adventure. I get to hang around men who believe as I do, and yet are different enough to be endlessly fascinating. I live in the house of my Father and learn from my brothers. And I get to sing the words of God in the voice of God."

The monk leaned forward, his strong hands resting on his knees.

"Do you know what I found here?"

Beauvoir shook his head.

"I found peace."

Beauvoir felt his eyes burn and sat back, deeply ashamed of himself.

"Why do you investigate murders?" Frère Antoine asked.

"Because I'm good at it."

"And what makes you good at it?"

"I don't know."

"Yes you do. You can tell me."

"I don't know," snapped Beauvoir. "But it's better than sitting on my ass or on my knees praying to some cloud in the sky. At least I'm doing something useful."

"Have you ever killed anyone?" the monk asked, his voice quiet.

Beauvoir, taken aback, nodded.

"I haven't," said Frère Antoine.

"Have you ever saved anyone?" Beauvoir asked.

Now Frère Antoine looked surprised. After a moment's silence he shook his head.

"I have," said Beauvoir, getting to his feet. "You just keep singing, *mon frère.* Keep praying. Keep kneeling. And let others stand up and do the saving."

Beauvoir left and was halfway back to the prior's office before he heard Frère Antoine's voice.

"There is one person I've saved."

Beauvoir stopped and turned around. The monk was standing in the dim corridor outside his cell.

"Myself."

Jean-Guy snorted, shook his head and turned his back on Frère Antoine.

He hadn't believed a word of it. Certainly hadn't believed the monk when he talked about his love of the monastery. It was impossible to love the pile of stones and the old bones that rattled around inside it. Hiding from the world. Hiding from their reason.

It was impossible to love singing the deathly dull music, or a God who required it of them. And he wasn't at all sure he believed Frère Antoine when the monk said he'd never killed.

Once inside the prior's office, Jean-Guy Beauvoir leaned against the wall, then bent over, placing his hands on his knees. He took a deep breath in. A deep breath out.

Chief Inspector Gamache returned to the prior's office carrying a new chair.

"*Salut,*" he said to Beauvoir, then placed the broken chair in the corridor, hoping a carpenter monk might find it and fix it. Gamache had things of his own to fix.

He indicated the chair, and Beauvoir sat.

"What did Superintendent Francoeur say to you?"

Beauvoir looked at him, astonished.

"I told you. Just shit about how incompetent you are. Like I don't already know."

But his attempt at levity sat on the desk between them. Gamache didn't crack a smile. Didn't take his eyes off his second in command.

"There was more, though," the Chief said, after considering Beauvoir for a few quiet moments. "Francoeur said more. Or insinuated. You need to trust me, Jean-Guy."

"There was nothing more."

Beauvoir was looking tired, drawn, and Gamache knew he needed to send Beauvoir back to Montréal. He'd find some pretext. Jean-Guy could take back the murder weapon and the vellum they found on the body. Now that copies had been made the original could go to the lab.

Yes, there were plenty of good reasons to send Jean-Guy back to Montréal. Including the real one.

"I think when people care about each other they want to protect them," said Gamache, choosing his words carefully. "But sometimes, like blocking a goalie in hockey or soccer, instead of protecting them you're just making it harder for them to see what's coming. Harm is done. By mistake."

Gamache leaned a fraction further forward, and Beauvoir leaned away, just a fraction.

"I know you're trying to protect me, Jean-Guy. And I appreciate it. But you have to tell me the truth."

"And you, sir? Are you telling me the truth?"

"About what?"

"About the leaked video of the raid. About how it got out. The official report was a cover-up. That video was leaked internally. But you seem to believe the official report. A hacker, my ass."

"Is that it? Did Superintendent Francoeur say something about the video to you?"

"No, it's my own question."

"And I've answered it before." He looked closely at Beauvoir. "Where did this suddenly come from? What do you want me to say?"

"That you don't believe the report. That you're privately investigating. That you'll find out who did it. They were our people. Your people. You can't just leave it like this."

His voice was spiraling out of control.

Beauvoir was right, of course. The video had been leaked internally. Gamache had known that from the moment it had happened. But he'd chosen to, officially anyway, accept the finding of the internal investigation. That some kid, some hacker, had just gotten lucky and found the video of the raid in the Sûreté files.

It was a ludicrous report. But Gamache had told his people, including Beauvoir, to accept it. To let it go. To move on.

And as far as he knew, they all had. Except Beauvoir.

And now Gamache wondered if he should tell him that for the past eight months he and a few other senior officers, with the help of some outsiders, were secretly, carefully, quietly investigating.

Some malady is coming upon us.

But in the case of the Sûreté du Québec, it had already arrived. Had been there for years, rotting away, from the inside. And from the top down.

Sylvain Francoeur had been sent to the monastery to gather information. Not about the murder of the prior, but to find out how much Gamache might know. Or suspect.

And Francoeur had tried to get at it through Beauvoir. Pushing and prodding and trying to thrust him over the edge.

Once again Gamache felt that lick of rage.

He wished he could tell Beauvoir everything, but he was deeply glad he hadn't. Francoeur would leave Jean-Guy alone now. Satisfied that while Gamache might still be up to something, Beauvoir wasn't. Francoeur would be satisfied that he'd gotten all he could from Beauvoir.

Yes, Francoeur had been sent with an agenda, and Gamache had finally figured out what it was. But Gamache had a question of his own. Who had sent the Chief Superintendent?

Who was the top boss's boss?

"Well?" Beauvoir demanded.

"We've been through this before, Jean-Guy," said Gamache. "But I'm happy to talk about it again, if it'll help."

He looked directly at Beauvoir over his half-moon reading glasses.

It was a gaze Jean-Guy had seen often. In trappers' cabins. In shitty little motel rooms. In restaurants and bistros. Burger and *pou-*

tine in front of them. And notebooks open.

Talking about a case. Dissecting the suspects, the evidence. Tossing around ideas, thoughts, wild guesses.

For more than ten years Beauvoir had looked into those eyes, over those glasses. And while he hadn't always agreed with the Chief, he'd always respected him. Loved him even. In the way only one brother-in-arms could love another.

Armand Gamache was his Chief. His boss. His leader. His mentor. And more.

One day, God willing, Gamache would hold his grandchildren in that gaze. Jean-Guy's children. Annie's children.

Beauvoir could see the pain in those familiar eyes. And he couldn't believe he'd put it there.

"Forget I said anything," Beauvoir said. "It was a stupid question. It doesn't matter who leaked the video. Does it?"

Despite himself he heard the plea in those last words.

Gamache leaned back, heavily, and watched Beauvoir for a moment. "If you want to talk about it, I will, you know."

But Beauvoir could see what saying this cost Gamache. Beauvoir knew he wasn't the only one who'd suffered that day in the factory, that day captured by the video and released into the world. Beauvoir knew he wasn't the only one who still bore the burden of survival.

"The damage is done, *patron.* You're right, we need to move on."

Gamache removed his glasses and looked directly at Beauvoir. "I need you to believe something, Jean-Guy. Whoever leaked that video will answer for it one day."

"Just not to us?"

"We have our own work to do here, and frankly, I'm finding it hard enough."

The Chief smiled, but it didn't quite cover the watchfulness in his brown eyes. The sooner Gamache could get Beauvoir back to Montréal, the better. It was dark now, but he'd talk to the abbot and send Beauvoir back first thing in the morning.

Gamache pulled the laptop toward him. "I wish we could get this thing working."

"No," said Beauvoir, sharply. He leaned over the desk, his hand gripping the screen.

The Chief looked at him in surprise.

Beauvoir smiled. "Sorry, it's just that I was working on it this afternoon and I think I've found the problem."

"And you don't want me to screw it up, is that it?"

"Absolutely."

Beauvoir hoped his voice was light. He

hoped his explanation was credible. But mostly he hoped Gamache would back away from the computer.

He did. And Beauvoir turned it around so that it faced him.

The crisis was averted. He sat back down in his chair. The chronic ache had turned into a sharp pain that tunneled into Beauvoir's bones and ran through his marrow. Like corridors, carrying the pain to every part of his body.

Beauvoir began wondering how soon he could be alone in the office. With the computer. And the DVD the Superintendent had brought. And the pills the doctor had left. He now longed for the next service. So that while everyone else was in the Blessed Chapel he could be in here.

They spent the next twenty minutes discussing the case, throwing around theories, throwing out theories, until finally Gamache got to his feet.

"I need a walk. Do you want to come?"

Beauvoir's heart sank, but he nodded and followed Gamache into the corridor.

They turned toward the Blessed Chapel, when the Chief suddenly stopped and stared, at the electric light bulb attached to the wall.

"Do you know, Jean-Guy, when we first

arrived I was surprised they had electricity here."

"Comes from solar and some hydro power they've hooked up to a nearby river. Frère Raymond told me. Want to know how it works? He told me that as well."

"Perhaps for my birthday. As a special gift," said the Chief. "But what I'm wondering now is how that light got there."

He pointed to the wall sconce.

"I don't understand, *patron*. How does any light get on a wall? It's wired there."

"Exactly. But where're the wires? And where's the ductwork for the new heating system? And the pipes for the plumbing?"

"Where they are in any building," said Beauvoir, wondering if the Chief had lost his mind. "Behind the wall."

"But the plan shows only one wall. The Gilbertines who built it took years, decades, to dig the foundation and put the walls up. It's an engineering marvel. But you can't tell me they designed it to have a geothermal unit and plumbing and that."

Again he pointed to the light.

"You've lost me," admitted Beauvoir.

Gamache turned to him. "In your home, in mine, there're two walls. The exterior cladding and the interior drywall. And between the two is the insulation, and the wiring. The plumbing. The vents."

And then it clicked for Beauvoir. "They can't have passed the wires and pipes through solid stone. So this isn't the outside wall," he pointed to the fieldstones that made the wall, "there's another wall behind it."

"I think there must be. The wall you examined for flaws might not be the one that's crumbling. It's the outer wall that's breached by roots and water. It isn't yet noticeable inside."

Two skins, thought Beauvoir, as they resumed their walk and stepped into the Blessed Chapel. The public face, and then the crumbling, rotting one behind.

He'd made a mistake. Hadn't looked hard enough. And Gamache knew it.

"Excusez-moi," a voice sang out, and the two men slowed, and turned. They were crossing the Blessed Chapel.

"Over here."

Gamache and Beauvoir looked to their right, and there, in the shadows, stood the Dominican. Beside the plaque to Gilbert of Sempringham.

The two Sûreté men walked over.

"You looked like you have someplace to go," said Frère Sébastien. "If I'm disturbing you we can talk later."

"We always have someplace to go, *mon frère*," Gamache said. "And if we don't we're trained to look as though we do."

The Dominican laughed. "The same with monks. If you go to the Vatican we're always hurrying down corridors looking important. Most of the time we're just trying to find a bathroom. The sad convergence of great Italian coffee and a shocking distance between toilets in the Vatican. The architects of Saint Peter's were brilliant, but toilets weren't a priority. Superintendent Francoeur has told me something about the death of the prior. I wonder if we can talk some more about it? I get the feeling that while Monsieur Francoeur's in charge, you do most of the actual investigating."

"That's a fair assessment," agreed Gamache. "What questions do you have?"

But instead of answering, the monk turned to the plaque. "A long life, Gilbert had. And an interesting description." He gestured to the writing. "I find it strange that the Gilbertines themselves, who presumably made the plaque, should make him out to be so dull. But way down here, as an afterthought, they say he defended his archbishop." Frère Sébastien turned to Gamache. "You know who that was?"

"The archbishop? Thomas à Becket."

Frère Sébastien nodded. In the uncertain light of the bulbs high in the rafters, shadows were distorted. Eyes became bleak holes, noses were elongated, misshapen.

The Dominican gave them a grotesque smile. "A remarkable thing for Gilbert to do. I'd love to know why he did it."

"And I'd love to know, *mon frère*," said Gamache, not smiling, "why you're really here."

The question amazed the monk, who stared at Gamache, then laughed.

"I think we have a lot to talk about, monsieur. Shall we go into the Chapter House? We won't be disturbed there."

The door to the room was through the plaque. Gamache knew it. Beauvoir knew it. And the monk seemed to know it. But instead of finding the hidden catch and opening it, Frère Sébastien waited. For one of the others to do it.

Chief Inspector Gamache considered the monk. He seemed pleasant. There was that word again. Inoffensive. Happy in his work, happy in his life. Happy, certainly, to have followed the Angelus bells and found this secluded monastery.

Built almost four hundred years earlier by Dom Clément, to escape the Inquisition. They'd faded into the Canadian wilderness and let the world believe the last rites were said for the last Gilbertine centuries ago.

Even the Church believed they'd gone extinct.

But they hadn't. For centuries these monks sat by the shores of this pristine lake, adoring God. Praying to him. Singing to him. And living lives of quiet contemplation.

But never forgetting what drove them there.

Fear. Fretting.

As though the walls weren't high enough, and thick enough, Dom Clément had taken one more measure. He built a room to hide in. The Chapter House. In case.

And tonight the "in case" had finally happened. The Inquisition, in the person of this pleasant monk, had found the Gilbertines.

"At last," Frère Sébastien had said when he first crossed the threshold. *"I found you."*

At last, thought Gamache.

And now the Dominican from the Congregation for the Doctrine of the Faith was asking a police officer to show him the secret door. To open it. To take away the Gilbertines' last hiding place.

Gamache knew it no longer mattered. The secret was out. There was no more hiding to be done. And no need. The Inquisition had ended. But even so, Chief Inspector Gamache was loath to be the man who after four hundred years opened that door for the hound of the Lord.

All this went through Gamache's mind in a flash, but before he could say anything, Beauvoir stepped forward and pressed the image of the intertwined wolves.

And the plaque clicked open.

"*Merci,*" said the Dominican. "I wondered briefly if you knew how."

Beauvoir gave him a dismissive look. That would teach this young monk to underestimate him.

Gamache stepped aside and gestured, inviting the monk to go first. They stepped into the Chapter House and sat on the stone bench that ran around the walls. Gamache waited. He wasn't going to start the conversation. So the three of them sat in silence. After a minute or so Beauvoir began to fidget slightly.

But the Chief sat absolutely still. Composed.

Then a soft sound came from the monk. It took just a moment for the Chief to recognize it. He was humming the tune Gamache himself had hummed over dinner. But it sounded different. Perhaps, Gamache thought, it was the acoustics of the room.

But he knew, deep down, it wasn't that.

He turned to the man next to him. Frère Sébastien had his eyes closed, his fine, light lashes resting on his pale cheek. And a smile on his face.

It felt as though the stones themselves were singing. It felt as though the monk had coaxed the music out of the air, out of the walls, out of the fabric of his robes. Gamache had the oddest sensation that the music was coming out of himself. As though the music was part of him, and he a part of it.

It felt as though all of everything was broken down and swirled together, and out of that came this sound.

The experience was so intimate, so invasive, it was almost frightening. And would have been, had the music itself not been so beautiful. And calming.

Then the Dominican stopped humming, opened his eyes, and turned to Gamache.

"I'd like to know, Chief Inspector, where you heard that tune."

TWENTY-NINE

"I need to speak to you, *Père Abbot,*" said Frère Antoine.

From inside his office, Dom Philippe heard the request. Or demand. Normally he'd have heard the old iron knocker against wood. But these were far from normal times. The rod had been declared the weapon that had killed Frère Mathieu, and taken away.

And word had spread that the prior had been alive when Simon had found him. Had received last rites, while alive. It gave Dom Philippe immense peace of mind to know that. Though he wondered why Simon hadn't mentioned it before.

And then he found out.

Mathieu had not only been alive, but he'd spoken. Said one word. To Simon.

Homo.

Dom Philippe was as baffled as anyone by that. With one word left to say in this world,

575

why would Mathieu say "homo"?

He knew what the congregation suspected. That Mathieu was referring to his sexuality. Asking for some sort of forgiveness. Some extreme unction. But the abbot didn't believe that was true.

Not that Mathieu wasn't a homosexual. He might well have been. But Dom Philippe had been his confessor for many years, and Mathieu had never mentioned it. It might, of course, have been latent. Deeply buried, and only came roaring to the surface with the blow to his head.

Homo.

Mathieu had cleared his throat, struggled to get the word out, Simon had said, and finally rasped, "Homo."

The abbot tried it. Clearing his throat. Saying the word.

He repeated it. Over and over.

Until he thought he had it. What Mathieu had done. What Mathieu had said. What Mathieu had meant.

But then Frère Antoine had entered and bowed slightly to the abbot.

"Yes, my son, what is it?" Dom Philippe rose to his feet.

"It's about Frère Sébastien, the visitor. He says he was sent from Rome, when they heard about the death of the prior."

"Yes?" The abbot indicated a seat next to him and Frère Antoine took it.

The choirmaster looked worried and had dropped his voice. "I don't see how that can be."

"Why do you say that?" Though the abbot had himself already worked it out.

"Well, when did you inform the Vatican?"

"I didn't. I called Monsignor Ducette at the archdiocese in Montréal. He informed the archbishop of Québec, and presumably the archbishop told Rome."

"But, when did you call?"

"Right after we called the police."

Frère Antoine thought about that for a moment. "That would make it about nine thirty yesterday morning."

It was, thought the abbot, the first civil exchange he'd had with Frère Antoine in months. And the abbot realized how much he missed this monk in his life. His creativity of thought, his passion, the debates over scripture and literature. Not to mention hockey.

But now it seemed restored, their common ground the death of Mathieu. And the arrival of the Dominican.

"I've been thinking the same thing," Dom Philippe admitted, and looked into the small fire in his small rooms. With the new geothermal they had central heating. But the abbot was a man of traditions, and preferred an open window and the warmth of the hearth.

"It was six hours later in Rome," said the abbot. "Even if they reacted immediately it seems unlikely Frère Sébastien could make it here this quickly."

"Exactly, *mon père*," said Antoine. It had been a long time since he'd called Dom Philippe that, having used the more stilted, more formal, colder *"Père Abbé"* for the past few months. "And we both know the archdiocese moves like continental drift, and Rome as fast as evolution."

The abbot smiled then grew serious again.

"So, why is he here?" Frère Antoine asked.

"If not because of Frère Mathieu's death?" Dom Philippe held Antoine's anxious eyes. "I don't know."

But for the first time in a long time the abbot felt his heart calm. Felt the crack that had caused him so much pain, closing.

"I'd like your thoughts on something, Antoine."

"Certainly."

"Frère Simon says that Mathieu said one word before he died. I'm sure you've heard that by now."

"I have."

"He said 'homo.' " The abbot watched for the choirmaster's reaction, but there was none. The monks were trained, and accustomed, to keeping their feelings and their thoughts to themselves. "Do you know what he might have meant?"

Antoine didn't speak for a few moments, and broke eye contact. In a place with few words, the eyes became key. To break contact was significant. But his eyes found their way back to the abbot.

"The brothers are wondering if he was talking about his sexuality . . ."

There was clearly more Frère Antoine wanted to say, and so the abbot folded his hands in his lap and waited.

"And they're wondering if he was referring specifically to his relationship with you."

The abbot's eyes widened just a little, to have heard it expressed so boldly. After a moment, he nodded. "I can see how they might think that. Mathieu and I were very close for many years. I loved him very much. I always will. And you, Antoine? What do you think?"

"I loved him too. Like a brother. I've personally never seen any reason to believe he felt any differently, about you or anyone."

"I think I know what Mathieu might have

said. Simon mentioned that he cleared his throat before speaking, then said 'homo.' I tried it a few times . . ."

Frère Antoine looked both surprised and impressed.

". . . and this is, finally, what I came to. What Mathieu might have been trying to say."

The abbot cleared his throat, or appeared to, then said, "Homo."

Antoine stared, shocked. Then he nodded. "*Bon Dieu,* I think you're right."

He himself tried it, clearing his throat and saying, "Homo."

"But why would Frère Mathieu say that?" he asked the abbot.

"I don't know."

Dom Philippe held out his right hand, palm up. And Frère Antoine, after the slightest of hesitations, took it. The abbot laid his left hand on top of that and held the young hand as though it might be a bird.

"But I do know it will be all right, Antoine. All manner of thing shall be well."

"*Oui, mon père.*"

Gamache held the Dominican's eyes.

Frère Sébastien looked curious. In fact, he looked deeply curious. But not anxious, thought Gamache. He seemed like a man who knew the answer would come, and he could wait.

The Chief liked this monk. In fact, he liked most of them. Or, at least, he didn't dislike them. But this young Dominican had a quality that was disarming. Gamache knew it was a powerful and dangerous quality and it would be folly in the extreme to allow himself to be disarmed.

The Dominican exuded calm and invited confidences.

And then the Chief Inspector realized why he was at once attracted and guarded. Those were, he knew, the qualities he used in an investigation. While the Chief was busy investigating the monks, this monk was investigating him. And he knew the only defense against it was, perversely, complete honesty.

"The tune I hummed at dinner comes from this."

Gamache opened the volume of mystical writing he'd carried with him since the murder, and handed the yellowed vellum to Frère Sébastien.

The monk took it. His young eyes needed no help reading it, even in the weak light. Gamache looked away for an instant, to catch Beauvoir's eyes.

Jean-Guy was also watching the monk, but

his eyes seemed almost glazed. Though that might have been the light. All their eyes looked odd in this secret little room. The Chief turned back to Frère Sébastien. The Dominican's lips were moving, without sound.

"Where did you find this?" the monk finally asked, looking up briefly from the page before his eyes dropped, yanked back to the paper.

"It was on Frère Mathieu when we found him. He was curled around it."

The monk crossed himself. It was rote, and yet he managed to invest it with meaning. Then Frère Sébastien took a huge, deep breath. And nodded.

"Do you know what this is, Chief Inspector?"

"I know those are neumes," he moved his index finger over the ancient musical notes. "And the words are Latin, though they seem to be nonsense."

"They are nonsense."

"Some of the Gilbertines seem to think the words are deliberately insulting," said Gamache. "And the neumes a travesty of a chant. As though someone took the form of Gregorian chant and deliberately made it grotesque."

"The words are silly, but not an insult. If

this," Frère Sébastien held up the page, "belittled the faith then I'd agree, but it doesn't. In fact, I find it interesting that the words never once mention God or the Church or devotion. It's as though whoever wrote this deliberately stayed away from that."

"Why?"

"I don't know, but I do know it isn't heresy. Murder might be your specialty, Chief Inspector, but heresy is mine. It's what the Congregation for the Doctrine of the Faith does, among other things. We track down heresy and heretics."

"And did the track lead you here?"

The Dominican considered the question, or more likely, he considered his answer.

"It's a long trail, covering tens of thousands of miles and hundreds of years. Dom Clément was right to leave. In the archives of the Inquisition there's a proclamation signed by the Grand Inquisitor himself, ordering an investigation into the Gilbertines."

"But why?" asked Beauvoir, focusing his attention. It seemed akin to investigating bunnies, or kittens.

"Because of who they sprang from. Gilbert of Sempringham."

"They were going to be investigated for

extreme dullness?" asked Beauvoir.

Frère Sébastien laughed, but not long. "No. For extreme loyalty. It was one of the paradoxes of the Inquisition, that things like extreme devotion and loyalty became suspicious."

"Why?" asked Beauvoir.

"Because they can't be controlled. Men who believed strongly in God and were loyal to their abbots and their orders wouldn't bend to the will of the Inquisition or the inquisitors. They were too strong."

"So Gilbert's defense of his archbishop was seen as suspicious?" asked Gamache, trying to follow the labyrinthine logic. "But that was six hundred years before the Inquisition. And he was defending the Church against a secular authority. I'd have thought the Church would consider him a hero, not a suspect. Even centuries later."

"Six hundred years is nothing to an organization built on events millennia old," said Sébastien. "And anyone who stands up becomes a target. You should know that, Chief Inspector."

Gamache gave him a sharp look, but the monk's face was placid. There seemed no hidden meaning. Or warning.

"If the Gilbertines hadn't left," said the Dominican, "they'd have gone the way of the Cathars."

"And what was that?" asked Beauvoir. But one look at the Chief's face told him it probably wasn't to Club Med.

"They were burned alive," said Frère Sébastien.

"All of them?" asked Beauvoir, his face gray in the dim light.

The monk nodded. "Every man, woman and child."

"Why?"

"The Church considered them free thinkers, too independent. And gaining in influence. The Cathars became known as the 'good men.' And good men are very threatening to not good men."

"So the Church killed them?"

"After first trying to bring them back into the fold," said Frère Sébastien.

"Wasn't Saint Dominic, your founder, the one who insisted the Cathars weren't real Catholics?" asked Gamache.

Sébastien nodded. "But the order to wipe them out didn't come until centuries later." The monk hesitated and when he spoke again his voice was low, but clear. "Many were mutilated first, and sent back to frighten the others, but it only hardened the Cathar resolve. The leaders gave themselves up, in an effort to appease the Church, but it didn't work. Everyone was killed, even people who just happened to be in the area. Innocents. When one of the soldiers asked how he was supposed to tell them from the Cathars, he was told to kill them all, and let God sort them out."

Frère Sébastien looked as though he could see it. As though he'd been there. And Gamache wondered which side of the monastery walls this monk from the Congregation for the Doctrine of the Faith would have been on.

"The Inquisition would've done that to the Gilbertines?" Beauvoir asked. He no longer looked dazed. The monk had hauled him back from whatever reverie he'd found.

"It's not a certainty," said Sébastien, though that seemed more wishful than real. "But Dom Clément was wise to leave. And wise to hide."

Sébastien took another deep breath.

"This isn't heresy," he looked down at the paper in his hands. "It speaks of bananas and the refrain is *Non sum pisces*."

Gamache and Beauvoir looked blank.

"I am not a fish," said the Dominican.

Gamache smiled and Beauvoir looked simply confused.

"So if it isn't heresy," said the Chief, "what is it?"

"It's a singularly beautiful tune. A chant, I think, though not Gregorian and not a plainchant. It uses all the rules, but then adjusts them slightly, as though the old chant was the foundation, and this," he tapped the page, "a whole new structure."

He looked up, first at Beauvoir then over to Gamache. His eyes were excited. The smile on his face back to its radiance.

"I think far from being a mockery of Gregorian chant, it's actually a homage, a tribute. A celebration, even. The composer used the neumes, but in a way I've never seen before. There're so many of them."

"Frère Simon made copies so that he and the other monks could transcribe the neumes into notes," Gamache explained. "He seemed to think the neumes were for different voices. Layers of voices. Harmonizing."

"Hmmm," said Frère Sébastien, again lost in the music. His finger rested, awkwardly it seemed to Gamache, on one place on the page. When the monk finally moved it, Gamache saw that the finger had covered a small dot at the very beginning of the music. Before the first neume.

"Is it old?" asked Gamache.

"Oh, no. Not at all. It's made to look old, of course, but I'd be surprised if this was written more than a few months ago."

"By whom?"

"Now that I can't possibly say. But I can tell you, it would have to be by someone who knows a lot about Gregorian chant. About the structure of them. About neumes, of course. But not a great deal of Latin." He looked at Gamache with barely disguised wonder. "You may have been one of the first people on earth to hear a whole new musical form, Chief Inspector," said Frère Sébastien. "It must have been thrilling."

"You know, it was," admitted Gamache. "Though I had no idea what I was hearing. But after he sang, Frère Simon pointed out something about the Latin. He said that while it's pretty much just a string of funny phrases, it actually makes sense musically."

"He's right." The monk nodded agreement.

"What do you mean?" asked Beauvoir.

"The words, the syllables, match the notes. Like lyrics, or the words of a poem. The meter has to fit. These words fit the music, but make no sense otherwise."

"So why're they there?" Beauvoir asked. "They have to mean something."

All three stared down at the sheet of music. But it told them nothing.

"Now it's your turn, *mon frère,*" said Ga-

588

mache. "We've told you about the music. It's your turn to tell us the truth."

"About why I'm here?"

"Exactly."

"You think it's not about the murder of the prior?" the Dominican asked.

"I do. The timing's off. You couldn't have come all the way from the Vatican this quickly," said Gamache. "And even if you could, your reaction when you arrived wasn't grief shared with fellow monks. It was delight. You greeted these monks as though you'd been looking for them a long time."

"And I have. The Church has been looking. I mentioned the archives of the Inquisition and finding the warrant ordering the Gilbertines to be investigated."

"Oui," said Gamache, growing guarded.

"Well, the investigation never ended. I have scores of predecessors in the Congregation who spent their lifetimes trying to find the Gilbertines. When they died another took over. Not a year, not a day, not an hour has gone by since they disappeared that we haven't been looking for them."

"The hounds of the Lord," said Gamache.

"*C'est ça.* Bloodhounds. We never gave up."

"But it's been centuries," said Beauvoir.

589

"Why would you keep looking? Why would it matter?"

"Because the Church doesn't like mysteries, except those of its own making."

"Or God's?" asked Gamache.

"Those the Church tolerates," admitted the monk, again with a disarming smile.

"Then how'd you finally find them?" asked Beauvoir.

"Can you guess?"

"If I wanted to guess I would have," snapped Beauvoir. The confined space was getting to him. He felt the walls closing in. Felt oppressed, by the monastery, by the monk, by the Church. All he wanted was to get out. Get some air. He felt he was suffocating.

"The recording," said Gamache after a moment's thought.

Frère Sébastien nodded. "That's it. The image on the cover of the CD. It was a stylized monk in profile. Almost a cartoon."

"The robes," said Gamache.

"*Oui.* The robes were black, with a small bit of white for the hood and chest, and draping over the shoulders. It's unique."

"*Some malady is coming upon us,*" quoted Gamache. "Maybe that's the malady."

"The music?" asked Beauvoir.

"Modern times," said Frère Sébastien.

"That's what came upon the Gilbertines."

The Chief nodded. "For centuries they've sung their chants, in anonymity. But now technology allowed them to transmit it to the world."

"And to the Vatican," said Frère Sébastien. "And the Congregation for the Doctrine of the Faith."

The Inquisition, thought Gamache. The Gilbertines were finally found. Betrayed by their chants.

The bells rang out and the peals penetrated into the Chapter House.

"I need to hit the toilet," said Beauvoir, as the three men left the small room. "I'll catch you later."

"Fine," said Gamache and watched Jean-Guy walk back across the Blessed Chapel.

"There you are."

Chief Superintendent Francoeur walked decisively toward them. He smiled at the monk and nodded, briefly, at Gamache.

"I thought perhaps we could sit together," said Francoeur.

"With pleasure," said the monk. He turned to Gamache. "Will you join us?"

"I think I'll sit over here, quietly."

Francoeur and Frère Sébastien took a pew near the front and Gamache sat a few rows back and across from them.

It was almost certainly discourteous, he knew. But he also knew he didn't care. Gamache glared at the back of Francoeur's head. His eyes drilling into it. He was grateful Jean-Guy had decided to pee instead of pray. One less contact with Francoeur.

God help me, Gamache prayed. Even in this peaceful place he could feel his rage grow at the very sight of Sylvain Francoeur.

He continued to stare, and Francoeur rolled his shoulders, as though feeling the scrutiny. Francoeur didn't turn around. But the Dominican did.

Frère Sébastien turned his head and looked directly at Gamache. The Chief shifted his eyes from Francoeur to the monk. The two men stared at each other for a moment. Then Gamache returned to the Superintendent. Undeterred by the gentle inquiry of the monk.

Eventually, Gamache closed his eyes, and took deep breaths in. Deep breaths out. He smelled, again, the scent of Saint-Gilbert which was so familiar, but slightly different. A marriage of traditional incense, and something else. Thyme and monarda.

The natural and the manufactured, come together here, in this far-flung monastery. Peace and rage, silence and singing. The

Gilbertines and the Inquisition. The good men and the not-so-good.

Hearing the bells had made Beauvoir almost giddy. Almost sick with anticipation.

Finally. Finally.

He'd hurried to *les toilettes,* peed, washed his hands then poured a glass of water. From his pocket he drew the small pill bottle and snapped off the top, no child-proof caps here, and shook two pills into his palm.

In one practiced move Beauvoir brought his hand to his mouth, and felt the tiny pills land on his tongue. One gulp of the water, and they were down.

Leaving the *pissoire,* he paused in the hallway. The bells were still sounding, but instead of returning to the Blessed Chapel, Beauvoir walked swiftly back to the prior's office. He closed the door and leaned the new chair against the handle.

He could still hear the bells.

Sitting at the desk he dragged the laptop toward him and rebooted.

The bells had stopped, and there was silence now.

The DVD in the machine started up. Beauvoir turned down the sound. No need to draw attention. Besides he had the soundtrack in his mind. Always.

The images appeared.

Gamache opened his eyes as the first notes arrived in the Blessed Chapel, along with the first monk.

Frère Antoine carried the simple wooden cross ahead of him and placed it in the holder on the altar. Then he bowed and took his place. Behind him the rest of the monks filed in, bowing to the cross and taking their places. Singing all the time. All the live-long day.

Gamache glanced at Frère Sébastien in profile. He was staring at the monks. At the long-lost Gilbertines. Then Frère Sébastien closed his eyes and tilted his head back. He seemed to go into a trance. A fugue. As the Gregorian chants and the Gilbertines filled the chapel.

Beauvoir could hear the music, but softly, from very far away.

Men's voices, all singing together. Growing more powerful as more voices joined in. While on the screen he watched his co-workers, his friends, his fellow agents, gunned down.

To the tune of the chants, Beauvoir watched himself gunned down.

The monks sang as the Chief dragged him to safety. Then left him. Dumping him there like — how had Francoeur described it? No longer useful.

And, to add to the injury, before leaving the Chief had kissed him.

Kissed him. On his forehead. No wonder they called him Gamache's bitch. Everyone had seen that kiss. All his colleagues. And now they laughed at him, behind his back.

As the Gregorian chants were sung in the Blessed Chapel, Chief Inspector Gamache kissed him. Then left.

Gamache glanced again at the Dominican. Frère Sébastien seemed to have moved from a fugue to a sort of ecstasy.

And then Frère Luc entered the chapel, and the Dominican's eyes sprang open. He was almost jolted forward in his seat. Drawn to the very young man with the divine voice.

Here was a voice in a million. A voice in a millennium.

The dead prior had known it. The current choirmaster knew it. The abbot knew it. Even Gamache, with his appreciation but limited knowledge, could hear it.

And now, the Congregation for the Doctrine of the Faith knew it too.

■ ■ ■ ■

Jean-Guy Beauvoir hit play, then pause. Then play again. Over and over he watched.

On the screen, time and again, over and over like a litany, a liturgy, Beauvoir saw himself fall. Saw himself dragged, like a sack of potatoes, across the factory floor. By Gamache.

In the background the monks chanted.

The Kyrie. The Alleluia. The Gloria.

While in the prior's office Beauvoir was dying. Alone.

THIRTY

After Compline, the last service of the day, the abbot took Gamache aside. Dom Philippe wasn't alone. To the Chief Inspector's surprise, Frère Antoine was with him.

It would be impossible, looking at the men standing together, to know that they were enemies. Or at least, stood on opposite sides of a deep divide.

"How can I help you?" Gamache asked. He'd been led to a corner of the Blessed Chapel. It was empty now, though the Dominican remained in his seat. Staring ahead as though in a stupor.

Superintendent Francoeur was nowhere to be seen.

Gamache placed his back to the corner, so he could keep a watchful eye on the darkened Chapel.

"It's about Mathieu's last words," said the abbot.

" 'Homo,' " said Frère Antoine. "Is that right?"

"It's what Frère Simon reported, *oui*," said Gamache. The monks exchanged a rapid glance, then returned their eyes to the Chief.

"We think we know what he meant," said the abbot. He cleared his throat very loudly, then said, "Homo."

"Oui," said Gamache, staring at Dom Philippe and waiting for more. "That's what the prior apparently said."

The abbot did it again. This time with a monumental clearing of his throat and Gamache had a moment of concern for the man's health.

"Homo," Dom Philippe repeated.

Now Gamache really was puzzled. He could see Frère Sébastien, the Dominican, looking over. If the noise from the abbot's throat had been loud to Gamache, it must have been monstrous when it hit the full glory of the chapel's acoustics.

The abbot stared intently at Gamache, his blue eyes piercing, willing the Chief to understand something he just couldn't.

Then beside the abbot, Frère Antoine cleared his throat. A guttural, desperate sound.

"Homo," he said.

And the Chief Inspector finally began to

grasp that it wasn't the word they wanted him to understand, but the sound. But it still meant nothing to Gamache.

Feeling extremely thick, he turned back to the abbot.

"*Désolé, mon père,* but I honestly don't understand."

"*Ecce homo.*"

The words came not from the abbot, nor from Frère Antoine, but from the Blessed Chapel, as though the room itself had spoken.

Then the Dominican appeared around one of the columns.

"I believe that's what the abbot and choirmaster are saying. Is that right?"

The two men stared at Frère Sébastien, then nodded. Their looks, if not outright belligerent, were uninviting. But it was far too late. This uninvited man from the Vatican was there. Indeed, he seemed every where.

Gamache turned back to the Gilbertines, standing side-by-side. Was that what had finally bridged the chasm between them? A common enemy? This pleasant, unobtrusive monk in white robes who sat so still but took up so much space?

"We think the prior wasn't clearing his throat," said Frère Antoine, turning from the Dominican back to Gamache, "but that he actually said two words. *'Ecce'* and *'homo.'*"

Gamache's eyes widened. *Ecce.* Eee-chay. But with the guttural Latin pronunciation. It could be.

The abbot repeated it, as the prior might have sounded. A man struggling to get out a word. A dying man with a throaty word, caught there.

Ecce homo.

The words were familiar to Gamache, but he couldn't call them up.

"What does it mean?"

"It's what Pontius Pilate said to the mob," said Frère Sébastien. "He brought Jesus out, bleeding, to show them."

"Show them what? What does it mean?" Gamache repeated, looking from Dominican to Gilbertine and back again.

"Ecce homo," said the abbot. "He is man."

It was almost nine in the evening, late by monastery standards, and Frère Sébastien left the three men and walked toward the cells. Frère Antoine waited a minute, for the Dominican to disappear, then after a brief bow to the abbot, he also left.

"Things have changed," observed Gamache.

600

Instead of denying that there was ever a problem, Dom Philippe simply nodded and watched the younger man stride off toward the door at the far end of the chapel.

"He'll make a wonderful choirmaster. Perhaps even better than Mathieu." The abbot's eyes returned to Gamache. "Frère Antoine loves the chants, but he loves God more."

The Chief nodded. Yes. That was at the heart of this mystery, he thought. Not hate. But love.

"And the prior?" asked Gamache as he walked the abbot to his rooms. "What did he love more?"

"The music." The answer was swift and unequivocal. "But it isn't quite that simple." The abbot smiled. "As you might have noticed, few things here are actually simple."

Gamache also smiled. He had noticed.

They were in the long corridor leading to the abbot's office and cell. Where at first it had seemed perfectly straight from one end to the other, now he thought he noticed a very slight curve. Dom Clément might have drawn a straight line, but his builders had erred, ever so slightly. As anyone who'd built a bookcase, or tried to follow a detailed map, knew, an infinitesimal error at the beginning can become a massive mistake later on.

Even the corridors here, he reflected, weren't as simple, as straight, as they appeared.

"For Mathieu there was no separation between the music and his faith. They were one and the same," said the abbot. His pace had slowed and now they were barely moving down the darkened hallway. "The music magnified his faith. Took it to levels of near ecstasy."

"Levels few achieve?"

The abbot was quiet.

"Levels you've never achieved?" Gamache pushed.

"I'm more the slow and steady type," said the abbot, looking straight ahead as they walked the slightly flawed path. "Not given to soaring."

"But neither do you fall?"

"We can all fall," said the abbot.

"But perhaps not as hard and not as fast and not as far as someone who spends his life on the ascent."

Again the abbot lapsed into silence.

"You obviously adore the Gregorian chants," said Gamache. "But unlike the prior, you separate them from your faith?"

The abbot nodded. "I hadn't thought about it until this happened, but yes, I do.

If the music was somehow taken away tomorrow. If I could no longer sing, or listen to the chants, my love of God would be unchanged."

"Not so with Frère Mathieu?"

"I wonder."

"Who was his confessor?"

"I was. Until recently."

"Who was his new confessor?"

"Frère Antoine."

Now their slow progress stopped completely.

"Can you tell me what Frère Mathieu said, in his confessions to you? Before he switched confessors?"

"You know I can't."

"Even though the prior is dead?"

The abbot studied Gamache. "Surely you know the answer to that. Has any priest ever agreed to break the seal of the confessional for you?"

Gamache shook his head. "No, *mon père.* But I'll never give up hope."

That brought a smile to the abbot's face.

"When did the prior switch to Frère Antoine?"

"About six months ago." The abbot looked resigned. "I wasn't completely honest with you." He looked directly into Gamache's eyes. "I'm sorry. Mathieu and I did have a disagreement about the chants, and that grew into an argument about the direction of the monastery and the community."

"He wanted another recording, and for Saint-Gilbert to be more open to the outside world."

"*Oui.* And I believe we need to stay on course."

"A steady hand on the tiller," said the Chief, nodding approval. Though both men knew, if you were heading into the rocks, a quick turn was often necessary.

"But there was another outstanding issue," said Gamache. They'd started walking again, toward the closed door at the end of the corridor. "The foundations."

Gamache had taken a step forward before he realized the abbot was no longer beside him. The Chief turned and saw Dom Philippe staring at him, surprised.

It seemed to Gamache that the abbot was on the verge of another lie, but in the breath he took before speaking he seemed to change his mind.

"You know about that?"

"Frère Raymond told Inspector Beauvoir. It's true, then."

The abbot nodded.

"Did anyone else know?" Gamache asked.

"I told no one."

"Not even your prior?"

"A year ago, eighteen months ago, he'd have been the first person I told, but not now. I kept it to myself. Told God, but he already knew, of course."

"Might have even put the cracks there," suggested Gamache.

The abbot looked at the Chief, but said nothing.

"Is that why you were in the basement yesterday morning?" asked Gamache. "Not to examine the geothermal, but to look at the foundations?"

The abbot nodded and they began their slow progress again, neither man in a hurry to reach the door.

"I waited until Frère Raymond was gone. I'm afraid I didn't need to hear him go on and on about the impending disaster. I just needed some quiet time to look for myself."

"And what did you see?"

"Roots," he said, his voice a study of neutrality. A plainchant voice, monotone. No inflection. No emotion. Just fact. "The cracks are getting worse. I'd marked where they'd been the last time I looked, a week or so ago. They've widened since then."

"You might have even less time than you'd hoped?"

"We might," Dom Philippe admitted.

"So what do you do about it?"

"I pray."

"That's it?"

"And what do you do, Chief Inspector, when all seems lost?"

Take this child.

"I pray too," he said.

"And does it work?"

"Sometimes," said Gamache. Jean-Guy hadn't died that dreadful day in the factory. Covered in blood, gasping in pain. Eyes pleading for Gamache to stay. To do something. To save him. Gamache had prayed. And Beauvoir hadn't been taken. But neither, Gamache knew, had he returned. Not completely. Beauvoir was still caught between worlds.

"But is all lost?" he asked the abbot. "Frère Raymond seems to think another recording would bring in enough money to fix the foundations. But you have to act quickly."

"Frère Raymond is right. But he also sees only the cracks. I see the whole monastery. The whole community. What good would it do to fix the cracks but lose our real foundation? Our vows aren't negotiable."

Gamache saw then what Frère Raymond must have seen. What the prior must have seen. A man who would not budge. Unlike the monastery, there were no cracks in the abbot. He was immovable, at least on this subject.

If the last Gilbertine monastery was to be saved it would have to be by divine intervention. Unless, as Frère Raymond believed, their miracle had been offered and the abbot, blinded by pride, had missed it.

"I have a favor to ask, *Père Abbé*."

"Would you also like me to approve another recording?"

Gamache almost laughed. "No. I'll leave that between you and your God. But I would like the boatman to come tomorrow morning, to take Inspector Beauvoir back with some of the evidence we've gathered."

"Of course. I'll call first thing. Assuming the fog lifts Etienne should be here shortly after breakfast."

They'd reached the closed door. The wood pockmarked by hundreds of years of monks asking for admittance. But no longer. The iron rod was gone and would leave the abbey for good with Beauvoir in the morning. Gamache wondered if the abbot would have it replaced.

"Well," said Dom Philippe, "good night, my son."

"Bonne nuit, mon père," said Gamache. The words sounded so strange. His own father

had died when Gamache was a boy and he'd rarely called anyone that since.

"Ecce homo," said Gamache, just as Dom Philippe opened the door.

The abbot paused.

"Why would Frère Mathieu say that?" Gamache asked.

"I don't know."

Gamache pondered for a moment. "Why did Pilate say it?"

"He wanted to prove to the mob that their god wasn't divine at all. That Jesus was just a man."

"Merci," said Gamache, and bowing slightly he walked back down the slightly curved hall. To think about the Divine, the human, and the cracks in between.

"Dear Annie," Beauvoir wrote in the dark. His light was out so that no one would know he was still awake.

He lay on his bed, fully clothed. Compline was over, he knew, and he'd retreated to his cell, until he could safely return to the prior's office, when everyone was asleep.

He'd found a message from Annie on his BlackBerry. A light-hearted description of her evening with old friends.

I love you, she wrote, at the end.

I miss you.

608

Hurry home.

He thought about Annie having dinner with her friends. Had she told them about him? Had she told them about his gift? The plunger. What a stupid thing to do. A crass, boorish gift. They'd probably all laughed. At him. At the stupid Pepsi who knew no better. Who was too poor or cheap or unsophisticated to buy her a real gift. To go to Holt Renfrew or Ogilvy's or one of the fucking snooty shops along Laurier and get her something nice.

Instead, he'd given her a toilet plunger.

And they'd laughed at him.

And Annie would've laughed too. At the dumb yokel she was screwing. Just for fun. He could see those eyes, shining, glowing. As she'd looked at him so often in the last few months. As she'd looked at him over the past ten years.

He'd mistaken that look for affection, love even, but now he saw it was simply amusement.

"Annie," he wrote.

"Dear Reine-Marie," Gamache wrote.

He'd returned to his cell, after looking for Beauvoir in the prior's office. The lights were off and it was empty. The Chief had spent half an hour there, making notes, copying notes. Preparing the package of evidence for Beauvoir to take out the next morning.

It was eleven o'clock. The end of a long day. He'd turned the lights off and taken the package back to his cell, after first tapping on Beauvoir's door. But there was no answer.

He'd opened the door and looked in. To be sure Jean-Guy was there. And sure enough, he could see the outline on the bed, and hear the heavy, steady breathing.

Deep breath in. Deep breath out.

Evidence of life.

It was unlike Jean-Guy to simply go to sleep, without a final check-in, a postmortem of the day. All the more reason, thought Gamache as he prepared for bed, to get him home as soon as possible.

"Dear Reine-Marie," he wrote.

"Annie. My day was fine. Nothing special. The investigation is moving along. Thanks for asking. Glad to hear you had a fun night out with your friends. Lots to laugh about, I'd imagine."

"Dear Reine-Marie. I wish you were here and we could talk about this case. It seems to swirl around the Gregorian chants and how important they are to these monks. It would be a mistake to dismiss the chants as simply music."

Gamache paused and thought about that. He found even just writing to Reine-Marie helped clarify things, as though he could hear her voice, see her lively, warm eyes.

"We had a surprise visitor. A Dominican from the Vatican. The office that used to be the Inquisition. Apparently they've been searching for the Gilbertines for almost four hundred years. And today they found them. The monk says it's just a loose end that needed to be tied up, but I wonder. I think, like so much else in this case, part of what he's telling us is the truth, and part isn't. I wish I could see more clearly.

"Good night, my love. Sweet dreams.

"I miss you. I'll be home soon.

"*Je t'aime.*"

"Talk to U soon," wrote Jean-Guy.

Then he hit send and lay in the dark.

THIRTY-ONE

Beauvoir awoke to the sound of the bells, calling the faithful. Though he knew the bells weren't for him, still he followed them through his bleary brain. Up, up he crawled to consciousness.

He wasn't even completely sure if he was awake, so vague was his border between conscious and unconscious. He felt confused, clumsy. Grabbing his watch he tried to focus on the time.

Five in the morning. The bells continued and if Beauvoir could've mustered the energy he'd have tossed his shoes at the monk who was ringing them.

He flopped back in the bed and prayed for the sound to stop. Anxiety gripped him and he gasped for breath.

Deep breath in, he begged his body. Deep breath out.

Deep breath — *oh, fuck it,* he thought. Beauvoir sat up in bed and swung his legs over the side, feeling his bare feet on the cold stone floor.

Everything hurt. The soles of his feet, the top of his head. His chest, his joints. His toenails and his eyebrows. He stared at the wall across from him, his mouth open and slack. Begging for breath.

Finally, with one jagged gasp, his throat opened and air rushed in.

Then the trembling began.

Oh, fuck, fuck, fuck.

He turned on the light and grabbed the bottle of pills from underneath his pillow, squeezing it tight. After a couple of tries he got it open. He wanted one, but the shaking was so bad two tumbled out. He didn't care. He tossed them both into his mouth and dry swallowed. Then he gripped the sides of his bed and waited.

His chemo. His medicine. The pills would kill what was killing him. Stop the trembling. Stop the pain so deep inside he couldn't get at it. Stop the images, the memories.

The fears. That he'd been left alone. And was still alone. Would always be alone.

He lay back in bed and felt the pills begin to work. How could anything this good be bad?

He felt human again. Whole again.

The pain receded, his brain cleared. The hooks and barbs released his flesh, and the void was filled in. As he drifted, Beauvoir could hear familiar voices singing.

The bells had ended and the service had begun. Vigils. The first of the day.

Two clear voices were singing now. A call and response. And Beauvoir was surprised to realize he now recognized it. His grip on the bed loosened as he listened.

Call. Response.

Call. Response.

It was mesmerizing.

Call. Response.

And then all the voices joined in. No more need to call. They'd found each other.

Beauvoir felt a tug deep inside. A pain not wholly numbed.

It was five thirty in the morning. Vigils had ended and Gamache sat in the pew, appreciating the peace of the service. He inhaled the incense. It smelled like a garden, not musky, like in most churches.

The monks had left. All except Frère Sébastien, who joined him in the pew.

"Your colleagues aren't as religious as you."

"I'm afraid I'm not religious either," said the Chief. "I don't go to church."

"And yet you're here."

"Looking for a murderer, I'm afraid. Not salvation."

"Still, you seem to find solace."

Gamache was silent for a moment, then he nodded. "It would be hard not to. Do you like Gregorian chants?"

"Very much. A whole mythology has grown up around them, you know. Probably because we know so little about them. We don't even know where Gregorian chant came from."

"Would the name be a clue?"

The Dominican smiled. "You'd think so, but you'd be wrong. Pope Gregory had nothing to do with the chants. Marketing, that's all. Gregory was a popular pope, so to curry favor some astute priest named the chants after him."

"Is that how they became so popular?"

"It didn't hurt. There's also a theory that if Christ heard any music, or sang any music, it would've been plainchant. Now there's a marketing tool. Endorsed by Jesus. As sung by the Savior."

Gamache laughed. "It would certainly give them a leg up on the competition."

"Scientists have even begun studying the chants," said Frère Sébastien, "trying to explain the popularity of the recording these monks made. People went nuts for it."

"And have they any explanation?"

"Well, when they hooked up probes to volunteers and played Gregorian chants it was quite startling."

"How so?"

"It showed that after a while their brain waves changed. They started producing alpha waves. Do you know what those are?"

"They're the most calm state," said the Chief. "When people are still alert, but at peace."

"Exactly. Their blood pressure dropped, their breathing became deeper. And yet, they also became, as you said, more alert. It was as though they became 'more so,' you know?"

"Themselves, but their best selves."

"That's it. Doesn't work on everyone, of course. But I think it works on you."

Gamache considered that and nodded. "It does. Perhaps not as profoundly as the Gilbertines, but I've felt it."

"While the scientists say it's alpha waves, the Church calls it 'the beautiful mystery.' "

"The mystery being?"

"Why these chants, more than any other church music, are so powerful. Since I'm a monk I think I'll go with the theory they're the voice of God. Though there's a third

616

possibility," the Dominican admitted. "I was at dinner a few weeks ago with a colleague and he has a theory that all tenors are idiots. Something to do with their brain pans and the vibration of the sound waves."

Gamache laughed. "Does he know you're a tenor?"

"He's my boss, and he sure suspects I'm an idiot. And he might be right. But what a glorious way to go. Singing myself into stupidity. Maybe Gregorian chants have the same effect. Make us all into happy morons. Scrambling our brains as we sing the chants. Forgetting our cares and worries. Letting the world slip away." The younger man closed his eyes and seemed to go somewhere else. And then, just as quickly, he came back. Opening his eyes he looked at Gamache, and smiled. "Bliss."

"Ecstasy," said Gamache.

"Exactly."

"But for monks it's not just music," said Gamache. "There's also prayer. The chants are prayers. It's a potent combination. Both mind altering, in their way."

When the monk didn't say anything, Gamache continued.

"I've sat here for a number of services now and watched the monks. To a man they go into a sort of reverie when singing the

617

chants. Or even just listening to them. You did it just now, just thinking about the chants."

"Meaning?"

"I've seen that look before, you know. On the faces of drug addicts."

That seemed to shock Frère Sébastien, who stared at Gamache. "Are you suggesting we're addicted?"

"I'm telling you what I've observed."

The Dominican got to his feet. "What you might have missed is the genuine faith of these men. Their commitment to God, to the perfection of the heart. You diminish it, sir, when you describe their solemn commitment as simply an addiction. You turn the chants into a disease. Something that weakens us, rather than strengthens. To characterize Saint-Gilbert-Entre-les-Loups as no better than a crack den is absurd."

He walked away, his feet, unlike the other slippered monks, rapping against the slate floor.

Gamache knew he might have gone too far. But in doing so he'd hit a nerve.

Frère Sébastien stood in the shadows. After stomping off he'd gone to the far door, opened it, then let it swing shut. Without going through it.

He'd stood in the crook of the church, the corner, and watched the Chief Inspector. Gamache had sat in the hard pew for a minute or so. Most people, the monk knew, had difficulty sitting still for thirty seconds. This quiet man seemed capable of sitting in the stillness for as long as he wanted.

Then the Chief Inspector had gotten up and without genuflecting, had left the Blessed Chapel. He'd walked to the door that led down the long corridor, to a locked door and the quiet young monk with the remarkable voice. Frère Luc.

Leaving Frère Sébastien alone in the Blessed Chapel.

It was now or never, the Dominican realized.

He started a slow, but steady search of the room. At the empty lectern he laid his hand on the worn wood, then continued the methodical search. Once he was satisfied the chapel was keeping no secrets, he stole down the corridor and into the prior's office, which the police officers had made their headquarters. There he rifled drawers, looked in files, opened folders. He looked under the desk, behind the door.

The Dominican turned on the computer, knowing what he was looking for would never be there. But he was determined not to have come this far and leave a stone unturned. Unlike the Gilbertines, who seemed satisfied to stay in the sixteenth century, Frère Sébastien was a child of his times. He could never do his job if he didn't know and admire technology. From planes, to cell phones, to laptops.

They were his tools, as crucial as a cross and holy water.

He scanned the files, though there wasn't much to see. The laptop wasn't connected, the satellite hookup too finicky. But before he could turn it off he heard a familiar whirr.

The DVD had kicked in.

Curious, the Dominican clicked and an image appeared. A video. The sound was turned down, which suited him. Besides, the images told the whole story.

He watched with growing dismay, repulsed by what he saw but unable to look away. Until the screen went dead.

He was surprised to find he wanted to watch it again. This horrible video.

What was it, he wondered not for the first time, about tragedy that made it so hard to look away? But the Dominican did. With a small but fervent prayer for the souls of those long lost, and those lost souls still walking among them, he turned off the machine.

Then he left the prior's office, and continued his search of the abbey of Saint-Gilbert-Entre-les-Loups.

He knew what he was looking for was there somewhere. It had to be. He'd heard it.

Thirty-Two

As he'd been speaking with the Dominican after Vigils, Gamache had noticed Francoeur in the shadows of the Blessed Chapel, walking quickly along the wall. Gamache was tempted to use the word "sneak," but it wasn't quite that. It was more stealth.

One thing was certain, Francoeur did not want to be seen.

But Gamache had seen him. When Frère Sébastien had stomped off, Gamache sat for a minute or so, to let the Superintendent get all the way down the long corridor and past the young monk at the door.

Then he'd followed him out the front door of the abbey.

Frère Luc had opened it without a word, though his eyes were filled with all sorts of questions. But Armand Gamache had no answers to offer.

Besides, the Chief had questions of his own, first among them whether it was wise to follow Francoeur. Not because of what the Superintendent might do, but what Gamache was afraid he himself might do.

But he had to find out what was so secret that Francoeur had to actually leave the abbey, and clearly not for an early morning stroll. Gamache stepped into the cold, dark morning and looked about. It wasn't yet six o'clock and the fog of the night before had become a heavy mist, as the frigid air hit the lake, and rose.

Francoeur had stopped in a copse of trees. He might have disappeared against the murky forest, but a soft bluish-white glow in his hand betrayed him.

Gamache paused, and watched. Francoeur's back was to him, and with the Superintendent's head bowed over his device it looked as though he might be consulting a crystal ball. But, of course, he wasn't. The Superintendent was writing, or reading, a message.

One so secret he'd had to leave the monastery, for fear of being found out. But he had been found, the message itself, in the deep dark of the morning, a beacon. Giving him away.

Gamache would give a lot to get that BlackBerry.

For a moment he contemplated quickly

covering the ground between them and grabbing it from Francoeur's hand. Whose name would he see there? What was so important that Francoeur would risk the bears and wolves and coyotes waiting in these woods for something vulnerable to make a mistake.

But Gamache wondered if that something vulnerable was himself. If the mistake was his.

Still he stood, and still he stared. And made up his mind.

He couldn't get the device out of Francoeur's hand, and even if he did, it wouldn't tell the full story. And at this stage, Gamache needed the full story. Patience, Gamache reminded himself. Patience.

And another tack.

"*Bonjour,* Sylvain."

Gamache almost smiled as he saw the glowing slab bobble in Francoeur's hand. Then the Superintendent spun around and any amusement left Gamache's face. Francoeur wasn't just furious, he was murderous. The phone, still on, made his face look grotesque.

"Who're you writing to?" Gamache asked, walking forward, keeping his pace and his voice even.

But Francoeur seemed incapable of

speech and as he approached, Gamache could see that there was fury there, but there was also fear. Francoeur was terrified.

And even more, the Chief wanted to grab that BlackBerry. To see who the message was to, or from, that an interruption would cause such distress.

For it was clear the Superintendent wasn't most afraid of Gamache.

In a split second Gamache knew this was his chance after all. He decided to make a grab for the phone. But Francoeur had anticipated him and with a swift movement, turned off his device and pocketed it.

The two men stared at each other, their breaths coming in puffs, obscuring the air, as though a ghost was forming between them.

"Who were you writing to?" Gamache repeated. Not expecting an answer, but wanting to make it clear that there was no more hiding. "Or were you reading a message? Come on, Sylvain, it's just us." Gamache opened his arms and looked around. "All alone."

It was true. The silence was so great it almost ached. It felt like they'd strolled into a void. No sounds. Few sights. Saint-Gilbert-Entre-les-Loups had even disappeared. The mist had swallowed even the stone monastery.

Only two men left in the world.

And now they faced each other.

"We've known each other since the academy. We've circled each other since then," said Gamache. "It's time to stop. What's this about?"

"I came to help."

"I believe that. But help who? Not me. Not Inspector Beauvoir. On whose orders are you here?"

Was there just the slightest flicker on those last words?

"You're too late, Armand," said Francoeur. "You missed your chance."

"I know. But it wasn't just now. I made my mistake years ago when I was investigating Chief Superintendent Arnot. I should've waited before arresting him, until I could get all of you."

Francoeur didn't bother to deny it. If it was too late for Gamache to stop whatever was happening, it was also way too late for Francoeur to issue denials.

"Was it Arnot?"

"Arnot's in prison for life, Armand. You know that. You put him there."

Now the Chief did smile, though it was weary. "And we know that means nothing.

A man like Arnot will always get what he wants."

"Not always," said Francoeur. "It wasn't his idea to be arrested, tried and sentenced."

It was a rare admission by Francoeur that Gamache, for a moment, had actually bested Arnot. But then had stumbled. Hadn't finished the job. Hadn't realized there were more to be gotten.

And so the rot had remained, and grown.

Arnot was a powerful figure, Gamache knew. Had powerful friends. And a reach well beyond prison walls. Gamache had had a chance to kill him, but had chosen not to. And sometimes, sometimes, he wondered if that wasn't also a mistake.

But now another thought struck him. Francoeur wasn't texting Arnot. The name, while respected by Francoeur, didn't evoke terror. It was someone else. Someone more powerful than the Superintendent. Someone more powerful even than Arnot.

"Who were you writing to, Sylvain?" Gamache asked for the third time. "It's not too late. Tell me, and we can wrap this up together." Gamache's voice was even, reasonable. He held out his hand. "Give me that. Give me your codes. That's all I need, and it's over."

And Francoeur seemed to hesitate. Moved

his hand to his pocket. Then let it fall, empty, to his side.

"You've misunderstood again, Armand. There's no grand conspiracy. It's all in your head. I was texting my wife. As I suspect you write to your wife."

"Give it to me, Sylvain." Gamache ignored the lie. He kept his hand out and his eyes on his superior. "You must be tired. Exhausted. It'll be over soon."

The two men's eyes locked.

"You love your children, Armand?"

It was as though the words had physically shoved him. Gamache felt himself momentarily off balance. Instead of answering he continued to stare.

"Of course you do." Francoeur's voice held no rancor now. It was almost as though they were old friends, chatting over a scotch at a brasserie on St-Denis.

"What're you saying?" Gamache demanded, his voice no longer reasonable. He could feel all reason escaping him, disappearing into the thick, dark forest. "Leave my family out of this." Gamache spoke in a low growl, and the part of his brain that could still reason realized the wild creature he thought was in the woods, wasn't. It was in his skin. He'd become feral, at the very thought of his family threatened.

"Did you know that your daughter and your Inspector are having an affair? Maybe you're not as in control of everything as you seem to think. What else don't you know, if that could get by you?"

The rage Gamache had been trying to control died out completely with those words. To be replaced by something glacial. Ancient.

Armand Gamache felt himself grow very quiet. And he could sense a change in Francoeur as well. He knew he'd gone too far. Had stepped too far from the reeds.

Gamache knew about Jean-Guy and Annie. Had known for months. From the day he and Reine-Marie had visited Annie and seen the little jug of lilacs on her kitchen table.

They'd known, and been immeasurably happy for Annie, who'd loved Jean-Guy from the moment she'd met him more than a decade earlier. And for Jean-Guy, who so clearly loved their daughter.

And for themselves, who loved both young people.

The Gamaches had let them have their space. They knew Annie and Jean-Guy would tell them, when they were ready. He knew. But how did Francoeur? Someone must have told him. And if it wasn't Jean-

Guy and wasn't Annie, then —

"The therapist's notes," said Gamache. "You read the files from Beauvoir's therapy."

They'd all been in therapy, since the raid. All the survivors. And now Gamache knew that Francoeur had violated not only Jean-Guy's privacy, but his own as well. And all the others'. Everything they'd said in confidence this man knew. Their deepest thoughts, their insecurities. What they loved. And what they feared.

And all their secrets. Including Jean-Guy's relationship with Annie.

"Don't you bring my daughter into this," said Gamache. With all his might he was restraining himself from thrusting out his hand. Not for Francoeur's BlackBerry, but for his throat. Feeling the artery throb, then weaken. And stop.

He could, he knew. Kill this man. Leave his body for the wolves and bears. Walk back to the monastery and tell Frère Luc that the Superintendent went for a walk. He'd be back soon.

How easy it would be. How good it would feel. How much better the world would be if this man was dragged into the woods by wolves. And devoured.

Will no one rid me of this troublesome priest?

The words of a king came back to him, and for the first time in his life he completely understood them. Understood how murder happened.

The malady was upon him. Cold, calculating, complete. It had overwhelmed Gamache, until he no longer cared about the consequences. He just wanted this man gone.

He stepped forward, then stopped himself. All the warnings he'd given to Beauvoir, he'd failed to heed himself. He'd let Francoeur under his skin. So that a man devoted to preventing murder had actually contemplated committing it.

Gamache closed his eyes for a moment, and when he opened them again he spoke, leaning forward and whispering, perfectly calmly, into Francoeur's face.

"You've gone too far, Sylvain. Exposed too much. Said too much. I might've had my doubts, but no longer."

"You had your chance, Armand. Back when you arrested Arnot. But you hesitated. As you hesitated now. You might've gotten the BlackBerry out of my hand. You could've seen the message. Why do you think I'm here? For you?"

Gamache walked past Francoeur, away from the monastery and into the woods. He followed the path to the edge of the lake and stood facing the water and the suggestion of dawn in the distance. With the dawn would come the boatman, to take Jean-Guy back to Montréal. And then he'd be alone with Francoeur. And they could finally have it out.

Every sea has its shore, Gamache knew. He'd been at sea for a long time, but now he thought he could finally see the shore. The end of the journey.

"Bonjour."

Gamache, lost in thought, hadn't heard the man arrive. He turned quickly and saw Frère Sébastien wave.

"I came to apologize for storming out of the Blessed Chapel this morning." The Dominican picked his way over the large rocks until he reached the Chief Inspector.

"No need to apologize," said Gamache. "I was rude."

Both men knew it was both true, and intentional. They stood quietly on the rocky shore for a few moments, hearing the far-off call of a loon, and in the near complete silence a fish jumped. The forest smelled sweet. Of evergreens, and fallen leaves.

Gamache had been thinking about his confrontation with Francoeur. Now he brought his mind back to the monastery and the murder of Frère Mathieu.

"You said you'd been assigned the task of finding the Gilbertines. To finally close that centuries-old dossier, opened by the Inquisition. You said the image on the cover of their Gregorian chants gave them away."

"That's true."

The voice was flat. It would skim and skip forever across this lake. Making barely a mark.

"But I think there's more you aren't telling me. Even the Church wouldn't hold a grudge that long."

"It wasn't a grudge, it was an interest." Frère Sébastien indicated the flat rock Gamache had been standing on, and the two men sat. "The lost children. Brothers driven away during a lamentable time. It was an effort to make amends. To find them and tell them they're safe."

"But are they? No man in his right mind would paddle on an unfamiliar lake, in the wilderness, at dusk, in a dense fog. Unless he had to. Unless there was either a lash at his back or a treasure in front of him. Or both. Why are you here? What're you really looking for?"

Light was filling the sky. A cold gray light, not doing much to penetrate the mist. Would the boatman make it?

"We talked about neumes yesterday, but do you know what they are?" the Dominican asked.

While unexpected, the question didn't totally surprise Gamache.

"It's the first musical notation. Before there were notes there were neumes."

"*Oui.* We tend to think the five-line staff was always there. Clefs, treble clefs, notes and half notes. Chords and keys. But they didn't just spring into the world. They evolved. From neumes. They were meant to mimic hand movements. To show the shape of the sound."

Frère Sébastien lifted his hand and moved it back and forth, up and down. It glided through the chilly autumn air, graceful. As he moved his hand he hummed.

It was a lovely voice. Clear. Pure. With a soulful quality. And despite himself, Gamache felt himself drifting along with it. Entranced by the movement of the hand, and the calming sound.

Then the voice, and the hand, stopped.

"The word 'neume' comes from the Greek for 'breath.' The monks who first wrote down the chants believed that the deeper we breathe the more we draw God into ourselves. And there's no deeper breath than when we're singing. Have you ever

634

noticed that the deeper you breathe, the calmer you get?" the monk asked.

"I have. As have Hindus and Buddhists and pagans for millennia."

"Exactly. Every culture, every spiritual belief, has some form of chanting, or meditation. And at their core is the breath."

"So where do neumes come in?" Gamache asked. He was leaning toward the Dominican, holding his large hands together for warmth.

"The first plainchants were learned orally. But then, around the tenth century a monk decided to write them down. But to do that he needed to invent a way of writing music."

"Neumes," said the Chief, and the monk nodded.

"For three centuries, generations of monks wrote down all the Gregorian chants. To preserve them."

"So I've heard," said Gamache. "Many monasteries were given Books of Chants."

"How'd you know?"

"They have one here. Apparently not one of the more remarkable."

"Why do you say that?"

"I don't," said Gamache. "The abbot told me. He says most are illuminated editions. Very fine. But he suspects since the Gilbertines were a minor order and very poor, they ended up with the tenth-century equivalent of a factory second."

"Have you seen the book?"

Frère Sébastien leaned toward Gamache. The Chief Inspector opened his mouth to speak, then shut it again and examined the Dominican.

"That's why you're here, isn't it?" Gamache finally said. "Not to find the Gilbertines, but to find their book."

"Have you seen it?" Frère Sébastien repeated.

"*Oui.* I held it." There was no use denying it. The book wasn't exactly a secret.

"My God," Frère Sébastien exhaled. "Dear God." He shook his head. "Can you show me? I've been looking all over for it."

"All over the monastery?"

"All over the world."

The Dominican rose and whacked the dirt and twigs off his white robes.

Gamache also got up. "Why didn't you ask the abbot or any of the monks?"

"I thought they'd probably hidden it."

"Well, they didn't. It normally sits on the lecturn in the Blessed Chapel, for all the monks to consult."

"I didn't see it there."

"That's because one of the monks has been keeping it with him. Studying the

636

chants."

As they talked they'd made their way back to the monastery, and stopped in front of the thick wooden door. Gamache knocked and after a moment they heard the bolt slide back and the key turn in the lock. They stepped in. After the chill outside, the abbey felt almost warm. The Dominican was halfway down the hall before Gamache called him back.

"Frère Sébastien?"

The monk stopped and turned, impatient.

Gamache pointed to Frère Luc, standing in the porter's room.

"What is it?" And then Frère Sébastien realized what Gamache was telling him. The Dominican began walking back, quickly at first, his pace slowing as he got closer to the porter's room.

Frère Sébastien seemed reluctant to take that last step. For fear, perhaps, of disappointment, Gamache thought. Or perhaps he realized he didn't really want the search to end. Because then what would he do?

If the mystery was solved, what would be his purpose?

Frère Sébastien stopped at the door to the porter's room.

"Would you mind, *mon frère*," the Dominican asked, suddenly formal, almost grave, "if I looked at your Book of Chants?"

It was not, Gamache knew, how the Inquisition of the past would have handled it. They'd have simply taken the book, and probably burned the young monk who had it in his possession.

Frère Luc stepped aside.

And the hound of the Lord took the last few steps in a journey that had begun hundreds of years and thousands of miles earlier. By brothers long dead.

He stepped into the dreary little room and looked at the large, plain bound book on the desk. His hand hovered over the cover and then he opened it and took a deep breath in.

Then a deep breath out.

A long, slow sigh.

"This is it."

"How do you know?" Gamache asked.

"Because of this." The monk picked up the book and held it in his arms.

Gamache put on his reading glasses and leaned over. Frère Sébastien was pointing to the very first word on the very first page. Above it was a neume. But where the finger was there was nothing, except a dot.

"That?" asked Gamache, also pointing. "That dot?"

"That dot," said Frère Sébastien. There

was a look of awe, of astonishment on his face. "This is it. The very first book of Gregorian chant. And this," he lifted his finger a fraction, "is the very first musical note. It must've somehow come into the possession of Gilbert of Sempringham, in the twelfth century," said the Dominican, speaking to the page and not the men around him. "Maybe as a gift, a thank-you from the Church, for his loyalty to Thomas à Becket. But Gilbert couldn't have known how valuable it was. No one would, at the time. They couldn't have known it was unique. Or would become unique."

"But what makes it unique?" asked Gamache.

"That dot. It's not a dot."

"What is it?" It looked like a dot to Gamache. He'd rarely felt so stupid as he had since arriving in Saint-Gilbert.

"It's the key." Both men looked at the young *portier* who'd just spoken. "The starting point."

"You knew?" Frère Sébastien asked Frère Luc.

"Not at first," admitted Luc. "I just knew the chants here are different than any I'd ever heard or sung. But I didn't know why. Then Frère Mathieu told me."

"Did he know this book is priceless?"

asked the Dominican.

"I don't think he thought in those terms. But I think he knew it was unique. He knew enough about Gregorian chant to realize none of the others, in all the literature and collections, had that dot. And he knew what it meant."

"What does it mean?" asked Gamache.

"That dot is the musical Rosetta stone," said Frère Sébastien, then he turned to Luc. "You called it the key and that's exactly what it is. All the other Gregorian chants are close. It's like getting to this monastery but not being able to get in the door. The best you can do is wander around the outside. Close. But not quite there. This," he nodded down at the page, "is the key that unlocks the door that gets us inside the chants. That gets us inside the minds and the voices of the earliest of monks. With this, we know what the original chants really sounded like. What the voice of God really sounds like."

"How?" asked Gamache, trying not to sound exasperated.

"You tell him," Frère Sébastien invited the young Gilbertine. "It's your book."

Frère Luc flushed with pride and looked at the Dominican with something close to adoration. For not only including him in this conversation, but treating him as an equal.

"It's not just a dot." Frère Luc turned to Gamache. "If you found a treasure map that had all the directions, but not the place to begin, it'd be useless. The dot is the starting point. It tells us what the first note should be."

Gamache looked back down at the book, open in Frère Sébastien's arms.

"But I thought the neume told us that," he said, pointing to the first squiggle above the first faded word.

"No," said Luc. Patient now. A born teacher, when working with something he knew and loved. "It only tells us to raise our voices. But from where? This dot is in the middle of the letter. The voice should start in the middle register, and go up."

"Not exactly precise," said Gamache.

"It's an art, not a science," said Frère Sébastien. "It's as close as we need to come and can come."

"If the dot is so important, why don't all the Books of Chants have it?" the Chief asked.

"Good question," admitted Frère Sébastien. "We think this," he hefted the book, "was written by musician monks, but that it was then taken and copied. By scribes.

Literary men who didn't appreciate the importance of the dot. Might have even thought it was a flaw, a mistake."

"So they left it out?" asked Gamache and the Dominican slowly nodded.

Centuries of searching, a near holy war, generations of monks dedicated to the hunt. All because of a missing dot, and monks who'd mistaken it for a flaw.

"The sheet of music we found on the prior's body had a dot," Gamache said.

Frère Sébastien looked at the Chief with interest. "You noticed?"

"I only noticed because you had your finger over it, as though trying to hide it."

"I was," admitted the monk. "I was afraid someone else would see the significance of it. Whoever wrote that piece of music knew about the original Book of Chants. And had written another chant in the same style exactly. Including the dot."

"But that doesn't narrow it down," said Gamache. "All the Gilbertines know about this book. They copy out the chants. They must know about the dot and what it does."

"But do they all know how valuable that makes this book?" asked the Dominican. "In fact, it has no value. It's priceless."

Luc shook his head. "Only Frère Mathieu might've known, and he wouldn't care. Its only value to him was the music, nothing else."

"You also knew," Gamache pointed out.

"About the dot, yes, but not that the book was priceless," said Frère Luc.

Gamache wondered if he finally had the motive. Could one of the monks have realized their old wreck of a book was worth a fortune? That the treasure within these walls wasn't hidden at all, but in plain sight, in plainchant?

Was the prior killed because he stood between the monk and a fortune?

Gamache turned back to the Dominican.

"Is that why you're here? Not for the lost brothers, but the lost book? It wasn't the drawing on the cover of the CD that gave them away, but the music itself."

The truth became clear. This monk had followed the neumes here. For hundreds of years the Church had been looking for the starting point. The Gilbertine recording of the Gregorian chants had unwittingly provided that.

Frère Sébastien seemed to be weighing his answer, then finally he nodded.

"When the Holy Father heard the recording he knew at once. It was the same in every way as all the other Gregorian chants sung in monasteries around the world.

643

Except, these were divine."

"Sacred," agreed Frère Luc.

Both monks looked at Gamache, their eyes intense. There was something frightening about that level of zeal. For a single dot.

In the beginning.

The beautiful mystery. Finally solved.

THIRTY-THREE

After breakfast Gamache approached the abbot. Not about the Book of Chants and its value. That he chose to keep quiet, for now. But about something else, of immeasurable value to the Chief himself.

"Did you get through to the boatman?"

He nodded. "Took a couple of tries but Frère Simon finally connected. He's waiting for the fog to burn off, but he's optimistic he can be here by noon. Don't worry," said Dom Philippe, once more correctly interpreting the tiny lines on Gamache's face. "He'll make it."

"Merci, mon père."

When the abbot and the others left to prepare for Lauds, Gamache looked at his watch. It was twenty past seven. Five more hours. Yes, the boatman would make it, but what would he find when he docked?

Jean-Guy hadn't come to breakfast. Gamache strode across the quiet chapel and out the far door. A few monks nodded to him in the corridor as they left their cells, heading for the next service.

The Chief looked into the prior's office, but it was empty. Then he knocked on Beauvoir's door and entered without waiting for a reply.

Jean-Guy was lying in bed. In his clothing from the night before. Unshaved, disheveled. Bleary-eyed, Beauvoir got up on one elbow.

"What time is it?"

"Almost seven thirty. What's wrong, Jean-Guy?" Gamache stood over the bed as Beauvoir struggled up.

"I'm just tired."

"It's more than that." He looked closely at the young man he knew so well. "Are you on something?"

"Are you kidding? I'm clean and sober. How many times do I have to prove it?" snapped Beauvoir.

"Don't lie to me."

"I'm not."

They stared at each other. *Five hours,* thought Gamache. *Just five hours. We can make it.* He scanned the small room but there was nothing out of place.

"Get dressed, please, and join me in the Blessed Chapel for Lauds."

"Why?"

Gamache was very still then. "Because I've asked you to."

There was a pause between the two men.

Then Beauvoir relented. "Fine."

Gamache left and a few minutes later Beauvoir, quickly showered, joined him in the Blessed Chapel, arriving just as the chants began. He dropped into the pew beside Gamache, but said nothing. Angered at being ordered about, questioned. Doubted.

The singing, as always, began from far off. A distant, but perfect, beginning. And then it drew closer. Beauvoir closed his eyes.

Deep breath in, he told himself. Deep breath out.

It felt as though he was breathing in the notes. Taking them to his core. They seemed lighter than round black notes. These neumes had wings. Beauvoir felt light-hearted, and light-headed. Lifted from his stupor. Lifted from the hole he'd rolled into.

As he listened he heard not just the voices, but the breathing of the monks, also in unison. Deep breath in. And then the singing, on the exhale.

Deep breath out.

And then, before he knew it, Lauds was over. And the monks had gone. Everyone had gone.

Beauvoir opened his eyes. The Blessed Chapel was completely silent and he was alone. Except for the Chief.

"We need to talk." Gamache spoke quietly, not looking at Beauvoir, but staring ahead. "Whatever it is, it will be all right."

His voice was confident, and kind, and comforting. Beauvoir felt himself drawn to it. And then he felt himself pitching forward. Losing all control. The pew leapt at him, but he couldn't stop himself.

Then Gamache's strong hand was on his chest, stopping him. Holding him. He could hear that familiar voice call his name. Not Beauvoir. Not Inspector.

Jean-Guy. Jean-Guy.

He felt himself slide sideways, limp, and his eyes roll to the back of his head. Just before blacking out he saw prisms of light from above, and felt the Chief's jacket against his cheek and smelled sandalwood and rosewater.

Beauvoir's eyes flickered open, the lids heavy. Then they closed.

Armand Gamache gathered Jean-Guy in his arms and hurried through the Blessed Chapel.

Don't take this child.

Don't take this child.

"Stay with me, son," he whispered over and over until finally they were at the infirmary.

"What's happened?" Frère Charles demanded as Gamache laid Jean-Guy on the examination table. All sign of the relaxed and jovial monk gone. The doctor had taken over and now his hand swiftly moved over Beauvoir, feeling for a pulse, lifting his lids.

"I think he's on something, but I don't know what. He had an addiction to painkillers, but he's been clean for three months now."

The doctor did a rapid assessment of his patient, lifting Beauvoir's lids, taking his pulse. He rolled back Jean-Guy's sweater, to get at his chest for a better sounding. There Frère Charles paused and looked at the Chief.

A scar ran across Beauvoir's abdomen.

"What was the painkiller?" he asked.

"OxyContin," said Gamache, and saw the concern in Frère Charles's face. "He was shot. The OxyContin was prescribed for pain."

"Christ," whispered the monk under his breath. "But we don't know for sure it's OxyContin he's on now. You say he's clean. Are you sure?"

"I'm sure he was when we arrived. I know this young man, well. I'd have known if he relapsed."

"Well it looks like an overdose to me. He's breathing and his vital signs are strong. Whatever it is, he didn't take enough to kill him. But it'd help if we had the pills."

Frère Charles rolled Beauvoir onto his side, in case he vomited, and Gamache searched Jean-Guy's pockets. They were empty.

"I'll be back," said the Chief Inspector, but before heading for the door he lightly touched Beauvoir's face and felt it chill and damp. Then he turned and left.

As his long legs took him back down the corridor, past staring monks, he looked at his watch. Eight A.M. Four hours. The boatman would arrive in four hours. If the fog burns off.

The mirthful light hadn't shown up today. Almost no sun made it through the high windows and Gamache couldn't see if the sky was clearing, or closing in.

Four hours.

He would leave with Beauvoir. He knew that now. Whether the murder was solved or not. According to the doctor, Jean-Guy was out of immediate danger. But Gamache knew the danger was far from removed.

It didn't take long to find the small bottle of small pills in Beauvoir's small cell. It was under his pillow. Barely hidden. But then, Jean-Guy hadn't expected to pass out. Hadn't expected his room to be searched.

Gamache picked the pill bottle up with a handkerchief.

OxyContin. But it wasn't prescribed to Beauvoir. It wasn't prescribed at all. The label had only the manufacturer's name and the name and dose of the drug.

After slipping it into his pocket, Gamache searched the cell and in the wastepaper basket he found a note.

Take as needed. And a signature. He carefully folded the paper, with more precision than necessary. Pausing at the window, he stared into the fog.

Yes. It was lifting.

In the infirmary Frère Charles was doing his paperwork and checking on Beauvoir every few minutes. The shallow, rapid breathing had become regular. Deeper. The Sûreté Inspector had moved from being passed out to merely sleeping.

He'd wake up in an hour or so, with a headache, a thirst, and a craving.

Frère Charles didn't envy this man.

The monk looked up and started. Armand

651

Gamache was standing just inside the doorway. And as Frère Charles watched, the Chief Inspector slowly closed the door.

"Did you find it?" the doctor asked. The Chief was looking at him in a way that the monk didn't like.

"I did. Under his pillow."

Frère Charles held out his hand for the bottle, but Gamache didn't move. He just continued to stare and the monk dropped his eyes, no longer able to hold the hard, heavy stare.

"I also found this." Gamache held the note up and the monk went to take it, but the Chief pulled it back. Frère Charles read it as it hung in the air between them, then met the Chief Inspector's eyes.

The monk's mouth was open, but no words came out. His face turned a deep red and he looked again at the note in Gamache's hand.

It was in his own handwriting. With his own signature.

"But I didn't . . ." he tried again and flushed more.

Chief Inspector Gamache lowered the paper and walked over to Beauvoir. There he laid his hand against his Inspector's neck, to feel his pulse. It was, the doctor recognized, a practiced move. A natural move. For the head of homicide. To establish proof of life. Or death.

Then Gamache turned back to the doctor.

"Is this your handwriting?" he nodded to the note.

"Yes, but —"

"And your signature?"

"Yes, but —"

"Did you give Inspector Beauvoir these pills?"

Gamache reached into his pocket and held out the pills, using the handkerchief.

"No. I never gave him pills. Let me see." The doctor reached but Gamache withdrew the bottle, so that the doctor had to lean in to read the label.

After examining it he turned and walked to his medicine cabinet, which he unlocked using a key in his pocket.

"I keep OxyContin in stock, but only for the worst emergencies. I'd never normally prescribe it. Filthy stuff. All my stock checks out. I have the records if you'd like to see what I've ordered, when, and what I've prescribed. There's none missing."

"Records can be faked."

The doctor nodded and handed a small pill bottle to the Chief, who put on his glasses and examined it.

"As you see, Chief Inspector, the pills are the same, but the dosage and the supplier is different. I never deal in the higher doses and we get our medications from a medical supply house in Drummondville."

Gamache removed his glasses. "Can you explain the note?"

Both men looked again at the paper in Gamache's hand.

Take as needed. And then the doctor's signature.

"I must've written that for someone else, and whoever left the OxyContin for your Inspector found it and used it."

"Who have you prescribed for recently?"

The doctor went to his records, but both men knew this wasn't necessary. It was a small enough community, and this would have been recent enough. Frère Charles almost certainly would remember, without aid of records.

But still, he looked it up and returned.

"I should demand a warrant for medical records," he said, but they both knew he wouldn't. It would just be postponing the inevitable and neither man wanted that. Besides, the monk never again wanted to experience that cold, hard stare.

"It was the abbot. Dom Philippe."

"Merci." Gamache went over to Beauvoir

once again and looked down at the face of his now-sleeping Inspector. After tucking the blanket snug around him, the Chief walked to the door. "Can you tell me what the prescription was for?"

"A mild tranquillizer. The abbot hasn't slept well since the death of Frère Mathieu. He needed to function, so he came for help."

"Have you ever prescribed tranquillizers for him before?"

"No, never."

"And for the other brothers? Tranquillizers? Sleeping pills? Pain medication?"

"It happens, but I watch it closely."

"Do you know if the abbot used the tranquillizers?"

The doctor shook his head. "No, I don't. I doubt it. He prefers meditation to medication. We all do. But he wanted something, just in case. I wrote that note for him."

Armand Gamache reached the Blessed Chapel but instead of walking through it, he paused. And sat, in the very last pew. Not to pray, but to think.

If the doctor was telling the truth, his note was found by someone and used to give Beauvoir the impression the pills were from the medical monk. Gamache wished he could convince himself that Beauvoir didn't know what he was taking, but the bottle was clearly marked OxyContin.

Beauvoir knew. And he took them anyway. No one forced him. But someone had tempted him. Gamache looked at the altar, which had changed in just the few minutes he'd been sitting there. Strings of light were dropping, like luminous acrobats, from above.

The fog was clearing. The boatman would come for them. Gamache checked his watch. In two and a half hours. Did he have time to do what was needed? The Chief Inspector spotted someone else in the chapel, sitting quietly in a pew by the wall. Not, perhaps, trying to hide. But not sitting out in the open either.

It was the Dominican. Sitting in the reflected light. A book on his knees.

And in that moment, the Chief Inspector knew, with distaste, what he had to do.

Jean-Guy Beauvoir was aware of his mouth before anything else. It was huge. And lined with fur and mud. He opened and closed it. The sound was mammoth. A mushy, clicking sound, like his grandfather in later years, eating.

Then he listened to his breathing. It was also unnaturally loud.

And finally, he pried open one eye. The other seemed glued shut. Through the slit he saw Gamache sitting on a hard chair, pulled up to the bed.

Beauvoir felt a moment of panic. What had happened? The last time he saw the Chief sitting like that Beauvoir had been gravely, almost mortally, wounded. Had it happened again?

But he didn't think so. This felt different. He was exhausted, almost numb. But not in pain. Though there was an ache, deep down.

He watched Gamache sitting so still. His glasses were on, and he was reading. The last time, in the Montréal hospital, Gamache had also been hurt. His face a shock to Beauvoir when he'd finally roused enough to take anything in.

It had been covered in bruises, and there was a bandage over the Chief's forehead. And when he got up to lean over Beauvoir, Jean-Guy had seen the grimace of pain. Before it quickly turned into a smile.

"All right, son?" he'd asked, quietly.

Beauvoir couldn't talk. He'd felt himself drifting off again, but he held those deep, brown eyes as long as he could, before he had to let go.

Now, in the monastery infirmary, he watched the Chief.

He was no longer bruised, and while there was and always would be a deep scar over his left temple, it had healed. The Chief had healed.

Beauvoir hadn't.

In fact, it now seemed to Beauvoir that the healthier the Chief got, the weaker he himself became. As though Francoeur was right, and Gamache was sucking him dry. Using him until he could be discarded. In favor of Isabelle Lacoste, whom the Chief had just promoted to Beauvoir's own rank.

But he knew it wasn't true. He unhooked the thought from his flesh and could almost see it drift away. But thoughts that dreadful came with a barb.

"Bonjour." The Chief looked up and noticed Jean-Guy's eye open. "How're you feeling?" He leaned over the bed and smiled. "You're in the infirmary."

Jean-Guy struggled to sit up, and managed it, with Gamache's help. They were alone. The doctor had gone off to the eleven A.M. mass, leaving Gamache alone with his Inspector.

The Chief raised the head of the bed, put some pillows behind Beauvoir and helped him drink a glass of water, all without saying a word. Beauvoir began to feel human again. His daze cleared, slowly at first then with a rapid succession of memories.

The Chief was sitting again, his legs crossed.

Gamache wasn't stern, wasn't censorious, wasn't angry. But he did want answers.

"What happened?" the Chief finally asked.

Beauvoir didn't say anything but watched with dismay as the Chief reached into his jacket pocket and withdrew a handkerchief. And opened it.

Jean-Guy nodded, then closed his eyes. So ashamed, he couldn't look Gamache in the face. And if he couldn't face the Chief, how was he ever going to face Annie?

The thought made him so sick he thought he'd vomit.

"It's all right, Jean-Guy. It was a slip, nothing more. We'll get you home and get help. Nothing that can't be put right."

Beauvoir opened his eyes and saw Armand Gamache looking at him not with pity. But with determination. And confidence. It would be all right.

"Oui, patron," he managed. And he even found himself believing it. That this could be put behind him.

"Tell me what happened." Gamache put the bottle away and leaned forward.

"It was just there, on the bedside table, with the note from the doctor. I thought . . ."

I thought it was a prescription. I thought it was all right since it was from the doctor. I thought I had no choice.

He held the Chief's eyes and hesitated.

". . . I didn't think. I wanted them. I don't know why, but I had a craving and they appeared and I took them."

The Chief nodded and let Beauvoir gather himself.

"When was this?" Gamache asked.

Beauvoir had to think. When was it? Weeks ago, surely. Months. A lifetime.

"Yesterday afternoon."

"It wasn't the doctor who put them there. Do you have any idea who else might have?"

Beauvoir looked surprised. He'd given it no thought, completely accepting they were from the medical monk. He shook his head.

Gamache got up and got Beauvoir another glass of water. "Are you hungry? I can get you a sandwich."

"*No, patron. Merci.* I'm fine."

"The abbot's called the boatman and he'll be here in just over an hour. We'll leave together."

"But what about the case? The murderer?"

"A lot can happen in an hour."

Beauvoir watched Gamache leave. He

knew the Chief was right. A lot could happen in an hour. And a lot could fall apart.

THIRTY-FOUR

Armand Gamache sat in a front pew and watched the monks at their eleven A.M. mass. Every now and then he closed his eyes and prayed that this would work.

Less than an hour now, he thought. In fact, the boatman might already be at the dock. Gamache watched the abbot leave his spot on the bench and walk to the altar, where he genuflected and sang a few lines of Latin prayer.

Then, one by one, the rest of the community joined in.

Call, response. Call. Response.

And then there was a moment when all sound was suspended and seemed to hang in mid-air. Not a silence, but a deep and collective inhale.

And then all their voices came in together in a chorus that could only be described as glorious. Armand Gamache felt it resonate in his core. Despite what had happened to

Beauvoir. Despite what had happened to Frère Mathieu. Despite what was about to happen.

Unseen behind him, Jean-Guy Beauvoir arrived in the chapel. He'd drifted in and out of sleep since the Chief had left, then had finally surfaced. He'd ached all over, and far from getting better, it seemed to be getting worse. He'd walked down the long corridor as though he was an elderly man. Shuffling. Joints creaking. Breath shallow. But every step took him closer to where he knew he belonged.

Not in the Blessed Chapel necessarily. But beside Gamache.

Once in the chapel, he saw the Chief at the very front.

But Jean-Guy Beauvoir's body had taken him as far as it could, and he slumped into the pew at the very back. He leaned forward, his hands hanging loosely on the pew in front. Not quite in prayer. But in a sort of netherworld.

The world seemed very far away. But the music didn't. It was all around him. Inside and out. Supporting him. The music was plain and simple. The voices in unison. One voice, one song. The very simplicity of the chants both calmed and energized Beauvoir.

There was no chaos here. Nothing unexpected. Except their effect on him. That was completely unexpected.

Something strange seemed to come over him. He felt out of sorts.

And then he realized what it was.

Peace. Complete and utter peace.

He closed his eyes and let the neumes lift him, out of himself, out of the pew, out of the Blessed Chapel. They took him out of the abbey and out over the lake and the forest. He flew with them, free, unbound.

This was better than Percocet, better than OxyContin. There was no pain, no anxiety, no worry. There was no "us" and no "them," no boundaries and no limits.

And then the music stopped, and Beauvoir descended, softly, to the earth.

He opened his eyes and looked around, wondering if anyone had noticed what had just happened to him. He saw Chief Inspector Gamache in one of the front pews, and across from him sat Superintendent Francoeur.

Beauvoir looked around the chapel. Someone was missing.

The Dominican. What had become of the man from the Inquisition?

Beauvoir turned to the altar and as he did he intercepted a brief glance from Gamache to Superintendent Francoeur.

Christ, thought Beauvoir. *He really does despise the man.*

Armand Gamache brought his gaze back to the monks. The chanting had stopped and the abbot was again standing front and center in the quiet church.

Then, into the silence, there came a single voice. A tenor. Singing.

The abbot looked at his monks. The monks looked at their abbot, then at each other. Their eyes wide, but their mouths shut.

And yet, the clear voice continued.

The abbot stood over the host and the goblet of wine. The body and blood of Christ. A wafer frozen in mid-blessing, offered to the air.

The beautiful voice was all around them, as though it had glided down the shafts of thin light and taken possession of the chapel.

The abbot turned to face the tiny congregation. To see if one of them had lost his wits and found his voice. But all he saw were the three officers. Scattered. Watching. Silent.

Then, from behind the plaque to Saint-Gilbert, the Dominican appeared. Frère

Sébastien walked slowly, solemnly, to the center of the Blessed Chapel. There he paused.

"I can't hear you," he sang in an upbeat tempo, much faster, lighter, than any Gregorian chant ever heard in the chapel. The Latin words filled the air. "I have a banana in my ear."

The music the prior died with had come to life.

"I am not a fish," the Dominican chanted, as he walked down the center aisle. "I am not a fish."

The monks, and the abbot, were paralyzed. Little rainbows danced around them as the morning sun burned through more mist. Frère Sébastien approached the altar, his head up, his arms thrust into his sleeves, his voice filling the void.

"Stop it."

It wasn't so much a command as a howl. A baying.

But the Dominican stopped neither his singing nor his progress. He continued, unhurried and unrelenting, toward the altar. And the monks.

Armand Gamache slowly rose to his feet, his eyes on the one monk who had finally separated himself from the rest.

The lone voice.

"Nooo!" the monk cried in pain. It was as though the music was sizzling his skin, as though the Inquisition had one final monk to burn.

Frère Sébastien came to a halt just below the abbot, and looked up.

"Dies irae," Frère Sébastien sang. Day of wrath.

"Stop," the monk pleaded. He'd stepped toward the Dominican and sank to his knees. "Pleeease."

And the Dominican stopped. All that filled the chapel was sobbing. And giddy light.

"You killed your prior," said Gamache quietly. "*Ecce homo.* He is man. And you killed him for it."

"Bless me, Father, for I have sinned."

The abbot crossed himself.

"Go on, my son."

There was a long pause. Dom Philippe knew this old confessional had heard many, many things over the centuries. But none as disgraceful as was about to come out.

God, of course, already knew. Had probably known before the blow was struck. Probably even knew before the thought was formed. This confession wasn't for the Lord, but for the sinner, the sheep who'd wandered too far from the fold. And been lost in a land of wolves.

"I have committed murder. I killed the prior."

Bugs were crawling all over Jean-Guy Beauvoir's skin and he wondered if the infirmary might've been infested with bedbugs or cockroaches.

He wiped his hand over his arms and tried to get at the ones crawling down his spine. He and the Chief were in the prior's office, doing the paperwork, making notes. Packing up. The final preparations before leaving with the boatman.

Superintendent Francoeur had officially made the arrest, taken possession of the prisoner, and called for the floatplane to pick them up. Francoeur was now sitting in the Blessed Chapel while the murderer monk made his confession. Not to the police, but to his confessor.

Beauvoir's discomfort came in waves. Getting closer and closer, until now he was barely able to sit still. Bugs crawled under his clothing, and waves of anxiety cascaded over him until he found he could barely breathe.

And the pain was back. In his gut, in his marrow. His hair, his eyeballs, his dry lips hurt.

"I need a pill," he said, barely able to focus on the man across from him. He saw Gamache raise his head from the notes he was making, and stare at him.

"Please. Just one more, and then I'll stop. Just one to get me home."

"The doctor said to give you Extra Strength Tylenol —"

"I don't want a Tylenol," shouted Beauvoir, his hand slapping the desk. "For God's sake, please. It'll be the last one, I swear."

The Chief Inspector calmly shook two pills into his hand and walked around the desk with a glass of water. He offered his palm to Beauvoir. Jean-Guy grabbed the pills then tossed them onto the floor.

"Not those, not the Tylenol. I need the others."

He could see them in Gamache's jacket pocket.

Jean-Guy Beauvoir knew he shouldn't. Knew this would be crossing a line which could never be uncrossed. But finally there was no "knowing" about it. Only the pain. And the crawling, and the anxiety. And the need.

He pushed himself off the chair with all the strength he had and grabbed at Gamache's pocket, thrusting the two of them against the stone wall.

■ ■ ■ ■

"I killed the prior."

"Go on, my son," said the abbot.

There was a silence. But it wasn't complete. Dom Philippe heard gasping as the man in the other half of the confessional tried to breathe.

"I didn't mean to. Not really."

The voice was growing hysterical and the abbot knew that wouldn't help.

"Slowly," he advised. "Slowly. Tell me what happened."

There was another pause as the monk gathered himself.

"Frère Mathieu wanted to talk about the chant he'd written."

"Mathieu wrote the chant?" The abbot knew he shouldn't be asking questions during a confession, but he couldn't seem to help himself.

"Yes."

"The words and the music?" the abbot asked, and promised himself that would be the last interruption. And then silently begged God's forgiveness for lying.

He knew there'd be more.

"Yes. Well, he'd written the music and then put in just any Latin words to fit the meter of the music. He wanted me to write the real words."

"He wanted you to write a prayer?"

"Sort of. Not that I'm so great at Latin, but anyone was better than him. And I think he wanted an ally. He wanted to make the chants even more popular and he thought if we could modernize them just a little, we'd reach more people. I tried to talk him out of it. It wasn't right. It was blasphemy."

The abbot sat in silence and waited for more. And finally it came.

"The prior gave me the new chant about a week ago. He said if I helped him I could sing it on the new recording. Be the soloist. He was excited and so was I at first, until I looked more closely. I could see then what he was doing. It had nothing to do with the glory of God and everything to do with his own ego. He expected I'd just say yes. He couldn't believe it when I refused."

"What did Frère Mathieu do?"

"He tried to bribe me. And then he got angry. Said he'd drop me from the choir completely."

Dom Philippe tried to imagine what that would be like. To be the only monk not singing the chants. To be excluded from that Glory. To be excluded from the community. Left out. His silence complete.

671

It would be no life at all.

"I had to stop him. He'd have destroyed everything. The chants, the monastery. Me." The disembodied voice paused, to gather himself. And when he spoke again it was so quietly the abbot had to lean his ear against the grille to hear.

"It was a profanity. You heard it, *mon père*. You see that something had to be done to stop him."

Yes, thought the abbot, he'd heard it. Hardly believing his eyes, and ears, he'd watched the Dominican walk down the central aisle of the Blessed Chapel. The abbot had been at first shocked, angered even. And then, God help him, all the anger had disappeared and he'd been seduced.

Mathieu had created a plainchant with a complex rhythm. The music had swarmed over the abbot's final defenses. Walls he didn't realize he still had. And the notes, the neumes, the lovely voice had found the chord at Dom Philippe's core.

And for a few moments the abbot had known complete and utter bliss. Had resonated with love. Of God, of man. Of himself. Of all people and all things.

But now all he heard was the sobbing in the stall beside him.

Frère Luc had finally made his choice.

He'd left the *porterie* and killed the prior.

Gamache felt himself propelled backward and braced himself. His back connected with the stone wall and the breath was knocked out of him.

But by far the biggest shock came in that split second before impact, when he realized who was doing this.

He gasped for air and felt Jean-Guy's hand go to his pocket. After the pills.

Gamache grabbed the hand and twisted. Beauvoir howled and fought harder, thrashing and wailing. Knocking Gamache in the face and chest. Knocking him backward again in a desperate, single-minded drive to get at what was in Gamache's pocket.

Nothing else mattered. Beauvoir twisted and shoved and would have clawed his way through concrete to get at that pill bottle.

"Stop, Jean-Guy, stop," Gamache shouted, but knew it was no use. Beauvoir was out of his mind. The Chief brought his forearm up and held it to Beauvoir's throat, just as he saw something that almost stopped his heart.

Jean-Guy Beauvoir went for his gun.

"All those neumes," Frère Luc slobbered, his voice wet and messy. There was a snuffle, and the abbot imagined the long black sleeve of the robe drawn across the runny nose. "I couldn't believe it. I thought it was a joke, but the prior said it was his masterpiece. The result of a lifetime studying chants. The voices would be sung in plainchant. Together. The other neumes were for instruments. An organ and violins and flute. He'd been working on it for years, *Père Abbé*. And you didn't even know."

The young voice was accusatory. As though it was the prior who had sinned and the abbot who had failed.

Dom Philippe looked through the grillwork of the confessional, trying to glimpse the other side. To see the young man he'd followed since the seminary. Had watched, from a distance, as he'd grown and matured, and chosen holy orders. As his voice had begun the long drop, from his head to his heart.

But, unknown to the abbot or the prior, that drop had never been completed. The lovely voice had gotten stuck behind a lump in the young man's throat.

After the success of their first recording, but before the rift, Mathieu and the abbot had met for one of their talks in the garden. And Mathieu had said the time had come. The choir needed the young man. Mathieu wanted to work with him, to help shape the extraordinary voice before some less gifted choirmaster got hold of him.

One of the elderly brothers had just died, and the abbot had agreed, with some reluctance. Frère Luc was still so young, and this was such a remote monastery.

But Mathieu had been convincing.

And now, peering through the grille at Mathieu's killer, the abbot wondered whether it was the voice Mathieu hoped to influence, or the monk.

Did Mathieu realize that the other brothers might be reluctant to sing such a revolutionary chant? But if he could recruit the young, lonely monk to the abbey, he could get him to do it. And to not only sing the chant, but write the words.

Mathieu was magnetic, and Luc was impressionable. Or so the prior had thought.

"What happened?" the abbot asked.

There was a pause and more ragged inhales.

The abbot didn't press anymore. He tried to tell himself it was patience that guided him. But he knew it was fear. He didn't want to hear what came next. His rosary hung from his hands and his lips moved. And he waited.

■ ■ ■ ■

Gamache grabbed at Beauvoir's hand, trying to loosen the gun. From Jean-Guy's throat came a wail, a cry of desperation. He fought wildly, flailing and kicking and bucking but finally Gamache twisted Beauvoir's arm behind his back and the firearm clattered to the floor.

Both men were gasping for breath. Gamache held Jean-Guy's face against the rough stone wall. Beauvoir bucked and sidled but Gamache held firm.

"Let go," Beauvoir screamed into the stone. "Those pills are mine. My property."

The Chief held him there until his twisting and bucking slowed, and stopped. And all that was left was a panting young man. Exhausted.

Gamache took the holster from Beauvoir's belt then reached into Jean-Guy's pocket and took his Sûreté ID. Then he stooped for the gun and turned Beauvoir around.

The younger man was bleeding from scrapes to the side of his face.

"We're going to leave here, Jean-Guy. We're going to get in that boat and when we get to Montréal I'm taking you straight to rehab."

"Fuck you. I won't go back there. And you think holding on to those pills will do any good? I can get more, without even leaving headquarters."

"You won't be in headquarters. You're suspended. You don't think I'm going to let you walk around with pills and a gun? You'll go on sick leave, and when your doctor says you're well, we'll discuss reinstating you."

"Fuck you," spat Beauvoir, the drool sticking to his chin.

"If you don't go willingly I'll arrest you for assault and have the judge sentence you to rehab. I'll do it, you know."

Beauvoir held Gamache's eyes, and knew he'd do it.

Gamache put Beauvoir's badge and ID card into his own pocket. Beauvoir's mouth was open, a thin line of spittle dripped onto his sweater. His eyes were glassy and wide, and he swayed on his feet. "You can't suspend me."

Gamache took a deep breath and stepped back. "I know this isn't you. It's the goddamned pills. They're killing you, Jean-Guy. But we'll get you to treatment and it'll be all right. Trust me."

"Like I trusted you in the factory? Like the others trusted you?"

And Beauvoir, even through his haze,

could see he'd scored a direct hit. He saw the Chief flinch as the words struck.

And he was glad.

Beauvoir watched as the Chief slowly put Beauvoir's gun into the holster and attached it to his own belt.

"Who gave you the pills?"

"I told you. I found them in my room, with the note from the doctor."

"They're not from the doctor."

But Beauvoir was right about one thing. He could get more OxyContin anytime he wanted. Québec was swimming in the stuff. The Sûreté evidence locker was swimming in it. Some of it even made it to trial.

Gamache stood still.

He knew who'd given Beauvoir the drugs.

"Ecce homo," said the abbot. "Why did Mathieu say that when he was dying?"

"It's what I said when I hit him."

"Why?"

There was another pause and another ragged breath. "He wasn't the man I thought he was."

"You mean, he was just a man," suggested the abbot. "He wasn't the saint you thought he was. He was a world expert on Gregorian chants. A genius even. But he was just a man. You expected him to be more."

"I loved him. I'd have done anything for him. But he asked me to help him ruin the chants, and I couldn't do that."

"You went to the garden knowing you might kill him?" asked the abbot, trying to keep his voice neutral. "You took the iron door knocker with you."

"I had to stop him. When we met in the garden I tried to reason with him, to get him to change his mind. I tore up the sheet he gave to me. I thought it was the only copy." The voice stopped. But the breathing continued. Rapid and shallow now. "Frère Mathieu was in a rage. Said he'd kick me out of the choir. Make me sit in the pews."

The abbot listened to Frère Luc, but he saw Mathieu. Not the loving, kind, godly friend, but the man overcome with rage. Stymied. Denied. The abbot could barely stand up to the force of that personality. He could begin to see how young Frère Luc might break. And lash out.

"All I wanted was to sing the chants. I came here to study with the prior and sing the chants. That's all. Why wasn't that enough?"

The voice became a squeak, unintelligible. The abbot tried to make out the words. Frère Luc cried and begged him to understand. And the abbot found that he did.

Mathieu was human, and so was this young man.

And so was he.

Dom Philippe lowered his head to his hands as the young man's sobs surrounded him.

Armand Gamache left Beauvoir in the prior's office and headed for the Blessed Chapel. With each step he felt his rage growing.

The drugs would kill Jean-Guy. A long, slow slide to the grave. Gamache knew that. The man who did this knew it. And had done it anyway.

The Chief Inspector yanked open the door to the Blessed Chapel so forcefully it banged against the wall behind it. He saw the monks turn at the sound.

He saw Sylvain Francoeur turn. And Gamache, as he approached with steely, steady calm, saw the smile fade from Francoeur's handsome face.

"We need to talk, Sylvain," said Gamache.

Francoeur backed away, up the steps and onto the altar. "Now's not the time, Armand. The plane will be arriving any moment."

"Now is the time." Gamache kept walking forward, his eyes never straying from Francoeur. In his hand he held a handkerchief.

As his long, steady strides brought him closer to the Superintendent, Gamache opened his fist to reveal a pill bottle.

The Superintendent turned to run but Gamache was faster, and caught him against the choir stall. The monks scattered. Only the Dominican stood his ground. But said and did nothing.

Gamache put his face against Francoeur's.

"You could've killed him," Gamache snarled. "You almost killed him. How can you do this to one of your own?"

Gamache had Francoeur's shirt in his fist, yanking it. He felt the man's warm breath on his face, in short, terrified puffs.

And Gamache knew. Just a little more pressure. Just a few moments more, and this problem would disappear. This man would disappear. One more twist.

And who would blame him?

In that instant, Gamache let go. And stepped back, glaring at the Superintendent. Gamache's breathing was shallow, rapid. With an effort he brought himself under control.

"You're fucked, Gamache," said Francoeur in a hoarse whisper.

"What's happened?"

Both men turned to see Jean-Guy Beauvoir clutching the back of a pew, staring at them. His face pale and shiny.

"Nothing," said Gamache, straightening his disheveled jacket. "The boat must be here. We'll pack up and leave."

Gamache stepped off the altar and made for the door back to the prior's office. Then he noticed he was alone. He turned.

Francoeur hadn't moved. But neither had Beauvoir.

Gamache walked back down the aisle slowly, looking at Beauvoir the whole time.

"Did you hear me, Jean-Guy?" he asked. "We need to get going."

"Inspector Beauvoir is, I believe, of two minds," said Francoeur, straightening his clothes.

"You suspended me," said Beauvoir. "I don't need rehab. If I go with you, promise you won't take me."

"I can't do that," said Gamache, holding Jean-Guy's bloodshot eyes. "You need help."

"That's ridiculous," said Francoeur. "There's nothing wrong with you. What you need is a decent boss who doesn't treat you like a child. You think you're in trouble now. Wait 'til he finds out about you and Annie."

Beauvoir spun around to Francoeur. Then back to Gamache.

"We already know about you and Annie,"

said the Chief. His eyes hadn't left Jean-Guy. "Have for months."

"Then why didn't you say anything?" asked Francoeur. "Are you ashamed? Hoping it'll be short lived? That your daughter'll come to her senses? Maybe that's why he wants to humiliate you, Inspector Beauvoir. Maybe that's why he's suspended you and wants to ship you off to rehab. In one *coup-de-grâce* he'll end your career, and your relationship. Do you think she'll want an addict for a husband?"

"We respected your privacy." Gamache ignored Francoeur and continued to speak only to Beauvoir. "We knew you'd tell us when you were ready. We couldn't be happier. For both of you."

"He's not happy," said Francoeur. "Look at him. You can see it in his face."

Gamache took a cautious step forward as though approaching a skittish deer.

"Yes, look at me, Jean-Guy. I knew about you and Annie because of the lilacs. The flowers we picked together and you gave her. Remember?"

His voice was gentle. Kindly.

Gamache offered his right hand to Beauvoir. A helping hand. Jean-Guy saw the slight quiver in the familiar hand.

"Come back with me," said Gamache.

There was complete silence in the Blessed Chapel.

"He left you to die on the factory floor," the reasonable voice floated toward them. "He went to help the others, and left you. He doesn't love you. He doesn't even like you. And he sure doesn't respect you. If he did he'd never suspend you. He wants to humiliate you. Castrate you. Give him back his weapon, Armand. And his warrant card."

But Gamache didn't move. His hand remained outstretched toward Beauvoir. His eyes resting on the young man.

"Chief Superintendent Francoeur read your files. The ones from your therapy," said Gamache. "That's how he knows about your relationships. That's how he knows all about you. Everything you thought was confidential, everything you told the therapist, Francoeur knows. He's using that to manipulate you."

"Again, he's treating you like a child. As though you can be so easily manipulated. If you don't trust him with a weapon, Armand, I do." Francoeur unclipped his own holster and approached Beauvoir. "Take it, Inspector. I know you're not an addict. Never were. You were in pain and needed the medication. I understand."

Gamache turned to Francoeur and fought

the urge to take out the gun now clipped to his belt and finish what he started.

Deep breath in, he told himself. Deep breath out.

When he felt it was safe to speak he turned back to Beauvoir.

"You need to choose."

Beauvoir looked from Gamache to Francoeur. Both stretched out their hands to him. One offered a slight tremble, the other a gun.

"Are you going to take me to rehab?"

Gamache stared for a moment. Then nodded.

There was a long, long silence. And finally Beauvoir broke it. Not with a word, but with an action. He stepped away from Gamache.

Armand Gamache stood on the shore and watched the float plane leave the dock with Francoeur, Frère Luc and Beauvoir on board.

"He'll come to his senses," the Dominican said, as he joined the Chief Inspector.

Gamache said nothing, but just watched as the plane bounced over the waves. Then he turned to his companion.

"I suppose you'll be leaving soon too," said Gamache.

"I'm in no rush."

"Is that right? Not even to get the Book of Chants back to Rome? It's what you came for, isn't it?"

"True, but I've been thinking. It's very old. Might be too fragile to travel. I'll give it a good, hard think before doing anything. Might even pray on it. A decision could take awhile. And 'awhile' in Church time is a very long time indeed."

"Don't wait too long," said Gamache. "I hate to remind you, but the foundations are collapsing."

"Yes, well, about that. I've had a conversation with the head of the Congregation for the Doctrine of the Faith. He was impressed by the abbot's insistence on keeping their vows of silence and humility. Even in the face of great pressure, including the possible collapse of the monastery."

Gamache nodded. "A steady hand on the tiller."

"Exactly what the Holy Father said. He was also impressed."

Gamache raised his brows.

"So much so that the Vatican is considering paying for the restoration of Saint-Gilbert. We lost them once. It would be a shame to lose the Gilbertines again."

Gamache smiled and nodded. Dom Philippe had his miracle.

"When you asked me to sing Frère Mathieu's new chant, did you know it was Frère Luc who'd react?" the Dominican asked. "Or was that a surprise?"

"Well, I suspected it might be him, but I wasn't sure."

"Why'd you suspect Frère Luc?"

"For one thing, the murder happened after Lauds. When I watched where everyone went after the service, it was clear only Frère Luc was alone. No one visited him in the porter's office. No one went down that corridor. Only Frère Luc could've gone to the garden unseen because everyone else worked in groups."

"Except the abbot."

"True, and I suspected him for a while too. In fact, right up until the end I suspected almost everyone. I realized while Dom Philippe wasn't confessing to the crime, neither was he completely exonerating himself. He told a lie he knew we'd uncover. Said he was in the basement looking at the geothermal. He wanted us to know he was alone."

"But he must have known that would make him a suspect," said Frère Sébastien.

"That's what he wanted. He knew one of his monks had committed the crime, and he felt some measure of responsibility. So he deliberately left himself open to take the blame. But that was another reason I suspected Frère Luc."

"How so?"

The plane was just skimming the waves. Beginning to get airborne. Gamache spoke to the monk, but had eyes only for the small plane.

"The abbot kept wondering how he could have missed it. How he didn't see it coming. Dom Philippe struck me from the beginning as an unusually observant man. Very little got by him. So I began to wonder the same thing. How could the abbot have missed it? And there seemed two possible answers. That he hadn't missed anything because he himself was the killer. Or, he had missed it only because the killer was the one monk the abbot didn't know very well. The newest among them. Who chose to spend all his time in the porter's office. No one knew him. Not even the prior, as it turns out."

The plane cleared the lake. The fog was gone and Gamache shielded his eyes from the bright sun. And watched the plane.

"Ecce homo," said Frère Sébastien, watching Gamache. Then his gaze shifted to the monastery, where the abbot had left the gate and was walking toward them.

"Dom Philippe heard Frère Luc's confession, you know," said the Dominican.

"Which is more than I've done," Gamache glanced at the monk before returning his gaze to the sky.

"I suspect Frère Luc will tell you everything. That'll be part of his penance. Plus Hail Marys for the rest of his life."

"And will that do it? Will he be forgiven?"

"I hope so." The Dominican studied Chief Inspector Gamache. "You took a risk, getting me to sing the prior's chant. Suppose Frère Luc hadn't reacted?"

Gamache nodded. "It was a risk. But I needed a quick resolution. I hoped if just seeing the new chant was enough to drive Frère Luc to murder, hearing it sung in the Blessed Chapel would also bring on some violent reaction."

"And if Luc hadn't reacted? Hadn't given himself away? What would you have done?"

Gamache turned to look him full in the face. "I think you know."

"You'd have left with your Inspector? To take him to treatment? You'd have left us with a murderer?"

"I'd have come back, but yes. I'd have left with Beauvoir."

Now they both looked at the plane. "You'd do anything to save his life, wouldn't you?"

When Gamache didn't answer, the Dominican walked back toward the abbey.

Jean-Guy Beauvoir looked out the window, onto the sparkling lake.

"Here." Francoeur tossed something at Beauvoir. "This's for you."

Beauvoir bobbled then caught the pill bottle. He closed his hand over it.

"Merci." He quickly twisted off the cap and took two pills. Then he leaned his head against the cool window.

The plane turned and flew toward the monastery of Saint-Gilbert-Entre-les-Loups.

Jean-Guy looked down as they banked. A few monks were outside the walls, picking wild blueberries. He realized he didn't have any of the chocolates to take back to Annie. But Beauvoir had a sick feeling that it no longer mattered.

As his head lolled against the window, he saw monks bowing down in the garden. And one monk outside with the chickens. The Chanteclers. Saved from extinction. As the Gilbertines had been. As the chants had been.

And he saw Gamache on the shore. Looking up. He'd been joined by the abbot, and the Dominican was walking away.

Beauvoir felt the pills take hold. Felt the pain finally recede, the hole heal. He sighed with relief. To his surprise, Beauvoir realized why Gilbert of Sempringham had chosen that unique design for their robes. Long black robes, with the white top.

From above, Heaven, or an airplane, the Gilbertines looked like crosses. Living crosses.

But there was one other thing for God, and Beauvoir, to see.

The monastery of Saint-Gilbert-Entre-les-Loups wasn't itself a cross. On paper Dom Clément had drawn it to look like a crucifix, but that was another medieval architect's lie.

The abbey was, in fact, a neume. Its wings curved, like wings.

It looked as though the monastery of Saint-Gilbert-Entre-les-Loups was about to take flight.

At that moment, Chief Inspector Gamache looked up. And Beauvoir looked away.

Gamache watched the plane until it disappeared from sight, then he turned to the abbot, who'd just joined him.

"I know how horrendous this has been for you."

"For all of us," the abbot agreed. "I hope we learn from it."

Gamache paused. "And what's the lesson?"

The abbot thought about that for a few moments. "Do you know why we're called Saint-Gilbert-Entre-les-Loups? Why our emblem is two wolves intertwined?"

Gamache shook his head. "I assumed it dated back to when the first monks arrived. That it was symbolic of taming the wilderness, or making friends with it. Something like that."

"You're right, it is from when Dom Clément and the others came here," said the abbot. "It's a story one of the Montagnais told them."

"A native story?" asked Gamache, surprised the old Gilbertines were inspired by anything they'd have considered pagan.

"Dom Clément relates it in his diaries. One of the elders told him that when he was a boy his grandfather came to him one day and said he had two wolves fighting inside him. One was gray, the other black. The gray one wanted his grandfather to be courageous, and patient, and kind. The other, the black one, wanted his grandfather to be fearful and cruel. This upset the boy and he thought about it for a few days then returned to his grandfather. He asked, 'Grandfather, which of the wolves will win?' "

The abbot smiled slightly and examined the Chief Inspector. "Do you know what his grandfather said?"

Gamache shook his head. There was a look of such sadness on the Chief Inspector's face, it almost broke the abbot's heart.

"The one I feed," said Dom Philippe.

Gamache looked back at the monastery that would now stand for many generations to come. Saint-Gilbert-Entre-les-Loups. He'd mistranslated it. Not Saint Gilbert among the wolves, but between them. In that place of perpetual choice.

The abbot noted the gun in Gamache's belt and the grim expression on his face. "Would you like me to hear your confession?"

The Chief Inspector looked into the sky and felt the north wind on his upturned face. *Some malady is coming upon us.*

Armand Gamache thought he could just hear the sound of a plane, way far off. And then that too disappeared. And he was left with a great silence.

"Not just yet, I think, *mon père.*"

ABOUT THE AUTHOR

Louise Penny is the *New York Times* and *Globe and Mail* bestselling author of seven previous novels featuring Chief Inspector Armand Gamache. Her debut, *Still Life,* won the John Creasey Dagger and the Arthur Ellis, Barry, Anthony, and Dilys Awards, and was named one of the five Mystery/Crime Novels of the Decade by *Deadly Pleasures* magazine. Penny was the first author to win the Agatha Award for Best Novel four times — for *A Fatal Grace, The Cruelest Month, The Brutal Telling* (which also received the Anthony Award for Best Novel), and *Bury Your Dead* (which also won the Dilys, Arthur Ellis, Anthony, Macavity, and Nero Awards). Her most recent novel, *A Trick of the Light,* received an Independent Literary Award and was named one of the Best Crime Novels of 2011 by *The New York Times, The Globe and Mail,* and *Publishers*

Weekly. Louise lives with her husband, Michael, in a small village south of Montréal.